IRON CITY

IRON CITY

Marion H. Hedges

with introductions by
Alan Wald
and
Frederick Burwell

Beloit College Press
Beloit, Wisconsin

Iron City, by Marion H. Hedges
ISBN: 1-884941-00-1
Copyright 1919, Boni & Liveright, Inc. Reprinted with permission of the
publisher, Liveright Publishing Corporation.
Printed and bound in the United States of America.

Cover illustration: *Strike, Fall River,* by Thomas Hart Benton, from the collection
of the New Britain Museum of American Art, Connecticut, bequest of Thomas
Hart Benton. Photo by Michael Agee. Design by Gregory B. Leeds.

Dedication: To Randolph Bourne.

First Beloit College Press edition: March 1994

Beloit College Press
Beloit College
700 College St.
Beloit, Wis. 53511

Foreword

Few liberal arts colleges enjoy the rich literary history held by Beloit College. Professor Marion Hedges' 1919 novel, *Iron City*, is a part of that history. It is a book of and about a particular time in the history of America, of American literature, and of the City of Beloit, Wisconsin and Beloit College. Impressively, after 75 years, *Iron City* is not only an enlightening window into a difficult time long past, but a good read to boot.

This is an appropriate time to take a fresh look at the impact of the radical American writers in the early 20th Century. *Iron City*, because it is an entertaining as well as representative work, is a good vehicle for such reflection. Our understanding of the novel is greatly enhanced by the two splendid Introductions in this edition. In the first, "The Radical Age of Innocence," Professor Alan Wald, a premier scholar on radical American literature, puts *Iron City* in both literary and socio-political context. Beloit College Archivist Frederick Burwell's Introduction, "The *Iron City* Controversy at Beloit," sets the novel in place and time.

Beloit College is indebted to Professor Wald and Mr. Burwell for their generous contributions to our understanding and reading pleasure.

VICTOR E. FERRALL, JR.
PRESIDENT, BELOIT COLLEGE

Author's Preface (1919)

I have endeavored to depict the unspiritual side of American life in the hope that when the details of the picture are assembled we shall see how far we have departed from our great tradition, and how at variance we are to our unconscious life.

The characters in this novel are composite portraits drawn from many diverse sources and should be read in that light only.

First Introduction

THE RADICAL AGE OF INNOCENCE
BY ALAN WALD

I.

Marion Hawthorne Hedges' 1919 *Iron City* is a social novel typical in literary form and inflecting the ideology of a turning point in the evolution of United States intellectual radicalism.[1] The year of the book's appearance under the imprint of the famous liberal publishing house of Boni & Liveright was a momentous one in the history of the political Left and, consequently, for the cultural Left that had taken its inspiration from the socialist movement of the era of Eugene V. Debs.

In 1919, only two years after the Russian Revolution, there were "soviets" in the Seattle general strike. Wesley Everett, an activist in the Industrial Workers of the World (IWW), was martyred in Centralia, Illinois. The infamous anti-Red raids and deportations began, directed by Attorney General A. Mitchell Palmer. And the Socialist Party split, leading to the creation of the new communist movement in the U.S.[2]

For writers on the Left, the signal development was the trans-

---

1   The most comprehensive survey of the 20th Century left-wing novel to date is Walter Rideout, *The Radical Novel in the United States* (Cambridge: Harvard University Press, 1956).
2   See James Weinstein, *The Decline of Socialism in America, 1912-1925* (New York: Vintage, 1967), pp. 234-57.

formation of the irreverent and carefree *Masses* magazine into the more serious *Liberator*, with its close ties to the Bolshevik Revolution. Famous pre-World War I literary radicals such as Jack London and Randolph Bourne were dead, but the best known surviving left-wing writers, Upton Sinclair, John Reed, Lincoln Steffens, and Max Eastman, embraced the spirit of "The Great Soviet Experiment" with both arms.

It is, of course, a rare novel that fully embodies historical forces of its time the moment its freshly printed book jacket goes on display in bookstore windows. Leon Trotsky's 1922 *Literature and Revolution* challenges the myth that literature anticipates rather than lags behind social development, using the memorable phrase, "all through history, mind limps after reality."[3] *Iron City* was, in fact, more nearly a retrospective on trends in literary, cultural, personal, and political radicalism that would unravel by the end of the next decade.

The politico-literary genesis of Hedges' novel is rooted in a time when the utopian vision of socialism was not confused with, or discredited by, the monstrosity that the Soviet Union would become under Stalin. Likewise, it expressed the mood of an era when the task at hand for the burgeoning labor movement was simply to become organized. The notion of a powerful and corrupt labor bureaucracy, willing to sell out its ranks in order to maintain its own power and privilege, was then barely thinkable among American workers.

In the realm of personal life, many radicals were inspired by dreams of freer, egalitarian, sexual relationships. A man and a woman, it was imagined, could live together in a mutual respect and trust unfettered by the hypocrisies of the past, and inequalities that would later be disclosed by the various "sexual revolutions" of the 1920s and 1960s.[4]

---

3 Leon Trotsky, *Literature and Revolution* (Ann Arbor: University of Michigan Press, 1960), p. 19.

4 See the discussions of feminism and sexual relations in Leslie Fishbein, *Rebels in Bohemia: The Radicals of the Masses, 1911-1917* (Chapel Hill: University of North Carolina Press, 1982), pp. 74-112, 127-59, and 193-204.

In literature, "modernism," evident primarily in new poetry, was characterized by self-conscious and difficult experiments in form, and was animated in part by postwar disillusionment and the growth of gloomy, psychoanalytically inspired meditations on the human condition. A radical novel like *Iron City* could still mobilize the forms and themes of the romance, the picaresque, sentimental novel and other earlier literary genres, yet bear on its cover a publisher's statement attributing to the radical critic and essayist Randolph Bourne the judgment that the work is "the finest first novel he has ever read, and one of the few great American novels."[5]

Iron City is innocent of the "proletarian realism" that Mike Gold would herald at the onset of the Great Depression and that can also be seen in Mari Sandoz's *Capital City* (1937), a work that extends some of Hedges' concerns into the era of expanding native fascism. It is also devoid of stream-of-consciousness and other Joycean techniques that swept expatriate literary circles in the 1920s and that blended with some versions of 1930s literary radicalism, as in the work of Henry Roth and James T. Farrell.

Yet, for all the ways in which it looks backward more than forward, *Iron City* cannot be classified a historically dated fantasy without relevance to the present. On the contrary, it has strengths that stem precisely from the fact that it is a work of art, free of the demoralizing and frustrating legacy of seventy years of political disillusionment suffered by the literary Left. It is not tainted by the "agony," to use Christopher Lasch's term, that grew as a result of periodic anti-radical campaigns such as the Palmer Raids and the McCarthy witch-hunts.[6] Iron City manages to capture and retain many of the ideals and visions that tell us what truly was important in the literary-radical impulse.

Indeed, the terrible failures of revolution in countries such as the Soviet Union and China, and the broken dreams of those

---

5 The jacket quote is mentioned in the review of *Iron City* appearing in *Catholic World* (February 1920), pp. 694-5.
6 See Christopher Lasch, *The Agony of the American Left* (New York: Vintage, 1968).

sections of the literary Left who imagined utopia on the distant shores of these non-industrial societies making a great leap forward into the modern world, have beclouded the fact that much of the core of the pre-World War I radical critique of contemporary capitalism remains valid. Thus, Marion Hedges shares a common agenda of concerns with the generation of students attending college at the end of the 20th Century, including the problems inherent in exercising power while maintaining integrity, and of finding fulfilling personal lives in a society marked by a huge disparity between haves and have-nots, where institutions intended to serve "humanity" can and have become controlled by ruthless and uncaring elites.

There is no reason why many of Hedges' dreams may not be recouped and harnessed to a new radical culture that has learned the lessons of, and refuses to be ensnared by, the catastrophic mistakes of the past. In a decade marked by the collapse of Soviet Stalinism, the victory of a reform slate in the International Brotherhood of Teamsters (the quintessentially corrupt U. S. union), and where the Nobel Prize for literature in 1993 has gone to a writer of the literary genius and moral sensibility of Toni Morrison, such hopes are, at the least, not totally without foundation.

II.

Hedges himself was a characteristic product of a generation fired with the dream of remaking the world. Born on September 14, 1888, in Winamac, Indiana, he received a B.A. from DePauw University in 1910. In 1912, the year before he went to Beloit College to teach English, he received an M.A. from Harvard, in close proximity to the classes producing John Reed (1910) and Walter Lippmann (1909). In his imagined world, Beloit becomes Crandon Hill College, an institution much out of touch with the issues of the day, and the young English professor becomes a sociologist, a discipline more accurately reflecting the growing concerns of the author.

This was Hedges' first novel, and he was only thirty-one years old at the time it appeared. Perhaps he was at least partly inspired in his ideals, as so many literary radicals have been, by Walt Whitman. In the manner of John Dos Passos, building upon Whitman just a few years later, Hedges is preoccupied with the negative transformation of indigenous U. S. ideals in the industrial age. His fictitious Iron City is a social organism founded by New Englanders; then, as the years go on, progressively inhabited by Welsh, English, French, German, and Irish, and finally, as manufacturing industries grow, by Italian, Eastern European, and African-American workers. Crandon Hill College, instead of responding constructively to the changing composition and needs of the city in which it is located, reacts conservatively, generating an irrelevant education, elitist faculty, and much social hypocrisy.

The first stirrings of change in the city are associated with the appearance of the young college instructor, whose activities raise the reader's, and at least part of the community's, awareness of labor agitation, unions, strikes, and the beginning of World War I. Moreover, the protagonist, John Cosmus, is a link between two women, the beautiful Margaret Morton and the modern Sarah Blackstone. The latter, an advocate of the new birth control movement, embodies the values that Cosmus will come to champion. "It has," she says, "been my position. . .that a teacher should do more than keep classes, that he should be a living link between the public and the best thought of the moment."[7]

Iron City is unabashedly a novel with a "message," aimed at solving a "problem." These are, surprisingly, virtually identical in content if not in form to the messages and problems of J. D. Salinger's *Catcher in the Rye* (1951) and Paul Goodman's *Growing Up Absurd* (1960). They concern the irrelevance of much of our educational system and the need for it to respond meaningfully to the authentic lives of people in the modern world.

---

7   Marion Hedges, *Iron City* (New York: Boni & Liveright, 1919), p. 40.

The form of *Iron City* is that of the classic "social novel," even though the social novel of Hedges' era was trapped among cross-currents. On the one hand, there is a kind of Whitmanesque celebration of a "bucolic America," strongly linked to sentimental and romantic fiction. Not unlike a Western adventure hero, John Cosmus, a gunless fighter for right and justice, a loner of uncertain origin, arrives as a stranger in the community to find love and strive to right the ills of the community.

On the other hand, the new consciousness of class society characteristic of radical thought as it matured around the turn of the century is just as evident in the novel through the protagonist's early encounters with poverty, ethnic prejudice, and the lure of big money and power. His desire to help his country by developing minds and his belief that college is the center of creative thought motivates him to change his life and enter the teaching profession. His name, Cosmus, suggests, in its echo of "cosmos," a broader and more integrated view of the world than that held by the narrow-minded citizens of Iron City. His plebeian class origins allow him to graduate from the "school of experience" even before his own encounter with higher education.

III.

Hedges' first novel (of two) was clearly highly autobiographical. John Cosmus's controversy with Crandon Hill College prefigures Hedges' own battle with the Beloit administration. The novel received remarkably favorable reviews,[8] considering its appearance during the postwar Red Scare. Despite the book's success and Hedges' popularity as a teacher, he left Beloit College the year after the book's publication. [The circumstances of his departure are described by Frederick Burwell in the

---

8   See the following: *Catholic World* (February 1920), pp. 694-5; *Dial,* Oct. 18, 1919, p. 358; *New York Call,* Nov. 16, 1919, p. 11; *New York Times,* Oct. 12, 1919, p. 24; *Springfield Republican,* Nov. 9, 1919, p. 15; *Survey,* Nov. 29, 1919, p. 43; *The Times (London) Literary Supplement,* Nov. 20, 1919, p. 673.

Second Introduction, which follows.] Hedges' unideological but pronounced left-wing convictions were still evident in his second novel, *Dan Minturn* (1928), praised in Walter Rideout's *The Radical Novel in the United States* for its expression of "the spirit of native radicalism."[9] At this time, Hedges was a contributor to the far left *New Masses*.[10] With the publication of *Dan Minturn*, his literary period ended and he embarked on a new career as a labor relations advisor and expert, and lobbyist for organized labor, a career he pursued until his retirement in 1954.[11]

Although *Iron City* is a work to be read in the pre-1930s context, the literary and political career of Hedges is rather characteristic of U.S. literary radicals of the first five decades of the 20th Century. A relative few—such as John Dos Passos, James T. Farrell, and Richard Wright—were able to sustain themselves as full-time novelists, but the vast majority, like Hedges, wrote only one or two books and were then subsumed into careers connected with the labor movement, the culture industry, or some previously developed skill. A few made comebacks in later decades, but most are forgotten until resurrected by an enterprising scholar whose work is not limited to the conventional big-name literary figures currently fashionable in academe. Marion Hedges is certainly the kind of activist and writer who merits attention by the new generation of students, readers, and scholars, who may see in him a spirit of iconoclasm bound up with a sense of social responsibility worthy of remembrance, and perhaps even of emulation.

ALAN WALD is a professor in the English literature department and in the Program in American Culture at the University of Michigan. He is author of *James T. Farrell: The Revolutionary*

---

9 Rideout, *op.cit.*, pp. 120-22.
10 *Ibid.*, p. 129.
11 See "M. H. Hedges Dies; Labor Expert, 70," *New York Times*, Jan. 9, 1959, 25:1.

Socialist Years (1978), *The Revolutionary Imagination* (1983), *The New York Intellectuals* (1987), and *The Responsibility of Intellectuals* (1992).

Second Introduction

THE *IRON CITY* CONTROVERSY AT BELOIT
BY FREDERICK BURWELL

On May 26, 1913, Beloit College President Edward Dwight Eaton announced in chapel that he had appointed a new instructor of English and rhetoric for the coming school year. The scholar, 25-year-old Marion Hawthorne Hedges, arrived in Beloit, Wisconsin, the following September for what was probably the quietest and most uneventful year of the seven he spent at the College.

Indiana-born, Hedges had received his bachelor's degree and Phi Beta Kappa honors from DePauw University, a master of arts from Harvard, and had taught for a year at Iowa Wesleyan College. The summer before coming to Beloit, he married the former Agnes Elisabeth Becker. In Beloit, they settled in a house on Park Avenue, close to campus.

The college Marion Hedges traveled to in 1913 was a fairly typical midwestern liberal arts school. Founded as "the Yale of the West" in 1846 by Yale graduates and based solidly upon the ideals and classical curriculum of that institution, Beloit College had gradually expanded to a residential population of a few hundred students. The City of Beloit itself had also grown and changed from a western frontier community settled in the 1830s, also by New Englanders, to an ethnically mixed, heavily industrialized, small midwestern city.

Hedges' entry into the life of the College was quiet and inconspicuous. He served as a judge for Shakespeare Society tryouts; helped organize Big Hill Day, the annual campus picnic; became secretary-treasurer of the faculty tennis club; and joined the faculty "All Stars" bowling club. Popularity with students came quickly, and he and his wife were invited to chaperon a number of fraternity and dormitory parties. William H. Short, class of 1922, recalls that Hedges "was a relatively short man, possibly five feet five inches tall, of medium build with a pleasant face and dark hair. His manner was open and friendly, and he seemed to be interested in you." A contemporary photograph of Hedges reveals a confident face with a strong chin and warm, but direct-looking, eyes.

Hedges was first assigned to teach two sections of the freshman course Introduction to the Study of Literature and a freshman class in rhetoric. In 1914-15, he began teaching a course in American literature open only to juniors and seniors.

The Beloit College student paper, *The Round Table,* dutifully reported the young instructor's publications, which, among others in 1914, included an article in *Forum,* entitled "The Physician as a Hero: William James," and, in 1915, one in *Play Book,* entitled "A Laocoön for the Movies."

In early 1915, *The Round Table* noted the founding of a new College literary society "composed of a dozen embryo geniuses who, under the guidance of Prof. M.H. Hedges, hold weekly meetings at which the productions of different members are read and discussed." The *Milwaukee Sentinel* picked up on the story, marking an eerie foreshadowing of *Iron City:* "For a time the activities of the group were shrouded in mystery. The secret at last leaked out. Every week the young writers grind out a chapter of 'A Step Higher,' a novel said to portray phases of Beloit College life." When interviewed, *The Round Table* reported, "members of the club unanimously refused to be questioned."

Two more significant facets of Hedges' life at Beloit College emerged in 1915. In April, he invited several students to his home to discuss organizing a local chapter of the journalistic fraternity Sigma Delta Chi. While a student at DePauw, Hedges had co-founded that society. A Beloit College chapter was chartered in June, and, according to *The Round Table*, Hedges assisted in the performance of its "mystic rites." In fact, Hedges "wrote the first ritual used in initiations of the fraternity." During the summer, Hedges and a colleague, Professor Karl T. Waugh, began writing weekly editorial columns for the local newspaper, the *Beloit Daily News*, under the heading "Saturday Night Thoughts." *The Round Table* described Hedges and Waugh as two "community-interested professors." In addition, Hedges took on publicity work for the College, writing two pamphlets, "The Great Adventure — Your Part In It," and "Beloit in the World's Work," as well as publishing "unique announcements" in *The Round Table,* copies of which were sent to dozens of high schools.

Hedges became increasingly immersed in College affairs and, apparently contrary to College tradition at the time, seemed at ease discussing College problems with students, both in his home and at local establishments such as the Blue Tea Room. He occasionally contributed articles to *The Round Table,* most notably a February 1916 comment entitled, "Dress The Round Table in New Clothes — An Open Letter On College Journalism." This article and his general outspokenness led to his first brush with controversy. Hedges urged the student newspaper to change from its staid, traditional magazine format, basically unchanged since the paper's founding in 1853, to a more representative "modern news sheet" style. "A change of form [means] a change in thinking," he wrote. "A change of thinking [means]. . . . constructive, not destructive thinking."

A scandal broke out when some students placed copies of an underground newspaper, *The Beloit Student,* on all the chapel pews. The "Yellow Sheet," as it became known, criticized in bold language both the administration and faculty of the College and demanded that *The Round Table* become a "news sheet." In the end, the perpetrators were never caught, Hedges was publicly exonerated of any involvement, and the flurry of discussion led in the fall term to the change in *The Round Table* format he had recommended.

Indications of Marion Hedges' radicalism also emerged in 1916, when *The Round Table* reported the formation of a local Socialist Society by eight students and two faculty members, Hedges and Sociology Instructor Lloyd Ballard. Within a few months, the society, "The William Morris Club," became a branch of the Intercollegiate Socialist Society. In March 1917, it brought Irwin St. John Tucker, an activist author and journalist with the American Socialist Party, to speak on campus.

In a 1959 letter to the College alumni office, Paul Pratt, class of 1918, recalled the Tucker visit:

> Irwin St. John Tucker made quite a talk — I have no recollection of what it was about — presumably it was socialist doctrine, which was anathema around the College in old Prexy Eaton's time. But it did greatly entertain the members of the class and in today's parlance was considered "terrific." There were a lot of us kids in the class, mostly boys, of course, and after class they all stuck around and decided that a guy that good ought to have an opportunity to speak at the morning chapel, which was a daily event back in those days.
>
> So — off we went, presumably incited cleverly by Mr. Hedges, who at that point discreetly withdrew to the background. Over to Prexy Eaton's we traipsed, impressed with the thought that here was a guy that all the world ought to hear. Prexy came to his door, listened to the "avant-garde" with his leonine head inclined and his shoulders

slightly bowed. The speaker paused for an answer. Then Prexy swept the eager faces of the class, assembled at his doorstep, his white-grey mustachio bristled alarmingly, and all he said, as I recall, was "Sorry gentlemen, Mr. St. John Tucker may not speak in chapel tomorrow morning." And the manner in which he said it indicated that he meant "or any other morning, ever."

Instructor Hedges became Professor Hedges in short order as his popularity as a teacher continued to grow. In May 1916, eighty-four freshmen signed a petition to President Eaton noting that, according to the College catalog, no courses offered by Hedges would be open to them in their sophomore year. "It is our desire to take further work under Mr. Hedges during the 1916-17 term," they wrote. In December 1919, *The Round Table* reported that in a "beauty and popularity contest," Marion Hedges placed first as the student choice for most popular faculty member.

William Short recalls Hedges' teaching style:

Professor Hedges was pleasantly objective and very interested, as if to say, "I'll give you a word picture of the subject. I find it interesting, and if you wish, I'll help you with it." I have a hazy recollection of being invited to confer with him at his home about a paper that I had written for his class. This was a bit unusual.

In July 1917, Melvin Amos Brannon became the third president of Beloit College, succeeding President Eaton, who retired after thirty-one years. Unlike his two predecessors, Eaton and Aaron Lucius Chapin, Brannon was not a clergyman. He was a scientist and administrator and had left the presidency of the University of Idaho to come to Beloit. He brought a different style to the College presidency that met with some resistance from old guard members of the faculty. Among other things, he instituted "progressive" curricular changes, including semi-professional and pre-vocational programs such as a department of journalism and courses in home economics. To a young radical like Marion Hedges, Brannon's statement that "a reasonable liberalism, properly guided, is essential for the world's progress" was certainly a welcome change.

Publication of *Iron City*

In an interview with the *Beloit Daily News* in 1940, Marion Hedges recalled that Randolph Bourne, literary critic and editor of *The Dial,* peddled the manuscript of *Iron City* from one New York publisher to another. Apparently it was Bourne's letter to Boni & Liveright that persuaded the firm to accept the book. "*Iron City* is the strongest first novel I have ever read and I consider it to be one of the few really great American novels," he wrote. Bourne died of pneumonia three days after the book was accepted.

On September 25, 1919, the *Beloit Daily News* announced the publication of *Iron City* under the headline "Prof. Hedges is Author of Strong Novel." The paper interviewed Hedges, who said, "When a writer wishes to express his sense of life's beauty, unity or significance and chooses the novel as a form, he does so because he wishes to secure the broadest canvas possible for his picture." He went on to explain why he wrote the book: "[I]n *Iron City* I have embodied the results of ten years' study of American life, and it is this background of national culture against which the story moves."

Boni & Liveright was a natural home for *Iron City.* The publishers were known for bringing out work avoided by the more established houses and had made their considerable reputation on books by such authors as Theodore Dreiser (in 1917, Hedges published an article on Dreiser in *The Dial*), T.S. Eliot, Ezra Pound, George Bernard Shaw, and even Leon Trotsky.

Although *Iron City* was not available in Beloit book stores until late October, Hedges gave President Brannon an advance copy.

Brannon read it and immediately spoke to the *Beloit Daily News,* praising the novel. He seemed quite aware that *Iron City* would provoke controversy: "[*Iron City* is] a courageous and direct attack on the inability of college education to take a dynamic hold on the world. . . . [U]nless we can have an open door policy in discussing intimately these things which are in all men's minds and hearts, we may as well write failure on the door of the entrance to civilization."

Brannon went on to praise Hedges' "ability and initiative," then admitted, "I read the book with probably less embarrassment than most others here. Any book that, dealing with a great problem, brings in sidelights on intimate things, is bound to embarrass judgment. The things touched on all happened prior to my coming to Beloit College and as a result leave me free to see the message and appreciate it."

The *Iron City* Controversy

Others, however, were not so appreciative. The Beloit College Archives has a number of letters to History Professor Robert Kimball ("Dickie") Richardson, detailing the reaction of various faculty members and others to *Iron City*. At the time, Richardson, a highly regarded faculty member, was on leave on the East Coast. In November 1919, Professor of Religion John Pitt Deane was the first to write Richardson about the controversy:

> . . . I need not say that I am profoundly disappointed in it. You know that I have always found Hedges stimulating and have believed in him. This, although I know his impatience with the church and most social institutions. I have attributed that to his earnest interest in the poor and the disadvantaged. . . .
>
> I know that it was probably written for a purpose, probably to jar something loose, to compel thought. But what possible excuse can there be for the parody and caricature of the local situ-

> ation and of the men with whom he is profession-
> ally associated? I resent with all my heart these
> caricatures. It seems to me that there is such a
> thing as professional etiquette, as professional
> decency, and that he has violated it many times.

Deane went on to say that he was certain that "[President] Brannon may wish that he had not endorsed the book so promptly. I imagine that something will happen as a result of it."

Another professor, J. Forsyth Crawford, made light of the great stir the book had caused: "In the town there is just now a bit of a flurry over Hedges' book. The situation is unpleasant, of course, but highly amusing. It will probably soon blow over."

In general, however, those who wrote Richardson were righteously indignant. Venerable Professor Almon W. Burr spoke for the "old guard" when he wrote:

> We are weathering the storm that the *Iron City* has
> brought. It has struck pretty deep into Beloit,
> alienated some of the College's best friends. I am
> still deeply indignant over it. I call it crude, cruel,
> crass and carnal. I would not have this author
> teach another day in Beloit. . . . [W]e are in
> trouble, and the other day the students voted that
> man "the most popular professor." It makes
> shivers run down my back.

Reviews of *Iron City* were generally positive, although some critics found Hedges' message heavy-handed. Without fail, however, all insisted that the young novelist showed great promise. *Survey* stated that "the author of this first novel has with one leap entered the highest realm of American social fiction." The *Chicago Tribune* agreed: "[*Iron City*] is far better than we dare expect any first book to be." *The Times of London* found *Iron City* "an authentic account of American life." Other reviewers praised the novel's "remarkable power," its "sense of real life and actual men and women" its "unusual merits in irony," and even the love story's "poetic charm," though a reviewer in the *Springfield Republican* found that "crudity, however, is apparent in many places."

The *New York Times* published one of the first reviews of *Iron City* and, even though critical and unfair to Beloit College, one of the most balanced:

> [T]he chief purpose of the book is to put into story form a scorching criticism of American methods of higher education and to charge them with failure to meet the demands of modern life. And it is evident that Mr. Hedges has had intimate knowledge of the inside workings of college faculties, or, rather, of some college faculty. Therefore his criticism deserves attention, and will undoubtedly receive it, since it is informed, constructive and aspirant for the best. . . . Mr. Hedges' criticism partakes of the nature of caricature; it is unfair in that it generalizes from one backward and unrepresentative institution. . . . Nevertheless, the spirit which he cauterizes does exist in varying degree in some, perhaps a good many, American educational institutions, and wherever it hides it deserves to be hunted out and spiked as thoroughly as St. George pinned the dragon to the ground.

Iron City sold well enough (at $1.75) to go into a second edition, for which the book's dust jacket was revised to include glowing excerpts from the many reviews. Years later, however, Hedges said that when the final copy was sold, he had earned the grand sum of $336.

On November 29, 1919, President Brannon tendered his resignation to Beloit College, ostensibly because of his failure to raise a "patriotic fund" of $110,000 for the College. Years later, however, Brannon said that the issue of academic freedom had much to do with his decision. Several professors had come under attack for their radical views, including Marion Hedges, and Brannon was under pressure to have them dismissed. In a letter to Richardson in 1949 (who at that time was writing a history of Beloit College), Brannon recalled that he had told the Beloit College trustees:

> Academic freedom is the most important thing in institutions of higher education. That is possible only when faculties are free to seek the truth, teach the truth, and have the respect of people who recognize that truth alone gives freedom to our world. Moreover, unless the president of the institution is allowed to decide whether his faculty is competent and trustworthy to teach the truth to youth, he can not make a success of his administration.

The College's Board of Trustees pledged its support of Brannon and his policies and asked him to withdraw his resignation. On the recommendation of President Brannon, they also granted leaves of absence to two of the professors accused of radicalism, Arthur E. Suffern and Clayton D. Crawford.

In a letter to the trustees dated December 1, 1919, Marion Hedges said: "After a conference with President Brannon, subsequent to your meeting on November 25, I in these words tender to you my resignation as professor of English in Beloit College to take effect on June 25, 1920, or earlier if you so desire." His resignation was not immediately accepted, and it appears that Brannon fought to keep him at Beloit.

In 1922, the well known novelist and political muckraker Upton Sinclair published his indictment of American education, *The Goose Step*. In a chapter titled "The Little Toadstools," Sinclair discussed the "singular fate" of Beloit College and *Iron City*. He described Hedges as a "young man of talent, who wrote a live novel. . . . Mr. Hedges declares that he did not indicate Beloit especially, and has received many letters from professors in other college towns, saying that the cap fitted them. But the gossips of Beloit insisted upon riveting the cap upon their own heads, and there was a dreadful scandal." Sinclair went on to describe the course of events leading up to Hedges' resignation, finally claiming that "three liberal professors were driven from the institution." Brannon wrote in 1949 that Sinclair "was right about some of the details, but totally wrong in regard to the ending." He insisted that those professors were not fired at all, but moved on to more financially lucrative positions.

Much of Brannon's correspondence from that period survives, including a few letters to him from Marion Hedges. One letter in particular, dated March 15, 1918, reveals many of Hedges' feelings and attitudes about his life at Beloit and presages some of what would appear in *Iron City* a year later. First he complained about the burdens of teaching 140 students each year, while also carrying on with extracurricular work with students, community service, and his own private projects: "It is not wise, I conclude, to take off years at the end of life to burn them at the present. . . ." He continued:

> In Beloit we are living in an era of fierce industrial expansion. The manufacturers have begun a new kind of activity calculated to leave them in a very real sense masters of the town. Much of what they are doing is admirable, but the result is, without a single doubt, the erection of barriers against ideas, and it is the business of the College to dispense ideas. If we are to have any real place in the community, if we are to be preserved as a *real* institution we have got to meet their activity with our united activity. . . . If I am to face my present state with no tangible promise of change [including a higher salary], I better, while I am yet young, seek some other field of employment.

Like his protagonist, John Cosmus, Hedges had an uneasy relationship with fellow faculty members. "I am aware in what light I am regarded by many of my colleagues," he told Brannon. "To them I am an educational adventurer, unbacked by any orthodox educational popery. How far is their power going to be allowed to circumscribe my usefulness?"

Also anticipating statements made in *Iron City* about the faculty in relation to the City of Beloit, he wrote: "I believe that the effectiveness of the College has been lessened by the persistence of the notion of a few members of the faculty that there is something sacrosanct about us, that we are a gentleman class — neuters, who have no definite duties to our times. Moreover, I believe that we shall never be fulfilling our full mission until we prepare industrial Beloit for the impending social and industrial changes which are coming, changes which are being very definitely resisted here."

Among the alleged "resistors" condemned by Hedges were local business leaders such as Alonzo Aldrich, who was the president of Beloit Iron Works, a manufacturer of paper making machinery (Crandon Iron Works in Iron City). Aldrich reflected the business community's perspective of dismay over *Iron City* in a letter to President Brannon, dated January 13, 1920:

> Most colleges have now connected with their staff of teachers, agitators that are as dangerous as any Bolsheviki or I.W.W. in the country; in fact, I think, more so, because they are genteel and therefore more insidious. I feel that every college should sever their connection with all such men as Mr. Hedges and several others of the type you have. . . . I believe the fundamental and particular business of all colleges and the part of the curriculum that should be stressed, is the teaching of Americanism, Patriotism, and Loyalty. . . .

President Brannon wrote back seeking to placate Mr. Aldrich. After noting that the trustees had Hedges' resignation at hand, he continued: "I can only say this now that it would probably mean a difference of about $15,000 to $20,000 a year to the income of the College if this resignation was accepted. . . . You may or may not know that Mr. Hedges has been voted the most popular man on the College faculty and that means something in the operation of a complex thing like an education institution."

Aldrich replied, asking for the method by which Brannon calculated the monetary loss to the College and adding, "the 'most popular man' vote does not impress me, only perhaps as a warning. You know some of our most noted rascals were models in gentility and suavity."

Brannon responded with meticulous calculations that he hoped Aldrich's "business mind will grasp," adding: ". . .Mr. Hedges has 150 students in his various classes [and]. . . . they share the same opinion with everybody acquainted with the inner workings of this college relative to the fact that Mr. Hedges is one of the most inspirational teachers on the Beloit College faculty, more than that, has few equals in America. . . ."

Early in 1920, an overwhelming majority of the Beloit College faculty signed a petition in support of President Brannon's retention. Among the few who did not sign, were Professors George Collie and Richardson. (Years later, Collie, the son of Beloit College's first student, described Marion Hedges as an "able man, but a natural-born troublemaker.") Probably sparked by the petition, Richardson wrote an angry letter to Brannon on February 2, condemning *Iron City* and criticizing Brannon's praise of it:

> With the general drift of the book's thought or imagery I am not here primarily concerned: what I would emphasize as serious is that you should have been led, from conviction or by surprise — and I believe the latter — to sanction

> by your praise and toleration a heedless, spiteful,
> or wanton literary exploitation of neighbors and
> colleagues: an exploitation which, in itself, is less
> "radical" than downright muckerish. . . . He
> [Hedges] fights with weapons of a type that oth-
> ers may not use. And one can but wonder what
> are the methods and results of his influence on
> students, in teaching, and in that conversational
> manipulation which he practices and recom-
> mends.

Three days later, Brannon replied saying that Richardson's
letter was an implied resignation. Richardson responded, on
February 9, by officially transmitting a notice of resignation letter
to the College trustees. Brannon, however, recommended that
the trustees not accept the resignation, and though Richardson
(and others for him) had looked for teaching jobs elsewhere, he
withdrew his resignation on March 21.

Even though he was just in his early forties, "Dickie" Richardson had aligned himself with the old guard among the Beloit
faculty. Like the College's founding fathers, Richardson was a
Yale graduate, and he revered the classical education traditions
and ideals they had championed. Though a very different sort
of teacher than Marion Hedges, he was also beloved by the
students, and his courses are legendary today. In a 1949 letter
to the then President of the College, Carey Croneis, Richardson
summed up his own feelings about the Brannon administration
and Marion Hedges:

> Dr. Brannon's own forward looking — and he
> always looked forward — made him kindly to
> freedom of thought on his faculty: and there was
> plenty of it. . . . Hedges was a great leader of
> students and doubtless an inspiring teacher. I
> think he had all the assurance of the typical
> young radical leader, and a complete contempt

for those who might disagree with him. And some of them found themselves used for examples of obscurantism and pig-headedness in his Iron City.

In March 1919, several months before *Iron City* was published, President Brannon wrote an assessment of Marion Hedges' abilities, describing his scholarship as "sound, thorough, and excellent," and his academic performance as "[e]xcellent in every respect." Brannon observed that Hedges had "[n]o habits or peculiarities which interfere with success" and summed up by stating his view of Hedges as "[a]n exceedingly high grade of man who can carry college work in the best institutions of the country." After *Iron City,* that man would never teach again.

Fiction vs. Fact

Just how closely was *Iron City* based on Beloit College and the City of Beloit? In his 1940 *Beloit Daily News* interview, Marion Hedges said: "People seemed to think that Iron City particularized about Beloit people and Beloit institutions. But it didn't at all. I was interested in the American scene and the things that I tried to write about were not Beloit scenes. But I couldn't convince some of my readers that this was so. So I was canned and had to pick up my life anew."

Hedges' protestations to the contrary, a careful reading of *Iron City* reveals dozens of similarities, to actual events, people, and places, too numerous to be coincidental. Hedges was well acquainted with the history of Beloit and Beloit College, having co-written in 1916 with Professor Theodore Lyman Wright, a Beloit pageant entitled, "From the Turtle to the Flaming Wheel." It covered the story from the pre-history of the Native American turtle mound builders,[1] to the present age of industry.

---

1   The Beloit College campus is dotted with effigy mounds built by the prehistoric predecessors of the Winnebago Tribe. The most famous is the Turtle Mound, a mound in the shape of a turtle. When it was first settled, in 1836, the Town of Beloit was, possibly because of the Turtle Mound, briefly known as "Turtle."

Like many authors of fiction, Hedges took what he knew well, made some changes, added liberal doses of imagination, and came up with a novel.

The reason so many in Beloit were outraged was that he was too obvious in his work. The history of Iron City too closely resembled the history of Beloit; Crandon Hill College President Crandon too closely resembled former Beloit College President Edward Dwight Eaton; and the great strike mirrored exactly the Beloit strike of 1902-03 in which the unions were broken by the "Beloit Citizens' Alliance."

Professor Richardson, in notes he made about the book, stated that "some of my own private conversation [with Hedges] is repeated." Richardson compared the funeral of Professor Christopher Mather early on in the novel to that of Robert Coit Chapin, the son of Beloit College's first president, in 1913, the year Hedges came to Beloit: "Even the pictures are accurately described as they hang in the room."

What surely bothered Beloit College History Professor Richardson most was Hedges' description of Crandon Hill College History Professor Charles Henry Clarke:

> Of all his colleagues, Clarke struck Cosmus as the strangest specimen of the academic mind; he always thought of him as a medieval Tory, if there were Tories in the middle ages. The psychology of Clarke was beyond his comprehension. How he could daily interpret the radicals of the past, and daily reject the radicals of the present, Cosmus could not see. It seemed to Cosmus that Clarke considered the middle ages a kind of Utopia from which mankind had moved forward like a crab.

That Marion Hedges would skewer a fellow faculty member in that fashion was beyond Richardson's comprehension.

Hedges Leaves Beloit

Hedges must have realized what his fate might be if *Iron City* were published. He was considering moving on many months before he resigned. In April 1919, for example, he wrote President Brannon, thanking him for his continued confidence in him, but adding, "I shall bring you a final decision as to my continuance here soon. Believe me the delay is not from a selfish motive; just now I am wrestling with an ethical problem, which I hope to solve soon." It is difficult not to surmise that the "ethical problem" was the upcoming publication of Iron City.

The social ostracism and subsequent "firing" of John Cosmus, the hero of *Iron City,* anticipated what befell Hedges. Hedges, however, believed he had something vital and worthwhile to say in *Iron City.* He probably summed up his perception of his own character when he wrote of John Cosmus: "There are some natures who find their happiness in the farther reaches of the spirit; in patriotism and in religion, and love of humanity. Cosmus was of such disposition. It seemed more important to him that justice triumph than that his own body be comfortable."

On April 23, 1920, President Brannon wrote to Marion Hedges: ". . . . the resignation which you tendered the Board of Trustees under date of December first, 1919, was accepted by the Board at the quarterly meeting held on April 20th. In accepting your resignation, the Trustees went on record as desirous of expressing their appreciation of your services to Beloit College and their good wishes for your success in your future undertakings." Brannon, too, thanked Hedges, but said no more. In contrast, in accepting at the same time the resignation of Professor T.W. Galloway, a less radical friend of Hedges, the trustees adopted a resolution praising at full length his "scholarly leadership" and "masterful teaching."

Also at the April 1920 trustees meeting, "it was moved and carried with enthusiasm that President [Brannon] be requested to withdraw his resignation. This the President consented to do." The Board also acceded to Brannon's recommendation that the trustees allow Richardson to withdraw his resignation.

The Round Table got wind of Hedges' resignation a few weeks before it was accepted and contacted Brannon, who declared, "Personally I regret very much that we shall lose Prof. Hedges. I consider him one of the best English teachers in America." An April 3, 1920 editorial in *The Round Table* described Hedges as "one of those rare men, best termed practical idealists." The paper went on to praise his work especially as a teacher, but also with the Beloit Players, the Shakespeare Society, *The Round Table,* and, ironically, his producing "some of the more effective college publicity matter." (Nearly 75 years later, Hedges' former student William Short agreed: "I have always felt that his classes were the most enjoyable and inspiring that I had at Beloit. I enjoyed the work and felt inspired to do my best. Professor Hedges seemed to me a practical idealist with a vision for mankind."

That the students would miss Marion Hedges, *The Round Table* was sure: "Considering all things, the resignation of Prof. Hedges means a great loss to Beloit College. We have not tried to say how great it will be, because that is impossible. But consider the facts and figure it out yourself." These lamentations, of course, came too late. In a month the paper announced that Hedges had accepted a position as special editorial writer for the *Minnesota Daily Star,* a radical labor newspaper owned by farmers and union members.

In early June, well before Commencement, Hedges and family packed up and left Beloit for good. The *Beloit Daily News* reported in its 1940 article that "after seven years on the faculty there had been only one staunch friend [presumably Galloway] at the station to see him and his family off." The article said he had not been back to Beloit in all that time.

In a letter to Professor Richardson, dated March 29, 1949, Brannon wrote:

> [Y]ou will state the absolute truth if you make a direct denial of Upton Sinclair's claim "that their

[Professors Hedges, Suffern, and Crawford's] liberalism, radicalism or conservatism" [had] anything to do with their leaving Beloit College. . . .
As you recall, the salaries at Beloit College were
very low — $2,100 for full professorships. . . .
Hedges went to a position with a Minneapolis
paper which paid twice as much as he received at
Beloit. . . . They were appreciative that I took the
stand I did with the trustees. They knew that it
was necessary for some president in the U.S.A. to
show that he did not let his own job stand in the
way of protecting academic freedom in higher
education. I did no more than my duty, of
course. However, we made history. I am not sure
that any other college or university president
followed the Beloit example.

In later published accounts, Hedges always insisted that he
was "canned" from Beloit College. He said that he was not only
fired, but also blacklisted in all the colleges and universities in
the country. His friend Galloway reportedly wrote personal
letters to the presidents of 165 colleges and universities asking
that Hedges be given a job. The "most popular teacher" at
Beloit College received not a single offer.

"I am glad of what happened at Beloit," Hedges said in 1940.
"It made me, but it did something else, too. It was stark tragedy
to me then, and to my family. Even yet the hurt is here. I
couldn't understand it then, and I can't understand it now."

After Beloit

Hedges pursued a varied and interesting career after leaving
the classroom for good. He lived for several years in Minneapolis, where, in addition to writing about public affairs and economics for the *Daily Star,* he served for eight months as special
investigator for Floyd Olson, then a Minnesota district attorney
and later a famed reform governor of the state.

From 1924 until his retirement 30 years later, Hedges was an active trade unionist, labor lobbyist, and leader in the American Federation of Labor. For 23 years he worked as the supervising editor of the International Brotherhood of Electrical Workers' *IBEW Journal.* Hedges also held the position of director of research for the IBEW, leading a staff of seven assistants from offices in Washington, D.C.

For a time, Hedges did not neglect his literary aspirations. Though *The Round Table* had announced in January 1920 that Hedges would publish a second novel, entitled "Mark Clifton's Daughter," in the fall, and in March reported the book would be called "The Great Undertaking," the book was never published. In 1928, however, Hedges finally published his second, and last, novel, *Dan Minturn.* Although it attracted less attention than *Iron City,* this story of a young labor leader in Minnesota who enters politics was published by the Vanguard Press to positive reviews.

Hedges maintained friendships and corresponded with notable authors, Carl Sandburg and Edgar Lee Masters among them, and continued to write articles on literary subjects for a variety of prominent magazines, including *The Nation, The New Republic,* and *The New Masses.* By the late 1920s he had begun to concentrate his writing on labor and economics topics, writing two more books; *A Strikeless Industry: A Review of the National Council on Industrial Relations for the Electrical Industry (1932),* and *Educating for Industry: Policies and Procedures of a National Apprenticeship System* (1946).

Among his many union activities over the years, Hedges traveled to Geneva, Switzerland, in 1935, where he was the first accredited labor representative to address the International Labor Conference. He was labor consultant to the Social Security Board (the predecessor agency of the Social Security Administration); special consultant on labor to the Tennessee Valley Authority (TVA), and planner for the Missouri Valley Authority. Hedges was also a founder and later vice chairman of the

National Economic and Social Planning Association and a recipient of its Gold Medal Award. He maintained a strong interest in social security legislation and workers' education. According to an article dated August 28, 1947, in the *Minneapolis Labor Review*, "Hedges' capacity for work astonishes his friends. When he testifies before Congressional committees, as he has on such subjects as housing, economic planning and public power, his knowledge of the particular field elicits the envy of his colleagues and the wholesome respect of members of Congress. The latter, in fact, learned quickly that they could not bait and heckle Hedges as they could other witnesses."

It was for his work directly on behalf of organized labor that Hedges ultimately became best known. According to the *Minneapolis Labor Review* 1947 article:

> [L]abor leaders credit Hedges with having laid the groundwork for an era of labor-management relations almost unparalleled in private industry. . . . Since the beginning of TVA, Hedges has presented every economic brief for the TVA workers. It is typical of this unassuming AFL leader that he wears an impressive diamond ring that he would consider too ostentatious to wear if it had not been given to him by 42,000 Tennessee Valley war workers a few years ago.
>
> The esteem and brotherhood of those 42,000 war workers was the sort of thing that a young sociology instructor was looking for in a novel Hedges wrote 28 years ago.

After he retired in September 1954, Hedges remained in Chevy Chase, Maryland. On January 6, 1959, he died of a heart attack at age 70.

The *Iron City* controversy expanded intellectual freedom at Beloit College, though it would be many years before some of the changes it pointed toward would take root. With the advent of a new, more traditional, administration in 1924, many of Brannon's "progressive" programs were dismantled.

The critic H.W. Boynton, writing about *Iron City* in *The Review*, may have best summed up Marion Hedges' legacy to both Beloit College and to literature: "For such a book, beginning and ending on a note of sane if impassioned inquiry, we may well be grateful."

FREDERICK BURWELL is the archivist of Beloit College. He is the editor of a series of publications dealing with the College's history and of the letters of former Beloit faculty member Joel Carl Welty, entitled *The Hunger Year in the French Zone of Divided Germany, 1946-47* (1993). Burwell also serves as an associate editor of the *Beloit Fiction Journal* and writes short fiction.

IRON CITY

Prologue

Late afternoon of a summer's day in a midwestern state. A young man, not over-tall but muscular, trudged along a telephone line that swept triumphantly in stately strides down the dusty road as far as he could see. The young man was weary; his feet dragged. He lifted himself heavily up his next post, and when he had crawled through the ten tiers of wires and perched himself upon the last cross piece at a height of forty feet, he sighed and fell into a position of relaxation.

The country swooned into the arms of the harvest. As far as he could see there were fields of grain, gold beneath the sun, peaceful, rich; and waving corn mellowing into fruitage. Into the distance, the fields stretched in the drowsy afternoon sun, a picture of bursting wealth; heavily uddered cows browsed beneath the trees; he caught the hum of insects from clover at the roadside; chickens cackled; hogs grunted from the farmyard a stone's throw beyond. He was lazily conscious of the white house behind the fruited orchard, the ample barn, the windmill, the engine shed, the dairy house near the spring. He saw beyond, too, a neat school house set well back from the road near a brook. The sight of all this wealth and comfort was very familiar to him and very commonplace.

But as he paused, resting, the imagination aroused by the play of sunlight on all that rural beauty lifted fields, cattle, houses into the high light of understanding. He revived, his nostrils were taut with deep breaths, he stretched out his arms in a gesture of rapturous submission. For a moment road, fields, barnyard, house, school building burst upon his mind in a flood of understanding, as America, his country.

Then incisively there cut across his revery the memory of the camp of shacks he had left four hours before at noon. The odor of long-used, unwashed clothes, of garbage, of human waste, of tobacco, smote him shudderingly, even in recollection. He remembered with a touch of aversion the row of thin, low wooden buildings, roofed with tar paper. The black-eyed passionate dagos, moody and suspicious, cursing, fighting, drinking, singing, lazy and repellent, handsome and potential; these seemed to intrude upon the countryside with a note at once awesome and discordant.

Who had brought them here?

The eyes of the young man followed the River of Wires as they traveled over the striding poles to the horizon's rim. Down the road to the edge of Dyer's place, and beyond they went; when the road turned, they turned; where the road crossed the river laboriously by bridge, they leaped; where the road mounted the hill, they climbed. On, on over the fields, river, through woods, to glittering cities, on, on, on.

He did not have it in his heart to condemn the energy that had brought the Italians here to build the line. What would the country be to him without the River of Wires? How it glistened in the sunshine! How it sang in the breeze! How it went on interminably! It goldened, as nothing else goldened, the commonplace countryside. It reached out its visible voice to all the beautiful capitals of the world, to Chicago, San Francisco, New York, Moscow, London, Paris, Rome, Bombay—the cities, the regal proud cities. The young man, though tired, never seemed alone when he worked along the great River of Wires. He went with it in his mind across field and stream. He pictured great avenues of the cities! He visioned the palaces! He mingled with the crowds! He sank himself in a great work there! He found minds like his own, keen, hungering, visioning.

"God!" he said audibly. "The world comes to me on those wires!" Suddenly he had an idea. He ran quickly down the pole to his kit of tools below. He selected a line-telephone, such as linesmen use in tapping wires. His nimble fingers soon had it adjusted at the top of the pole to the continental wire. He would listen to the world talk. First he heard a strange buzzing, then, very clearly, the voices of two men conversing.

"This is Collins in New York," one was saying.

"Hello, Collins," the other voice answered. "I am at the Auditorium in Chicago. Did you get my man?"

"No, I didn't," the first voice came again. "I don't know of a man in the world just now who can fill that job. Twenty-five thousand dollar brains are scarce, you know."

A light came suddenly into the young man's face. He disconnected the apparatus, and sat thoughtfully for many minutes looking out over the fields; then he climbed down the pole and picked up his tools. He untied no more wires that day, nor thereafter. He went back to the ill-smelling camp, past the dago shacks, past their occupants,—his comrades,—to the foreman's office.

"I want my time," he said simply.

"Why, John Cosmus, I hate to lose you," exclaimed the bluff boss. "What are you going to do?"

"I am going to college, and become a twenty-five thousand dollar brain."

The foreman did not laugh. "Johnny, my boy," he said, "you've got the right idea."

He paid the young man, and watched him go slowly up the hill toward the town. He shook his head. "I lost my best climber there," he said softly.

But Cosmus went on singing. At the top of the hill he paused and looked back. He saw the blue smoke curling from the shacks, he saw the swooning fields, and beyond the River of Wires, shining—on, on to the proud cities, and further through his dreams.

1 An American City

When Jones & Jones, merchants of Iron City, hung out their flag on the Fourth of July, the event was of civic magnitude. The city editor of the *Republic-Despatch* gave one column front to the happening, for Jones & Jones had been in business in the same building for forty-two years, and every year had hung out at precisely the same hour the same identical flag. Moreover, it had been recorded that with Jones & Jones was an eminent clerk, who had served the firm for thirty-two years at a salary of $75 a month, who owned a Ford automobile, and still had forebears in New England. Iron City boasted at least one eminent maid; she lived with the respectable Taylor family and was a heavy tax-payer, for she owned three houses and lots. And among the other notables there was also Thomas J. Cruisenbarry, eminent sexton of the First Congregational Church. He was the third generation of Cruisenbarry to have custody of the city cemetery. His father before him had served the city thirty years, and at his death had received formal tribute from the city council for his services, as had his father, in turn, before him. Cruisenbarry III, in acknowledgment of the family's high services, received one hundred dollars a month, an increase of twenty-five dollars over the salary of his father. No other facts reveal so clearly the stiffness and inertia that imperceptibly was beginning to creep numbingly over the foundation stratum of this progressive American city.

Outwardly Iron City gave no evidence of the stiffness of its joints. To the sallow eye of the British traveler, who once had stopped in the city and had telegraphed back to his London journal, Iron City was "new and uncouth." It had its "loop" district, built in the form of crossed S's, in which were congested all the shops, banks, hotels, hospitals and offices for a city of thirty thousand. Bass River, cutting transversely the business section, freshened this quarter and furnished water power for numerous mills. Nothing was done to beautify the stream; facing the banks were back stoops and unsightly factories. The city park, containing a statue of the donor, was up town, not along the river. The residences lay further to west and east, on the high bluffs and flats beyond. True, along the Front road a few mansions had arisen and the country club with golf links spread its august length across one of these wooded knolls. Of course, these residence districts were more pretentious than the shops down town. These were small, and still did business, as Jones & Jones did, on a personal basis. Strictly speaking, there were few firms, no corporations. It was Jones's store, or Dailey's store. Most of the upper circle of Iron City had charge accounts at Marshall Field's and at Carson's, some hundreds of miles distant, and many of the middle class shopped from large, fat catalogues of mail order houses. But the local shops did not suffer. The upper circle was small, and proprietors knew well how to cater to the trade of the workers. They resented far more the competition of Woolworth's Ten Cent Store, which had set up its flaming front some ten years before.

In spite of these competitors, the shops were thriving as the banks testified. There were four banks in Iron City, all bulging at the sides. And if one were looking for a metaphor to describe this American town he could find none more accurate than the hackneyed "bee-hive."

Iron City was a hive. The owners of the shops were not at all aware of the city's importance. But the seven millionaires, who sat well back in the shadow of community affairs, or who perceived its life through beveled glass of private office or limousine, knew that Iron City was on the map.

These seven millionaires were not all Iron City "boys," but most of them were, and they were proud that seven nationally advertised industries had their home offices in Iron City, and that four continental railroads were kept busy carrying Iron City products to Bombay and Damascus, as well as to Oklahoma City and Portland, Maine. These captains of industry were self-made; and to the inhabitants they were still Tom and Joe. But though they did not lie wholly apart, they evinced little real desire to mingle closely with Iron City life. They contributed money to the new Y.M.C.A. building,—and spent their winters with their business. Iron City remained a middle class town although no inhabitant would listen to its being called middle-class. There were no poor, no slums. There was no vice, no legalized home of prostitution in all Iron City, though the curse of Babylon stalked the streets. After all, its sin was not so much the sin of ancient Nineveh or Tyre as the sin of Sybaris,—the sin of being too comfortable and too content.

R. Sill and Son owned the largest manufactory, a plant worth five million, which employed five thousand men, mostly of alien birth, "foreigners." This was a manufactory of engines; and it lay sprawling out close to the "swell" residence district along the river to the north. Automobiles, paper, shoes, machinery and clothing were the other premier products of the City.

It was these manufacturing concerns that were fast giving the town the aspect of a metropolis, were feeding it and clothing it, erecting its public buildings and churches and schools, uniting it with the great outside world beyond the turn of the northern railroads; but it was these same factories that were giving Iron City its one problem, turning its sabbatical peace into clamor, and reforming, with the thrust of a giant, the entire social fabric of its life.

Factories to have existence must have workers, and workers could not come from among the ranks of Iron City's native population. And so industries began to import workers; and the workers had to live, and finally they began to trickle through the interstices of the older population. A series of importations during a period of thirty years had brought over thirty alien races to Iron City. Twenty-two worked in the factory of R. Sill and Son alone. They came of necessity, imperceptibly—dogged, grave, gay, licentious, potential, dreamy, dirty, diligent, lazy, patriotic—and they stayed. And when the glacier of immigration passed, one could find the story of their coming in the strata of Iron City society.

One can see the symbol of that society in an inverted cone. At the apex, the foundation stratum, represented by merchants like Jones & Jones, and eminent clerks and sextons, was the thinnest and shortest; it was composed directly and purely of New England stock. One evidence of its Puritan genesis was the three well established Congregational Churches in the city, and the fact that the millionaires belonged to the First Congregational, and not to St. Luke's. This Puritan stock supplied all the preachers, teachers and most of the big professional men of the community. It had built Crandon Hill College. It was the Brahmin caste, the upper circle, ringed round by thirty alien peoples. It saw its light gradually darkened. The Blue Laws were broken. Baseball and moving-drama became acceptable on Sundays. Through various avenues new standards of continental living began to shape its youth.

The president of the National Bank recorded the change in standards in a letter to the *Republic-Despatch.*

Mr. Editor:

The writer attended the "Follies" given in the assembly room of the High School last evening. While Longfellow, Emerson, Bryant and Holmes looked on (and perhaps heard) from their picture frames on the wall, a very nice little girl was allowed to sing a song about how her beau was all right, except that he didn't know how to kiss. There were some other songs about love and girls and kisses. There was no semblance of genuine talent or refinement in the program.

Puritanism is dying in Iron City, just as everywhere, but I had not looked to see the schools push it so soon into its grave. It is gone with the coming of "refined ragtime" and moving drama, and automobiles.

And so, Mr. Editor, the new order comes to Iron City.

OBSERVER

Perhaps the President of the National Bank was not honest enough, or perhaps he did not see that the same industries that filled his vaults with treasure had brought the alien and the new order to his native city. And so the Puritans saw their influence waning; the story was out of their hands. R. Sill, if he saw, could not turn back; the wheels of industry had to be kept going.

Superimposed upon this ground of New Englanders, were the more ancient incomers, the Welsh, English, French, German and Irish. They, except for a greater moral liberalism and a sterner political conservatism, were as much Americans as the older inhabitants. They worked in linen mills. The French and Irish supported the three Catholic churches; the English and Welsh went to St. Luke's, the Germans to the two Lutheran churches. All these churches resented the most recent comer—the white, substantial Christian Science church. The children of these races of the second stratum were to all appearances thoroughly and utterly assimilated. Superimposed upon this layer of alien life, were the Scandinavian, Swiss and Scotch, to all appearances Americanized; on them a tier of Italians, large, dynamic, floating, but ever present, though isolated from active participation in the affairs of the city. True, a small church had been built for them recently, the first mark of their permanency. On these strata were superimposed, Greeks, Lithuanians, Austrians and Slavs, scarcely English speaking, and wholly foreign. The final tier of the cone placed there by an exquisite stroke of irony was the recent horde of American negroes.

The Puritans had built Crandon Hill College. It should have been the chief agency for the integration of the whole conglomerate. It was over a hundred years old, rich, dignified and proud. Among its graduates were great editors, bishops and missionaries, authors, senators, congressmen, and governors, poets and hymn writers, teachers and thinkers. Its faculty had a national reputation. The trustees were millionaires, brokers and insurance magnates, in the neighboring metropolis. By their stewardship in Iron City itself, it was connected with such well-known men as P. O. Smithkins, president of the Utility Company, and Senator Matt Tyler. It was the fine flower of American civilization of a generation back. Its students came from the "good" homes of the city and immediate vicinity. Perched on a hill overlooking the river near Guy Street, the thoroughfare of "hunyocks," not far from the factory of R. Sill and Son, it drew its skirts about itself and shrank from all the sordid life of factory and immigrant.

But with all its Phariseeism, it was the great heart of the city, lying still; and it must receive most of our attention in this little epic of an American commonwealth.

Iron City was traditionally though restrainedly proud of its college. To tell the truth Iron City was proud of all its institutions. It extolled its Carnegie library, churches, public schools, Masonic Temple, K. of P. Hall, banks, Modern Woodmen, National Guard, saloons, of which there were fifty, street car system, natural site, its city poet, who though forty had never voted, its baseball teams, etc. It said nothing about its trade unions, its industrial fermentation, its intellectual poverty, artistic barrenness, and religious sterility.

Iron City was too busy and too comfortable to face problems. It preferred to drift. It visibly had a destiny; it somehow would be carried through. To mention problems was to "knock" and knocking was the cardinal sin in Iron City. The Commercial Club, at one time seriously alarmed, started secret propaganda against any critics bold enough to find fault with Iron City. "Boost, boost, boost; publicity, advertise"—these made up the creed of this American commonwealth. What if the aliens were not taken care of; what if there were heavy murmurs out of the depths of Sill's mill? Sill who was known to have spent $30,000 to defeat the passage of the Workman's Compensation bill. What if gas was $1.30 per unit? What if the city was unintegrated? What if art was a bastard among these people? What? What? What?——

If one were to figure in stone an image of the commonwealth of Iron City, one could do no better than to carve a youth in his first long trousers, neither boy nor man. One would need to make this figure loll back in a speeding machine, his face set with strength not light, his hands strong, prehensile like a man's, his eyes clear, filled with no dream, his destination yet unknown.

2 John Cosmus, Student of Society

John Cosmus, when he arrived in Iron City one September morning in 1913 to take up his duties as instructor in Sociology at Crandon Hill College, could not by any chance have been taken for a personification of the city itself. He was young enough to be sure, immature, if you will, but he was not lacking in poise; he had also a quality, spiritual, not fully developed perhaps but more than suggested by his firmly knit figure, clean gray eyes, and thoughtful face. Plainly he did not belong to the breathless nervousness of Iron City; he was not below nor above, but beyond it. Without in the least degree suggesting the academian, he was in a homely way self-possessed and distinguished; he was distinct in outline, he was himself. Seven years of arduous self-conquest had burned out, even in one so young as he, the dross of insincerity.

But like all those who are direct, Cosmus saved himself from priggishness by not knowing what he was. As he stepped off the express from Chicago he sighed with relief when he discovered few students on the station platform. He was self-conscious. Here and there were groups of young men and women laughing and gesticulating, assuming the boisterous prerogatives of the college student. John thought that the young men were better dressed than himself. He glanced nervously at his somewhat worn suit and recalled a little bitterly the fact that manners are acquired before one is fifteen, and that the school of experience, even when topped off with Harvard, does not teach one how to wear clothes. He stood awkwardly for a minute. Lost in the unreality of all those last seven years,—his college course, his graduate work, his first bitter experience in the far West teaching, and now Iron City, "new and uncouth" but impressive. He glanced regretfully at the rapidly disappearing train and saw beyond the telegraph wires, beckoning amicably.

A cab driver tried to take his bag; Cosmus objected, saying that he was looking for Samuel Curtis. The ancient cabman obligingly pointed him out and simultaneously Curtis saw Cosmus. They looked at each other, Curtis fleetingly, turning his shifty black eyes away at once, Cosmus searchingly as was his wont. Cosmus wanted to cry out, "How sad you are!" He had the habit, feminine he laughingly characterized it, of seeing people in terms of vivid exclamation. And sad Samuel Curtis was; that was the sum total of him. His gray suit, old but well kept, his stiff shirt with its high round collar, such as clergymen wear, with its four-in-hand, half unclasped, could have no affiliation with anything but a day that was dead and gone and sad. His fine face, with its high brow, was grown prematurely grave; the deep, black eyes under their bushy brows, furtively searched one's face and, instantly disappointed, searched elsewhere; his features suggested a thwarted personality; but when he spoke, Cosmus could not believe that such a voice came from such a man; it was high and dull, it whimpered and whined; it savagely butchered its native English.

The two men paused for a moment on the platform, and this gave Curtis a chance to say that he was glad Cosmus had written to him ahead for rooms, because "accommodations" were scarce; and allowed him to get his guest's baggage and tumble them all into a wide-seated phaeton, drawn by a wheezy red horse.

Cosmus often thought afterwards that his triumphal entry into Iron City had something peculiarly symbolic in it. The tedious pace of the nag, the rattling wheels of the ancient vehicle, seemed to run counter to Iron City life. Everywhere he saw flitting automobiles, marks of influence and affluence, and well dressed crowds, busy streets, and bustling life. The city was at the height of its tide, moving serenely toward its undemocratic destiny, and Curtis and Cosmus, in their old-fashioned phaeton, seemed twin apostles, each in his way, of an ancient and dying and of a new and budding democracy.

They did not talk much. After Curtis had asked the customary questions concerning his guest's journey, and how he had left his people, he relapsed into silence. Nevertheless he fascinated Cosmus; he seemed to breathe out mystery as well as sadness. Finally Cosmus said, "I was just thinking that it doesn't look like the usual college town."

"Times do change. I remember," and Curtis began and slipped garrulously into reminiscences of the past, full of plaintive notes. Here Cosmus was first aware of another strange attribute of Curtis;—although but fifty he assumed on the slightest provocation the role of the aged. Was that not the key to him, thought Cosmus as they drove along; is he not a somnambulist of a vanished dream?

The Curtis house was located near the campus in the "good" section of the town, on what was known as the Bluff. Here was the center of the New England nucleus of the city's life. The Curtis house was a great, rambling old mansion of the style of 1872, overlooking a stagnant brook and the flats that stretched in undulations to the far-off wooded ground line. On the flats, near the brook, Curtis carried on extensive gardening. The house was as quaint as its owner, clean, and airy. Cosmus—"Professor Cosmus," as Curtis called him—was to have a large bedroom overlooking the flats on the East.

Cosmus was delighted with Mrs. Curtis. She was a hearty, motherly woman of great vivacity and irrepressible cheerfulness, and she made him wonder abruptly if the old saying, successful marriages are opposites, held true here.

"Now I just want you to make yourself at home, Professor. Everybody does who comes here. You're not much older than my boy, you know, and he is a freshman just this year, too." John was doubtful about the "too," but there could be no question of her cordiality. "If you want anything," she went on, "you must get it for yourself; I am not going to make you company, but if you need anything that you can't find, just let me know."

She spoke with such warmth and sincerity, that Cosmus was completely won. "It is good to find a home so soon," he said sincerely, "I know I am going to be happy here."

"I know you will," she smiled back. "Sarah Blackstone says home is not a place but a spirit, and so one can have more than one home perhaps."

Cosmus thinking that, perhaps, Sarah Blackstone was a new author he had not read, asked,

"Who is this Sarah Blackstone?"

"You'll meet her, for she is on the faculty, too."

John was shown to his room, and soon had his baggage unpacked and his things put away. He found on the table a book that interested him. It was the New Testament in Greek, margin-marked and thumb-worn, and he wondered who could be reading it. Perhaps it had been left by some former student-occupant of the room. He tossed it carelessly into a drawer. A little later after he was settled, Mr. Curtis came up to the room and awkwardly invited him to go for a ride in the afternoon—"to see our little city." John consented, but Curtis did not leave immediately.

"Say," he said nervously, "did you see anything of an old book around here?"

"Yes, I did. This Greek testament, you mean?"

"Yes, that's it," said Curtis, taking it eagerly, and preparing to depart.

"Do you read Greek?" called out Cosmus pleasantly. Curtis was embarrassed. "Well—well—I used to," he whimpered in the strange shrill way of his; "I still read this old New Testament sometimes. It's kind of a keep-sake." And he passed out in the atmosphere peculiar to him.

After lunch, Cosmus threw himself down into a chair to rest.

He consciously tried to compose his mind to make it fit into the hurly burly of new impressions. He wanted to feel at home, but he did not. He felt awkward, and new; he lacked mastery. He had not lived long enough to know what self lay down deep beneath the folds of his being; he could not forecast his own reactions; he was not sure what he yet was, or was to be. Although he had had a so-called higher education and a year in Harvard graduate school, he was still a ghost to himself, groping tremblingly for a *milieu* to move in. He dreaded, with positive pain, the thought of entering the class room and facing the rows of upturned faces. He dreaded to be called "professor." He cringed beneath the imagined stares of the crowds at chapel. He was a coward. Cosmus had taken up teaching (and here he saw himself with a touch of irony), because he imagined that the American college was the focal point for the mother-brains, the creative minds of the race; he wanted to be a creative mind, and he wanted to shape minds with the gift for creation. Ever since the time long, long ago when he had heard over the telephone wires, the call for a twenty-five thousand dollar brain, he had shaped his career with that idea dominating him; then he had eschewed business or the law, accepting a position at twelve hundred dollars a year, for the simple reason that he believed that the American college was a place for the creative minds of the age. He was very humble as he contemplated his opportunity at Crandon Hill College; he looked forward, with rosy pleasure, as the mind will, when it hangs between sleep and waking, to a long life of unapplauded service, to a home and perhaps later a wife. His head nodded. He dozed.

He was awakened by voices. He tried not to listen, but he could not help it. Samuel Curtis was saying in his high shrill voice, "I can not do it, I can not do it. It would be a travesty on father for me to play his part. I can not." And then came Mrs. Curtis's gentle voice, "I did not mean to hurt you, dearie, but wouldn't it be a greater travesty for some one else to act father's part!" "No, no, no," groaned Samuel Curtis, "I can not. I can not."

"There, there, dearie," consoled Mrs. Curtis. Cosmus heard the heavy steps of the master of the house, and a door slammed. He arose and washed his face wonderingly.

The carriage ride that afternoon was no less than a personally conducted tour, Samuel Curtis, the least dictative of men, seeming somewhat arbitrary in his itinerary. Of course he drove Cosmus to the campus. Nine or ten buildings, representing stages of architecture from 1830 to 1900, from the grave ecclesiasticism of Central Hall to the imitative Greek of the Carnegie Library, impressed the stranger as unusually handsome. Central Hall, Curtis explained, had been built with the bare hands of the first trustees and faculty. A significant fact, thought Cosmus. The campus, from a rare vantage point on the bluff, overlooked the river. For miles the eye could go past the dam and the mills, past the huge establishment of R. Sill and Son, which was like one great, grimy forge, lightened by lurid glares,—beyond, to the cooling angles of woodlands, and the hazy prairie hills. Curtis said that he never got tired looking at that view. As they paused to look they were accosted by some one evidently of authority; he ignored Curtis with deliberate rudeness, Cosmus thought.

"Mr. Cosmus." he said, "don't you think this is the prettiest campus you ever saw?" Without giving time for an answer he continued, "I am not waiting for an introduction, because I am on official business. I am Professor Reed, secretary to the faculty. Our good colleague, Doctor Mather, died suddenly yesterday in the Canadian Rockies; he is to be buried here the third day hence and the president is anxious for the new men to be present at the funeral, both as a mark of respect, and because Professor Mather summed up, as it were, Crandon Hill spirit."

All this was said as if it had been learned, in the mechanical feelingless tone of the functionary.

Bowing himself away, Professor Reed cut across to Central Hall, without so much as acknowledging Samuel Curtis's tardy salutation. Now that he was gone, Cosmus turned and looked at his companion. His face was very pale, and his lips worked without forming words. Finally Curtis said, as though speaking to himself:

"So Chris Mather is dead. Yes, yes, dead. I went to school with him. Fine boy. Fine boy." He seemed lost in the past. He cast a spell over Cosmus's imagination. Sadness was the heart of him. It was strange that this gardener, this boarding-house keeper, could be so disturbing to one, who had not known him twelve hours, even to the point of teasing him with mystery.

Curtis, in a mechanical way, followed (throughout the city) an itinerary which obviously had been carefully mapped out. He drove from the campus to the Historical House, a compact, gray frame building of the Civil War period. Presidents and governors and generals had been entertained there. Then to the Crandon Iron Works, the second manufactory in size and importance. As they passed, Cosmus caught a glimpse of marble corridors through the awninged windows of the office building. Hence to Iron City's Savings and Trust Company, and then by the prettiest residence street, home.

Three days later, John attended the funeral of Professor Christopher Mather. The Mather house had manorial spaciousness, and the dignity of a day long passed in house building. Austere, substantial, venerable, it faced the campus like some ghostly guardian of the past.

Curtis and Cosmus found seats in what must have been the library, and the latter noticed, with fastidious accuracy, every detail of the room. What dampness! What sickening odors! Hyacinths, with their message of death, suffused the air with their fragrance. Sunlight seemed quenched in the heavy twilight of the long rooms. The musk of books and rugs and closed rooms mingled with the scent of flowers. Far away in a shadowy part of the house, some rich male voice was intoning: "The Lord is my Shepherd, I shall not want." There were no songs. Only silence— the restless silence of mourners, broken by the creak of chairs under nervous masculine backs, the rustling of silk, a slowly indrawn sigh, the buzz of an insect, the murmur of leaves outside far away along the walk. The atmosphere made John feel dull and heavy. His mind ran along glassy surfaces of impressions and symbols. The Past, he mused, this is the visible embodiment of the Past. These are the sentient walls of an old house; its history is, perhaps, the history of America's intellectual life, its pioneer hopes and fears, and frontier struggles. Its walls went up when Emerson broke the fetters of European intellectual dominance with his "American Scholar"; its roof repelled rains when Lincoln unbowed his head at Gettysburg and poured out in three minutes the charity of his great heart; its enfolding ivy was planted when James J. Hill began his empire in the great Northwest. It has persisted through storm, rains and change—yet to persist? Cosmus glanced up, almost as if he felt the gaze of some one's eyes to stare directly into a pictured face; it was a Puritan face, at least "Puritan" as visioned by French in his figure of stone—calm, reverential, unafraid.

"Is that a picture of Professor Mather up there?" he whispered to Samuel Curtis.

"No," Curtis answered, "his father, the first president of Crandon Hill College," and then he added irrelevantly, "There have been only three since."

Cosmus renewed his scrutiny of the painting with fresh interest. So from father to son, the torch of civilization had been handed! From son to whom?

And then as a postlude to these thoughts, a voice in another room, far away and ghostly, began to read the life of Christopher Dwight Mather: "Christopher Dwight Mather, son of Ellery Dwight Mather, first president of Crandon Hill College, was born in Iron City on September 14, 1864. He attended the public schools of Iron City and the Plainfield Academy, and later, in 1881, entered the college here. Professor Mather was distinguished by an ardent love of literature, and began at an early age to record his thoughts and impressions in a journal. His life, so outwardly calm, is best revealed through this chronicle."

Then followed some passages which showed vividly the simplicity, the democracy, the ardent idealism of the college of a generation ago. One passage stuck in Cosmus's mind long after.

"March 5, 1897. The election of Major McKinley illustrates conclusively the bad effect of the Civil War. Most of us Americans, lost in sentimentalism, fail to see that the Civil War was baneful. With no exception, this war made every president up to Major McKinley himself, a soldier. It served as an excuse for a high protective tariff, which allowed expansion and development of natural resources. It permitted tremendous condensation of capital in the hands of a few—and now all our problems, God help us, the problems of living in New York City, and the problems of education at Crandon Hill, turn on the greater problem of condensation of capital. I am not sure that old Professor Jason was not right when he said, 'Science is from the devil.' Science has invented machines which have killed handicraft, and when handicraft goes, art goes. Science has intertangled nations with eloquent wires. Science, and its methods of generalization, have taught men how to think in the large, and build huge dynasties of riches. There are hard times before you, O Republic, and before you, O Crandon Hill College. Education is mechanized. We have lost our soul. Why can't we go back to the old ideals of my father!"

"The entries in the diary break off in 1901. Professor Mather served his college loyally up to this year, 1913. He went last June to the Canadian Rockies, never to return. Those of us who knew him personally, who felt the daily electric shock of his personality, can only bow our heads now, as he would have us do, in silent submission."

The funeral made a deep impression upon Cosmus. It brought him face to face with the college of the past—the sabbatical, simple, reclusive student life which he had already dimly felt. He came to the swift conclusion that if this funeral were typical of its life, Crandon Hill College must be a fossil imprisoned in a rock.

Long after he had blown out the kerosene lamp that night,

Cosmus sat in the dark, overlooking the moonlit flats, thinking and planning. Life seemed so simple and easy just then. For one who had met the jagged edges of life in his earlier years, Cosmus was unusually innocent of the world. He thought it a place for the working out of simple justice; he had not yet discovered that there were men who were utterly unlike himself in their patriotism. To him there were no inscrutable mysteries, save the simple mysteries: the passing of time, the perpetuity of the past in the present; reproduction and love. All else was clear, under the solvency of man's mind. He sat immersed in his thoughts until he saw a figure come up from the flat below, and stand for a moment, looking up at the stars; silhouetted clear against the light, the body could be clearly seen bent heavily, revealing as the blurred features could not, utter dejection of spirit. Cosmus could not take his eyes away; in the stillness of the night he heard the sigh which fell from the tired lips of the man under the trees below. Once the figure lifted up its arms in silent imploration, then dropped them submissively, and disappeared in the shadow of the house. The night was empty now: it seemed impotent to speak its thoughts. Cosmus mused; he wondered if he must go on forever feeling sorry for Samuel Curtis.

3 Sarah

One morning before school opened, while John Cosmus was
dressing in his room, Mrs. Curtis came to him greatly agitated.
When John had persuaded her to be seated, and while he was
still finishing shaving, he tried to disentangle the strands of her
snarled story. She had come to tell him that Sarah Blackstone
was to be relieved of her position as instructor in history at
Crandon Hill College, but her indignation made her at times
incoherent.

"And what I want you to do, Professor Cosmus, is to go and
plead her case."

"But I don't know Miss Blackstone," he protested "and I am
a stranger here."

"So much the better. They will listen to you impartially, because you can see the thing as right, not personally, you know."

John could not help smiling at the naive absurdity of Mrs.
Curtis's request; but he took the thing too lightly, perhaps, when
he said, "But how do I know that Miss Blackstone deserves to
remain on the faculty of Crandon Hill College? A faculty, you
know, Mrs. Curtis, is a very dignified, ultra-respectable body,
which must uphold the best traditions and noble customs of the
past."

"Sarah Blackstone," she broke in, not perceiving the irony in
his words, "is the truest sweetest——"

"Yes, but what is the charge preferred against her?"

"That she don't go to church."

"Doesn't go to church?"

"Yes, and she is a religious person, Professor Cosmus. I know she has peculiar notions about church, and I don't exactly agree with her, but that makes no difference; she is really good. You see I belong to Reverend Mr. Dingley's flock—the First Congregational, the biggest church in town. I have been serving as deaconess—visiting the sick, and relief work, all that sort of thing," she interpolated, not sure that he knew what the work of a deaconess was, "and would you believe it, everywhere I go I find myself anticipated—Sarah Blackstone has been there scattering good—not letting her right hand know what her left hand doeth—but Reverend Mr. Dingley don't see that this is being religious. Well, I do wish Sarah would go to church, too, and not cause all this bother."

"I can't believe that any such charge would relieve Miss Blackstone of her position; Crandon Hill is no longer a church school, it is on the Foundation. Are you sure there is nothing else?"

"Well, there is something else. Sarah has been distributing tracts on the limitation—let's see—well, on not having so many babies, you know," she said, looking hard at John.

Cosmus thought a moment. "I see. Tracts on the limitation of offspring?" Mrs. Curtis nodded.

Finally he said, "I will go, Mrs. Curtis, if you think I can do anything."

But when Mrs. Curtis and John rapped at the door of Sarah Blackstone's house a little later, they were told that she had gone over to see President Crandon at the college. John felt some reluctance in intruding farther into such a matter, but the nature of the charge against Miss Blackstone made it more than a private affair. Any one with a social consciousness, he thought, must feel an interest in this case. And then Mrs. Curtis said:

"I don't mind going over to President Crandon's office one bit. I have known him all my life; he was a great friend of my father's, and Reverend Mr. Dingley will not resent it—besides this will be a good way for you to see the real Sarah Blackstone."

John allowed himself to be led along. When they arrived at the library, Mrs. Curtis knocked at the President's office door, and when it was opened, calmly walked in. Drawn up about the long mahogany table, there were four persons. John recognized the Reverend Mr. Dingley, a youngish man, fastidiously dressed, singularly handsome. His voice was noticeably deep and fine, and he seemed to delight in playing upon it. Hugh Crandon, president of Crandon Hill College, who sat at the head of the table, was a man well toward sixty. He was the dominating figure in Crandon Hill life. He looked his part, tall, square, alert, with gray hair and mustache, and refined manner. His face had lost, if it ever had possessed it, anything of ministerial look; it wore an expression of calculating shrewdness. "A corporation lawyer," some one once called him in John's presence. Yet with the shrewdness, or rather as a part of it, was a kind of immobility behind which the real Hugh Crandon always retreated. John felt this remoteness of personality in his first meeting with President Crandon and at his last. The president now introduced Mrs. Curtis and John to Miss Georgia Summers, Dean of women. Though she smiled and dimpled, she did not conceal her displeasure at Mrs. Curtis's intrusion. The other person at the table was Miss Blackstone, whom John met for the first time.

President Crandon was above annoyance; he said that they were met there to consider some common interests of the college, but that these could wait, if the business of Mrs. Curtis and Mr. Cosmus was urgent; he would retire with them to another room.

"With your permission, President Crandon," broke in Miss Blackstone, "I would like to speak before my friend, Mrs. Curtis, and before Mr. Cosmus, a member of the faculty. I am afraid we differ as to the nature of this conference. I consider it wholly a public matter."

President Hugh Crandon was plainly disturbed. "A public matter, Miss Blackstone? I don't understand. It is customary, you know——" He paused, as if hoping she would understand as if by telepathy, and not prolong the disagreeable controversy.

"I understand," she said. "It is customary to consider Crandon Hill College a private institution, when in reality, it is entirely a public one. It is my belief that every member of the faculty should consider himself a public servant."

"No doubt, they do," replied the president.

"I am sure they do," said Reverend Mr. Dingley.

"I am sure that duty to the public is uppermost, as it were, in the heart of every one of Crandon Hill's professors," chanted Dean Georgia Summers.

"Then there can be no possible reason why Mrs. Curtis and Mr. Cosmus may not stay, and why I cannot explain at once—very simply, why I have stayed away from church, and have distributed tracts on the limitation of offspring among the Italian and Lithuanian women of Iron City. Those are the charges, I believe?"

President Crandon looked uncomfortable.

"There were no charges, Miss Blackstone. As is the custom, we merely wanted to talk over certain matters relative to your general effectiveness as a teacher."

"May I ask what matters?"

"Yes," said Reverend Mr. Dingley. "Apart from your ecclesiastical views, do you not think that you would be a greater force in the community, a better example to the students, if you united yourself with some church of your choice? The college, I beg to remind you, my dear Miss Blackstone, had its genesis in the church, was furthermore fathered by the church and should still acknowledge, though superficially estranged by the Foundation, its connection with the church."

"May I ask you a personal question, Mr. Dingley?"

"Yes, of course."

"How many sermons have you heard in the past year?"

"Well, now, that is hard to say. One or two, I judge."

"I have heard five. I hope you won't think I am impertinent, if I point out that if goodness is dependent on hearing sermons"—she paused. There was a dazzle in Miss Blackstone's eyes that John liked to see.

"But Miss Blackstone, the sermon is the smallest part of church-going; the real thing is the acknowledgement of one's connection with the community."

"I agree, but I prefer to acknowledge my connection with the community by working in it—by distributing tracts, for instance."

John Cosmus was delighted with this little drama. He was content to be a spectator; but he saw the eyes of President Hugh Crandon meet those of Reverend Mr. Dingley across the table in full understanding. The president arose, and said affably, "I believe we thoroughly understand each other, Miss Blackstone, and I think there is no longer any reason to prolong this discussion."

A change came over Miss Blackstone. She no longer bantered, but hardened into seriousness.

"Before I am dismissed, President Crandon, I feel as if—as if I must justify myself before my friend, Mrs. Curtis, and Mr. Cosmus, who may be said to represent the public. It has been my position in this matter that a teacher should do more than keep classes, that he should be a living link between the public and the best thought of the moment. That is all I have tried to do, and if I am discharged from Crandon Hill College, I shall simply state the reasons as I see them, to the press."

"Why, my dear Miss Blackstone," said Dean Georgia Summers, "who ever thought of discharging you? I am sure we all think of you as one of our most effective teachers."

"Yes, indeed," said President Crandon.

"Then," said Miss Blackstone sweetly, "will you please say I have resigned? I am going home to accept a position that Mr. Boyne of the Crandon Hill Iron Works offered me this morning."

Cosmus later acknowledged that he was somewhat amazed by Miss Blackstone's audacity. Had she leaped beyond him? Had this young woman out-thought him, determining educational values that were unknown to him? To tell the truth, Cosmus was shocked by her decisiveness. College to him had always been something sacred, something to give his life to, and her disloyalty, flippant on the surface at least, seemed at this moment almost a sacrilege. Was she courting trouble? Was this girl all head and no heart?

President Crandon, urbane, immobile ever, expressed, as in a sermon, perfunctory regret that the college was to lose the services of Miss Blackstone and bowed them out.

On the steps of the library Mrs. Curtis beamed upon Sarah Blackstone and Professor Cosmus and re-introduced them. It was the beginning of what was to be something more than a pleasant acquaintance. As she stood talking for a few minutes with Mrs. Curtis, Cosmus had an opportunity to study Sarah Blackstone's face unobserved. It seemed to him that the striking characteristic of her singularly delicate face was clearness of design. Unlike herself some faces are distinguished by one or two fine features; perhaps the eyes are deep and large, while the chin may be weak and slanting; sometimes the nose is regal, and the mouth is a straight, short line. Not so with Sarah's face; every feature stood out in relief: rich brown hair, distinct dark brows over deep blue eyes, skin of warm, rosy texture. These features, clearly designed, belonged together; the face was handsome; it was beautiful because these parts formed a harmonious whole.

Clearness of design bespoke clearness of spirit. As the days of their acquaintance passed, when he was away from her, Cosmus thought of her in cooling symbols: a mountain lake, a snow-capped mountain of soft contour, a Greek statue, symbols of beautiful, inspiring things far removed. When he was near her, he thought of a clean-lipped, clean-limbed little brother that he once had had—and lost.

But though she did not lack geniality or companionableness, she possessed a faint, impersonal quality, a distantness, a vague elusiveness, which he felt but could not analyze. On their walks, he was just as happy to feel her bound alone up the hill beside him, nostrils taut, her cheeks flushed, as he would have been if he had dared to put his arm about her and move up together limb to limb.

Cosmus sometimes longed for some show of weakness, of human need on her part. Such self-sufficiency was, he thought, uncanny in a woman. Often, as a result of her aloofness, they engaged in badinage, under which lurked a more solemn symbolism. One day when he came down stairs at Mrs. Curtis's, he found her at a window. She turned and faced him.

"You have come to play with me, little girl?"

She caught his mood.

"No, I don't play with little boys. I came to see Mother Curtis."

"But I want you to play with me, to see the sun and shining air. The hills are waiting for us. Let us go!"

"But I dare not. Old Grandmother Convention said, 'Child, you must never go until you have——'"

"I know what you are going to say, but grandmother is dead now, and anyway, she never practiced her own advice." Pleadingly, "If you will come I'll show you something."

"What?"

"Will you come?"

"Show me first."

"You promise?"

"Yes."

"My crooked finger." He held up the marked hand.

"Poor boy," she said. "How did you hurt it?" This with exquisite solicitude.

They went out into the tonic air. Cosmus never had seen such a splendid creature. With half the length of stride, she kept pace with him; her eyes sharp and clear; her breast deep and full; she looked like an incarnate figure of Womankind.

"Where do you play oftenest?" he asked, to break a silence that was not at all awkward.

"Wouldn't you rather go where I play best?"

"Yes, please take me."

"Only he who has a boy's soul can go," she said.

He was silent. They went on past children dancing on a lawn, where every grass-blade shook silver sundrops down.

"Have you a—a boy's soul?" she asked mischievously.

"I have a soul, I know it. I just discovered that this evening."

"But a child's soul," she insisted.

"You answer that. You're sitting as judge!"

She laughed.

"Then you can hear my symphony."

"Your symphony? Then you play, do you?"

"There, you betrayed yourself. You can't make believe. Your soul is the soul of a man. Take me home, sir."

Cosmus looked at her, and saw she had slipped into seriousness.

They turned about, and silently tramped to town. At the gate of the cottage, at which he left her, Cosmus, with deference, said:

"Miss Blackstone, have I been rude? When I find the soul of a boy that is gone, may I come again?"

"I'll ask Grandad Convention," she retorted, and flashed into the house.

John found rest and satisfaction in her. Without reservation, he could give her full allegiance. She seemed able to follow him into ways of tortuous thinking, excursions he liked to take now and then into abstract knowledge. Her spirit, too, it seemed to him, was not cut off, as his was not, from the poet heart of humanity. Yet, there was something lacking in her, a baffling something that he searched to find. It was her mystery.

One day, when they were in the midst of crowded Cambridge Street, a dirty child toddled up and clutched Sarah's dress. Its upturned face, tear-stained and pitiful, its wistful helplessness, filled John at once with the most intense pity. Sarah looked down at the child, not unkindly, then bent and carefully unloosed its hand.

"Go find your mother, child," she admonished.

Cosmus was not satisfied. Was that the key to her mystery? Not that her body lacked vitality, but that she had chastity, so profound, that she shrank from motherhood. Was Sarah Blackstone but an Attitude, a Spirit?

He tried to get her to talk about herself, but he failed. Here, too, her self-sufficiency asserted itself. She spoke of her home in the metropolis; of her family, of friends; but the allusions were always vague and impersonal. She had a kind of wistful interest in many persons in Iron City. She it was who told Cosmus about old Professor Jason, first professor of philosophy in Crandon Hill College, who had committed suicide when science courses were first introduced into the curriculum. Her interest in people, though, seemed to John more intellectual than friendly; more sociological than maternal.

He had no trouble in talking of himself to her. When he congratulated her on her strength in resigning from the faculty of Crandon Hill College, she replied that she had merely suited her own pleasure, pointing out laughingly that he was still in prison and she free.

"I've discovered this week," he answered, "that I am not getting along very well with my classes. It's a questionable joy standing before a group of people and pouring out the best you have on inattentive ears. The students sit negligently for the hour, courteously quiet, save for an audible breath, now and then, or the scraping of feet. But not once can I strike fire. The world is so wonderful to me," he asserted boyishly; "it is filled with so many problems and is dangerous with so many impending changes, so momentous with opportunities that I expect all young men and women to be moved at the sight of it."

"I understand," she answered.

"I have a deep sense of limitation," he went on, "in this new field at Crandon Hill College. It began my first morning at chapel. I entered confidently—inflated perhaps, a little youthful, you know, and mounted the platform to take a seat. I was met by President Crandon. 'Mr. Cosmus,' he said, 'the faculty are seated according to rank, and instructors sit down there.' His thumb pointed peremptorily to a row of seats among the students. I colored; some students laughed; and I obeyed his gesture. It was awfully humiliating, if it was only a trifle. I have tried to see the philosophy that lay behind it."

"The college, you know," Miss Blackstone replied, not without a touch of irony, "is an emanation of the home, and must be patriarchal in its form of government. You, as youngest in the family, must sit at the foot of the table."

"So I discovered. There seem to be six tiers of eminence in Crandon Hill life: assistants, instructors, assistant professors, professors, deans and president—all rigidly observed. No professor's wife would make the mistake of inviting a mere instructor to tea. I thought," he concluded with a smile, "that I had graduated from the democracy of manual labor into the democracy of learning years ago, and instead I find it is a monarchy."

"Not a despotism?" she asked, smiling.

By this time, the two had made a detour and had come again to the city. The town lay in the valley, cut by the sweeping river; there were the towers of the college on the Bluff, a few scattered church spires, bridges, the red-bricked shops, and the smoldering factories. It lay still frozen into calm, like a painted thing far removed from the sordidness of daily life, as beautiful as Wordsworth's London, as tranquil as Keats's marble town. For a moment it seemed to John a dream, with Sarah the only reality. Then he remembered the streets filled with busy life, the gutters running with filth, the factories full of restless, discontented thousands, the churches, unattended, the cramped quarters for the negro, the dago shacks along Guy street. "Submerged hatred, decaying democracy, class feuds, social parasitism, gross materialism"—these broken phrases flowed through his mind, and when he glanced at Sarah, she seemed filled with the same emotion. They passed down into the town, trod the busy streets, and came to her door, both conscious of the difference between the painted city of the hill and the city of reality; and they felt very near to each other.

Cosmus spent much of his spare time with Sarah Blackstone in the first months of his struggle at Crandon Hill College. She was an inspiration to him, and so he did not heed the inevitable buzz of censure that arose from his colleagues on the faculty. But one evening on returning from a walk, Mrs. Curtis accosted him at the door. As usual she treated him to a long recital of petty happenings in her customary delightful vein of motherliness. She was one of those women with a deep, unsatisfied, maternal feeling; perhaps this accounted for both her charm and her unattractiveness; her quick human sympathy and her gossiping restlessness. This evening amidst the flow of small things, there was one question the significance of which did not strike him until nearly an hour later.

"Has Sarah ever told you about her friend Sidney Haynes?"

When that question suddenly returned to him he was sitting at his table reading a new treatise on the Single Tax. He immediately went in search of Mrs. Curtis, and asked her what she had meant.

"Why, you dear boy," she said, "Sarah has referred so often to Sidney Haynes, I thought maybe you ought to know about him." She paused, and then added, "Seeing that you are with her so much."

The explanation was worse than the question, and Cosmus was uncomfortable.

After this conversation with Mrs. Curtis he went out for a walk. He followed the lighted street until there were no lights, and he went into the country, down the dim road, past the brown fields and the silent brown farm houses. When he returned the city was asleep. All the houses were dark, save where panted the great factories on the edge of town. At the corner of College and Zackary Streets, a patch of light in a large square house indicated that some one was stirring behind the blind. As John passed opposite, the blind was raised and a girl in a night gown, her hair in two flowing braids, paused for a moment to look out into the night. Cosmus stepped into the shadow of the tree. The girl was beautiful; he could see her limbs beneath the diaphanous folds of her gown, like a nymph's through water; she was almost a vision. He stood tremblingly staring until the lamp winked out, and it was dark in the great house, too.

Just as Cosmus turned into the Curtis yard a few minutes later, he detected the figure of Samuel Curtis down in the flats below, walking among the cornrows. Sad and strange as ever.

John lay awake long after midnight that night. He could hear clearly the throb of the engines, the clang of steel on steel, from the great factory of R. Sill and Son blocks away to the north. His senses alert, his mind strangely pitched in a mood of wonder, as it often is at midnight-waking, he felt a sudden warm intimacy between himself and the unseen workers yonder. He tried to visualize the great dusty, lurid workrooms, the glare of molten metal, the buildings towering up in the smoke and flame like shadowy shelters, the noise, the wonder, the fatigue, the inarticulate marvel of industry. He seemed to know the men, their mute loyalty to the task, their aching discontent, their sullenness; their dogged tenacity, simplicity, comradeship.

He seemed to understand for the first time their narrowness, pettiness, flightiness. He thought of the college, dumb and quiet on the Bluff; its richness of life, its ideals, its dreams.

And as he lay wondering, his mind racing with symbols, inarticulately as waking minds at midnight will do, he heard the wind beat against the wires, in its old chant of progress.

The River of Wires, Cosmus thought, flowing on and on, between the cities—between Iron City and Chicago, New York and London—on and on.

And he thought, suddenly thrilled, "What is the River of Wires going to bring to the boys and men in the factory on the hill?"

But when he slept he did not dream of factories or cities, but of a forest glade, and a girl more beautiful than all the rest.

4 Margaret

Cosmus put the question guiltily at the breakfast table.

"Who lives in the large square house at the corner of College and Zackary?"

"Carl Morton," Mrs. Curtis told him.

Strange to say, that same morning in the Carl Morton house at the corner of College and Zackary, a girl was asking to go to college in order to take courses in sociology.

Carl Morton was foreman of the smithy gang in the factory of R. Sill and Son. He was a type of man that it is good to see. A life of labor had given his body a massiveness and symmetry and his face refinement. He might have been figured by St. Gaudens, to fit into a drawing of industry by Pennel. Of English stock, he had been brought to Iron City from Yorkshire, when he was eight years old, a half century before, and his services at the Sill plant were almost coincident with its life. Therefore he could be pardoned, perhaps, for his over-warm pride in the Sill manufactory. Some inherited respect for authority, coupled with a sense of proprietorship in a business in which he had no real share, made him an ardent supporter of R. Sill. He invariably spoke of "our plant"; and he always justified every arrangement that Sill made in his own favor with his men. Every morning Morton walked through the office and said "Good morning, Mr. Sill," and got in reply a brusque, but not unkindly, "Good morning, Morton," "Good morning, foreman." Morton never had had any sympathy with organized labor, he was one of the chief agents through which the office—that vortex of mystery and authority—worked in resisting the entrance of unions in the plant of R. Sill and Son. When the company was buzzing over the clash between the Railroad Brotherhoods and the magnates over the eight-hour plan, Morton stood for the railroads.

"If a man can't work ten hours, he's a weakling—that's all he is." He drew himself up to his full height and knotted the great muscles about his neck and chest. "I have worked ten hours a day for thirty-eight years, and I haven't suffered." And then wagging his head sadly, he concluded, "I don't see what the laboring man is coming to."

No one who saw Carl Morton could question his views. The fine product of a system, he and old Sill were the flowers of the feudalistic industrial order fast falling into decline: master and man, the baron and his squire.

But if Morton resisted any sort of organization among the men, he carried his conservatism no farther at the factory. Like a hound, he smelt out faults in the composition of his department. He improved here, and improved there; he espoused the tactics of efficiency, and lived them mercilessly, yet kept the regard of his men. He saw the smithy grow from a hand-operated forge to the great, roaring furnace room with ten forges and pneumatic hammers that did the work of hundreds. Every day Carl and his assistants put into the fire and beneath the great six-ton hammer, four three-thousand-eight-hundred pound engine shafts. Such work, day in and day out, amidst the white glare of the forges, and the drumming of the huge hammers, commanding and guiding, flowered Morton into a leader of men.

Carl carried his conservatism into the education of his only child, Margaret. To him, the rearing of a child was simple. Reared himself under a somewhat simple régime, in an environment that might be best described as pioneer, it never occurred to him that in complex Iron City a hundred forces beyond his control played upon his child, which in a way had never touched his own life. The movies, countless story magazines, innumerable associates, a flux of undigested opinions, new standards of sex, new judgments in religion; these, unreckoned with by the parent were calculated to offset much of the old-fashioned training that Morton clung to. He believed implicitly in Margaret because he loved her madly, to a point little suspected by himself, and because he judged that his own excellent example, and the constant inculcation of a few well-tried maxims, would hold her true. "Serve God," "Mind your manners" and "Respect your betters" were the elements of Morton's teachings. And it must be said that "Respect your betters" received the most emphasis. Morton left the first precept to St. Luke's, the second to Mrs. Morton, a frail woman, who was a recent convert to Christian Science, much to Carl's comfort and chagrin, and the last to himself.

Hence he was horrified when Margaret came home from a party and said, "I had five dances with Raymond Sill, and I think he is horrid."

"Tut, tut, daughter."

"And he flunked out at Yale, too."

"What have I told you, daughter, about respecting Mr. Sill's son?" Carl Morton did not see the impish tongue thrust out at him through his daughter's pretty teeth.

Margaret tried to obey her father in all things; but when obedience to the axiom "Respect your betters" stood in the way of membership in the Country Club, and an automobile, she rebelled. Her father, applying his own philosophy to himself, hesitated about allowing himself the illustrious privileges of automobiles and a country club, questioning whether it became a foreman of a smith gang to assume such airs. Old Sill himself, at one time, had belonged to the Country Club, and Morton wondered whether it would not be an affront to his master if he belonged. Margaret did not care for such twaddle, yet she was puzzled to know how to encompass her designs. Then suddenly she discovered her father's loyalty to her. She fell sick with a high fever, and Carl sat by her bed night and day, taking one of his rare absences from the factory, that he might nurse her. One night she watched him through half-closed eyes, and saw the profound paternity shining in his face; it startled, frightened and pleased her.

When she recovered, she again took up the question of the automobile, and found him obdurate. Without hesitation, she went to the Rex Garage and left word that Carl Morton wanted an agent to call that night at seven, that he was on the market for a machine. When the agent arrived, he inadroitly stated that "your daughter, Mr. Morton, says you want a machine."

Carl's loyalty to Margaret, and an innate fineness, kept him from betraying his daughter. He accepted the agent's statement, and in a few days Margaret had her car, and in a few weeks the Country Club membership.

The mistake Carl Morton made was in not taxing his daughter with deceit.

That had happened two years before. The education of Carl by Margaret went on, and when she asked to go to college, largely because the *Theta Kappa Chis* were rushing her, he did not demur, although to him the world seemed somewhat strange when the daughter of a foreman no longer kept her distance from her betters. And so it was finally arranged that she should enter the second semester.

It was inevitable that John Cosmus would find Margaret Morton out. She was in his elementary course and he often found her great eyes disconcerting as he set forth the principles upon which society was based. He noticed her immediately the first morning. Fire in form, was what Cosmus thought of first in reference to Margaret Morton. She was not large, but well developed, massive in daintiness. He loved to watch her move as one would a fine animal; at times he caught a glimpse of a clean slender ankle and the bulging calf above her shoe tops. The taut folds of her waist over a full breast, the depth of chest and the shoulders wide like a boy's; the movements of well-formed hips set him to answering, deep within him, undisguised calls. One day it became necessary to meet her in conference on an assigned topic. Cosmus sat in his office waiting. Outside he could hear the water dripping from the eaves, and the sing-song of the wheels from the paper mills across the river.

All the time that Margaret and John were talking—surface talk, routine of school matters—each was saying to the other deep, unuttered, primitive things.

John thought, "What great eyes, how exquisitely molded her nose and mouth!"

They were very happy. They seemed floating in a great sea of pleasure, a sea that was electric with currents that throbbed and beat in one heart as well as in the other. The same yellow sunshine fell through the dusty window, the same shadows quivered on the wall, the same sing-song of the engines came in through the window, the same harsh voices of distant teachers beat in upon both of them. It was a day very commonplace and drab, but to them how different; they knew not that it was drab. He watched her lips perceptibly parted, her lids fallen low over her eyes as if they were curtains to shut in the out-peering soul, her startled breath moving the lace which fell low over a swelling bosom. Images floated in his mind like music. He saw a stream and two bodies moving in unison with the shining water; a garden sweet and fragrant, and they two lying close together looking up at the flying clouds; a Norwegian bathhouse, and he smiting her flushed flesh with odorous pine boughs.

She seemed a different creature, breathing marble, flesh surcharged with impelling power—eloquent. She, who was so mute, spoke now in this moment a language which he understood too well.

If any one had looked in at that moment, at No. 12 Central Hall, he would have seen only young Professor Cosmus pausing in his learned discourse to catch his breath for a moment, and a confused freshman girl, wisely inattentive. In reality a man and woman were sitting there shaken by the eternal whirlwind so full of passionate meaning.

"You see, Miss Morton," he was saying perfunctorily, "sociology in a sense may be thought of as the philosophy of philosophy. The biologist makes certain generalizations about life, the psychologist does likewise; the theologian, the economist, just in so far as they generalize are to be thought of as philosophers. Then it is the office of the sociologist to take all of these views, and harmonize them in respect to one unifying standard, namely their practical significance, to human society—to our living together."

Wisely she did not raise her eyes, nor close her lips, nor steady her trembling limbs. She just sat mutely calling to him. When he stopped his formal discussion, she did not even feel it incumbent upon her to take up his conversation where he left it, but feverishly began to rattle off little vague frivolities incident to school life.

"You see, Doctor Wheaton put me in his advanced French class, and I have had only one year." Cosmus thought she must speak French delightfully. "And French is so musical. Did you know that Professor Palmer is sick?" she asked. "Isn't Mr. Kimbark a strange, dear, green man?"

And then they lapsed into meaningful silence until they were conscious again of the inaudible world about them, and feebly tried to break the chains which bound them, making an effort to speak. The words were flat and blatant in their ears. She at length rose to go and Cosmus with an uncontrollable gesture reached out as if to take her hand. He could not see, his breath struggled in his throat. He groped for a chair and sat down heavily, his face hooded with his hands, his frame shaking as with cold.

He felt her hand on his head. It calmed him. He looked up into her deep eyes, and saw her transformed.

"Why you, you are a woman," he said.

She smiled down on him, and touched his hot forehead with what he thought was indescribable gentleness. He took her hand; again they were conscious of the inaudible world, eloquent with vast meanings, shutting down over them. John Cosmus fixed his eyes on the shadows that quivered on the wall. They seemed almost like a coil of serpents. He dared not look at her, but he could feel her heart throb in her hand.

Then true to another impulse, he arose suddenly and said, unsteadily, "Yes, Miss Morton, if you should take that subject, and give it some thought, I believe you would find it advantageous."

Mere trite phrases that floated in his whirling mind.

"Good afternoon, Miss Morton."

She stood in the doorway, the light of the inaudible world still on her face, her eyes afire, it seemed, beneath her lowered lids, her bosom tossed by her breathing.

"Won't you come and see me sometimes?" she asked, and then he heard her light foot on the stairs.

When she had gone, Cosmus looked at his watch abstractedly, and brushed his hand across his eyes and forehead; he experienced a sense of deep loss, of want. One question stirred in his mind, "What am I doing? I, John Cosmus? . . ."

Margaret Morton possessed an unconscious gift for unchastity. From some obscure ancestor had descended into her all the pull and witchery of sex. She belonged to the dynasty of beautiful women. She was two women. Her surface self ran slightly above the average; she was only an ordinary girl, prattling of dances, engagements, machines, her favorite actress. Her unconscious self ran into racial deeps; she excelled all her friends in that she had a genius for attracting men; and she never knew by what power she held them. She knew she affected them profoundly, but she did not know just how she affected them. If she had been called a girl with a capacity for evil, she would have been as much shocked as her father would have been. She attributed her popularity to personal charm. She did not know that she had concealed in her a mystery that had undone statesmen, leveled thrones and desolated empires.

So she affected Cosmus. In contrast to the thought of Sarah Blackstone, the thought of Margaret Morton made him restless.

She awakened in him moods, such wild gypsy longings that life in Iron City sudden ran stale. He wanted to be off to another fairer place; his work was drudgery; life a sham. And yet, never to him before had the world of tree, sky, and field looked so enchanting. This world was a dazzle of changing loveliness. How could he endure so much beauty? He felt stirring within an impulse to go to Margaret, confess his love, and elope with her And all this time, his keen, dry intellect sneered and chuckled over him.

About this time he came to know Ezra Kimbark better. Kimbark was the Professor of English Literature, and to Cosmus the most interesting man in the faculty. They had met the fall before, in a manner that afterwards to the friends seemed dramatic. Cosmus had been caught in a storm on the campus and Kimbark appearing suddenly, apparently from nowhere, had taken him home with him.

"I am Ezra Kimbark, and you are Cosmus. Some rain, isn't it?"

Cosmus had known, in that moment, that he would like Ezra Kimbark; there began then that intercourse of minds that men of intellectual tastes crave and delight in.

But Kimbark was not an antidote for Margaret. That malady had to run its course. One day Cosmus received a note from President Crandon calling attention to the unwritten custom at Crandon Hill that the instructors should not have any social intercourse with students. He had written Cosmus that while it was, of course, far from his purpose to impose his will upon another, yet he felt sure that Mr. Cosmus would be sensitive to the fine standards of the institution.

Nevertheless, though not unconscious of the proprieties, and fully aware of the weight of sentiment against his friendship with the Mortons, John called frequently at the house to see Margaret. He was delighted with her father; Carl's poise and simplicity, his ready tongue, and his familiarity with a field that is alluring to every young man—Big Business—made the blacksmith interesting to the teacher. Cosmus accepted with alacrity Morton's invitation to visit the Sill manufactory—"our plant," the foreman said.

The presence of Margaret did not satisfy. She was like some delicious poison, distilled in the blood, that only blurred one's powers. He could not find peace away from her. He who had not known women was at last helpless before this girl.

He knew fits of depression, too. The world, he watched with keen eyes; and he felt a tightening of world consciousness in the early months of 1914. Was it possible that in this strange subjective passion for Margaret, he was merely feeling the strain and tug of the world consciousness ready to pass into momentous changes? There was a furor of dancing all over the country, and Margaret, unrestrained by college restrictions, tangoed every night. Cosmus intervened in behalf of her health. They quarreled. She called him "an old mossback," and he replied in kind—and then repented—and then quietly philosophized that the dancing craze was but another manifestation of the cosmic nervousness of which he was so aware. Strikes; vast aggregations of men in commotion; syndicalism, socialism, internationalism, world peace to the keen-eyed student of society were but phenomena that reflected like mirrors impending cosmic changes.

"If you want to get spiritual chorea," he said to his friend Ezra Kimbark, "pick up any one of the American magazines which purports to be a review of the week or month; let opinions, controversies, counter-opinions, hopes, fears, discoveries, scepticism beat in upon you, without finding in all that swirl of talk one authoritative note. What America needs is a single commanding voice in the name of the spirit, and I fear that the very nature of our commonwealth forbids its rise."

Seeing so clearly the trend of the world, and by nature being dynamic rather than receptive, it was exquisite torture to Cosmus to sit still and do nothing. Some one has said that college professors as a class are the unhappiest individuals in the world; it is because they see and can not do.

How far should one be docile? Did the analogy between a

mother and a college hold entirely? Should one love his college as one would his mother, because he had no other? Was education no great, vital function? Should the college be its own judge and jury, always acquitting itself?

John's reasoning broke down. He was at sea. Of this, however, he was sure—Crandon Hill College was not affecting the life of its generation to the point of exercising social control. He came to recognize his malady and resolved to shake it off, and act, and then fell upon him the blighting vividness of Margaret again.

Strange to say, in this condition, he craved once again the companionship of Sarah Blackstone, whom he had seen only occasionally for the last few months.

Yet he saw no irrelevancy in the fact that he felt a passion so low in the physical order as jealousy, in reference to a creature so much a spirit as Sarah! He avoided her company when he craved it so much, for he had never questioned the truth of Mrs. Curtis's insinuation concerning Sidney Haynes.

One Friday, late in February, on an excuse to be in the open air, he took a gun and went into the country to hunt. Ten miles east of Iron City there lay a rolling country of uncultivated fields and oak woods of a wildness which exhilarated him. The morning was cold and brilliant, snow lay in a light crust over the ground. Cosmus walked briskly. He felt freer and stronger than he had for weeks; than at any time since he had begun his strange relations with Margaret, pretending he was her teacher, when in reality he was but a lover. He saw little game, but he tramped on enjoying the wild road as it climbed and wound through the heavily oaked hills. Soon after noon the wind shifted suddenly to the south, and in an hour it was raining—a warm rain for February, but chilling to John as he slushed along in the melting snow. At three he was ten miles from home in a wild strip of country, with the winter day, hastened by the storm, fast drawing to a close. He had not yet entered the strip of heavy forest which he saw ahead, when he heard a shrill whoop from behind, a cheerful honk-honk, and a machine, with lights aglow, slipped up beside him. It was Margaret, who had come out to look for him.

In the car it was comfortable and cozy. Margaret could not drive fast because of the mud, but he did not care. He was glad to have her beside him, in the wild romantic country, certain of her regard for him. It seemed to him a charming instance of her growing thoughtfulness that she had come out in the storm to guide him in. She looked more beautiful and more dangerous than ever in her rubber-coat, her rich hair tucked under the round rain cap, its wet tendrils blown about her flushed face. The jolt of the car threw her warm, heavy body against his, and he felt an impulse to hold it there. By this time they were passing through the oak-woods. Cosmus suddenly remembered that when he had passed there that morning, he had seen a log cabin some paces from the road; and now he had it on his lips to suggest that they get out, go to the cabin and build a fire to dry their clothes.

Suddenly there flashed through his mind the real motive for that suggestion. His face flushed. He spoke almost sharply.

"I must get out and walk," he said, without looking at her, "I'm cold."

For a moment she did not understand; then struck, perhaps, through the avenue of her quick instinct by something in his face or manner, she answered, "Oh, I know what you can do. You get in the back seat, and wrap the buffalo robe around you."

Tremblingly, he did as he was told, and they rode home in silence. At the outskirts of the city she stopped the car.

"I guess you had better get out here, and walk," she said. "I don't want President Crandon to fire you."

When he had climbed down, he stood for a moment with his hand on the open car door, trying to trace her beautiful features in the dark. For a moment their spirits met in indissoluble bond, then she said, in a tone that was not strange then, but in his memory was strange ever after, "Isn't it hard to be good, even when one wants to be?"

He stood on the road watching the red light of her car blur

away in the rain.

In that moment his brain cleared in regard to Margaret Morton.

5 Crandon Hill College Faculty

As Cosmus stood in the cold rain watching the light of Margaret's machine blur away into the distance, he remembered suddenly that he must go that night to a reception at the home of President Crandon. It was good to get into clean linen, and to assume the respectability of evening clothes. At receptions Cosmus hid his shyness under the guise of the amused spectator. Cynical, as youth ever is where it sees pure idea shatter itself against superficiality and convention, and with senses alert, he watched the life of the whole college flow by like a procession.

He had learned much in six months and he had been disappointed. Idealist though he was, he was not a thin idealist, and consequently he resented the monkish remoteness from life, the abject worship of the past, the class feeling of the American College; he himself was a victim of it. As an instructor, Cosmus held low rank in the college life, and he was never allowed to forget it. Even at the reception, ladies seeking him out in his corner patronized him until he felt complete loss of self-respect. He was made to feel by many of the faculty that sociology was a raw and untried subject, of such modernity as to make it suspicious, and President Crandon never failed to let him know in many various subtle ways that he had incurred the administration's displeasure in his independent ordering of his own private affairs. Feeling himself entirely an outsider, it was no wonder that Cosmus, as he stood alone surveying white necks against broadcloth shoulders, numbed by the chatter in treble and bass, smiled a bit cynically at the scene about him; he watched young Mr. James, assistant in the chemical laboratory, at one thousand a year, father of two, expecting a third, listen respectfully to the Professor of Latin, father of none, pompously expatiate on the evils of birth-control, and his sixth tour of Europe. As two men passed, he caught a fragment from their conversation—it was the Professor of History defending high protective tariff; to one side he could hear the Professor of German denouncing the "Masses;" and the Professor of French decry vocationalism and Max Eastman; and above all the other voices there rose Dean Georgia Summers's, ecstatically chanting "Music is love in search of a word." How many, Cosmus thought, of all these masters of arts were really masters of anything at all?

The reception took on extra interest due to the fact that the president and host gathered the men in an upper room, and announced that he found it necessary "to intrude upon their merriment to transact a modicum of business which came too late for the last faculty meeting and was too urgent to postpone." Professor Reed, as secretary of the faculty, then arose and read a resolution.

"Whereas Guy Street, once a respected thoroughfare fronting the campus of Crandon Hill College, had lately become foul through Greek, Italian and negro tenantage, be it resolved that the faculty suggest to the board of trustees, as agents of the corporation, to petition the city council for permission to close Dover Street, which transversely cuts the campus, in order thus to divert much of the overflow from these tenements on the way to the factories from the campus into Sixth Street."

The resolution was passed without demur, for instructors had no vote; and the social felicities were resumed. There was music and recital. Dean Georgia Summers sang one of "Schumann's exquisite heart songs."

Sought out in his vantage corner, Cosmus was spoken to, though often very briefly, during some part of the evening by every individual present. Hither flowed Mrs. Dingley, wife of

Reverend Mr. Dingley, a *grande dame* minus the pince nez, discoursing on the "perquisites and immunities" of a minister's wife and the joys of having once lived in New Haven; elongating her white arm toward him, she said to Cosmus, "You know New Haven, do you not, Mr. Cosmus?"

"No, I am a Westerner."

"Oh," and she passed on, obviously disappointed.

"I was just saying to Mrs. Reed," said Mrs. Stokes, a thin lady in black with penciled eyebrows, "that the new incumbent in archeology was a Dwight, and you know the Dwights, Mr. Cosmus, are directly descended from Jonathan Edwards."

She also moved on, and then came Dean Amos Witherspoon, a noble figure of Roman calm and quiet sadness. He spent five minutes explaining to Cosmus his plan of making Crandon Hill a rich man's school.

"We must do it; it is the next step in the development of the privately endowed college. We simply cannot compete with the state schools, and we must find a field distinctly our own in education. We must serve only the best families."

Dean Witherspoon was replaced by Charles Henry Clarke, professor of history. Of all his colleagues, Clarke struck Cosmus as the strangest specimen of the academic mind; he always thought of him as a medieval Tory, if there were Tories in the middle ages. The psychology of Clarke was beyond his comprehension. How he could daily interpret the radicals of the past, and daily reject the radicals of the present, Cosmus could not see. It seemed to Cosmus that Clarke considered the middle ages a kind of Utopia from which mankind had moved forwards like a crab. To-night Clarke said something of the "lack of background in the West"; he thought it no wonder that the students were vulgar and listless, or they had no appreciation of intellectual things.

"Just look at the state building at the capital," he exclaimed. "Actually, Mr. Cosmus, they have carved beeves on its façade—raw, beefy beeves—rather than the stately figure of Justice."

Across the room, Cosmus saw the president, looking his part, tall, handsome, still wearing the mask of immobility behind which Hugh Crandon lived. And Cosmus wondered what was the secret power of the man, what was his ruling motive and hope? Was it true that an institution was the shadow of one man? Hugh Crandon, then, had a heavy responsibility on his shoulders.

Like most men, John Cosmus saw what he looked to see, but it must not be supposed that he did not see justly enough to perceive the spots of color in all this drabness. His eyes rested with tranquillity on the young professor of Economics, his back against the wall, as if defending something. Cosmus knew him as an incorrigible democrat; and even then, he caught his words: "The harder the lid is clamped down, the bigger the explosion." Cosmus was not content until he spied little Professor James, of philosophy, disciple of Dewey, whose life had been one long struggle to interpret democracy and give America a soul. While he was thinking of these two pioneers of the new order, he was joined by Kimbark. "You're smiling," he said as he came up.

"I was just wondering what would happen if a faculty were suddenly endowed with a sense of humor," Cosmus answered.

"Be sober, perhaps."

"Or laugh themselves to death at their own collective unwisdom."

"That's treason."

"From me? There's something wrong with all this. What is it?" Cosmus spoke with sudden earnestness.

"I just heard Professor Clarke say that the American college is being assassinated in its own household."

"By a woman, I suppose," Cosmus answered cynically.

"You mean Sarah Blackstone? I wish she were here."

"She doesn't."

"Does she puzzle you, too, with her self sufficiency?" Kimbark asked. "I never saw a woman who was so utterly a woman, and yet so much a man. You know she has been ostracized by her own sex. She thinks too much. I hear she is doing great things at the

Iron Works."

There flashed into Cosmus' mind the image of Sarah, as she had stood that evening on the hill, pliant, strong, and the memory of their fugitive understanding. What wonderful power she had to make him strong! How he needed her!

At that moment Dean Georgia Summers was quacking in his ears. "Ah, my dear Mr. Cosmus, have you heard that Dame Rumor is connecting Mr. Boyne's name with Sarah Blackstone's? Too bad, isn't it, that Mr. Boyne is not college bred. You were speaking of the dear good working men, I suppose?" she asked, including Kimbark in her stereotyped smile. "Isn't it strange they persist in defiling our campus? One would think they would move to some better part of the city."

Cosmus's loyalty to the college snapped completely. There was something wrong. He must find where the wrong lay.

On his way home that night, he saw the light in the Mather house, guarding the campus like the torch of ancient culture, and across the city to the North, the red tinge of the factory over the black pipes, and up above, the line of wires purling along between the world cities.

6 An American Industry

The morning after the reception, Carl Morton was to take Cosmus to the factory. When he called at the Mortons' he found Margaret in the garage washing the machine. Apparently she did not mind the cold; she looked robust and pretty in her snug, red jersey; and for the first time, Cosmus noticed that wistfulness of figure which is the poetry of girlhood. He knew, then, what he had experienced the night before in reference to her was that she was a human soul, with its serious frailties, struggles and aspirations, and that she possessed something of that high spiritual quality that Sarah Blackstone had. He wanted to say, "Little soul, you are safe with me." Instead, he said, "Were you late for supper?"

"No. Were you late to your party?" and seeing him shake his head, she added: "A faculty party must be funny. Do you dance or play kissing games?"

He was aware of her vulgarity.

When finally her father came out and they were leaving, she called out after them, "I hope you like the bull-dog."

Carl flashed her an angry glance, as he said, "Maggie, how many times have I told you not to speak of Mr. Sill in that way?"

"How do you know I meant Mr. Sill," she retorted, laughing. "Perhaps I meant Buster!"

Night after night, day after day, at any moment—midnight or noon—wherever he was, John could pause for a moment in work or play and hear above the usual hum of Iron City life the pant and throb, the whistle and bell of the Sill plant. Twice a day, at five o'clock, crowds of men, on bicycle or afoot, carrying dinner pails, streamed from its gates.

Until this morning that was all that Cosmus knew of the manufactory—save, of course, that it occupied blocks of buildings to the North, and turned its high picket fence, surmounted with barbed wire, formidably to the world. What was the motive power behind this tremendous activity? Production? Was it food to fill mouths? Shoes to clothe feet? Lumber to build houses? None of these. The answer lay in the hundreds of automobiles that lined Iron City's streets on Saturday night.

When man discovered the energy that lay in wood and coal, seething under water, he ushered in the age of steam; when he discovered that explosive power lay in a fluid—a mobile energy—which he could safely carry in a tank, he ushered in the age of gasoline which made possible the lighter-than-wood and heavier-than-air machines. John knew before he put foot into the office of R. Sill and Son that no man could take in account any national culture, art and philosophy that did not find a background in the great industrial order. R. Sill was re-forming as well as clothing and feeding Iron City. And Cosmus was sensitive enough to share Carl Morton's admiration for this great throbbing center of life that stretched its nerves out to the cities of the world.

"We shall be visitors, and make a complete tour," Carl said.

The office building was a great brick, oblong, arsenal-like, with awninged windows and a flag-staff. In the vestibule, a girl at a switchboard near a barred gate coordinated the life outside with the many departments within. On Carl's magic request a ticket was issued to Cosmus, click went the gate, and they stepped into a corridor, connecting great, well-lighted rooms filled with busy typewriters; then into a court. It was here that a curious thing happened. In the empty court they saw a man in overalls, bareheaded and carrying a dinner pail, rapidly approaching them. Cosmus's curiosity was instantly aroused because the man seemed drunk, or sick, or crazy; his intelligent face was very pale, and from his mouth came a stream of incoherent sentences. Instead of passing he stopped abruptly in front of the foreman; and slamming his dinner pail against the wall, he began to curse so passionately, yet quietly, that Cosmus wondered at the force of it. He was a powerful man in a kind of steel-like, wiry way; not tall but admirably built, dark-eyed, and smooth-faced. A single lock of gray hair, flowing down through jet black locks, like a kind of anadem, and a deep scar above the left eye made him particularly striking looking. Facing around to see if he were attracting attention from the office, he stuck his face close to the foreman's, and delivered, almost in a whisper, a tirade that was terrible. "You are at the bottom of this, you damned rat. You spied on me, you sneaking, dirty, son-of-a——".

As he stood there stamping and cursing there was such hatred in his face that John feared violence. He was surprised to see that Morton flinched under the words and trembled, but that he showed no anger. Instead he tried to calm the man by ignoring his madness. "Come, Walt. This is Professor Cosmus of the college."

The man stopped short, and shot a hot glance from under his brows straight into John's eyes. John saw his white hands—he wondered that they were white—working spasmodically.

"Damn such a school as that is; it ought to be burned to the ground." Wheeling on his heel, he picked up his dented bucket, entered the office and was gone.

"He's been warned several times to keep still," explained Morton, not wholly untroubled. "He's always shooting off his mouth among the men, and now they have caught him, and given him the walk.

"A socialist, probably; anyway, he's been caught several times talking union. Why can't he leave the men alone; they're satisfied. We can't have them tampered with. It's demoralizing to business."

"What's his name?"

"Kuhns—Walt Kuhns."

With that Morton dismissed the matter, and led the way up a flight of steps to a lookout window

As Cosmus looked out over the Sill plant, he felt a thrill of admiration for all the energy mobilized in this single teeming center of trade. He saw a settlement of black, low buildings, pierced by thousands of sooty windows, stretching for many blocks to the north, meeting on its eastern and western rim a belt railroad, upon which trains were moving. Above these buildings was a cluster of tall black pipes, belching smoke, which even amidst the grime, strangely resembled the tubes of a great organ. Colossal steel girders and huge derricks in the yards belittled the locomotives and cars creeping beneath them. Clanging bell, shrill whistle, snorting engine, whirling wheel, ringing hammer beat up to them, where they stood enthralled. How vast, how powerful, how beautiful! Who would not thrill to be a part of this great movement in productive cooperation? Had not R. Sill been a giant to build this with the sweat of his own human brain?

There was pride in Morton's voice as he pointed out shop after shop, this time-saving device, that wise utilization of natural power, and in particular, when he succeeded in making John see the smithy, a squat stone building on the farthest side of the yards.

They descended. Morton was careful to lead his guest into every department of the business. They entered the pattern-room, comparatively quiet, leisurely, well-lit; beyond, the core-room, with its well-tended garden of trenches. In the pouring room adjoining, giant kettles, carrying tons of white, molten metal, suspended from moving cranes, glided swiftly from mold to mold, filling them. Men, like demons, pushed tiny wagons not wholly unlike tea-carts, filed with the glowing stuff, and there where the kettles were filled, a river of lava danced over by thousands of fireflies flowed from the furnace's crimson mouth. John could scarcely tear himself away from the fascination of this spectacle.

Next they came to the assembly room—a vast building almost one-third of a mile in length (a corridor not unlike our national capitol's in dignity) filled with moving cranes built on a tremendous scale. The raw material in the form of heavy ingots came in at one end and emerged at the other as living engines.

Thence the visitor passed to a smaller building—the finishing room. Here workmen, like gnomes in masks, scraped and brushed parts of engines. Morton shouted above the roar, "We can't get only foreigners to work here. It gets 'em." The forge room with its colossal automatic hammers, its white-hot furnaces and Vulcan-like workers came next, and here Morton had Cosmus see every detail of the intensely interesting work. What handsome fellows the smiths were! How they belittled the work of the mind—John's work—at the desk playing with ideas.

Cosmus saw it all: the paint-room where large engines were sprayed in ten seconds with smooth coats of paint; the shipping room, the efficiency, advertising and chemical departments. And the last section. The last section visited was the hospital, clean and white and spacious.

"How many do you serve a day?" John asked the nurse.

"Averaged 80 a day, last year," she answered with a show of pride.

Eighty a day—it made John suddenly sober.

Then, as if saying "Let's see the man behind all this," Morton led Cosmus back to the office, through swinging doors of leaded glass, where they were finally admitted to R. Sill.

He was not what Cosmus expected to see—this baron; from appearance, he little deserved the name bull-dog, which the ready tongue of Margaret had given him that morning. There was nothing in his look and manner that suggested ruthlessness, cruelty or vulgarity—qualities which have been attributed to the entrepreneur of Sill's eminence. He suggested respectability, quiet power, and a poise that put to shame the creature trembling and cursing, beside itself with rage, which they had met in the yard an hour before. R. Sill was tall and massive with a large and fine head; features a trifle soggy, and eyes not too clear, nevertheless suggesting strength. There was lordliness in his manner, no haughtiness.

"I have just one thing against you college people," he said, leveling a look straight at Cosmus. "You don't keep up with the times. After all, a college is just another factory like this one. The trustees, I take it, are the board of directors; the president is the general superintendent; you faculty are the business-getters, and the students are the patrons. Are you all the time studying how to bring in the greatest return on the dollar? Now, do you people up there on the bluff have an efficiency department?"

He smiled, somewhat morosely. "From the samples of your men I get there, I take it you don't. Do you know, Mr. Cosmus, that some of my foremen won't accept college men in their departments."

Cosmus asked why.

"They don't stay; they are discontented and untrustworthy."

This concluded their conversation but as they turned to go Morton tarried for a minute at the mahogany desk. Through the glass doors John heard the two voices.

"You know about Kuhns?" the foreman asked.

"I gave orders this morning."

Cosmus detected a new note in R. Sill's voice, the husky quivering "C" of deep emotion, ending in metallic hardness.

"Those fellows get worse all the time." Morton ventured to add.

"Let them. What have I told you? Their efforts are spasmodic, and will end. They can't hold out. Everything's against them. We'll break them this way always."

At the door opening into the court, Morton left Cosmus, who decided to take a turn about the engine room before passing out of the yard-gate which the workmen used. Crossing the court, he turned sharply to the left, and stood marveling at the wheels revolving noiselessly through their magnificent orbits.

"May I see your ticket, sir?"

The voice in John's ear was meticulously tuned to carry insult. Looking up, Cosmus saw a squat, heavy figure of a young man in a fashionable suit that seemed glaringly fresh and clean in contrast to the surroundings. His round, tilted head with its coarse pompadour was without a hat; the eyes were narrow and shifty; the nose pug and strong. A young business man's mustache, a gold tipped cigarette in a mouth of straight line; this much John took in as he turned and faced the custodian. Coarse, flat-footed independence, a kind of worldly charm and conscious power, delighting in authority, emanated from him.

He stood coolly sweeping Cosmus up and down with his keen eyes, carelessly knocking the ashes from the cigarette with a little finger.

"Have you a ticket, sir?" This time more patronizingly.

Cosmus at once recognized old Sill's son and knew that Raymond must have known him. This was studied insult then.

The two stood looking at each other, aroused to antagonism. Biologists interested in personality assert that behind a single sentence may be an inherited background of special characteristics. Was the sentence that Raymond Sill cast in the face of John Cosmus that afternoon the product of inheritance or training?

7 The Sill Family

"The Sills," R. Sill the first was wont to boast, "have an instinct for strong women." It was a mature acknowledgment of woman's place in his own life and affairs. This R. Sill, the first, Raymond's paternal grandfather, was a country physician—a graduate of Dartmouth medical school in the class of 1843. Like many a second son of a New England farmer, he left the homestead to take up a profession, equipped with strong nerves, keen mind and a convenient theology; no tenet of Calvinism forbade sagacious manipulations of the law of supply and demand, the exacting of compound interest. At Millers Falls, Mass., where the young physician settled, he found promise of a fair field of development in his profession—and Patience Conway. Patience Conway was the miller's daughter. She received silks and satins every half-year from Paris, and she was the belle of the neighborhood, pretty and substantial. She had been to Boston to school. Dr. Sill paid her attention, of course, and they drifted into a relationship that old Mr. Conway, who considered Dr. Sill a good match, wanted to force into an understanding. Sill might have married Patience Conway, had he not met Maude Randolph, a school mistress from the back lands, whose birth was shadowed in mystery. A "strong woman," she made Patience Conway seem insipid. As youth will, away over the hills in the doctor's chaise, they went one afternoon before tea to Attleboro, and married suddenly. Then by some inexplicable whim, some gypsy in the blood aroused by romance, they never returned to Millers Falls.

The winter of '48 they started west in a sleigh, stopped off in Vermont to see Sill's parents, thence on to Montreal, to Detroit, to Chicago, finally settling near Iron City, which was called Nassau then. In all that wild wedding journey, in the dead of winter, under chill December stars, over unbroken tracks, through wolf-packed forests, in sad, silent places, the doctor never once was disappointed in his bride. She never whimpered, never complained, but arose every morning ready for the far places. At Iron City they found Indians, a French trader married to a squaw. And a few men from Ohio had started a mill. Staying until midsummer, the doctor's Maude died in child-birth, and was buried under an old oak not far from the campus of Crandon Hill College. The doctor never escaped her sweet influence. It was a tribute to her memory that kept this man lonely and single until he was fifty years old. What share Maude Randolph might have had in his subsequent career as a financier cannot be guessed. She was a strong woman, and might have saved him from the pursuit of power which he now began.

Young Dr. Sill did not stay in Nassau, but went back to Chicago, and later became a kind of circuit physician throughout north-western Illinois. Here he laid a basis for his fortune. With a keen sense of values in human nature, a steady temper, and ambition in a country wild and new—what could not be accomplished?

He became an incorrigible backer of Illinois soil. He used to ride along the heavy roads, leap from his horse, pick up the spongy dirt between his fingers, press it tightly into his hands, and wonder at its give. "That is an Eden," he would say, sweeping his long arm over the flat dreary prairie land.

The inhabitants did not believe him. They found the land only a treacherous bog, from which lifted a miasma by dawn and sunset, that bred disease and death. They believed in nothing; they were incorrigible pessimists, as malaria-ridden folk always are. Doctor Sill, in his dry, casual way, later used to say, "The inhabitants of Illinois were so full of malaria that they never needed to call me; all I had to do was to ride by their cabins and, if their windows shook, I went in!" For these pioneer farmers, Dr. Sill had three prescriptions; he gave them quinine; he gave them money; he dispensed optimism. Out of the saddle bags came a pile of the drug; out of the doctor's boot came the long black purse; across the shrewd face came the inevitable smile. "That is an Eden," he would say over and over again. And the quinine and the money and the smile won. The malaria was conquered, the fields tilled and prosperity reigned.

R. Sill, the first, suddenly found himself an itinerant bank. The long black purse became an institution founded on personality. The convenient theology allowed the physician, when he was dispensing optimism, to charge twelve and fifteen per cent interest, until, one day in the early fifties, he found himself rich and looking for investments. His mind reverted to youth, to the wedding journey with Maude Randolph, and he remembered the rich timber lands in Michigan, through which they had driven with clasped hands under the still Western stars.

In 1864, he took two important steps in his career. He made his first investment in Michigan woods, and he married Maude Stone, his secretary. Maude was never the first Maude to him, but through long association she knew his idiosyncrasies and shared his aims. And she gave him what he counted his right to have—a son.

Long before 1882, R. Sill the first had given up his practice and retired. He lived in Chicago—a backwoodsy pioneer type afloat in the new great metropolis. What a spectacle he had seen! What a colorful, various procession of men and events had streamed across his retina. What a miracle to behold a frontier fort leap into a world metropolis.

About Chicago, he ever remained an eccentric figure. He appeared at the best clubs and cafes in the same old boots, carrying the same old long black purse. He was petulant and impudent. He thought nothing of saying to a clubman,

"I don't like that tie; take it off, sir," or of squabbling with the cashier about a penny, and of tipping him with a gold-back. He was rough, honest, shrewd; one of those rare specimens of the individualist which the frontier so often breeds.

One night in his eightieth year, he dreamed of Maude Randolph, and on arising, a prayer of his mother's ran through his troubled brain. He wrote a letter that morning.

Two days later, on May 2, 1882, to be exact, young Reverend Hugh Crandon, newly elected president of Crandon Hill College, hitched up the horse to the surrey and drove through the drowsy streets to the post office for mail. Reverend Mr. Crandon was already facing a crisis in his affairs. The college was on the verge of bankruptcy. Founded by the church, it had served the good purpose for which it was intended by furnishing ministers, and teachers to a nation rapidly becoming self-conscious. The college was able, then, to adumbrate America's crudeness with a feeble but genuine culture. But in 1882, that era was closing. There were vague world-whispers of other needs and moments. Science had brought new ideas and tools; and a few mighty empire-builders were conscious of the vast wealth of this America, and of the leverage that lay in cooperation of capital, in the utilization of labor. These world-whispers were disturbing to sabbatical colleges. Neighboring institutions had heard, and were active in tapping the rapidly accumulating fortunes of the overnight millionaires. Crandon Hill College was tottering under the guidance of a board of trustees composed of ministers only. As Reverend Mr. Crandon rode along through the elm fringed streets, he cogitated. How could he replace his present trustees with wealthy and influential laymen, and how could he unite the field of education, the center of light and culture, with the youthful and powerful industrial aristocracy about to mature? And as he cogitated, an answer was dropped into his lap. The post-girl brought him Dr. Sill's letter, and he read:

Reverend Hugh Crandon,
  Crandon Hill College,
  Iron City.

Dear Sir:

If I give you $100,000 could you raise a like sum? For God's sake don't blow about it. I'm that kind.

R. SILL.

Perhaps it was the grim Calvinistic conscience at work in Dr. Sill, perhaps it was the memory of the grave under the oak tree near Crandon Hill campus; at any rate, he kept his promise, and Crandon Hill College was saved. That was only the beginning of a series of gifts.

In 1882 R. Sill, the first, owned eight million dollars. He vowed that he and his wife would die without a cent in the world. And so R. Sill the second became penniless.

R. Sill, the second, was an active, handsome boy interested in machinery. He turned his room into an experimental station for dynamos and engines; he never gave his father any trouble. When Dr. Sill told him that he intended to give all his fortune away and thus set him free to make his own mark in the world, the son merely commented impersonally.

"I didn't know you had as much as eight million, Father."

Like his father, he seemed more interested in making money than in spending it. He went to Crandon Hill College at his own suggestion, and worked his way through; and there it was that he met Patience Conway Wood, of Millers Falls. It was not until several years later that he learned that she was the daughter of Patience Conway. She it was, who discovered his passion for engines, and though she loved the arts and was a musician and painter herself, she advised him to give up college. He quit at the end of the freshman year, married Patience Wood and took a job with the then newly organized Enterprise Pumping Company of Iron City. In ten years he had diverted the energies of the plant into making gasoline engines, and he had acceded to managership and possession.

Everywhere he found helping hands stretched toward him; he seemed born in the right generation; he was asked to swim with and not against the current.

His particular virtues—enterprise, taciturnity, expert knowledge in a new field, thoroughness—were everywhere in demand. Brother manufacturers spoke to him of identical interests; brilliant Judge Matt Tyler went out of his way to talk with him on the street; Haskell, editor of the *Republic-Despatch,* offered him space in his columns free, merely in order to boost Iron City business. Even the government consented to high protective tariffs to encourage his lusty business. No wonder R. Sill, the second, in time developed a philosophy of radiant optimism. He and Iron City and America were favored by God; he knew, because they all were prospering; also, there somehow arose in his mind the notion that business was sacrosanct. He thrilled with secret joy when he heard enthusiastic advertising men speak of the Romance of Business, the Internationality of Business, the Empire of Business and even the Religion of Business.

All this was in the first two decades of his career—the happiest of his life. His son Raymond was growing up, a strong, promising boy, and his wife had not yet fallen ill. The novelty of commanding vast materials and men and the novelty of success had not worn off. It was just after the Spanish war that he struck his black year. Moving with the current, pursuant of the common policy of consolidation, he established factories at Toronto, Three Rivers and Dallas. Then it was that R. Sill, the second, first became aware that there was such a thing as envy in the world. A spirit, at least, which he called envy. There were persons vulgar enough not to appreciate the sacrifices he had made, not to enjoy his success, not to perceive the beauty of Big Business. These persons were raising their heads in politics, and they made R. Sill nervous. He was not a statesman, he admitted that; he was a specialist, and all he asked was to be let alone. In the first clash with envy in his state, he lost, and he then decided that it was time to give the new menace careful attention. He gathered his friends together—Haskell of the *Republic-Despatch,* Judge Matt Tyler and others, and laid the situation before them. They saw as he did, the danger to expanding industry, to the "very life of the Nation," as Tyler put it, and they decided because of that phrase, that Tyler ought to go to the Senate. The little matter was carried through without a hitch and Sill breathed easier.

It was after this black year, that President Crandon approached Sill to fill a vacancy on his Board of Trustees.

"I'll give you five thousand dollars toward a business college," Sill told him, "but I haven't time or inclination to serve as a trustee."

President Crandon did not allow his annoyance to be seen; he smiled, expressed adequate regret that "a business man, so eminent, and an alumnus, and a son of a noble friend of the college" could not serve on more intimate terms with the institution. When he learned that business college in Sill's mind meant a department of stenography and book-keeping, he delicately steered clear of the offer and the matter was closed.

Long before Sill became delegate to the National Republican Convention for his district, one of the way stations in his career, he stopped going to church. He still contributed to Reverend Mr. Dingley's salary each Sunday, but he would say, "Mother, I am tired this morning. You go." And he and Raymond would take the small car and go for a ride, or he would work in his office.

When John Cosmus met R. Sill, the second, that February afternoon, he crossed Sill's career when it was already past the zenith. Sill was a hammerer on the will. He was just a little tired of life, and vaguely certain that he had missed something, he knew not what. He still clung tenaciously to his optimism; he thought himself a great patriot; he was a believer in law and order, but he was not above breaking the law, when by so doing he saved trade, the life of the nation, from the zealous and envious; he was a good husband, a good citizen, a fair employer. In short, Sill was a specialist with illusions, playing a large part in a large world, yet moving narrowly in a little world, barren of great ideas.

Somehow Sill's weariness and sense of loss were connected in his own mind with his son, Raymond. After Raymond's rather disastrous career at Preparatory School, he watched the boy narrowly for signs of revolution. He longed to see him assert his will, and make a choice of a career. But he waited in vain. Raymond was twenty before Sill gave up hope. Then they had a talk.

"You must go to work in the plant," R. Sill told his son.

"Send me to Yale instead," was Raymond's answer.

Sill secretly was so pleased at the boy's manifested desire, that Raymond was sent,—but stayed only a year. In the vague background of that year at Yale, which the father later saw, a woman moved darkly, and the boy came home. He did not seem even to catch the subtle insult in his father's question, when old Sill asked at their midnight interview, "Raymond, did you learn anything from those academic fellows about inheritance? Can some old ancestor from a generation or more back affect a son? Your grandfather was a great man, you know."

Wasn't R. Sill, the second, wrong? Moving uncertainly among ideas, had he not failed to see? Wasn't Raymond after all a Sill?

R. Sill, the first, given the freedom of frontier life, suddenly expanded through native shrewdness to mastery, into a financier. In a half century, he made and dispersed a vast fortune. R. Sill, the second, though he treasured the illusion that he had surmounted great obstacles, in reality climbed an easy grade against no opposition. He swam with the current. Grandfather and father both loved power. But no more than did Raymond. Raymond loved power better than anything else in the world. But he felt unconsciously, in the capitalistic world, which his father had helped to mold, certain centrifugal forces of unexpected strength, and he shrank from them and therefore from a business that did not offer him the expansive field of freedom that it had offered his father. To be sure, Raymond did not reason about the situation; he felt it. He was not weaker in will than his progenitors; he merely faced more opposition and more competition than they had.

The only other talent, buried in the folds of Raymond's personality, which might have swept into fruition and made him a man—was the artistic. From Patience Conway Wood, he had received a love of beauty. Even after she became an invalid, his mother still painted. She lay in her bed, a sweet, slender figure that carried the fragrance of roses, making little sketches of scenes from Millers Falls. "What did you daub to-day, Mother?" old Sill would say tenderly, and she would hold up some bit of field or wood, delicately tinted. "I always try, Father, to make trees just like Corot's but I never, never can." What impetus was there in Raymond Sill's environment to make him an artist? What use had Iron City for art? And so he hid effectively his too warm love of beauty.

Raymond had at hand adequate instruments for the expression of his love of power and his love of beauty, now deteriorated into mere love of sensation. When the big Stutz was added to their garage, the boy was almost satisfied. With that he could sweep over highways like some great new creature neither bird nor beast, drinking in color and loveliness in huge gulps of power. But even the Stutz did not hold Raymond entirely. One day he was moved to confide in Margaret Morton. "I think I've just about got the Big Chief in the notion of letting me have a plane," he told her.

With the accumulation of great capital had come machines which satisfied, too easily perhaps, the sense of power and beauty. At any rate, Raymond was a Sill.

And yet, how can he who believes in democracy, who has come to believe too in that *float* of ideas, that great sea of human consciousness, which in one manifestation or another, we call public opinion, how can he doubt that Raymond's environment shaped him, and crushed him into that meanest of all things—a parasite? Raymond, a product of the capitalistic order, had become the chief element in its disintegration. He was the great anarch.

It was he then, R. Sill, the third, who stood there coldly

measuring John Cosmus. And perhaps Cosmus, through avenues of unconscious power, understood something of what Raymond was, in lineage and in effect; at any rate, he had an impulse
to strike him as he would a puppy. But the fetters of civilization
held, and instead he quietly handed out his card of entrance.

As he turned away, Raymond said, "You will need this to get
out, Professor Cosmus." But Cosmus did not return to take the
ticket.

8 The Outcast

From the engine room, where Cosmus had left Raymond Sill, to the yard-gate it was perhaps two hundred feet. A warm blooded man could walk that distance in about thirty-three seconds, long enough for one, brimming with indignation, to store his mind with many images. A moving picture of Cosmus's mind those seconds would have been interesting.

Pictures of the factory, and workmen, simple, childlike, weary; Margaret dimpling and radiant, Old Sill not as he had seen him, but as he imagined his face must have looked, to match the hardness in his voice when he had said, "We shall break them this way always"; Morton, faithful and honest; Raymond, puglike, sneering, hiding his best self in some dark corner of his soul; but clearest of all, Walt Kuhns, his eyes deep and fine, a crown upon his head, but with courage enough to rebel.

Somehow as he walked ashamedly away from Raymond Sill, Cosmus felt very near to Walt Kuhns.

He expected to be held up at the yard-gate, but when he got there he found the gate unguarded; in the street a few steps away, there was a group of excited men gathered around a police ambulance. Cosmus caught muttered imprecations and a groan; he saw the glitter of brass buttons, and police stars in the early winter twilight. He drew nearer. Two officers were lifting a man into the ambulance; the other men seemed to be employees of the Sill plant. Cosmus heard the door click, and saw the machine bound away.

The workmen were returning slowly up the walk toward the gate talking excitedly. As they passed Cosmus, he heard one of them say, "He had the nerve to try and walk in; what does he think we are ?"

"I got him one square between the eyes—"

And then another man broke in,

"I don't care, Walt Kuhns is a good scout after all."

The next morning Cosmus scanned the pages of the *Republic-Despatch*, but he found no word of a fracas at the plant. Buried away in the court items he did find notice of a case of the State vs. Walt Kuhns, for malicious trespass.

Moved by a hidden bond of sympathy and by natural curiosity, Cosmus resolved to call on Kuhns at the cell. He had no difficulty in gaining entrance to the man. Judge Carr, who granted the order, and with whom he chatted a few minutes, seemed to see nothing more in the incident than bad blood between some working men; he thought Kuhns would probably go up for ninety days.

When Cosmus entered the lock-up, he had to look twice at the man sitting in repose next to the iron barred window before he recognized him. Was that Kuhns? The light that trickled through the windows fell upon a face of singular calmness; the prisoner was unagitated, and filled with a dignity and submission which were quite noble. He did not seem surprised at seeing Cosmus and there was no trace of resentment in his voice as he greeted him.

"Come in," he said, "I remember, you were with Morton yesterday morning. Cosmer, Comer—was it?"

Cosmus told him his name.

"You saw me at my worst yesterday. It's my failing. I'm like that when I get tired fighting. Those spells of wrath are like drunks, I guess. But they're mistakes; they make me less fit for the work."

"Would you believe me, Mr. Kuhns, if I told you that I took quite seriously what you said about the college yesterday morning?"

"What did I say?"

"You said you wished all such colleges as Crandon Hill——"

"Yes, don't repeat it; I remember. I'm not a college man, and perhaps you think I was presumptuous—that I ought not to judge——"

He paused, as if recollecting,

"Mr. Cosmus," he said earnestly, "I'd like to make you see this thing as we do. It's a long story——" he paused and seemed to hesitate. Then feeling the interest and sympathy in Cosmus's manner, he went on again. "Let me tell you a little incident—one of the things which has made me feel as I do——

"Can you see a room in a miner's hut on a late spring night? A man is sitting there with grave, thin face and burning eyes, writing. He has just given orders to the striking miners to resist the militia. It has hurt him to do it because he is an idealist, and hates bloodshed, and all these men are his comrades;—he has worked in the mines with many of them. There is a knock at the door, and he says, like a friend, 'Come in.' A man dressed in cool flannels, and a lieutenant of the guards enter. The man is from Pittsburgh—of the higher-ups;—he believes as they all believe, that every man has his price. He is carrying a satchel crammed with bills of large denominations and gold coin. He has come to buy out the leader of the miners; he wants him to sell out his comrades. The higher-up takes a chair; the two men talk; they even laugh; they touch on every subject imaginable but not once upon the subject nearest them. Why doesn't the Higher-up get busy? Why doesn't he open the mouth of his satchel and pour its glittering contents upon the bare table? He doesn't, he is sizing up his man. He is using strategy; all the time the Master is calm, courteous, sincere. Presently the Higher-up gets up and it looks as though he were going to open his satchel. But he doesn't. Instead, he puts on his hat, shakes hands with the leader, takes his satchel and goes out. He is beaten. For once he finds a man who has no price; he did not even open his proposition. The lieutenant of the guards stays; he goes to the leader and shakes his hand; but that is not enough; he says something. It is this, 'I promise to resign from the guard, and enlist with you!'"

John Cosmus filled the pause with a question, "He kept his word, of course?"

"I am that lieutenant," Kuhns answered. "I was a boy then. I enlisted in the militia for a lark, and it was no lark. That fall I should have entered a seminary of the Protestant Episcopal church. I didn't, and I am not sorry. I am in a nobler army, a higher church."

The eyes of Walt Kuhns burned, but he showed no other signs of excitement. He was calm and unaffected. These statements seemed from him the merest commonplaces.

"It is great to work with a man like the Master. He says that each one of us is a pioneer, a Columbus. We are in the van of democracy. He offers no reward save the service. What he did for the Higher-up, he does for all men; he impresses them with his nobility, and honesty. He is another Lincoln it seems to me, an obscurer Lincoln."

"Is this war so large?"

"Large? Why, friend, when the first blood was spilt on the bodies that were brought in, it seemed to me, after having seen the Master, that this skirmish was greater than Bull Run."

Cosmus was thinking of R. Sill when he asked the next question,

"And the movement is not sporadic?"

"The Master does not say much when he is moved deeply, but that night as he cowered over the body of a comrade, he said, 'It is a holy thing to die for liberty!' When a man talks like that"— Kuhns finished with a gesture.

"I see," said Cosmus.

When Cosmus had left Walt Kuhns and found the street, Iron City life was at its flood. Machines were honking, newsboys crying extras, shoppers carrying their packages, children in carriages, all were hurrying past in prosperity, peace—and indifference.

John Cosmus, a student of society, was thinking of two faces, the face of R. Sill as it must have looked when he said, "We shall break them in this way always," and the face of Walt Kuhns when he had repeated his master's words, "It is a holy thing to die for liberty."

Then he remembered that he had not received an answer from Kuhns to his question, "What of the college?"

Here was a pretty problem, indeed, for a student of society.

9 On the World Horizon

In June, after the close of the first year at Crandon Hill College, John Cosmus went to Lake Keewasee, near to the capital of a neighboring state, for the summer. Here was the middle west at its fairest; leagues of blue water, green rolling fields, commodious farms, golden harvest fields upon which the visitor suddenly emerged from coverts of deep, cool woods, amber-dim, rich with the hum of bees. Here was range enough for his cramped spirits and mind; he could regain normality and adjust perspectives. Ostensibly he had decided on this retreat to write his Book, "Theory of the Standardization of Wages," but in the first weeks he slept, ate, swam, played tennis, or loafed with the imperturbable animals.

He liked to cast his eyes over the fifteen miles of blue water to the city at the side of the lake, where rose the capital like a marble lily; not far beyond, peeping above the trees, were the towers of the University. A boat from the city with a faint flavor of habitations, business and the world of men, stopped at the pier before the Burkhardt cottage every morning to bring mail and papers.

Mr. and Mrs. Adolph Burkhardt and their two young sons Karl and Gustav, were his hosts. He had met Mr. Burkhardt in a Chicago reference library, struggling with a book on business psychology. Burkhardt was a mild, self-conscious, little man, a first violinist in the Symphony Orchestra.

"Perhaps, you can help me with this," he had said to Cosmus, placing a page on "Sensation" before the student. "I can't understand Münsterberg—in English. You see I must be more practical in America and so I take a course in beesiness at the University."

Burkhardt's self-conscious effort to become practical was the evidence of his impracticality. But he was generous, kind and hospitable. His love of music was unaffected, and his loyalty to Cosmus genuine. Mrs. Burkhardt was motherly and refined; the sons, Karl and Gustav, were two young Indians, who preferred any sport to music, and often used Cosmus as a buffer against their ardent father. They did not want to practice, but they always did. Day and night Cosmus heard the scrapings of the violin. Sometimes the father would improvise little vagrant melodies that caught the very spirit of the place—harvest fields, little crinkly waves and swirling leaves; or he would draw the face of night itself in his great sweet sound waves. One favorite piece that he loved, and which he played well, too, was Massenet's "Elegie." Often before sleep came, Cosmus in his cottage adjoining heard the first breathing of this great song. He always saw a procession of women mourning, the procession of the ages, passing through desolate streets of desolate towns. Adolph never played this save at night; it was then that Cosmus was most glad for the music. Sometimes in the midst of morning work it was disconcerting.

Cosmus thought most of Margaret Morton in such moments as the "Elegie" inspired. Margaret's womanliness in spite of her youth, maternity shadowed deep beneath, linked her with the profound. When he had left her some weeks before, they had been on no different basis. He had asked her to write and she had given no definite promise. "I'll send you a postal from Pike Lake. Raymond and I are going there to a house-party, you know." She had not sent a letter or a postal. Cosmus, in a spirit of banter, had been sending her postal cards ever since. When he was in the city he sought out the gayest conceits, as he would for a child. After all, wasn't that what his changed relations with Margaret—since that night when she had picked him up in her machine—meant? Hadn't he found the child in her? Somehow he had never since been so shaken by the winds of passion. Still Margaret was for the night. She haunted the moonlit wood, bent above him in the lake; her body must have slept on that tuft of moss; his drowsy head must have been pillowed on her bosom. The earth deep witchery of sex crossed darkened distances; absence only sharpened desire, however chastened by the soul.

Margaret for the night, and Sarah for the day. Cosmus had left Iron City one June morning by the electric. He was glad to go—"darned glad"—as he told Kimbark, who was to study in France that summer—for, although Mr. and Mrs. Curtis were kind to him, Cosmus was not happy in Iron City. The straightened, artificial life shut down on him like a prison. As the car sped North past the Crandon Hill Iron Works, he saw Sarah at an awninged window, evidently superintending the placing of more window boxes, gay with geraniums A desire to see her before he left, seized him. He signaled the motorman, and left the interurban at the next corner. He never had any trouble in being direct with Sarah.

"I am going away for the summer; may I write?" he asked.

She flashed him a look of such friendliness that Cosmus for a moment imagined that it was tender.

"Oh, I wish you would," she answered.

Then he did not stay. He plead some errand, and walked the streets about the factory waiting for the next car.

They had been writing all summer in an irregular fashion. Whatever whim or mood dictated, they put down on paper and sent. Sometimes Cosmus drew pictures to illustrate his own wit and humor. Sometimes he culled paragraphs from his "Theory of Standardization of Wages" and sent them intact; once he sent her a red-clover blossom, and she replied with a leaf. In return she sent him newspaper clippings and once a poem which had pleased her. Her letters were always vivid, gay, penetrative, impersonal. She connected him with the outer world; occasionally there was a reference to the heat and the men sweating at the machines; she told him of her successful effort to get Mr. Boyne to install motor-driven fans in all departments, etc., etc. Her letters would not let him forget the submerged struggle between Walt Kuhns and R. Sill, the second.

One day, pondering on Walt Kuhns, Cosmus suddenly saw what he thought was a solution to the problem. He wrote to Sarah Blackstone:

"Here we moderns are utterly neglectful of the most powerful instrument in the hands of society—the float of ideas, which is the sum total of the thoughts and feelings of men. The sea of accumulated consciousness is society; it affects men against their will penetrating to the sub-conscious. Through it, men become automatons. Once in a generation, this force breathes through a nation in time of war, and we see men, the creatures of this Great Spirit, throw themselves willingly into the abyss of death. The problem is to get men to feel the Spirit in time of peace. The problem in a democracy is to let loose this wash of ideas, without despotic control of press and school. Indeed this great float of ideas is the only medium in which democracy can exist.

"When I look at America, the sanctuary of national faith, fragmentized by scores of aliens, broken into political parties, criss-crossed by feuds between labor and capital, cut into fifty commonwealths, I wonder how we can ever imagine that we have a democracy.

"We are children yet in our understanding of this great instrument, which is mastering us, but which we may master. The thoughtful, the creative minds, must fill the strategic positions of the world in order consciously to control this solution of ideas, not for themselves but for society.

"In other words the next great movement of society, as I see it, is from an ego- and class-centric into a socio-centric world.

"R. Sill is ego-centric; Walt Kuhns, perhaps, is ego-centric; President Hugh Crandon is ego-centric,—(more the shame, for the college, now groping for a mission in the world, should serve to usher the nation peacefully into a socio-centric era)—all are shut up in their stifling class worlds, gasping for the larger spaces of a socialized world.

"In this way we will achieve this democracy. This is America's job, and the fact is, that when we stand for this kind of democracy we are pleading for internationalism, too, the ultimate world-consciousness."

Sarah's letter in reply contained one sentence—a personal one—which made Cosmus think. "Your letter," she had written, "cheered my day." He got a vision of her straight, strong figure, and he wondered if Sarah ever needed cheering. She seemed so self-contained. Was she after all often weary? Did she go home from the stifling office tired and broken? He tried to fancy Sarah weary—crumpled, perhaps, and depressed. He was filled with shame. He was here where it was cool, thinking; she was there in the heat, doing. Something of the loveliness and need of the woman became clear to him. He knew an impulse to take her in his arms; to make her his child too....

The morning that the news of the invasion of Belgium reached Cosmus, he was thinking that he had never seen so peaceful a world. He had arisen earlier than usual and had gone before dawn through the dewy woods up through the newly-cut fields, where the wheat stood gold in the shock, the pigs grunted and chickens clattered comfortably. A farm-girl and boy were starting off to the barn with pails and a man hallooed melodiously to a neighbor a quarter of a mile away. The sun burst up out of the lake, and he watched it mount the dome of the capitol until it flashed on the gold image of justice at the far top. In that moment Cosmus experienced again the sense of identity with the earth, with the general life of the people, and with this, his country, and as he stood, there at the farthest mist-robed hill, the River of Wires glinted in the sun.

When he got back to the cottage, the mail boat had just come to the Burkhardt pier. Adolph was standing with trembling hands and livid face, scanning the first page of the paper. He turned to Cosmus. "Der must be some meestake—some meestake," he said, still pondering over the paper.

Cosmus read as in a dream. Adolph Burkhardt went mechanically into the house, and soon Cosmus heard the strains of "Elegie"—the procession of women mourning through desolate streets of war-emptied towns.

Cosmus read the paper greedily inside and out where he stood, and then he went back to the cottage. It was not the same world that he had moved so confidently in a moment before.

Student that Cosmus was, familiar as he was with the situation in Europe, the initial impression of the unreality of the war never left him. It was a dream no more real than the flow of images inspired by Adolph's music. He consciously tried to bring his mind to bear upon it as a reality—an event at that moment enacting; he tried to close his eyes and force his imagination to see the imperial army like a gray mist floating down over Belgium—every soldier identical with the rest, a tin cup as the paper said, "dangling at the same identical angle from each soldier's belt." But he could not. War could not be, this was merely some gigantic cinema unrolling before his eyes —not reality—not the actual drama of modern civilization. The world was too far advanced for that; the soldiers themselves would come to their senses in time; the socialists would save the day; this would stop! But it went on.

The next morning unwonted constraint hung over the Burkhardt household. There was no practicing of music; by unseen power of gravitation the whole family, including Frau Burkhardt and Cosmus, were drawn to the pier to await the coming of the boat.

"Any extras?" Cosmus called out to the boatman.

"None this morning."

They had to be content with one paper. Breakfast went cold on the table. They shared the sheet in silence, and then sat down to eat. Unable to think through this catastrophe, one by one they fell back upon their instincts.

"Dis German Armee," Herr Burkhardt volunteered, "ist one

fine machine, hain't it?"

Cosmus thought that the eyes of his host had never looked so small, and yes, overnight they had grown cunning, and his spine-thick face, coarse and greasy. He did not answer Burkhardt's question; something inhibited complete acquiescence. He tried to bring his mind around to the scholarly ideal of neutrality; he wanted to weigh each side, and arrive at a just conclusion, but something within him rebelled; a deeper something recoiled in horror at the sight of conquest and devastation.

When Adolph said again, "It was Russia; she has been planning this for years. Germany will save the world from the Bear," Cosmus answered, "Belgium attacked Germany, I suppose?"

When Sunday came they were left without a paper. The mail boat did not make the trip. Cosmus actually suffered. He could not understand how news from Europe had become so important in his eyes.

He remembered the Balkan Wars in 1907, and how they scarcely ruffled the surface of public opinion in America. But this was different. He did not have to be very wise to deduce that this war was destined to change the very fabric of the world, to reach out and touch him directly, to modify Iron City and America. All morning he was restless. He tried to read, or to write. He abandoned tennis with Karl because it was too hot. At noon he decided to walk over to the Boy's camp, a mile distant, to borrow a paper. Arriving there he was again disappointed; they had been into town but had been unable to buy a single paper. Vague rumors were afloat. The Germans were in Brussels and some said that there had been a great sea-battle which left the Prussian fleet free to bombard London; their cavalry were even approaching Paris.

Cosmus went back to the Burkhardt cottage. On the porch Frau Burkhardt was reading a German Bible; she looked up, her kind eyes filled with tears.

"Oh, Johnny," she said, "I wish it hadn't come. It's so useless."

By evening Cosmus felt he must have news. The lights of the

city winked on one by one; Cosmus was sure that some terrible thing was impending. He asked Frau Burkhardt if she thought it foolish for him to walk to the city.

"I need exercise," he said.

She told him to go. The still road followed the lake; now and then he met an automobile, but, walking, he had time to think, and as he walked he became calmer, more dispassionate and less fanciful. About ten o'clock he caught a car at the outskirts of the city and rode down town. At the *Journal* office he found turmoil, but he succeeded in getting a paper. There was no news; the situation on the Belgian front remained unchanged.

The next morning, Cosmus did not go back to the Burkhardt cottage. He wrote an elaborate letter, explaining his need to do some work in the University library.

As a matter of fact there was work in the library for him to do. He was bent on finding out the truth behind the war. He began a systematic study of Europe of the nineteenth century. That became his summer's task. Day after day went by in August and September, and he was there turning over many books and periodicals. He did not allow the heated current articles which were beginning to flood periodical literature, to prejudice him. He read the books that were conceived and written before 1914. Books on German education, books on German philosophy, books on German trade theories and practices, appraisals of German literature; German socialism and state theories; lives of Krupp, Ballin, and the Hohenzollerns; German art and religion—these books were studied, mastered. As he read, three truths began to stand out—truths to him patent and undeniable; first, the war should not have been a surprise, for it was foreseen by prophets; secondly, the war was not inevitable; and thirdly, if any human force was guilty, that force was Germany. Germany was guilty.

But what did the war mean? Could any one say? Was there any explanation to be had? The force of such racial movement left the individual weak—almost cowering in the sense of his own insignificance. One night before it was time to go back to Iron City, Cosmus stood watching the traffic twinkle by through the rainy streets. Yes—the crowd—was that a key to the war after all?

He thought of signs; an editorial written with a believing heart by a young reporter; a novel of prophecy written by a young man not yet thirty; a bookstore hidden away in an obscure city street, which had but one purpose, the dissemination of radical social theories; the discharge of a college professor for facing his duty; establishment of new magazines distinguished for radicalism; the tremors of the artistic life of America; the surge and thrust of labor and capital.

And now—the mass movements of men in turmoil, of continental battles which split the universe asunder.

These were signs that stirred, that lifted up and cast down.

No man had a right to think only of himself in such a year, for if these signs, that flared up and painted the horizon, meant anything, they meant this:

The individual is nothing.

The race is all.

The race—the future—demands all: love, peace, pain, possession, comfort, culture, life.

Did the war then not mark the passing of the egocentric world, and the beginning of the new society?

10 Inflammable Youth

"Oh—it's you."

She stood with Boyne's great black safe for a background, a trim figure in steel-blue tailor made, a jaunty feather in a toque that fitted tightly her head which some called too large, but which could not be thought anything but magnificent. Sarah was something to find satisfaction in, a beautiful woman. Cosmus had never realized before that a figure not over five-feet-five could carry such dignity. Her smile was reassuring.

"Of course, I'll go," she answered. She slammed down the rolled-top of her desk, covered the typewriter, and they raced like children down a corridor to the street. September night; they found an acrid smell of burnt leaves in the air, a great moon, and a spirit of adventure everywhere. They found, too, suddenly as they laughed together over nothing in particular, that they had grown closer together during absence. Those letters so frank yet so impersonal had linked them mysteriously, and they were feeling in unison, pulsing together over trifles. It was as if they were strangers to Iron City's familiar streets, and were seeing them in the light of a fresh new romance. The shop windows were interesting; the long rows of automobiles lining the thoroughfare were interesting. Through the fresh air they paced rhythmically apart, step by step as two men might in the exhilaration of physical exercise.

Here were negroes in the gaudy colors they liked so well; Italians, their olive skin and dark eyes set in passionate faces, no longer attracting attention; Chinese, cues gone, immaculately dressed in American pinch-backs, intelligent, alert—less immobile than their wont; they passed a Hindoo, still in native costume, dignified, mysterious; Jews and Greeks vociferating; gaunt faced, solemn-eyed Slavs; large, placid, blonde Scandinavians and Germans. Here in provincial Iron City on Saturday nights was enacted the pageant of nations. Its immense implications silenced them. Cosmus felt again that nearness to the general life—and loyalty to America, which like a mother enfolded all the races.

Sarah, seeming to understand his thoughts, said, "Oh, yes, I know a German who has married a Greek; a Greek who has married an Irishman; an Irishman, who has married a Russian Jew. What is to become of the races? It's the unification of the world!"

They always seemed to find each other, somehow, in that mood—in that passion for the general life.

"Do you know Dickens Street?" she asked.

"No, take me."

She turned sharply off from Main Street, swarming with shoppers, into a by-street, to which somehow, Cosmus never before had penetrated. Here they found twilight, stillness; three streets converged to form a triangular plot, where stood a statue; these streets were lined with dingy ware-houses, with staring windows, quaint shops, which had the unmistakable air of something distinctly antique and foreign.

"Look sharp, sir," Sarah said gayly, "or Mr. Micawber will walk out of that door to allow you the inestimable pleasure of contributing to an indigent gentleman's happiness."

There was the joy of living in her laugh. Cosmus first became aware of two virtues in Sarah Blackstone. She carried her own world with her and her happiness did not depend on things.

They found a restaurant up a flight of stairs, to which music and a Japanese waiter added a touch of the outré slightly beyond Iron City's convention. It was the only place in town which might by the most charitable stretch of the mind be called Bohemian. Here one could sit as long as he liked over tea or coffee, listening to Hungarian music, chatting undisturbed.

They stood for a moment before the window and watched the throngs below jam in and out of shop and theater.

"This is pay-night," Sarah explained. "That accounts for the crowd. It's strange how all our life whirls not about the college but about R. Sill and Son's plant."

"Iron City doesn't seem much affected by the war."

"It isn't really; when the first news came the *Republic-Despatch* got out an extra, and Mr. Sill in an interview stated that he would not manufacture munitions. I learned later from Mr. Boyne that his Dallas and Toronto plants were transferring all their engine business here, and that they were doing the manufacturing of shells—we don't scorn war-brides in Iron City, but that is all we care about the war. It's meaning—as for that—well!"

She removed her coat, and sat down; their eyes met across the table.

"But that is being serious, and I promised myself not to be serious tonight." Then she added, "We don't play enough, Mr. Cosmus."

He was doubtful about the "we." Who do not? He and she? or Iron City folks in general?

"Suppose I tell you, you are unusually beautiful tonight."

It was a clumsy attempt at play, he afterwards recognized. She looked frightened, annoyed, and he despised himself for his bluntness of perception. He was afraid that he had rudely brushed away the tenuous threads that subtended their happiness. But she smiled back bravely.

"Let's not do that either,—we both are too poor at it."

After that there was a little breathless silence while the waiter brought the tea; then they settled back in comfort. They were happy, shyly happy in a calm, natural manner. There was no storm of feeling beating up through him for expression; he was content; completely harbored; totally answered.

"Do you know," he said suddenly, "this makes me think of home."

Her lids fluttered again a moment, then her eyes faced him squarely in man-fashion.

"It does, doesn't it? One gets so tired of cafeterias and boarding houses."

He liked to see her eat—unashamed of hunger. He liked her strong hands, like a mother's he thought. To be in her presence was as a walk at dawn in fresh rain-cleared air. And yet her imperious innocence was there to guard against every advance of sex.

She broke a piece of white bread; she broke a piece of brown bread and dexterously made a sandwich. A third virtue; she was herself.

Five minutes later, on the street, they were filled again with magnetism borrowed from the crowd—folk intoxication—and allowed themselves to be carried gayly along to the entrance of the Green Jewel. They went in. Ah, here was magic. Dimness and music and an interesting story inducted into the mind with meticulous ease. Here was reading together—reading of no high order to be sure—but reading together under the most thrilling conditions; a kind of Grand Opera of Fiction. On the screen, in bewildering array, were flashed processions of Arabs in white solitopias, cities by the sea, stretches of beach and breakers, mountain roads, cities burning, a harem with realism carried almost too far—sea nymphs, led by the Modern Venus; one saw the flash of her naked body like the blade of a fish in the shining water and then she stood dripping on the sands clothed in nothing but her innocence and hair. There were battles and shipwrecks, and finally the last close-ups of lovers in each other's arms.

"If you will pardon the intrusion of a sociologist upon this American Night's Entertainment, I must remark," Cosmus said mockingly, "that if this be a revelation of our national life—then America is a cross between a child and a roué. This show was nothing but a fairy tale held together by a thread of sensuality."

"I suppose so," she answered, "but nudity somehow seems no more objectionable on the screen than it does in the Louvre. And you must remember that that film was not made for professors but for girls—say— like Margaret Morton."

Cosmus felt uncomfortable. He searched her face. Surely she was not piqued.

"You know Margaret then?"

"Yes, I see her often at the Country Club, and I think she is one of the two really beautiful women I ever saw outside the movies."

"Yes, she is beautiful," returned John thoughtfully.

The crowds were thinning in the streets when they came out. Iron City, after all, was but a country town pushed into the pose of a metropolis. The crowds were thickest at nine, and from then on thinned; at eleven all of the pretentious bustle was over.

"Well, Mr. Sociologist, if you are in the high-brow mood, let's go and see the paintings."

"Paintings?"

"Yes, paintings—an exhibit from the Chicago Art Institute, with a real-live lecturer attached."

They arrived too late for the formal address, but they found the lecturer commenting informally on the pictures. The exhibit was Iron City's first venture into the field of art; and Iron City had ventured boldly. Of course, the Woman's Club had brought the exhibit as a part of its "uplift program." Iron City needed art, not a shallow imitation but a virile, living art that could reproduce the wonder of factory pipes against the autumn sky. In a world as it might be, Raymond Sill might have been such an artist;—he had virility and life and love of beauty.

The small auditorium in the Carnegie Library, where the pictures were hung, was crowded with women. Besides the lecturer there were three men in the place. A ministerial personage, a helpless drooping individual with his wife, and a homeless, shabby painter with eager face. The last was holding a sketch, evidently his own, up to the lecturer for criticism. Sarah touched Cosmus's arm, "Oh, I want you to meet Silly Dodd."

She meant the painter. They sought him out and Cosmus was introduced. John saw the sketch. It was done on a piece of wall-paper with pencil, and filled in with smeary pigments. The criticism the lecturer offered was that Dodd had used black where he ought to have used purple.

"But, sir, I had no purple."

Dodd spoke thickly and indistinctly; there was something feeble and underfed about his person, something feeble in his manner, but no intimation of imbecility.

"Why do they call him Silly?" John inquired of Sarah, when they were in the street again.

"I suppose because he doesn't know enough to keep clean. Dodd isn't a success, but I find him interesting. He won't work. They tell me he was in the Spanish War, had the yellow, and worked at Sill's plant until they put in the efficiency system. He was married once, married a widow who owned an apple orchard in Michigan; but Dodd wouldn't pick apples; he preferred to paint them, and she sent him about his business. I laugh yet when I think of what that marriage must have been. I suppose Dodd is the least desirable person in Iron City. I suppose mothers hold him up as the pattern of shame to their children, and yet, Dodd's whole life has been one long passionate pursuit of a spiritual ideal. Think of painting on wall-paper with colors bought at Woolworth's!"

"Has he had any training?"

"Yes, he worked with Charles Francis Browne years ago. Suppose he were a great artist? Wouldn't it be just the same for him in Iron City?"

They had lost their gaiety; folk intoxication had gone with the crowd. Carloads of shoppers passed them, and the streets were emptying. They were aware of the expansive night, the remoteness of the skies and the vastness of the world. But they had lost none of their sense of comradeship. Silence did not bother them. They drifted homeward. In the Park where a few leaves were fluttering down over the newly erected statue of R. Sill, M.D., they sat down on a bench. They were loth to go in; here was peace.

Sarah took a pin from her hat and rolling her collar up around her white throat, pinned it snugly. The air was sharper. John watched her, fascinated. Every move of hers was decisive, strong. She knew well how to take care of herself. When she spoke, after a time, it was of Dodd again.

"It must be no picnic for Dodd to be so impractical when every one around him is so practical."

"True."

"Iron City must stifle him. I sometimes think that the school, the church and money-getting are great conspiracies against freedom. It must be terrible to lose one's love of freedom," she paused, "I suppose when one does, one is old."

That she would get old seemed preposterous to him.

"You'll never get old," he told her.

"It is very nice of you to say that, but already I feel that I have missed something, and the pity of it is, I don't know what it is."

A note of wistfulness had crept into her voice. She seemed reaching out to him like a child, but when he looked at her she was marble. Her clean-cut beauty was remote; her charm was power. She did not, could not need him. She was a refuge. She was to be respected, adored, not loved as men love women. He failed to answer her.

She said, "There, I was serious, and I had promised not to be serious." And when she said that a barrier closed between them and she arose and started home. Cosmus was not ready to go in, but he did not say so; he walked along beside her—content. The last few steps in the vast moonlight seemed to him like a benediction. At the gate, they parted quickly. She turned back as if to shake hands; he didn't see her outstretched hand in time; then embarrassed by his blindness she went into the house without a word.

Cosmus was happy. In bed he fell asleep quickly, and slept soundly, but not before he had time to think; her presence seemed everywhere round him, her lips, her eyes, throat and hair. Then he laughed, "Funny, and I have never touched even her little finger."

Sarah did not sleep. She sat in the dark by the window and watched the moonlight. As Ezra Kimbark had said, Sarah was a man's woman. Like many another modern woman, she had acquired that reputation because she let her mind rule her heart. Such a reputation must have come with her up from childhood, but it wasn't quite authentic.

When she was two years old her father had died. As far back as she could remember, his absence made her heart ache. Even her mother did not know how she missed him, for little Sarah began building up an outer armament of steel. She envied the fathers of the other girls and shyly tried to adopt one, but never succeeded. "A self-willed little miss," they called her. On rainy afternoons she often went up to the attic to the big trunk, and looked over her father's photographs. She built together fragmentary impressions of him until she had a preternatural grasp upon his personality; but such a fleshless parent did not answer her need.

When Sarah was seventeen, her mother died. To her mother death did not come suddenly, but slowly and cruelly. Mrs. Blackstone had taught school for fifteen years after her husband's death, and teaching had brought on a slow disease. The two of them, Sarah and her mother, in the last three years of her life had moved from sanitarium to sanitarium, from east to west seeking a hopeless relief. Sarah was forced to live with strangers, and to assume mature duties when all the time her child's heart was crying for understanding. The child's uncle in Cleveland said, when mother and daughter were at San Antonio, "Oh, sister will be safe down there, for Sarah is just like a grown-up and assumes responsibility with delight." On her death-bed Mrs. Blackstone gave Sarah a letter to be opened after the funeral. It was a wild, passionate cry such as only a stricken mother could have made. It frightened Sarah. She sat with white face and did not weep for days. Then she silenced her heart, locked up the child she was in a dungeon and riveted another layer of steel about her clinging womanhood. Sarah could not recall those days now without pain.

She went to live with the uncle in Cleveland, who had five daughters, and although he said, "Dear, you will be just like my own little girls," somehow, Sarah never fitted into the machinery of the household. They never understood her and she suffered much. "She is independent," the uncle said, "she doesn't need much fathering." And so Sarah at nineteen was just a little unwomanly—that is unlike most women—with a vein of cynicism running deep, and an atheistic bent.

At college, she distinguished herself in debate, eschewed belles-lettres, took a course in economics and history, and became the leader of her set. She was the all-around girl. Men did not care much for her—though not quite that. She was popular with them,— but popular differently; she never seemed to need them. They counted her their pal. She could defeat them at their own peculiar game of logic, and she played tennis with exceptional vigor. When she received her master's degree the president said: "Sarah Blackstone will be a great dean in five years." So she would have been, no doubt, if she had not run counter to the artificial thinking of Reverend Mr. Crandon. In business, she found the contact with living reality, which she craved, but was it calculated to save her from dying inwardly, as she had told Cosmus she was afraid she would?

With all her perspicacity, her interest in and knowledge of other persons, Sarah Blackstone did not know what she lacked. She was blind to that quality of hers, which held men off, just as much as Margaret Morton was unconscious of the mystery that allured them.

She sat at the window a long time and thought of John Cosmus. She considered him but a boy, but it was his inflammable idealism, his faith in life which attracted her. She had had a broader experience than his, and she knew that idealism and faith in an age of agnosticism were all too uncommon.

When she finally arose, she did not undress in the dark as was her wont. She turned on the light, and cast little sly glances at herself in the glass. What she saw did not displease her.

"I don't care, I am not scrawny," she thought, and then added, "I suppose I am just a natural-born old maid." But she did not sigh. Something stirred within her. Inflammable youth tingled in her veins; life and power beat up from unprobed depths. Her heart fluttered in her throat, and a blush dyed her silver flesh, Then laughing, she turned off the light, threw open all the windows, stood gulping in a deep draught of air, then jumped into bed and slept.

11 Raymond and Margaret

Margaret Morton sat at her dressing table. Her room was the
most luxurious in the great old-fashioned house. Soon after she
had won the automobile and the membership to the country
club from her father, she had asked him to allow her to remodel
and decorate two rooms under her own supervision. Carl had,
of course, consented. Margaret sent for a contractor, and had
hardwood floors, now handsomely waxed, laid over the old, soft
pine, previously covered with carpet. She hung mahogany doors
and had the woodwork finished in white; with soft curtains, a few
rich rugs, she managed to throw over the rooms the air of
sweetness and refinement. She had bought her furniture at
Field's one day, when she was in the city, a few pieces of bird's-eye
maple which to her seemed very fine. Her ideas for the room she
had gotten from a house at Pike Lake, where she had gone to a
house party. From off the room a bath with showers was elabo-
rately appointed.

   Margaret had just emerged from the shower, and sat in her
flowered kimono before her dressing table, doing nothing in
particular. She was waiting for Raymond; they were to drive over
to Spotswood for supper, and return in the October dusk. She
was not thinking of any one or anything. It was a bother to think.
She had a sense of warmth and well-being. The shower must have
been a little too warm, for she was languorous. Ideas refused to
climb up above the threshold of consciousness. Her lids drooped
down over her eyes, but did not touch her cheek. She could peep

out beneath the lashes; with satisfaction, she saw how long and dark the lashes were; the perfect curve of the lips, and of the shapely arms. She smiled—the dimples came. She tried posture after posture, expression after expression, all beautiful, all satisfactory to her, for she laughed out loud like a child. It must have been a rehearsal.

"I must dress," she thought, "Raymond will soon be here;—shall I put a patch on to-day? How soft silk is. I wonder if Professor Cosmus is in town. Lavender always becomes me. How I love old rose."

Then she sank back again into relaxation—warm, comfortable, her senses alert, drinking in all the sweetness of the little room. She took up a silver file, and opened a scented box, but her hand stopped midway in the act, her lashes drooped again; she was all rosy in her dream. She brushed her nails languorously; then she trailed across the room, and opened a wardrobe door. From an array of dresses, she selected two; a lavender and an old rose. These she laid fastidiously on the bed and stood pondering, her hands above her head, the sleeves falling back from her lovely arms. Which should she wear? She moved back to the dressing table, fumbled in a jewel case and produced a dingy copper cent. "Heads for rose; tails for lavender."

She tossed. The penny struck the head of the bed, rolled across the floor, spun awkwardly, and set.

"Just my luck—tails."

She knit her brows, then laughed, tossed her head in defiance, and put the lavender dress back into the press.

She sat at the edge of the bed, holding a silk stocking listlessly, her eyes caught by something out of the window. They rested on an uncompleted Gothic church, the new St. Luke's. The spire rose like a carved needle into the sky, and the gaping windows seemed like beautiful slits the shears had made in the lovely granite fabric. Margaret crossed herself devoutly. Then her eyes closed in a dream again; she saw the church finished ready for a bridal party; a new awning led from the curbing to the door;

contrary to all precedent it was hung with flowers; a limousine drew up at the church; it was followed by a score of machines—all glistening; from the first, a beautiful girl alighted—there was a gasp from the crowd; was there ever such a lovely bride? And the groom! As he gleamed and danced in and out of her dreams, first, he was Raymond Sill and then John Cosmus, or some mysterious, more wonderful personage, whose face was not clear. Up the steps——

The dream was interrupted by her mother's voice.

"Maggie, Raymond's here."

"Already? Tell him I'll be down in three minutes."

"Can I help you?"

"Oh, no, Mother, I'm almost dressed. Tell him he'll find the last *Cosmopolitan* under the pillow on the davenport."

And in twenty minutes, Margaret came down stairs in the old rose dress, her eyes all mirth.

Raymond sat on the davenport with the magazine in his hand talking to Mrs. Morton, looking like a sportsman in his neat tweed. Outside the big Stutz still panted impatiently, stroked down to ten miles.

Mrs. Morton was the kind of woman who was admirable for her insincerity. By chance revelation some years before she had suddenly seen what she really was, and had at once decided to build herself over. Though she was timid, she sought to appear aggressive—something of the executive; hurt and frightened by life, she pretended that she was strong and unafraid; preferring to keep silent, she talked volubly; anything but strong or well, she preferred to boast of her good-health. But wasn't all this feigning admirable, when she was thereby improving nature's handiwork?

"Now children—let's see," she examined her wrist watch, "it is a quarter of five. I shall expect you back not one minute later than eight o'clock. You will have plenty of time even then, and will not have to drive like mad."

"All right, Mother," replied Margaret, "but if the machine

should break down, or something—don't forget your Christian Science." With that, they were off.

There was an irrepressible gayety about Margaret Morton that was wholly natural, not attained. Some secret spring of energy seemed to supply her with a superabundance of spirits which no reserve could hold in check. She laughed and talked ceaselessly, but melodiously. It was good to hear her—not for sense but for music. No doubt, this was one of her great points of attractiveness.

She was saying to Raymond:

"You can't guess what I dreamed last night. I dreamed that I was walking along College Street, and I saw men and girls staring at me, and shaking their heads. They whispered, too, and giggled. Finally I heard one say gloomily 'what a shame, such a fine girl, too, could go with any man she pleased, and all that, and now she is a grind.'"

Margaret's voice trilled off into laughter. "What do you think of me as a Phi Beta?"

"I thought you wanted to be, Mag?"

"How's that?"

"You stick so close to Professor Cosmus."

"Anyway, he's not rude to me like you are," she pouted.

Spotswood lay twenty miles west over good roads, through a region of quiet farms, and wooded hills. Raymond drove like mad.

"You'll kill yourself some day," Margaret shrieked in his ear, as they swerved down a hill, and around a corner.

"Not in an auto."

"Why not?"

"A hunch is a hunch, you know. Just can't do it."

She liked best to dash through villages, Raymond to take the hills. To her there was a thrill in dropping down upon a cluster of human habitations, so swiftly that the houses seemed to leap to the eyes, and to sweep through the streets with the gaze of all the inhabitants upon the strange machine. She delighted in attention. That was the joy in these trips for her. She was playing the grand lady grandly. Raymond seemed touched by the beauty of the autumn world more often than she. Sometimes he slowed down to a walk and pointed out a field or glade, some stretch of painted woods, or farmhouse that she might have missed. It was at such moments that Raymond felt nearest to Margaret; he would let his arm drop on her shoulder and she would let it rest there. Though he was not unsusceptible to her charms, theirs was not yet a sentimental relationship; it was one that had begun in childhood's comradeship and had thus far stopped at reciprocal interests. Raymond gave her excitement; she gave him gayety.

Spotswood reached at sundown, they found the Spotswood House, a hotel that tried to capitalize its dingy antiquity by the sign, "The House that Lincoln Chose." They hurried into the dining room and found the table reserved for them. Margaret did not remove her veil; she liked the air it gave her. They lingered long over their meal—these two young hearts, finding joy in pretending that they were world-travelers, oblivious to the real world; the world of war and struggle that lay behind the gloomy embers, which they were watching in the west.

When they came out upon the hotel piazza, the last red of the sun had died at the end of the street. The air was sharp and fragrant. They must be off. Margaret felt free and strong. She could go on like this forever. Why should they go in? She loved the night—the flight through its mystery on winged wheels.

"Say," she said, "we've just got to go home by way of Trinway."

He glanced at his watch. It was nearly seven. At the best they could not touch Trinway to the east and get back to Iron City before ten. He looked at Margaret, the pretty, teasing face atilt to him.

Soon they were careening over the star-lit roads, silent, impassioned, thrilling. Once they narrowly missed collision with a wagon, once they would have capsized in a ditch had it not been for Raymond's cool twist of the wheel. But such escapes were part of the pleasure. On the edge of the village precincts, Raymond always slackened speed a trifle. It was near Twelve Mile that they met the major adventure of the evening. Although Raymond had slowed down, it was not enough to give him easy control of the heavy car. As they turned a corner they saw a boy dart into the lane of light made by their lamps, falter, hesitate; Raymond whirled the wheel, they paused. There was a scream behind. Visions of a crumpled human form swept through Raymond's brain. He slowed down. Margaret grasped his arm, frantically.

"Don't stop, Ray, don't stop; Mother must not know we were out here."

He touched the throttle and they fled guiltily out of the town upon an unfrequented road. Mile after mile they put between them and the village. Finally Raymond felt that he could slow down to a walk. They were sober and silent; some awful calamity suddenly towered above them. By some reflex of Margaret's gayety, she laughed nervously and said.

"I don't believe we struck him; I looked back quick, but I couldn't see."

"He screamed."

"He was only scared. Please don't be worried, Ray."

They reached home soon after ten. They saw there the lights of Raymond's factory painting the sky; there were lights in the Morton house, too.

Mrs. Morton met them at the door.

"What did I tell you, Maggie," she began severely.

"Well, Mother, we couldn't help it. We had to carry water a half a mile to cool the engine."

"Why, you poor children, you actually look fagged out."

Margaret did not sleep. She lay staring up at the ceiling, calculating the chances of their being found out. Oh! What if they had killed the boy?

The next morning she had a headache, and yet she dressed to go down to breakfast. She was on the stairs when she heard her father's big voice above the clatter of coffee-cups say,

"The *Republic-Despatch* says that a boy was run down by a strange machine at Twelve Mile last night. Lots of excitement; the whole town is indignant because the driver did not stop. A person who would do that," he said emphatically, "is nothing more or less than a human skunk."

Margaret did not go down. She crept back to her bed-room, undressed and lay still, white and distraught.

At his father's office, Raymond scanned the morning papers. Yes, there it was—a news story and an editorial on "vampires of the road." Raymond's face flamed behind the paper. Thank God! only the boy's leg was broken.

About eleven Margaret received a telephone call. She lay still, feigning sleep, inwardly fearful that it was an officer of the law. Her mother called.

"Raymond wants you, Maggie."

"Oh."

At the phone Raymond was saying

"The boy only had a leg broken."

"Oh, I'm so glad."

"And they don't know who did it."

"Gee. I'm so glad, Ray."

That night when Ray dropped in to see Margaret, they suddenly saw themselves in a new relationship. They had a secret. They were linked by a common guilt; some vaster, darker fate had joined them. They saw themselves in the livid light of melodramatic romance. They enjoyed its novelty. When Raymond left, he stooped and kissed Margaret's willing lips for the first time. With that kiss, they laid aside the boy-and-girl relationship; it sealed their entrance into manhood and womanhood, and opened an alluring and mysterious world.

12 Substantial Citizens

John Cosmus, in his room at the Curtis house, one November evening, held open before him a letter from Frau Burkhardt, which said "Six weeks after you left, our dear Karl sailed from New York to Sweden. He is only an under-officer in the 346th Prussian Guard, but it does us good to know that we can do that much for our Vaterland."

The letter brought with it the turmoil of a world at war. To be sure Cosmus had been wrestling with the abstract problems which such a catastrophe would usher into a mind of his type; but here in this quiet letter was concrete contact with the blood and stir and havoc of the battle itself.

Karl—little Karl—was perhaps at that moment either giving or taking life. Outside a November moon congealed the world to marble. There trailed through his mind, by some irrational connection, thoughts of Babylon, the strong which had ravished beauty from the world and had, in passing, not left a stone; the mystery of time; the passing of civilizations; and the unfathomable mystery of war.

He turned from the window, picked up the newspaper clippings, which Frau Burkhardt had so graciously sent him, glanced over them, and tossed them into the grate. "Mere propaganda!"

He found in Iron City many persons more susceptible than he to the seduction of the *Continental Times,* and other pro-German media. There was a mild indifference generally as Sarah had said, but of those who thought at all, many strongly sympathized with the Prussian government. Why shouldn't they? They found in that magnificent military machine that glided down over Belgium and France the embodiment of much of what they worshiped in their own civilization; largeness, speed, efficiency, and conscious destruction of competitors. Iron City had been paying obeisance for years to the same Gods as Germany. As one citizen put it, "Fritz can lick the world because he is the best business man in the world."

To all this Cosmus returned surprise. He had traversed a large field of thought,—history, economics, science, religion and literature; and before the war, he had been striving to do what thoughtful men of his generation everywhere were consciously or unconsciously trying to do; to adjust society to the sudden wrench which Darwinism had given the world two generations back; to build a philosophy, firmly imbedded in fact, yet inclusive of spiritual values. Forced as he had been from boyhood into contact with hardship,—he had had to work with his hands,—he had grown to respect things as they are. He recognized the immutable laws of the universe. But he never failed to see the pulsing inner life of man, its needs, intentions, shadowy passionate aspirations; he believed that man was the arbiter of his own destiny. The hope of society, he believed, was the attainment of mobility—a propensity for flowing, with the least wrench, into the convolutions that the immutable power of the universe had set for it. Cosmus saw Germany, therefore, a detriment to the larger mobility—because, in the transition from class-thinking to social thinking, Germany was just another colossal class-mind, inimical to socialization. But subtly specious Germany was, because she seemingly had attained socialization within herself. As a matter of fact, she had not; in a nation where there was no free, quick circulation of ideas, there could be no real socialization.

When Cosmus found so much sentiment for Germany in Iron City, he was troubled. He could not understand how Americans could fail to see the issue. Was Democracy decadent? He concluded that Iron City was the victim of class thinking, being, as it was, but an emanation of Sill's factory—the embodiment of largeness, efficiency, and conscious destruction of competitors.

He sat thoughtfully in his room late one night by the fire—troubled. America was jeopardized; whether she saw it or not, she was imperiled by her own supineness. Shut in, in provincial Iron City, he seemed alone in his passion for America. But if he had only known it, young hearts and minds East and West were throbbing with the new dream of a great Democracy.

The next evening he sought out Sarah Blackstone. He had formed that habit lately;—she was so much that which Iron City was not. They were sitting over coffee in the little cafe, with its half-Bohemian flavor. He was tired; the eternal grind of the classroom, relieved only occasionally by inspiration, had exacted its toll. His mind beat feverishly in and out of abstract problems—as a teacher's mind will—spinning wildly in the web of dilemma, seeing only the everlasting return of circumstance. Only vigorous altercation with a medicine ball or contact with the cooling presence of Sarah was able to cure him when he was in that state.

"Why is it," he was saying nervously, "that, when the solution of all social problems depends on education, we do nothing whatsoever with the problem of education?"

She pushed her chair back from the table, folded her hands in her lap in her peculiar way, smiled across at him, and said,

"Tell me about it."

"Well, President Crandon informed me yesterday that there had been several complaints against my approach to Labor Problems."

"So?"

"Oh, of course, he didn't say so directly; he never does. Ostensibly he came to commend me for the way I edited the catalogue, but he said, by the long road around, 'We must guard our departments from any taint or suspicion of class prejudice.'"

Sarah smiled.

"Oh, the blindness of the man. Class-prejudice." John was

getting shrill, then recollecting himself, he stopped, shrugged his shoulders, turned out his hands. "You know," he said quietly, "that they got the injunction through to close Dover Street."

"Yes, I know."

"Dean Georgia Summers's eyes will no longer be assailed by the sight of the dear working men."

"You despise that woman?" There was half-concealed amusement in Sarah's voice.

"She seems to me to have fed her life-long on the dregs of Victorianism. After all," John continued, "the problem is summed up by your own phrase—private and public duty. Crandon Hill College acts as a private institution, existing of and for and by a class, whereas education by its very nature, if its object is attained, is a public enterprise. Think of our opportunity here in Iron City to do something for the alien peoples, and to extend the democratic principle. Think of our duty to adjust America to the colossal events of war. But if we so much as broach the subject, a hue and cry of socialism is raised, until one feels like kicking himself out of the profession."

"Which I should never do—being a man," Sarah said with a smile. She liked Cosmus for his vehemence.

"The college should be pouring such a flood of impersonal, scientific knowledge upon the situation, reflecting truth so clearly without the aberration of class-minds, that the disintegration of America would be impossible."

"They don't see, Mr. Cosmus—that's all. You forget that you are an expert in social conditions. And say what you will, truth is illusive, metaphysical. Take old Mr. Sill, do you fancy that he looks upon himself as a vile plutocrat? No, he treasures the pretty illusion that he is a leader in society. Does President Crandon consider himself a failure as an educator? Hardly. He has his pretty illusions, too. The whole problem is to make them see."

"See!" John answered bitterly. "In other words to solve the problem of education one must educate. Just so. You have brought me back to where I started this morning. I have been moving in that toxic circle all day. You, even you, have failed me."

Sarah did not let this emphasis on "even you" go unnoticed.

"I suppose I have," she said, sad for no reason whatsoever. "But you forget youth. You forget yourself, and the thousands like you, young and strong, and seeing. They will bring the new age soon, very soon."

As she spoke Cosmus saw past her face now radiant, through the window to where the River of Wires gleamed, a link between unseen cities.

"And you'll never stop trying to make them see—that I know. You won't get tired; you won't fail, you'll go on."

It wasn't what she said that renewed John's strength, it was she. Something passed from her to him, it seemed, and made him strong. He felt the fever and the fret vanishing, and ambition renewed.

"That reminds me of an experience I had with Professor Clarke yesterday," he said smiling; "Clarke, you know, believes in the divine right of professors. He was deploring the rising ripple of self-government among the students, and he said: 'God gave Moses to the children of Israel, and they took him.' I answered, 'But that was God!' And he didn't see the joke."

They laughed. The atmosphere was cleared and they were happy. When they arose to go, before leaving the room, Cosmus turned to her fervently.

"You did help me after all, Sarah."

Perhaps he did not know that he had called her Sarah for the first time, so seldom had he called her anything else in his mind. But Sarah knew. It filled her with strange exultation, and when he turned to her again, her eyes were dancing, her cheeks radiant. . . .

As John Cosmus looked back upon that second winter at Crandon Hill College it seemed one long stretch of exasperation. Upon one side, he saw America's pitiable need of a great unifying passion, on the other, the immobility of the college, its servile worship of the past, its short-circuiting of great ideas. He did not escape despair, or that withering sense of failure, which comes to all men who see principles rather than things, masses rather than individuals. He would awake out of his struggle trying to reassure himself: Wasn't he making quite too much of this? Iron City was perfectly happy. There was no problem at R. Sill's plant! The college was contributing a trained citizenry,— minds capable of facile changes of thought and of social control. Why should one take education seriously when no one else did? Then he would return to the round of duties to run face to face with indifference, provincialism, and class-hatred. If it had not been for Sarah Blackstone, Cosmus might have despaired utterly. She furnished much of the motive force that drove him on in those months. He turned to her habitually, and yet, he always found the same barrier between them. They were greater friends, but lesser lovers.

One winter evening when he called for her at Boyne's office, he found her bowed over the desk, her head resting on her arms. She arose with a start, and a none-too-brave smile.

"You're tired," he said. "You'd better not go out to-night. I'm a dog to think of asking you."

"I'm all right. I can go."

"What is it, Sarah?" Strange, to him she often seemed two women—one, masterful, and strong, one only a child.

"Nothing." Then she added with that quick smile of hers, "when I was a child, I did not receive a single gift on my tenth birthday, and I remember still how I felt. I still feel that way sometimes."

He experienced again the impulse to take her in his arms, and again the thought intervened, that there would be something preposterous in caressing Sarah Blackstone. When he spoke it was quite impersonally,

"Come in and get a cup of coffee. That will brace you up."

And he was not above laying upon her his own vexing problems.

In late November before Senator Matt Tyler, trustee of Crandon Hill College, went to Washington, Cosmus had an opportunity to talk with him concerning the educational situation.

"My dear son," replied the Senator, not unkindly, "like most boys you are taking the whole matter quite too seriously. If you'll just ease up a bit, things will come out all right. They always do. You will find that the college is still the bulwark of the state, that there are a lot of older and wiser heads than yours thinking on these same problems. What our noble public document, the Declaration, says about all men being created free and equal, you will find is quite true in these United States."

Senator Tyler was scrupulous in his personal attire. Broadcloth, linen, a rose in his buttonhole, were evidences of exacting taste. He was ruddy and not portly—a handsome figure. Cosmus had his eye on the diamond shirt stud as he asked,

"Don't you sometimes suspect, Senator, that our Declaration and Constitution as ready-made plans are not quite adequate for all present needs? And don't you ever grow impatient at the lack of large, generalizing minds that should come out of schools? Aren't we producing specialists, rather than administrators—real leaders in the state?"

Senator Tyler smiled broadly, and tapped Cosmus's knee with his elegant finger.

"It's a good thing you talk that treason only to one who is as good natured as I am, young fellow." He winked jocosely. "No, you go back and get interested in the development of your own department, and let these vexing matters go. They will take care of themselves." He arose and saw Cosmus to the door. "Don't judge these matters too important. Good-by, come again."

Senator Matt Tyler evidently did not consider this interview unimportant. He was sober when he sat down in his swivel chair; his brows were knitted; and he scribbled something on a pad of paper. Two or three days later when he met President Hugh Crandon at dinner he whispered in the midst of Haskell's best story, "Young Cosmus seems a little restive."

"Yes, he hasn't put himself in harmony with the large historical background of the college."

"Oh, that's it, is it?" The Senator murmured; their eyes met understandingly.

One evening after the Christmas vacation, Mrs. Curtis told Cosmus that her friend, Mrs. Hilton, matron of Mather Hall, had been discharged.

"I wonder if you can't do something to get her place back?" Cosmus smiled; Mrs. Curtis was always attributing to him influence in the college which he did not have.

"I'm afraid not, Mrs. Curtis. Why was she discharged?"

"Well, she wanted to buy fresh supplies—that is, milk, butter and meat—from Holdon & Holdon, and the college authorities wanted her to buy them from the Iron City Consumer's Company."

"She gets them cheaper, I suppose," Cosmus asked "from the Consumer's Company."

"No, dearer."

"Dearer?"

"Well," Mrs. Curtis spoke almost defiantly, "Mrs. Hilton told me that she had it straight from one of the clerks at the Consumer's, that Mr. Smithkins holds the controlling interest in the Consumer's Company."

"You mean in the Utility Company?"

"No, both."

"I can do nothing, Mrs. Curtis."

Cosmus remembered where he had last seen P. C. Smithkins; it was at prayer-meeting at the First Church. Tall, elderly, volatile, Mr. Smithkins, trustee of Crandon Hill College, was asserting, apropos of nothing, that "We have no literature in America, because America is too prosperous."

By such indirect means, Cosmus was inducted into the central fact of college life. He knew that when one formed an opinion about anything so subtle as the spirit of a place, there was always danger of allowing the personal equation to count too much, but here fact piled itself on fact in convincing preponderance. Though hot with the impatience of youth, he was never blind enough to attribute to Sill, Crandon, Tyler and Smithkins, conscious collusion, or even so much as tacit understanding. To Cosmus, the most culpable of all was President Crandon. Under his guidance, the college should have been creating a quick current of large ideas, which would have purged society of injustice and made democracy real. But President Crandon, amiable and formal, made education a mere massing of conventionalities and intricate artificialities. Some mysterious antipathy drove him, the youthful instructor, and Hugh Crandon, the president, asunder. From Crandon, the president, from Tyler, the trustee, from his colleagues, Cosmus received only antagonism. Even Ezra Kimbark, though friendly, Cosmus found did not understand. To Kimbark, education was the passionate pursuit of an aloof and painted past.

The only element which saved Cosmus from complete discouragement was a few students. He thought often of the words of Sarah, "But you forget youth. You forget yourself, and the thousands like you, young and strong—seeing. They will bring the new age soon, very soon." There was Jenkins, a freshman, whose father was a coal operator in Illinois; Jenkins openly sympathized with the men when they were out on a strike and sought to bring them and his father into an amicable settlement. There was Weaver, dynamic and brilliant, fearlessly setting himself to the study of society in the hope of arriving at some practical egress from the maze of social problems. These and others like them gravitated to Cosmus, and compensated for hours of discouragement.

Not so Raymond Sill. His entrance into college in the fall was a signal for rejoicing on the part of football enthusiasts. No one ran the team like Raymond, nor played the mandolin so pleasingly. Under Margaret Morton's urging, he elected Labor Problems with Cosmus. In the classroom Raymond sat back often with a mocking expression on his dark handsome face; or he would mischievously try to sidetrack all discussion of current problems into consideration of abstractions.

He would interrupt: "Don't you think selfishness is at the bottom of all acts? Should one man be blamed then more than another?"

He had a sluggish but, when aroused, trenchant mind, and a disconcerting gift for analysis. Cosmus honestly tried to answer his difficulties until he was convinced that Raymond was quibbling. When he turned upon him the full battery of his anger and impatience, Raymond relapsed into silence and later tried to precipitate a mutiny. Often he did not appear for days.

When the semester ended, Cosmus was forced to flunk Raymond Sill. There was a rule which automatically cut off any student who failed from participation in college activities. When the mandolin club went on its spring trip, however, to his surprise, Cosmus discovered that Raymond was the leader.

"By special courtesy of the president," he was told by Dean Witherspoon.

There is no deliberative body so little understood as a college faculty. Formed of individualists and specialists, it feeds on technicalities; it has no sense of humor, and no soul. It is inclusive of all points of view, but incapable of accepting any. Every member insists on speaking on every subject. Its individual wisdom is rivaled only by its collective unwisdom. It rivals the German Reichstag as a debating society. In the two years in which John Cosmus had sat on the faculty of Crandon Hill College, he had never once seen the ghost of an educational policy stalk across the well-set stage, upon which so many orators strutted and fretted. He, however, had heard the faculty spend two hours discussing whether "successive," had logical or chronological meaning. President Hugh Crandon, polished and forbearing, patiently guided the orators through the Dædalian maze of parliamentary procedure. Now and then Cosmus thought he saw the wraith of a twinkle in the president's eyes. What was this president's power? What was the real Hugh Crandon who hid behind the mask? Once Cosmus had heard Mrs. Crandon indiscreetly say, "Yes, Mr. Crandon allows all the faculty to have their say, then he does as he pleases anyhow."

At one of the regular faculty meetings early in the spring, Cosmus, goaded by the indifference of his colleagues into bringing before them problems of Iron City's life, made his maiden speech. Direct always, he said:

"Mr. President, I consider the greatest mistake Crandon Hill College ever made was the closing of Dover Street to the alien workers that used to pass through the campus. In itself, it seems nothing; in reality it has become a symbol of our aloofness from the vital life of our city. We have stamped ourselves with the insidious insignia of class."

Such sincerity, interpolated into an assembly whose policies were masked by insincerity and politeness, was freezing. For a moment, it looked as if no one were to accept the challenge. President Crandon, calm and dignified always, recoiled; his eyes contracted into hot slits. Then Professor Clarke, the whip of the house, arose.

"Mr. President, I do not wish to prolong this discussion (Professor Clarke always preluded his remarks thus) but I feel——" Here he paused, drew himself up to his full height, threw back his head as if about to deliver a blow with it, and then thundered, "that such remarks are out of order. Indeed, I consider them a violation of professional etiquette. The closing of Dover Street had the due consideration of the faculty, Mr. President, and of the administration, Mr. President, and of the Board of Trustees, Mr. President. Such unanimity makes Mr. Cosmus's remarks nothing short of impertinent."

There was a general rustle of applause. The "whip" continued to strike. "Moreover, gentlemen of the faculty, you have been all witnesses to the vulgar intrusion upon the privacy of this institution. Actually Mr. President, I myself have seen foreign mothers sitting upon the senior bench suckling their infants. What a spectacle for the young women of this college!" Dean Georgia

Summers tried hard not to blush. Professor Clarke was just a little outspoken. "In view of these facts, I consider Mr. Cosmus's remarks ill-taken."

He sat down. Others clamored for the floor. Professor Erickson was recognized.

"It seems to me," he said caustically, "that Mr. Cosmus when he spoke of education had a Chautauqua, not a college, in mind."

There is something damning in a phrase. Professor Erickson's was of that kind. It dissolved all opposition into laughter. And it endured. Thereafter the "Chautauqua brand of education" appeared in every one's mind when Cosmus's name was mentioned.

So Cosmus failed to make them "see." Three months of the second year went by in sight and hearing of the great outer drama of a world in flux. Never a note seemed to pierce the calm of Crandon Hill College, or the complacency of Iron City. Cosmus, alone save for Sarah Blackstone, despaired. Many a day he resolved to resign, and go to France for service. After the faculty meeting that course seemed more imperative. But he was loyal to the few students who were seeing, and he was aroused into a fighting humor. And above all there was Sarah. He met Walt Kuhns, labor leader, again.

13 Family Councils

"Raymond, son, how should you like to go to Massachusetts and spend the summer with grandfather Wood?"

Mrs. Sill, in laces, reclined on a *chaise longue;* sunshine fell through the beveled glass of French windows in spots of iridescence. Raymond saw them from where he was sitting near the window overlooking the street. He had willingly stayed home from chapel to talk to his mother.

"I don't know, Mother, it is pretty there."

Patience Wood Sill with her daintiness and tranquillity always brought to the surface in Raymond a sense of peace and loveliness.

"You'll go then?" She spoke eagerly.

"No, I think not, Mother; it's too dull."

She was disappointed.

"How about the trip up the Allegash that Stephen Tyler spoke of?"

"Why should I leave my own home town at all, Mother?" He said this as one would give a challenge. For he was familiar with his mother's tact; he knew that something deeper than appeared lay in her solicitude for his summer plans.

She replied, "Raymond, I have never forgiven your grandfather, Dr. Sill, for not marrying my mother. She wasn't happy, you know, with Father." Raymond had not known this particular side of that episode, and what had that to do with vacation?

"Well, Mother?"

"The Sills are no judges of strong women, that's all?"

"You, Mother, were——"

"I'm not sure, son; I think I married your father."

Patience Sill often resorted to frankness when it was needed to carry an argument.

"But, Mother?"

"You, Raymond, are a Sill."

He saw now what was coming, and yet he would do nothing to avoid it.

She went on, "You are seeing too much of the Morton girl—"

No third person, least of all a mother, is capable of understanding the relation which exists between two souls. By implication, Patience Sill thought Margaret Morton weak, and nothing, therefore, that Raymond could say would alter her opinion. This he knew. He was silent.

"What do you see in her?"

"She's a good kid."

"Yes, I know, but not half as attractive as Hazel Tyler."

"It's according to your point of view."

"The Morton girl, Raymond, is the kind that women are instinctively suspicious of."

"Jealous of, you mean?"

His mother's talk had served to give Raymond an objective on his relationship with Margaret. For the first time, he was seeing it from the outside. Previously he had accepted Margaret as something he wanted—as he accepted food and air. She fed something deep within him, something that had to be fed, and something he did not purpose to leave unfed. And he was surprised, in a sense, at his mother's serious consideration of his association with Margaret, as much, perhaps as he would have been if she had said, "Why, Raymond, you are breathing air!" But now that he saw himself and Margaret as a third person saw them, there was an impulse to resent his sweetheart. It was the same impulse which makes a little boy turn and slap the little girl that he is caught playing with. Whatever regard Raymond had for Margaret it was not one that would make him sacrifice for her.

"Don't you think you are taking this too seriously, Mamma?"

"You are a Sill, dear."

She said this significantly.

Raymond suddenly saw that here was an opportunity to get something he had wanted for a long time. Perhaps, by making a concession to his mother in regard to Margaret Morton, he could win her allegiance to a new project; so he said,

"Mother, when I leave Iron City the next time, I go to France."

"To France! What are you thinking of? To fight?"

"Yes, to fight."

Perhaps Raymond was not wholly serious. What he wanted was not to go to France, but to get an aeroplane.

"But before I go, I want to learn to fly in this country. Can't you get Father to let me have a plane?"

She answered shrewdly.

"So that you can break your neck, and thus rid yourself of that Morton girl?"

"No, Mother. I should have to go to Chicago to learn, you know. It would take six months."

Both enjoyed this bout of wits.

"We'll see, Raymond."

Raymond knew, and had known since he was a lad, that when his mother said "We'll see," the thing was settled in his favor. He went over and kissed her.

At the door she called him back.

"You won't get mixed up with her, will you, dear?"

She said this imploringly. Raymond was touched by her concern. He said seriously—more seriously than he had said anything else:

"Never fear, Mamma. I'll not marry Margaret. She's a jolly kid, but——"

He went out. She heard his short, heavy step on the stairs, and his whistle. But she did not appear at rest; she had not liked something which she had seen in her son's face when he had said "Margaret."

If Patience Sill could have followed Margaret Morton's thoughts during the chapel service at college every morning, she might have had evidence against her son's sweetheart more tangible than mere instinct. That morning Margaret had not heard a word of the service; in fact, she scarcely ever did unless the speaker was young and good-looking. Then she listened after a fashion. She often wondered why John Cosmus never led chapel, for she was not aware of the precise distinctions in rank in the college hierarchy. While Scripture was being read, Margaret often stared amicably at him, hoping to get in public a response which was intimate. She was not given to analysis, but if she had been, she would probably have been aware that she regretted that she no longer held Cosmus by bonds of intimacy. And she probably would not have been honest enough to confess that it was her own fault that she no longer continued to hold him. Somehow he forced her to turn her better side toward him. Her ruminations consisted not so much of ideas, as recollections, sensations and promised pleasures.

Often when she returned home from chapel, Mrs. Morton would say, "Who talked at chapel this morning, Margaret?"

And invariably Margaret would answer, "Let's see, I forget." Or she would supply the deficiency of memory by any name that came to mind. Once she had said, "That funny Professor Kimbark."

"What did he say?" Mrs. Morton had persisted.

"I couldn't hear well; you know he 'barks'."

"Margaret," Mrs. Morton exclaimed impatiently, "I wish you would be more serious, and take more interest in religion."

"I'm waiting until St. Luke's is completed," and her daughter glanced out of the window to where the handsome Gothic church, the center of much of her dreaming, still stood windowless.

Mrs. Morton was usually routed in these contests.

If Margaret did not care for Scriptural exhortation at chapel, music did have meaning for her. The organ with its breadth of feeling, and deep reaches into the unconscious, awoke in her, selves she did not know she possessed. She veritably believed that this was true religious feeling; it was the nearest approach that Margaret, in the flower of adolescence, ever made to religious feeling. In reality music spoke to her in terms of images; spirit voices spoke to her. On the largest stained glass window behind her, little leaves danced in the morning wind. They let a soft amber light through; Margaret could hear them sigh and rustle. Under the spell of music these leaves became countless hands that caressed and loved her. She could close her eyes, and sink back in an ecstacy of experience, seeing and hearing nothing. Often at home she spoke of the pleasure organ music gave her. She said that it made her feel so religious, which pleased her father.

On the particular morning when Raymond had failed to appear at chapel because of the conference with his mother, Margaret, on returning home, was confronted by Mrs. Morton and a letter.

"Oh, I know what it is, Mother—from Dean Witherspoon. Are they going to jerk me up on the green carpet?"

"Daughter, this is serious. He says you are in danger of failing in three subjects."

"Did that Professor Cosmus flunk me?"

"No, his is a C."

"It's history, then?"

"Yes."

Mrs. Morton was perturbed. She thought her daughter on the verge of disgrace, and what was more she dreaded Carl's anger should Maggie be forced to leave school.

"Now, Mother, you know as well as I do that this is not serious," Margaret reassured her. "It's mere bluff on the part of the office. They always do this in order to get you to study harder. No one is ever fired."

"But, Maggie, that isn't the point. You've got to do better for your father's sake."

"I suppose I should, but studying is so beastly dull."

"You are going out too much."

"Not half enough."

"Maggie, when I was a girl your age—one date a week until ten o'clock sufficed."

"No wonder, there was nothing to go to."

This angered Mrs. Morton for some reason, and once in a while, in a fit of anger, she would exert parental authority.

"Well," she said firmly, "just the same, you can not have another date this week, you understand."

Margaret, seeing what she held dearest suddenly taken away, burst into tears, and delivered herself of an unmaidenly storm of words, ending by throwing herself headlong on the davenport. From the depths of the pillow, she struck back.

"Yes, yes, yes. I suppose you want me to be old and ugly like you are before I'm twenty. All right, Mrs., I will, I will."

More tears—this time Mrs. Morton joined in. She had been insulted by her own daughter. She sat down limply in a rocker, and put her handkerchief to her eyes. Oh the cruelty of youth! In time she controlled herself and said with feigned composure,

"I suppose you will never know how cruel you have been until you have a little girl of your own. You will never appreciate your mother till then." This in self-pity; then in a kind of jealous scorn, "Suppose you had a mother like Patience Sill, always lying around in laces, and mixing paints; who'd take care of the house while you were gadding round then? I'm twice as sick as she is."

Some hidden chord of sympathy sprang up between mother and daughter. Perhaps Margaret suddenly saw the pathos of her mother's position, or rather she perhaps caught some glimpses of herself—Margaret, gay, color-loving, exuberant—suddenly struck down by disease. Perhaps, she even saw the truth in her mother's words. Margaret knew that her mother was really a sick woman. Many a time, Mrs. Morton was on the verge of losing her feeble hold on Science, almost determined to consent to an operation. Instantly she was on her mother's side.

"Of course you are, Mother dear," she said, "and you are a thousand times better than Mrs. Sill. I hate that woman."

That was a good deal for Margaret, and it contented Mrs. Morton. Reparation had been made. They gradually lowered their tones, dried their tears and by the time Carl came home all signs of the storm had vanished. Morton looked tired.

"Margaret, get my slippers. It's a wonder you don't think of your father once in a while," he said. He never would have spoken to Margaret thus, had he not been very tired.

"What is it, Carl?" said his wife.

Morton seldom "brought business home."

"I am not sure," he said "I fear trouble. Sill thinks it is nothing, but I know."

"Oh, I guess it'll come out all right, Father," Mrs. Morton replied with her usual optimism.

At the supper table, the telephone rang. Margaret answered it eagerly. Mrs. Morton listened.

"Oh, is that you, Ray?"

*   *   *   *

"Oh, quit your kidding."

*   *   *   *

"Why, Ray, I——"

*   *   *   *

"What time?"

*   *   *   *

"Yes, I guess so."

*   *   *   *

"Of course, I'm crazy to."

*   *   *   *

"Good- by."

She heard Margaret's voice trail off into tenderness. She suddenly saw her daughter in a new light.

Mrs. Morton understood. She got Margaret's eye, when she

came back to the table. That look seemed to say, "Say nothing to father. He's tired."

Margaret knew that she had won.

In the kitchen, Mrs. Morton asked, "You made a date for to-night?"

"Yes, I thought you wouldn't mind. It's the Country Club dance. I'll swear off to-morrow."

"Is it with Ray?"

"Yes."

"All right."

14 *Misunderstandings*

During the winter that followed, Cosmus wondered often about
P. C. Smithkins's remark: "We have no literature in America
because America is too prosperous." Indeed Iron City, as part of
America, seemed too prosperous to know in any way the depths
of life. Gloom or tragedy, it could not know; hustling, energetic,
progressive, it was for all the world like a boy who had never
encountered grief, poverty, death. The dim corners of a vast
world gave back vaguely echoes of a world-war. Iron City lay with
its specious sides turned up to the sun a warning to knockers,
muckrakers and agitators. Problems? There could be no problems; for proof, look and see. There were no slums—at least save
that bad row of houses along Guy Street; the street cars ran
regularly; gay crowds thronged well-paved streets; the factories
had more than they could do; the banks were bursting; there had
never been a panic in the city. Where were the problems? For
the onrush of the human tide seeps through the social break-wa-
ters so gradually that one scarcely discerns in the tiny capillary
at one's feet the beat of the agitated sea beyond. Even Cosmus,
trained student of society that he was, often was tempted to close
his eyes and drift, so trifling at times are the concrete incidents
through which the great principles beat, and reveal themselves.

One evening at work in his room, Cosmus was interrupted by
the shambling feet of Samuel Curtis upon the stairs. In the two
years that Cosmus had lived at the Curtis home, he had come no
nearer to solving the mystery of the landlord. Sad always, retiring

always, thwarted by life, Curtis remained an enigma.

Was he going by? Cosmus listened. No, he stopped outside the door. This time Curtis, always formal, did not knock. He slowly opened the door, and stood nervously upon the threshold. Without looking once at John, he began in his high, shrill voice to stumble into a denunciation.

"You'll have to leave this house, Mister Cosmus. I'm sorry, but we can't keep you here any longer. You'll have to leave. I understand that the Missus across the street wants roomers. You had better go over there. I'll set you in the street in a minute, do ye hear me?"

Cosmus thought it was some ill-timed joke. He tried to smile. Curtis in a kind of subjective agitation continued his shrill invective, his voice rising higher and higher, finally breaking at the top, then beginning the crescendo all over again.

"This house can't shelter you any longer, Mister Cosmus. This is the house of Curtis, sir, and it can't shelter you any longer. It always has had the pleasantest relations with the college, with Crandon Hill College. But times do change."

"But, Mr. Curtis, explain yourself."

"You can get other rooms across the street, Mister Cosmus. We can't shelter you any longer. Please go, or I'll set you in the street; I'll set you in the street myself!"

Anger, so foreign to Samuel Curtis, seemed to rack his frame. He stood so sad and antique, so tremblingly in the doorway, that Cosmus could only pity him. It was useless to argue with him while in this unnatural humor.

"You know me well enough, Mr. Curtis, to know that I don't deserve insult at your hands. I refuse to budge until you prefer some charge that I can answer."

"This house can't shelter you any longer——"

"Yes, I know. But why?"

"I'm sorry to say it, Mr Cosmus, but you hain't fit to teach at Crandon Hill College—you with your notions about woman's freedom, labor and anarchy— you with your vilifying of good

President Crandon behind his back, and your talk about a world-order. You hain't fit, that's all. I'm sorry to put you in the street, sir, but the Curtis family have always had pleasant relations with the college. You go."

Samuel Curtis had never seemed more of an enigma than he did in that moment. Cosmus, accustomed as he was to the analysis of human nature, found himself baffled. He stood irresolute, his mind running back over the months he had spent in Iron City, the first impression of Curtis at the station, his ride with him about town, his cry "It would be a travesty on Father," his nocturnal vigils in the garden. With these reflections came, too, a mild melancholy, always incident to reminiscence and the sudden realization of change-growth. He had come two years ago into this room an uninformed boy; he was leaving it a man—a rebel, made so by men like Samuel Curtis.

"Very well," Cosmus said. "Come back in fifteen minutes, and you can help me set my trunk into the street."

Curtis seemed surprised. He turned and paused.

"I hate to do it, Mr. Cosmus," he said haltingly, "but Father would——"

"No trouble at all. I thank you for the diversion."

And so it happened that Cosmus found himself bag and baggage in the street, the long rays of the afternoon sun falling across the lawn and Sarah Blackstone coming up the walk.

She seemed to take the situation in at once. At any rate, she paid no attention to the baggage.

"You haven't seen anything, Mr. Cosmus, of a Bertha Livinsky, age sixteen, have you?" She smiled. "You see I have been out adventuring this afternoon, looking for a lost Polish girl."

Curiously enough, in that moment Cosmus remembered that he had never asked Sarah about Sidney Haynes.

"Here is a nice problem in practical sociology for you, Professor Cosmus." Her humor was irresistible; she stood before him the highly trained, sagacious woman of the new century; and yet to Cosmus the rare delicacy of her beauty was never more ingratiating.

"I'm always interested in problems." He wanted to call her Sarah. "Go on, tell me."

"It's strange," she answered, "but the whole problem of Bertha Livinsky—of all Berthas, Gretchens, for that matter—is pretty much a question of priest and lover. I was talking to Father Sobieski the other day and he said quite philosophically, 'I try to collect Easter money, I can't. But wait, at death I get them.' The pressure of our economic world is too much for some of the aliens; they find that they are not so efficient when they come from the parochial schools; so they go over to the public."

"They learned the meaning of our phrase, 'It pays.'"

"Yes, and little else. They are pitiable in their ignorance. This morning when I went to see Mrs. Livinsky, across the lower St. Paul tracks, she was sitting on the back-porch looking dismally out over the filthy yard.

" 'Where's Bertha?' I asked.

" 'Don't know. Gone to get work,' she said sullenly.

" 'When?'

" 'Three days.'

" 'What work?'

" 'Don't know. She read in paper.'

" 'Which paper?'

" 'Don't know,' and that is all that I could get out of her at first. She just sat there stolid and suspicious until she found out that I wasn't from the Board of United Charities, and that I had known Bertha at the Machine Works. Then she crumpled up and cried."

"And you have found no trace of Bertha?"

"Oh, yes. I've learned something. You see here's where the lover enters; in most cases there's a man."

She did not pause here, but Cosmus's mind strayed for a moment away from Bertha to the woman before him. At times, he was apprehensive of the energy contained in her—the thrust and whip of her mind. "And who is the man in your case, Sarah

Blackstone?" he was thinking. An then he remembered again that he had not asked her about Sidney Haynes.

"You see marriage in most European nations is a social and family matter. Here in America it is individual and romantic. Bertha's mother can not advise her, because she was not wooed as Bertha is wooed. And Bertha can not help herself, because she has lost touch with the social significance of marriage. Affairs like hers as a rule are little short of seduction. If she is lucky, poor thing, she gets money for her child, and then she begins all over again to conquer that world where woman's happiness begins and ends."

John was thinking of education, and the part Crandon Hill College might play in the life of Bertha Livinsky.

"And if you found Bertha?"

She shrugged her shoulders impatiently. "If I did, I could do little. That's the pity of it. Sometimes I suspect myself, am afraid that I'm out to find happiness for myself only. You see, when a person is endowed with energy, sitting at a desk all day does not satisfy her; I am afraid that in the vague hope of helping Bertha, I am trying to do something for Sarah."

She had analyzed that social problem, Cosmus thought, with a directness and objectivity quite masculine, and yet he was keenly aware again of an almost child-like wistfulness in her tone and face.

"If you know the man—there's marriage."

She shot him a swift glance.

"Marriage! Do you think I should want to condemn her to life with a man like Bill Daggett?"

"You know him, then?"

"Yes, it no doubt was Daggett."

"Who is he?"

"A foreman at Sill's plant, and, to tangle your skein of things the more, philosopher, a college man for two years." She paused, and became self-conscious a moment, as if aware of what Samuel Curtis would think of her if he knew what subject they were discussing. "No, I think too much of marriage to condemn Bertha to slavery. She's better off alone. When she comes back, I shall try to show her, if I can, that she has not strayed into unpardonable shame, and save her from the despair that has been woman's lot all these years."

Cosmus was never more sure of the fineness of the woman before him. Before they could resume, a dray drove up for his trunk.

"I'm moving, you see," he explained.

She did not answer.

The drayman bawled, "Where to?"

Cosmus was at a loss. He did not know what to say. In the excitement that Curtis had caused him, he had overlooked the important trifle of a roof over his head. He hesitated. The drayman repeated his question, impatiently.

Sarah whispered, "Why don't you go to the Y.M.C.A.?"

Why, of course. Just the thing. He felt grateful to her, spoke to the drayman, and turned. "May I walk along with you?"

When they were out of sight of the Curtis house she turned to him eagerly and said, "You mustn't be too hard on Samuel Curtis."

"You know all about it, then?"

"No, I only guessed. You see, knowing Samuel Curtis, I knew the clash was inevitable."

"I can't make him out. He's 'queer', isn't he?"

"Yes, queer, if to live in a world apart from the real is to be queer. You see, Professor Cosmus, you are aiming to destroy the last vestige of his older world."

"I?"

"Yes. Curtis was once owner of the R. Sill plant long ago—and Sill destroyed the semblance of the thing he loved. Now you are laying your hand on the college—his college."

"His college? I don't understand."

"Well, you see the elder Curtis was a promoter of the finest type. He was a professor in the college, but in addition, an organizer outside. He established the Iron City Savings Bank and Trust Company—it took him ten years to create the sentiment, write the bills, introduce them in the legislature, and establish the institution. He secured patents for pumps that laid the foundation for the Enterprise Pumping Company, which R. Sill later acquired. He went to the legislature—and was a candidate for governor. . . . Well, it's not easy to be the son of a father like that."

Cosmus recalled vividly his drive with Samuel Curtis, and the man's careful itinerary, reviewing all his father's monuments. "But I can't understand why it should make Curtis a fool."

"Curtis—the son, I mean—had a controlling share in the Enterprise Pumping Co. and could have passed on into Sill's regime, but he shrank from the sordidness of business. His wife didn't help him any—she was an Eastern woman. Curtis saw that R. Sill wasn't a gentleman; at least after his father's kind. Business oppressed him, Sill towered over him. The game wasn't worth the candle—he let the business go for nothing. Such things happen, you know."

"I see. Curtis is an ancestor worshiper, or a sort of l'Aiglon?"

"A misfit, I should say; a product of culture for its own sake. They say he was the best Greek scholar in the college. What that plant might have been up there, if he, not Sill, owned it."

"It's curious, but there seem to be just two facts in Iron City; that factory and this college."

"It's our bias, I suppose."

They had come to Sarah's door, but had passed on by tacit understanding out the leafy street to the fields. Sarah had managed even by her dispassionate narrative to rehabilitate the Curtis Cosmus first had known, the night wanderer on the flats. After all, there is nothing more thrilling or sobering than vagrant glimpses into other personalities—and Cosmus felt that he had at last seen the real Samuel Curtis. All impatience with the man was gone.

"I suppose," he said, "that I should respect Samuel Curtis for setting me in the street. For a man who inherits his ethics, theology and manners, that was a pretty bold act. For once he was original. But the college, what of the college?"

Sarah turned to him, her face alight, and impulsively clasped his arm. "I wanted you to say that," she said.

"You're a good friend, aren't you?"

She did not answer. He was sensible of her warm touch upon his arm, and in a minute, when she dropped her hand, he reached down and drew it through his arm again.

"You might fall," he said.

They both seemed satisfied with that explanation. Sincere as they were with each other in all human matters, they practiced deception when it came to emotion. Tremblingly they were reaching along racial avenues of speech, groping dimly for each other—like children—in that vaster world of instinct and love. So they walked silently, thrilling to the beauty of later evening. It seemed to Cosmus as if he had passed out of the world of factories, crowds, problems, into a great, wide plain peaceful and dim, where he walked with one whose mind he knew without speech. And that one was almost God.

And yet, how far apart these two were. They were of such natures that they could not trust mere feeling or sentiment; they had to translate those sublime stirrings of sex into words and deeds. And so they were kept apart. If Cosmus had trusted his mood, and had lifted her then in his arms, and kissed her, he would have found the eager passion of a deep and pure woman meeting his. He did not. Out of such relations as theirs may come poetry; but the ecstasy of passion is postponed and perhaps never comes. So Carlyle missed the fullest union and broke Jane Welsh's heart.

When Cosmus had brought her to her gate he had courage to say:

"Sarah, who is Sidney Haynes?"

He heard the quick intake of her breath, but there were no signs of embarrassment when she said:

"Mother Curtis told you; she's so curious."

She paused. He waited.

"John, I'd rather not tell you. You might not understand— and—he's no——"

It was the first time she had called him John, but that did not make up for his disappointment. He felt as if she were obliged to tell him, if she had had another lover. That was the trouble with them; since they depended on a medium so treacherous as words, words so many had to pass between them, that they had to suffer much before they reached that higher ground of sure and permanent understanding. With her refusal, the inexplicable barrier was erected again between them. The chords that were flowing like music from one to another snapped. He seemed to see her only as the keen, self-contained, above all forbidding woman of the world. Perhaps jealousy, or some sublime sense of being thwarted, aroused him; at any rate, he was angry—coolly, but passionately angry. He intended to hurt her when he said:

"Some people are all mind and no body, and they somehow have a great capacity for hurting their friends."

He could see her figure, even in the dim light, straighten and tighten.

"What?" she said in startled tones.

He was ashamed. He did not want to see her that way. He turned to look up the street where the colonial spire of the First Church scraped the sky, and then he spoke again, as calmly as he could:

"Oh, yes, I have been waiting to tell you that Walt Kuhns has come back to organize a union, and I have decided, if I see a way, to help him all I can."

He paused, "It's only right." There was no answer. What was the matter? Was she going to be a fool? He turned. She was gone!

15 A Conference of Races

One morning when Jerry Mulvaney, machinist, walked into the machine-shop at the Sill plant, he found Bill Daggett, foreman, bending over the form of his pal Callahan. The big foreman's knee was planted on Cally's chest, and his heavy fingers were closing over the little workman's windpipe. Already Cally's eyes had begun to bulge.

"What 'cher call it, Bill," Mulvaney said to Daggett, "a Jew picnic?"

"No, Callahan here says that during Lent he's game not to swear, and I just bet him a dollar that he would swear before seven o'clock."

Mulvaney was not a Catholic, but his ire was aroused at the sight of the punishment his pal was getting.

"Auh, no, you don't. Take your knee off his chest, you big stiff."

Daggett looked up, mystified, his little eyes blinking in his large head, the great bellows of his chest working beneath his sweater. He was a huge man—all of six feet four in height, and close to three hundred and twenty pounds. Princeton College remembers him as the star fullback of the late nineties.

Mulvaney was near the lathe, fingering a piece of lead pipe, and looking nasty about the gills.

Daggett relaxed his hold on Callahan's throat, rose heavily, and stood eyeing the two Irishmen. He was mad with humiliation, and what had begun in cruel jest gave promise of ending in war.

"Whew!" snarled Daggett through set teeth. "I can whip both of you little devils."

"No, you can't either, you big tub," said Mulvaney coolly. "You can't even handle me."

Daggett, like a huge bear, moved cautiously towards Mulvaney. Callahan arose dizzily, and, paying no attention to the irate foreman, went to the hydrant to wash his face; Mulvaney threw down the lead pipe, and retreated behind the lathe.

"What's the matter, splinter, 'fraid of me?" asked Bill.

"No, you hogshead, I'm not afraid of you," said Jerry. "I'm going to wear you out chasin' me, and then I am going to sail in and give you the worst lickin' of your life."

Daggett, all the angrier, tried to reach across the machine to seize his antagonist. The light-footed Irishman easily eluded him. Round and round the machine they went, Mulvaney smiling derisively, and keeping up a spirited fire of insult.

"Go to it, log-foot."

"Don't spill your guts, Tub."

"Hi, there, fire-truck."

In time the tactics of the Irishman began to accomplish their purpose. Already, either from anger or weariness, Daggett's breath was coming in gasps; and passion had risen to blind his eyes with confusion.

"Tongue hanging out, bullock," sneered Jerry.

He suddenly moved easily out into the clear space between the lathe and the door. Daggett lunged for him; there was another round of foot-work. Like master wrestlers, feinting for a hold, little Irishman and giant foreman circled back and forth. Other workmen came in, and stood grouped about the benches, enjoying the fight. The room was awesomely silent.

Suddenly Mulvaney's arm shot out fiercely, straight to Daggett's vitals. Down came the big man's hands over his stomach, and his breath sang through his teeth.

"Ah."

In a flash, Mulvaney's arm swept through an arc from his heel to his opponent's chin in an uppercut that was a marvel to all who saw; and down went Daggett's big form to the floor. It was a wicked blow, and the foreman lay dazed under the lathe, like a pitiable thing.

He was not desperately hurt. In five minutes he had picked himself up and had the men at work.

That noon Bill Daggett was taking bets that Jerry Mulvaney could whip any man in the plant. The news of the fight spread as on underground cables, and no one covered the offer. Daggett and Mulvaney became friends. Daggett, with the large geniality of big men, found in the smaller one much to fear and admire, and Mulvaney, shrewd and self-seeking, accepted and enjoyed the homage. Daggett was not a bad fellow. He seldom showed his brutish nature and he hid his passions well. He sang tenor, pounded the piano, and recounted gridiron exploits with considerable rough charm.

Not long after the fight, Mulvaney said to his newly-made friend:

"Look-a-here, Bill, you've got to come into the union."

"Go to hell, will you; none of that crowd for me. They're crooked, all of them—and it costs too damned much."

It was said that Daggett could swear longer and louder than anybody in the plant. He himself was reported as having said:

"My English prof used to say that my vocabulary was damned limited, but he was mistaken. I can talk to men all right with these"—here he held up his heavy fists, and let loose a string of oaths.

But Mulvaney, knowing his man, was not to be frightened by the vigor of his expletives. "That's all right, Bill; I understand how you feel. But have you looked into this matter? You've never been a member of the union, have you?"

"Naw, don't want to be. I was beaten up in Dayton once by a crowd who was just going out, and I don't intend to forget it very soon."

Daggett looked ugly. Mulvaney was not discouraged. He saw the advantage of having Bill Daggett with them. Daggett was popular, huge, and a foreman, and moreover, he was a particular friend of R. Sill's. Sill was inclined to have favorites among the foremen.

Bill continued, "I'd advise you, Mulvaney, to leave this business alone. That man Kuhns don't know how to manage men, and anyway, he's an intruder—never worked in a factory in his life, did he?"

"Leave that to me, I'll stand by Kuhns, but, by God! if you peach on us, I'll smash every bone in your body."

Daggett knew that Mulvaney meant what he said.

"Who's goin' to peach? But as a friend, I'd advise you to keep out of it. Look here, you can get what you want if you'll only handle old Sill right. Why, I've made him look like a monkey for four years. Shine up to him and say 'Morning, Mr. Sill, wonderful plant you've got here.' It gets him every time; all these God-Almightys love taffy."

"Yes, you're a hell of a college man, you are," Mulvaney answered, "gettin' your way by bunk and graft. But what of us others; there are four thousand men getting only $2.65 a day, and eighty of us go to the hospital a day."

"Well, you don't get me," he said defiantly.

Mulvaney was disgusted. He turned away, for a moment beaten, and then he bethought himself of another approach to the big foreman. He came back, and stood solemnly in front of Daggett.

"Daggett," he said slowly, "once more, you better come in." He paused and then added with heavy finality, "I know about Bertha Levinsky."

The face of the big foreman was a picture of woe, anger, humiliation. He looked as if he would like to destroy his companion.

"—damn you, for mentioning that to me." He couldn't speak further. Taking a stogie out of his pocket, he bit at it savagely, then lit it.

Mulvaney stood coolly staring at him.

Daggett spoke at last, smiling. "Well, when do you meet?"

"To-night, above Willard's saloon."

So it was that Daggett was won for the union. It might have been better if he had stayed out, but Mulvaney in his zealousness for the cause, and in his Celtic eagerness for power, thought well of forcing Daggett in. No one could doubt Mulvaney's loyalty to the union idea (his father had suffered years before at Bridge-port for the cause). But the project afforded, too, an outlet for his peculiar love of persuasion, and when that failed, of coercion, and Daggett presented a subject for coercion hard to resist.

That night Walt Kuhns drew his comrades about him. There were Mulvaney, and Daggett, and a socialist by the name of Grover, and Duke, a negro, and, most interesting of all, Mary, the Lithuanian woman.

Mary, as everybody called her, was a statuesque, queenly sort of a woman, with quick comprehension, broad grasp upon human affairs, and a passionate regard for what she called her community. She spoke thirteen languages fluently, and had done much through them to hold the more recent aliens to a responsible citizenship. From her small grocery store—presided over by Peter, her husband—she reached out in every direction into Iron City's life.

There was a kind of stubborn fearlessness, a vivacity of utterance, a fervid love of fellows that marked her as exceptional. Though she had been reared a Catholic, she had rebelled against the Church and was sending her children to the public schools and to the Baptist Sunday School. Kuhns had given her a Cause, a something that appealed to her quick maternal feeling.

Next to her was Duke. He was a recent negro acquisition to Iron City. All his life had been spent in migratory occupations. He knew the rolling population of America as few knew it. He had been born in an Iowa boarding house for transient negroes; he had sold papers on the streets of New Orleans, threading the maze of the underworld. And for thirty years a porter on trans-continental trains, he had seen the white man off his guard—away from his own town—in the first abandon of vacations. He had seen bishops drunk, preachers seeking the alluring immunities of women, statesmen seduced by flattery. He always saw human nature weary from travel, turning uppermost its petty side, and he had come to believe that the white man shared the frailties of the negro and had merely arrogated to himself, through numbers, the position of superiority.

And yet Duke was not filled with race hatred. By fraternizing with the whites, he became like them. He had erased all accent from his speech; was alert and affable in manner, yet reserved and self-contained. He took genuine pride in his race and family—"The Dukes of Virginia, sir,"—not "sah"; and he had become a rare judge of men and women. He had obtained, too, much information in his travels, and, by becoming the official intimate of cultivated people, the frequenters of Pullmans, he had come into vivid touch with the thought, the trend of public sentiment, and the gossip of the day.

Duke had quit portering to set up a store on Osgood Avenue, where the negroes were segregated. He saw a good business chance, but he saw, too, a chance for helpful leadership among the blacks. He was ambitious to play an elegant part in the race drama. He often said that Booker T. Washington's relegation of the negro to mere manual labor was wrong; the Afric imagination was fit for literature, the arts and politics.

He had come to Walt Kuhns's conference at his own request, to plead for the inclusion of the colored workers in the Union. Across from him sat Grover. He was not of the caliber of the others, but a studious local personage, who had an intellectual interest in labor and socialism.

Walt Kuhns sat at the head of the table, which with the chairs were the only pieces of furniture in this rough room above Willard's saloon. He was intensely conscious of the power represented in this little group of people. Mary could speak for the

Slavs, Austrians, Italian and Greek peoples of the city; Mulvaney and Daggett for the Irish, Welsh and English; and Duke for the negro.

He, as leader, was not unaware, though, of the racial antipathies current at that moment. It was Mary who had slipped into the vacant chair beside the negro after Grover, Daggett and Mulvaney had passed it by. Daggett sat back, silent and bored. Between even them—the big foreman and Kuhns, the leader—there were repellent forces at work.

Duke was saying: "Gentlemen, eighty per cent of my blood is white, fifteen per cent Indian, and five black, and yet I am to be discriminated against as a negro. Some people don't like Duke because he speaks out, but I believe in being plain. You will make a mistake if you don't let the colored man in the union. He has come to Iron City and has come to stay."

Daggett sat back, his surly eyes not intent upon the negro, but upon Walt Kuhns, as though to forbid his granting Duke's request. Kuhns treated Duke with courtesy, and promised to take the matter up with the council as soon as it was formed. With that the negro bowed himself toward the door with a good deal of a flourish. "The war, gentlemen," he continued, "has given the colored people a chance, and they have came to Iron City to stay. Don't forget that."

"The hell we won't," growled Daggett softly.

Mulvaney, to cover up Daggett's ill-nature, began to inquire at once into the details of organization. Instantly Kuhns was besieged with questions: "Who was going to be shop-committee man? When were the street meetings to start? What did he hear from Boyne's factory? Was he in touch with the head council?"

Mary made a brief report of her activity among the Italians that day. Daggett sat in silence, sucking on an unlighted cigar. Kuhns's strategy was to secure secretly the allegiance of the mechanics—the higher grade workmen—in the various plants and then when these men were enlisted, to announce openly that chapters were to be formed in Iron City. Having won the skilled labor, he expected to enlist the others with ease and to be strong enough to force recognition of the union principle. He counted greatly upon the scarcity of all kinds of labor to carry the campaign through. A newspaper was to be established and a trades council; there was also to be a dynamic executive committee unifying all the working classes.

"I don't believe you can do it," put in Daggett. "The time hain't right. There are too many ignoramuses in that shop to join the unions, honyocks and niggers."

"Shut up, Bill. You know we can," responded Mulvaney quickly. Kuhns fastened his quiet eyes upon the big foreman.

"Mr. Daggett does not believe in our cause perhaps. If not, he is in the wrong place. We want only believers here, men willing to sacrifice."

"Sure, Bill's all right," Mulvaney assured him.

"Of course I'm with you," Daggett asserted, "or I wouldn't be here. Do you realize that I may lose my job tomorrow morning?"

There were other parleys; then Walt spoke quietly to them about the larger aspects of their cause. He was a prophet by nature, and he had the gift of speaking sincerely and deeply without sentimentality. He told the story again of his conversion to unionism, repeated the words of his master, advised moderation, patience, and above all, largeness of view. How Iron City, with its closely "in-bred" control of industry, was one of the few communities of importance where union labor was not recognized. Then they went home.

Kuhns lingered at the table. As he turned his head toward the dusty, narrow window, he could see the crowd in the street below—the tide of life running even here in this backwater of the world, apparently aimlessly. A big automobile—mark of power and affluence—swept by; he could see it preempt the thoroughfare; the smaller machines as if by instinct gave it way. It stood in his mind for the facile, mobile power he was fighting. How strong and sure it was! It daunted him!

He felt for a moment the staleness of living that all brave men feel now and then when they suddenly relax their hold upon the engaging task of their whole life. With that relaxation comes disillusionment, the re-grouping of men and things about another ideal. He saw Mary, Duke, Mulvaney, Daggett and Grover, as they really were—petty souls—reaching for a greater share of the world's things; incapable of rising above the immediate needs of themselves and their class. And worse, he saw himself as a mere sentimental seeker after an unattainable end. He felt tired and beaten, incapable of accomplishing the coalition of the alien crowds of Iron City. Why go on! Why give one's self to insult, defeat and despair, sacrificing family, home and peace! Let the world drift to hell. The strong were too strong, and would have their own way in spite of him and his kind. God! What a nasty world it was, with its nuzzlers, slaughterers, flatterers, seducers and kings.

Then by some irrelevant twist of mind he thought of Cosmus, and the thought gave him comfort. Cosmus was fighting the battle too, there among the strong, and for the first time the labor leader felt as if his moment were at last being recognized and given a semi-official endorsement.

"Comer," he murmured; he never could remember Cosmus's name. "Comer is all right. He is working there, too."

And he went down the rickety stairway, past the saloon from which the fumes of stale beer emerged, to the attic room at the Johnson House, strong again.

In six weeks there were thirty-four hundred union men in Iron City.

16 The Wedding

Spring came, with its pagan spirit waking the gypsy in the blood. It is as if it furnished anew the wide dingy chamber of the world with fresh scents, dainty chintz of flowers, soft green coverlet and sky-flung windows, and said: "Children, here is the place of nuptials." And youth always enters with sighs and kisses, and suddenly finds itself in new accord with nature. All its veiled mysteries—earth and body, night and stars, desire and frustration, covetous longings and killing despairs, seed and soil—stand naked and revealed.

From the moment that Raymond and Margaret entered the mysterious world whose sesame is a kiss, silence entered. As they drove past the black stacks of Sill's factory, out upon an unfrequented road to Pike Lake—they did not talk much; and what they said was fragmentary, yet charged with heavier meanings. Margaret lay in the hollow of his arm, feeling the heart of the engine beat through them until it seemed at times as if they were one mechanism. That fancy was characteristic of her in this new world: she suddenly found herself playing with fantasy—moving in a land of shadows and illusion. All of her old gayety, her thoughtless badinage, seemed deployed in achieving a new dignity of womanhood. She was happy. Raymond was her lover, won and possessed. And with that came abandon—not wantonness. If one could have looked into Margaret's mind and seen the image of herself which was there, one probably would have seen only another heroine, like those who are flashed upon the screen every night before countless thousands. She was true to her ideal and standard. She was living up to the world that most nearly answered her desire. To ride along the dim road, pressed close to Raymond's body, seemed quite the natural thing to her.

"I'm glad you don't drive fast," she whispered.

He bent over her tenderly. His arm tightened.

"You mean," he said, "so I can——"

"Yes, of course, that too; but I was thinking of the accident at Twelve Mile."

"Boys ought not to be allowed to play in streets."

"Sure not. But I'm glad he got well."

Somehow their secret did not lose its potency. Through that they began anew the luxury of walking down the long avenue of common experiences.

Pike Lake, which they reached soon after sunset, was an unusual stretch of water for the Middle West. Spring-fed, crystal clear, it lay between great bluffs, like a mountain pool. No one could suspect that, receding from this water, the prairies broke away in unending monotony. The lake was a glorious geographical blunder, which furnished a haven for the prairie-fagged inhabitants of Iron City—and also for Chicago millionaires. Lining the east shore of Pike Lake were imposing estates, with pretentious piles of masonry and ornate gardens. All private—all shut off from the gaze of the vulgar. But Raymond knew just where to drive to get forbidden glimpses, across wide lawns, at awninged mansions. Such views gave them a thrill, put them in touch with the gay life of the metropolis, which they both craved. The banality of middle-class Iron City preyed upon them. Although R. Sill was rich enough to keep up such an establishment, he had no desire to do it. He loved the shop and factory too much to dawdle over a country home. But Raymond!

"I understand, Mag," he said, "that you can buy any of these places for a song."

"You can!"

"Yes, you can. You see they were built by the packers and those people long ago, and the younger set don't care for 'em."

"They don't? Those lovely places?" Margaret was incredulous.

"I don't blame them; take Lake Superior—it's always cool up there, and you know Pike Lake sure can get hot."

"It can, can't it?" she agreed.

"But what's their loss is our gain. I've been thinking that when we are married, we might take one of these for a few summers. It would be good enough for a while." Raymond said this with the assumed dignity of manhood.

"Oh, Raymond!"

They had spoken often of marriage lately; they had drifted into it, first in jest, then in reality. It somehow seemed the natural thing—and, perhaps, the proper thing. But it meant little. They made no plans; they were never formal in vow or promise. It was part of the drama. To Margaret, marriage meant scarcely more than the vision of an "adorable wedding" at St. Luke's. To Raymond, it meant nothing more explicit perhaps, but something more concrete. It thrilled him with a sense of power and ownership and inspired a vague forward-reaching ecstasy. He looked down at Margaret; he could see her round head, sweet profile, and tapering figure, and he was satisfied. Margaret was a beautiful girl and Raymond loved beauty.

They went to one of the smaller hotels—the Yale Hostelry, to which Raymond had telephoned ahead for reservations. As they entered, Margaret experienced as always the stir of delight at feeling admiring eyes upon her. She walked boldly up to the desk with Raymond, and stood quietly waiting while he got the tickets. She preferred that course to being hidden away in the "Ladies' Parlor." Margaret never lost her poise. She seemed made to inhabit just this environment. She heard the clerk say:

"Oh, yes—Mr. Sill?"

"I telephoned at ten from Iron City," Raymond explained.

"Let's see," the clerk answered as he ran through the list. "How many, just you—and—wife?"

Without hesitation, Raymond replied, "Yes, two."

Margaret's heart beat fearfully! How sweet and strange it sounded. But outwardly she never flicked an eye. There she stood in her long blue motor-coat, like incarnate ice.

"Did you hear what he said?" whispered Raymond.

"Yes, and you didn't correct him, naughty boy."

"I didn't acknowledge it, did I?"

They laughed joyously. At the table, Raymond would not let Margaret forget. He liked to see her blush.

"Maggie."

She did not take her eyes off the soup.

"Oh, Maggie."

"What is it, sir?" she answered, still refusing to meet his gaze.

"You *are* my wife, aren't you?"

She glanced up—aflutter at what she saw in his face.

"You hungry man! Eat your fish."

An inexplicable bond was laid between them in that moment. In silence they spoke to each other something never uttered before.

As Margaret whispered to him later, as they wheeled slowly home, in the dark, "It was just as if we were married, dear."

"Married?"

Somehow the word from her frightened Raymond now.

"We can't be, you know, until after I return from France!"

"You'll not go to France."

"Oh, yes, I will. I'm serious."

"No, you won't."

"Why?"

She reached a tender arm around his neck, pulled his ear down to her lips and whispered:

"Because you're so spoony, you couldn't."

They were emerging from a deep wood, and suddenly turning a corner, they found themselves looking across leagues of unbroken prairie lands. A new moon swam up in the filmy sky, over which fleecy clouds sailed. Directly before them a daisy field trembled in the sweet light. A breeze sprang up, like a voice, and thrilled them. Raymond drew up the car to the side of the road. They climbed out and stood, their arms around each other, looking into the face of nature's mystery. The world suddenly seemed alive. It flowed through them, and it crushed their bodies together in passionate embrace. They crossed the fence, Raymond lifting Margaret over. Through the mystic light they walked, among the daisies, limb to limb. As Margaret stooped to pick a flower, the moon slipped beneath a cloud, a breeze sprang up, a hot lush breeze from the south, that seemed to burn them.

"Why, it's like summer," she murmured.

Raymond did not hear. He swayed toward her, groping, their lips met. He lifted her in his arms, she pressed close to him, then suddenly they turned and walked fast to the machine. The engine started, he threw open the throttle, and they dashed on for minutes at full speed—as if fleeing from something—which, alas, they carried with them.

That event in the daisy field opened door after door into a more alluring, more mysterious world. Margaret said:

"What did you run away for?"

"I won't—the next time."

And so they confidently stepped on further into the world of mystery and danger.

It must have been ten-thirty when the lovers reached town. Stillness had already settled over Iron City, and the early evening fire had gone out of the factory pipes. In the calm they heard the clinkle and clang of forge and derrick, blended into nocturnal music. They were vividly alive—these two—to sound and color and odor. The senses, dilated with the turbulent breath of desire, drank in the night's charm. They seemed to belong to the night—the machine slipping along in the dark, carrying limp bodies tortured by tempestuous hearts. Hurrying through still streets, they yearned to each other, loath to go in.

At last Margaret remembered that her father and mother had gone to one of their few parties at the Country Club.

"If that's the case," Raymond suggested, "let's drive the old boat to our garage, and walk home."

"Then the neighbors won't know," she replied.

Somehow a sense of guilt was ushered in—guilt that was pleasurable. In the garage, they stood for a moment, their arms about each other; then they went hand in hand through the Sill garden, careful to step only on grass. They took the long way to the Morton house, and when they reached there, they sat upon the porch in the heavy shadow of the oaks. Something would not let them go—the world of mystery shut down over them, like the night, its currents sensitizing their bodies to every touch and sound and breath. How beautiful everything was!

"I didn't know an arc light could look like that," Margaret whispered.

"Nor I."

They heard the clock in the college tower strike eleven. Somehow the experience on the lonely road, long before, with John Cosmus, flashed through Margaret's mind. She leaned her head against Raymond's shoulder. How far away college seemed! That world of books, classes and parties had retreated into obscurity; the world of mystery was the only reality now.

The clock recalled Raymond to duty. He must go. Yes, he must go. It was eleven-thirty before he stood up to depart, but she pulled him down beside her again, as if to keep her warm, whispering:

"Father and Mother are not home yet. Stay."

He obeyed, until the clock again intruded. Then he arose quickly, said good-night, went down the path without a word, and disappeared in the shadow. Was he gone? No, he must not be gone!

Margaret stood tremblingly on the porch, every sense expanded, listening. Was he gone? Why had he gone? There came to her as she stood there, her wild young heart yearning, some knowledge of the fragility of pleasure and the brittleness of life and beauty. And she sighed.

"Maggie!" She turned. There was Raymond at the other end

of the porch, holding out his arms to her.

"Dearest."

"I couldn't go."

"I'm so glad."

"Take me for a walk," she whispered.

"Oh!"

With their arms around each other, they went down the shadowy street, their senses dulled to every sight and sound, save to each other's body.

It was a mad walk; they knew not where they went. They only knew they had to be together. Through the spring night, avoiding zones of glare, and any late pedestrians, they stumbled on into the world of mystery. In time the moon went out, and a wind sprang up, with rain in it, and suddenly all the lamps winked out.

"One o'clock."

"Where are we?"

"You're hurting me."

They looked around in amazement. Big drops of rain began to fall and the wind was fitful and cold. Raymond's arm tightened about her waist. They got their bearings.

"Three blocks from home."

"Let's not go in."

"I could go on forever."

"You little thing."

They had been walking in a circle. They quickened their steps—and then Margaret saw dimly as through tears that they were not turning into her yard, into her house, but were mounting the steps of the new St. Luke's. Could she hesitate? There beat in upon her brain the image of the wedding party—awnings decked with flowers, the big line of limousines glistening, the bridal procession, music, flowers, the bride. She went up the steps. She saw the night sky, wild and fitful, through the unglassed windows; her heart beat frantically, but she went in; she went up the aisle. Her dress caught on something; she pulled it loose. She could feel Raymond breathing deep beside her. The rain fell.

By some stroke of irony, by some strange crossing of associa-
tions, the last conscious idea which came to Margaret, to whom
books meant nothing, was the story, read long ago, of an ill-fated
queen, chanted by a Roman poet:

> "The queen and prince as love or fortune guides,
> One common cavern in her bosom hides,
> Then first the trembling earth the signal gave,
> And flashing fires enlighten all the cave;
> Hell from below and Juno from above,
> And howling imps were conscious of their love.
> From this ill-omened hour in time arose
> Debate and death and all succeeding woes."

At the altar, Raymond and Margaret sank down together into
a sea of ecstasy.

Arrived home, the Mortons sat for a moment in the parlor
wondering if Margaret had preceded them. They did not see her
"things" hanging in the hall.

"I bet she is, Mother," said Carl, and mounted the stairs to
peep into Margaret's room His tender hand, fumbling on the
bed found it smooth and soft.

Slowly and thoughtfully he came down stairs.

"Yes, she is in, Mother. You go to bed. I shall be up in a minute.
I want to look over these papers of Sill's."

Mrs. Morton took him at his word, and went to bed. Carl sat
down in the Morris chair, flung a paper over the lamp to dim it,
and waited. His mind ran on education, training—"home-train-
ing," he called it—and he wondered if Margaret were really
getting what she ought to get. He was troubled—he did not
understand the generation in which he found himself, and he
still clung passionately to his three broad axioms of education:
"Serve God; mind your manners; respect your betters." So he
sat. He fell asleep, and when he awoke the day was just about to

dawn. He stooped and removed his shoes, and went softly to the door, opening the screen. The morning was fresh and sweet; birds were beginning to awake and to tinkle in the trees. He went out. In the porch swing his little daughter Margaret lay asleep, her arm tucked under her pretty head, as he had seen her sleep ever since she was the tiniest child. She stirred.

"Sh," he said, putting his finger on lip.

She rubbed her eyes and sat up.

"I lay down here, Father, because I couldn't get in. I didn't want to wake you."

"Go up to your room softly. Don't wake Mother."

Together they tiptoed up the stairs, neither to sleep. Margaret lay watching the sunlight slowly creep into the room. She tossed back and forth until her brown hair was a tangle of curls. She got up, drew up a blind, and looked out. St. Luke's glistened in the sun.

"Oh! my wedding!" she thought, passing her hand weakly across her mouth, as persons often do who are confused in thinking.

Was everything quite right after all? There was a sickening sense of loss—of missing something, and alas! of having nothing to which she could look forward. It seemed almost as if it were the end of life's perpetual picnic.

She crossed the room and sank heavily on the bed, her hot head buried in her arms.

Carl's mind, as he lay stiffly beside his wife, still beat feverishly on the problem of Margaret's education. Shouldn't the movies be stopped? Perhaps Margaret might do better at a girls' school in the East? Had Margaret been asleep, he questioned? Was Margaret honest? Shame on you, Carl Morton, for questioning her. And Raymond Sill?

Yes, Raymond Sill. How many moralists less austere than Carl Morton would have extenuated Raymond Sill? Yet after all, Raymond, by the unconscious gleaning of the mind, had only caught the spirit of his age. The predatory philosophy of his father and his father's world had unconsciously become his own. To take what you want where you find it, seemed simple enough, washed around as Raymond was by such ideas. Wasn't Margaret beautiful, and didn't Raymond love beauty?

Perhaps, too, by the way of chance, Margaret, deflecting her father's teaching through her own personality, was merely living in her own way the axiom: "Respect your betters." At any rate, there were at least two troubled hearts in Iron City that morning.

17 The Anarch

Margaret was surprised, when she awoke, soon after noon, on the day after the ride to Pike Lake, that she was charged with such a sense of well-being. The world was no different. That sense of loss, which she had experienced a few hours before, was gone. Life stretched before her with the same old possibilities of sensation. The same? With added zest and danger. And with added meaning? Hardly. To Margaret, the meaning of life was unimportant. She did not discern that meaning might include sensation. There was her room, sweet and clean, and the cool, white bath-room, and her lovely dresses, and the soft, white bed, just the same. Mother did not know, and Father! Father had been so good and kind last night; he always was. A throb of something like remorse made her start. No, Father would be proud and happy that the son of R. Sill loved her. Dear Dad!

How good it was to bathe, and don fresh linen! It never had felt cleaner! How good it was to come down into a darkened parlor, where it was still and cool, and to find Mother ready with a kiss, and not a sign of rebuke. How good it was to find a bite to eat in the pantry! The world was no different, after all.

"Has Raymond called up?"

"No."

"Are you sure?"

"The phone hasn't rung this afternoon, Maggie."

Perhaps he was sick! She trembled at the possibility! She put by every other thought. He must be sick or he would have called.

He had to be sick.

The afternoon dragged by. She tried to read a magazine; she forced herself to be unusually amiable to her mother. Poor Mother, how pale she looked.

Some girl friends came in and there were the usual giggles, confidences and gossip. They played and danced and sipped lemonade. One of them who knew her better than the others demanded suddenly, "Is Ray going to France, Mag?"

Margaret did not reply at once. Somehow she did not feel quite so confident as she had last night that he would not go. She hesitated, until another girl put in:

"Don't break your neck to answer, kid; when is it comin' off?"

"What?"

"I bid for maid of honor, Mag."

Laughter followed. There was interchange of banter, and more confidences. Margaret showed them some "fancy work" she was doing.

"You ought to be knitting for the soldiers," one said significantly. There was a shout of merriment.

When they left, Margaret was glad. They seemed so noisy somehow—and Ray might call up at any time.

Ray did not call before supper. The three Mortons sat at the table pretty much in silence. Margaret thought that her father must be worried about the men at the plant. She tried to be amiable. She talked well, telling them about Pike Lake, and related many amusing incidents, mostly fabricated; but pretense did not bring back old times. If her father only would not be so silent!

They pushed back the chairs, left the dishes standing, and went to work in the garden. Presently Margaret slipped off, went into the house, to the telephone, and called the Sill residence.

"Is Raymond there?"

The maid found Raymond in his mother's room. They were laughing over the latest volume of Professor Leacock. Previously Patience Sill had re-opened the question of his going to Massachusetts for the summer.

"When you come back, Raymond son, I promise to have Father get you the plane."

The proposition did not seem so bad.

"Do you want me to go very badly?" he asked. "I'll think it over, Mother."

"The phone, Mr. Raymond," the maid announced.

"For me?"

"Yes, sir."

He went out, closing the door softly behind him. At the telephone a voice said:

"Ray, this is Margaret."

There was a pause of expectancy.

"Well?"

"Aren't you coming up?"

"Why, Mag, I just promised Steve and Hazel Tyler that I'd go to the Green Jewel with them."

"But, Ray."

"I'll see you soon, dear."

What business had she to cry like that? What business had she to call him up anyhow? Couldn't he have one evening alone? He had been awfully good to go down to the Mortons' as much as he had in the past three months. He had spoiled her, that's what he had and she didn't appreciate it.

Raymond was all resentment. It seemed a pretty affair that Margaret should have shown such feeling over just one evening at home. With him there was not the dawn of obligation. Margaret, no doubt, could look out for herself. She always had.

When he returned to his mother's room, he stood for a moment in the doorway, to light a cigarette. Then he said:

"Mother, I guess I'll take you up on that proposition, after all."

Her face lighted up.

"I knew you'd come to your senses, Raymond son."

When R. Sill came home an hour later than usual, Mrs. Sill called him into her room.

"Well, what is it?" he said roughly.

She gave Raymond a meaningful look, and said something about her last painting; she did not want to approach R. Sill when he was in this mood.

"What's wrong, Father?" asked Patience Sill.

R. Sill had something he wanted to say to Raymond.

"Let's go out and look over the Stutz together," he said to his son, more as a command than a request. Then added, "We'll be back in a minute, Mother."

Raymond's first thought was, "I wonder what's eating the Big Chief now?"

Something had disturbed R. Sill that afternoon. Morton had come to him shortly before the hour to leave the office, with a surprising bit of news; Morton was white when he announced it.

"I have just learned that this whole town has been unionized, that a labor sheet called 'The Labor Defense' will appear to-morrow for the first time, announcing the organization of the Iron City Trades Council, which is only a union of unions—and a mass meeting to be held in the Opera House Tuesday."

R. Sill's first impulse was to be angry, to strike out and wound something, some one, for allowing this terrible menace to exist. But he restrained himself. He made it a rule never to show fear or anger before subordinates. True to his type, he surrounded himself with something of the pomp and show of kings.

"Where did you get this?"

From Daggett.

"You know Daggett likes his little lie!"

"This is straight. He belongs to the Machinists' Union himself! Here's the list."

Morton handed a memorandum to his chief.

"Nearly six hundred of ours affected!" Sill exclaimed.

"Mostly machinists," Morton said significantly.

Sill read:

"Team drivers 36
Molders 40
Painters 100
Blacksmiths.................... 47
Pattern-makers 32
Machinists.................... 312
Core-makers 32
_____
599

Morton was plainly worried.

"We simply can't fire that bunch," he said. "It's all our skilled labor."

R. Sill fixed his hard eyes on his foreman, dropped his chin on his chest. He spoke in the metallic tones of angry hate.

"Don't say 'can't', Morton. I don't like it. We will fire every one of them." He stood up proudly. "You know, my father died a poor man. He threw a million dollars away on education. I'll be willing to spend every cent I've got in breaking them. They can't run me. It's a cause, Morton, that's what it is!"

Morton had never seen his chief quite so moved, and he gazed at him in admiration. R. Sill was magnificent. Sill himself felt that he somehow had distinguished himself; he had struck just the right note.

"Send Daggett in!" And, being pleased with himself, he added, "And, Morton, don't you worry!"

Morton, thus dismissed, went out satisfied.

In five minutes Daggett came in, smiling and genial.

"Daggett," said R. Sill coolly, "how did it happen that you were so late in putting us next to this union business?"

"I wasn't late, Mr. Sill. Kuhns——"

"It's Kuhns, is it?"

"He's been in town but a few weeks."

As a matter of fact, Daggett had just been able to shake himself free from fear of Jerry Mulvaney; it had been a struggle between fear and cupidity— cupidity had won.

"All right, Daggett! I guess that won't make any difference. Keep us in touch, will you?"

"Sure. I believe, Mr. Sill," returned the big man obsequiously, "that those fellows have no right to strike when you've been treatin' 'em so well. I don't know any plant where the men get so much for their diggin's."

Sill smiled.

"You see, Daggett, not all of them are so sensible as you."

"So long, Mr. Sill."

"Good afternoon."

Creature of habit, inspired by a sense of leadership, Sill had merely acted in his usual decisive fashion. In reality, he was not so confident or so sure as he appeared. Instinctive fear of the crowd, so prevalent in his type, stirred him to uneasiness. A massed force of six hundred men was different from the impact of isolated workers and agitators. And Sill felt that there was something in the situation that was new; this perception of difference worried him most of all; the habit-mind, ruled by custom, cannot brook change. Somehow the formation of six hundred men into an organization in six weeks indicated to him a mysterious madness in men, which he connected dimly with the war. And to Sill, though it was doubling his wealth, the war stood as the great unexplained. Sill was afraid—as men always are of that which they cannot understand.

He sat crumpled in his chair—feeling tired and misused. He felt resentment toward Morton, Daggett, Kuhns—and toward Iron City. It was the ingratitude of men that allowed them to unionize at this evil time. They were unappreciative and unpatriotic.

He nestled there, a lonely man, old before his time. The stenographer in the outer office came and tapped on the door, but he did not hear. The late afternoon sunlight fell through the windows, and the five o'clock whistle blew before R. Sill stirred himself.

Then all his resentment, all his weariness, the defection of the men, the madness of the generation, centered themselves in Raymond. Raymond was the weak point in his defense. If he only were a proper son, like Steve Tyler; if he only were ready to meet these new forces, which R. Sill did not understand. He groaned in self-pity and humiliation. Raymond was a failure.

It was this mood which R. Sill brought home with him into the peaceful sitting room of Patience Sill, and which he carried out into the garage lest his wife should see.

When father and son had reached the privacy of the garage R. Sill said without preliminary:

"Ray, I want you to stop all this nonsense about going to Massachusetts, this running round with the Morton girl, and this folly of college—and come into the business with me."

"But, Dad, I don't want business—"

"I don't care what you want. It's time that you tied yourself to something."

Raymond, quickly detecting a new spirit in his parent, and realizing that his mother was not near to abet him, looked around helplessly.

"I suppose I'll become treasurer, or something?" he added.

"No. You go into the Efficiency Department."

"But, Dad, Mr. Boyne made Al treasurer right off over at the Iron Works."

"I'm not Boyne—and, what's more, you're not Al. You'll go where I put you."

Raymond, seeing that he was routed, fell back upon Fabian tactics, often employed. He had learned that if he did not resist his father, he gave a chance for the despotic in R. Sill to subside and a chance for the parental to assert itself. At any rate, delay would give him time to see his mother. So he said meekly:

"All right, Father. I suppose you need me—the whole town is buzzing about that Walt Kuhns's new gang."

Sill reacted at once as Raymond supposed.

"That's sensible; now you go in the house and tell Mother."

R. Sill felt better after this conference; he was handling the new situation, and Raymond no doubt would turn out to be a Sill after all.

That night, though, he did not find sleep readily; darkness magnified his fears, and getting up, he knocked softly at Patience Sill's door.

"Is that you, Ray?"

Her answer sent a pang through Sill.

"No, it's me—Father."

"Come in. What's wrong?" She was anxious.

He came over and sat down upon her bed.

"Mother," he said, "I've been thinking that perhaps I was a little hard on Raymond this evening. You can tell him to-morrow that he can have the plane."

"I knew you would, Father."

"But he ought to tie to something."

"He's only a boy yet."

"But I don't like a floater, Patience."

"What?"

"Down at the mill, the workman's a floater when he don't stay at a job for any length of time. He floats from one factory to another; he's no good—he never ties to an employer."

"Ray's not like that."

R. Sill answered sadly. "I'm afraid sometimes he is."

Whatever R. Sill's faults were, his great virtue was loyalty. He was intensely loyal. To be sure, loyalty to his country merely meant loyalty to his class, to business—still he was primarily loyal—vicariously loyal. He would suffer for a cause—and suffer long.

Patience Sill stroked his hand.

"Don't worry, Father."

Sill went out and closed the door. That night he lay awake for hours suffering as only a disillusioned parent can suffer. Was he right? Was Raymond without loyalty?

It would seem that he and Margaret Morton had discovered the same fact about Raymond on the same day.

18 Professor Ezra Kimbark

The mass meeting at Johnson's Opera House, under the auspices of the Iron City Trades Union, brought but one question to John Cosmus—the same question he had been asking himself for weeks: What of the college? He had become fully aware of the inert mass of sentiment that lay within the college circle, reflected as it was by the unprecedented action of Samuel Curtis, a person only remotely connected with the college, in ejecting Cosmus himself from his house, and yet he could not believe that thinking men would withdraw themselves from an event as moving as the unionization of Iron City's workers. If nothing more, it was dramatic—a flaming bit of contemporaneous history.

Besides himself, there had been just three members of the college community present at the meeting, Professor James and two students, Jenkins and Weaver.

Cosmus was going home pondering on this indifference when he was attracted by a crowd of boys congregating at the entrance of an alley. The fitful light from the arc across the street was bright enough to reveal a man lying prostrate in the mud. Drunk or sick? As Cosmus came nearer he saw that the boys must have decided that the man was drunk. Moved as boys are by an instinct to mutilate a personality already desecrated by drink, they were making sport of him. For them it was amusing to throw pebbles and sticks at the heavy form, and at the same time to speculate whether the still figure moved a finger, or perceptibly stirred.

"There! His foot shook."

"No, it didn't."

"It did, too! I saw it."

"Say, fellows, is he breathin'?"

"Drunks never do."

When Cosmus came up, one boy, bolder than the rest, had lifted the leg of the sleeper, much as a blacksmith does for a horse he is shoeing, and was pounding vigorously on the sole of the shoe. The man groaned, and laughing, the boy dropped the lifeless limb. Cosmus saw that the foot was small, and encased in good shoes. There was something, too, familiar in the whole figure, as it lay stretched comfortably there in the shadow. Cosmus pushed his way through the crowd, and turned the man over. He gave off an odor of brandy. He lifted the face into the light. What he saw startled him. It was Ezra Kimbark.

In a few minutes he had frightened the boys away, sent the oldest after a cab, and had driven to the side entrance of the Y.M.C.A. Inside Cosmus explained the case to the secretary, and had Kimbark helped to his room.

There was something pathetic in the limp figure, sprawled heavily on the bed, the strangely gnarled face, the dark rings under the myopic eyes, the oozy lips, the degradation of the whole form in a kind of brutish impotence. As best he could Cosmus loosened the soggy shoes and socks, damp coat and waistcoat—covered the sleeper over with comforters and rug, and sat down to wait.

As he waited, the ironic humor in the situation came over him and he laughed. Professor Ezra Kimbark, of all men—drunk!

In the months past, in which acquaintance with Kimbark had become a friendship founded on admiration, there was nothing that would prepare him to see his friend like this. And yet he was not astonished. Kimbark always had somehow a gift for surprise that might well be called theatrical. It had characterized their first meeting in the storm, when Kimbark had broken upon him like an apparition; that seemed now a prelude to the man. He was a vivid being, carrying his atmosphere with him, with enough reserve to make Cosmus never sure of him. In the limbo which lay behind his vivid personality there was room, Cosmus thought, for drunkenness, women, yes, and perhaps wrong. The human heart is always willing to suspect evil and romance and genius of its fellows.

In the last year, because Cosmus had been engaged in what Kimbark called "stirring the froth of modernity" (Kimbark loved such metaphors), the two had not seen so much of each other. Kimbark did not care for problems; Cosmus was not much interested in abstract beauty. So the two had fallen apart.

Now, Cosmus, dozing in his chair, was suddenly awakened; Kimbark had stirred; his unseeing eyes, now of a luster like a fish's, were peering out of half closed lids. The effect was horrible. Cosmus went down the hall, and came back with a glass of water; he tried to get the sleeping man to drink. Kimbark's brow was burning; he stirred restlessly. The night was long; in the morning, early, Cosmus brought a physician. After examining the patient, he turned to Cosmus and said, gravely:

"I am afraid of pneumonia."

Cosmus did not want to remove his friend to a hospital because he was afraid of talk. To avoid it he assumed the responsibility of nursing him, and announced to the college that Professor Kimbark was confined to his home with a bad cold.

Late in the afternoon of the third day, Kimbark's fever broke. Cosmus, sitting in the room alone, suddenly found his friend's eyes, previously so wild, now questioning and sane. His first words were:

"Well, what do you think of me now?"

Cosmus smiled and answered jocosely:

"You're a sly dog, but you mustn't bark now. To sleep with you."

Cosmus could see that Kimbark was troubled considerably, not with physical pain but by the thought of his moral weakness. When he awoke two hours later, he resumed the topic where he had left it.

His mind seemed impaled upon the one thought of disgrace. "I'm done, Cosmus: I'll never go back."

"Pshaw! You're taking the matter too seriously. You're not a drunkard and you're too valuable to lose."

"You don't understand. I'm a failure, that's all."

"Because you slipped up once?"

"It's another case of the preacher's son gone wrong," Kimbark answered grimly. "Some men drink for taste. I drink for exhilaration. I find relaxation in it, a recovery of much of what I want to be and cannot. I'm not going to entertain you with a story of debauch. The drinking, John, is but a symptom. I know myself. The malady lies deeper and there is no remedy."

As men at rare times will, Kimbark began to confide in Cosmus.

"Father was a preacher in Indiana—yes, I was born midst the flat, dingy Middle West, and I guess nature shouldn't produce my kind; at least we were never intended for America. Business, industry, with its refinement on nature's bitter law of survival, doesn't mean for us to survive. But there are lots of us, nevertheless.

"Well, I accepted Father's plan to enter the church, but all the time I was pursuing my own little private end: to see beauty, and then to create it. Well, I didn't find much beauty in the corn lands, but I managed to find it in books and personality. Words I loved; I love them still. I smile at the students sometimes. I seem but a fossil floating in a thin, watery existence. In reality, I am tinglingly alive, a denizen of life's thick, sensuous medium. All through words, I get all men's experience through these windows of life."

John interrupted.

"Aren't you a little hard on the Middle West, Ezra? I have often wondered why so little of just that stuff,—cornfields, barn yards, pigs, tranquil mediocrity,—ever got into American books?"

"Thank God!"

Cosmus let him go on; it was doing him good.

"In the Eastern Seminary I found a good deal of bad theology and little religion; and then I had a genuine religious experience. At least that is what I call it. At any rate, I felt in a new way. It was when I saw the sea for the first time at night; it lifted me into new regions of generalization, the parts of the world flowed into one, and I knew peace. After that I couldn't go into the church; it was too narrow, and if I ever was free, it was in that moment on the shore. I wrote and told Father. It nearly killed him, I guess, and strange to say, I began drinking then, for I switched over into the graduate school, and there was plenty of chance."

John Cosmus remembered Walt Kuhns and his story of giving up the church.

"By the way, what do you think of the church, Cosmus?"

"I think a good deal about it."

"You never go."

"You know President Crandon has taken me to task for that."

"I guess I go out of habit, or something," Kimbark admitted.

"I stay away out of principle."

"How's that? I suppose you think Christ but a myth?"

"On the contrary, I believe in Him, in my way, and believing in my way makes the church idolatrous."

"Idolatrous! You're a devil of an iconoclast, Cosmus."

"What I mean is this. The church seems to believe in only Christ's body. I believe in Christ's spirit. Ritual, creed, belong to the body. If men would give up these things to the understanding of the spirit, why, I believe that we would not have a dis-united and fossilized institution, but a great brotherhood."

"Well?"

"The great contribution of Jesus is not an idea, but a mood. As I see it, it is pity for the world, coupled with great consuming desire to work a change, and work inspired by pity is but sacrifice. And what is the crucifixion and resurrection but sacrifice dramatized? If Jesus had never lived, crucifixion and resurrection would still be a universal symbol of the soul's perennial willingness to work and to die for the race's good. Christ is in our bosoms."

"Where did you get this?"

"Look within you. It is there."

"Then there are Christians everywhere, John?"

"Of course, in places we least expect to find them—the Italian mother in Guy Street, among the soldiers in the trenches."

"And in the churches?"

"I wish I could believe you—yes, there too. But I have a suspicion of institutions. They get so set. Many men go to church, sit in silence, soothed with music, luxuriate in emotion and come away satisfied that they have sacrificed—what? A few moments of egotistic pleasure. On Monday they solve their business problems after the way of all flesh. Take Smithkins."

"There. There. I'll take your word for Smithkins."

"But I am interrupting you. What about the graduate school?"

"That can wait."

"No, it can't. I may not see you again."

Kimbark beat the coverlet with nervous fingers. "Well, it was torture. I had to do something and so I chose literature. You know the system. Endless dissection, cold linguistics, suspicion of passion. I stuck at it. I went through the mill, and came out—a professor. My impulse to create was there all right."

He leaned on his left elbow, clenching the fist of his right hand above his head, as one who curses.

"You know, Cosmus, all tragedies are subjective. There are no others. That's the reason we Americans have never written great drama. We care too little for souls and too much for things. I have suffered. I suffer yet. When I start to write, my failures stand up before my eyes, and stare and stare. There is Milton before me sneering, and Wordsworth. They ridicule every word I pen. Demoniac ghosts, they drive me out of my room, under the stars, to recover in the great heart of nature the soul I would have been if sophistication had not laid its syphilitic kiss upon me. . . .

That's what education has done for me . . . Drink! Why shouldn't
I drink?"

"Write your own story, man."

"I am too weak even to dramatize my own failure."

There was genuine pathos in the man, lying weak and trembling, his terrible face spasmodic under the stress of his own pity.
For want of something kinder to say, Cosmus suggested, platitu-
dinously:

"Perhaps, Ezra, that is what you must sacrifice."

"I get your argument. I must sacrifice the only talent worthy
of contribution to the race—to God. No irony in that, to be sure,"
he said contemptuously. "That's the trouble with you, Cosmus.
You do nothing but think. You and the rest have ceased feeling."

John was silent. He had to acknowledge the truth of his
friend's accusation. Kimbark ushered him into the presence of
life's vast disharmonies. When the individual is forbidden by the
very forces which the race creates—to make contribution to the
race—that is tragedy indeed. But why murmur? Why complain?
The individual was nothing.

He looked up. Ezra was sleeping heavily, like one exhausted.

When they resumed their conversation the next day, Kimbark
said wearily, "Can't you see that the only thing for me to do is to
go to France? I love her. She alone gives me the beauty I crave.
Perhaps there I shall find the fulfillment I seek. If not, then the
lovely sacrifice you speak of."

It seemed to Cosmus as if Kimbark had grown doubly bitter
in the last few days.

"You know Cosmus, the State guards its scientists behind the
lines, but its poets—" he snapped his fingers. "Anyway, I'm not
a poet. I'm a dog-gone failure."

And so, three days later, when Cosmus came hurriedly into his
room, he was not altogether surprised to find it empty. Upon the
table was a book; in the book a note.

Dear John:

I leave you holding the bag. Be a good sacrificial beast, and tell old Crandon I have gone to France. God bless you, Cosmus. Keep up the fight. I feel better than I have for months.

KIMBARK

It was then that Cosmus saw the book plate. It bore the image of a dungeon window, solidly barred, cut in heavy stone, opening on a sea of far horizons; on the sea's rim a ship danced and beckoned in airy freedom.

Poor Kimbark!

The night that Cosmus heard that the machinists of the city had walked out he went home with Margaret Morton from the college library. Margaret had been suddenly taken sick in the stacks and the librarian had asked Cosmus to help her home.

As she walked beside him she was unusually silent. She seemed like a little gray mouse in her oils, stealing along in the mist. Cosmus attributed her silence to a headache, but she would not let him call a taxi. Presently she said, "Father's all worked up about the strike. It's a new thing for Iron City—this union business."

Cosmus was non-committal. She continued:

"Somehow I don't much blame the men."

"I don't, either."

Then they lapsed into silence again. The magic and the mystery of Margaret were gone with the laughter in her voice and the spring in her step. Cosmus wondered. At the gate, she said quietly:

"Professor Cosmus, I'm not doing well in school. Wouldn't you advise me to stop?" All this was colorless; then a new note crept into her voice, a beseeching note, near anguish. "What I need is a fresh start. I need to begin over again. Don't you suppose that if I should go to France to nurse, I would come back more ready for college?"

Cosmus did not guess the depth of feeling behind those questions.

"You're too young, Margaret," he said.

"But I want to be older; that is, I want to be different."

"If I were you, I would fight it out here."

He left her standing on the veranda, watching the lights tremble and blur in the tiny pools of water in the streets. Cosmus walked the wet streets, his mind in a turmoil. To him only the potentialities of men seemed important, and the only tragedy unfulfillment.

In Margaret, Samuel Curtis, and Ezra Kimbark, thwarted as they were, rested the problem of education. They had never been led out. The unfathomable sea of energy in them had never been sounded. In that sense, and that sense only, they were lost souls.

Before his eyes they merged and blended into rank on rank, file on file, of the great unfulfilled—the masses—the people— the thwarted of the ages. All pity for Kimbark or Curtis or Margaret was engulfed now in the larger pity for the crowd, the human foundation upon which all art, culture, science, progress, had been vicariously built. The struggle of Walt Kuhns against R. Sill, minimized by comparison, shrank to a trifle, in this larger perspective of the ages. Unions! What of the trade guilds of the Middle Ages? Socialism! What of the syndicalism of Wycliff? In the tedious and painful spiral ascent of society upwards, life renewed itself in similar forms. The people were always struggling for fulfillment. And the one common impulse—which could never die—was the democratic. He only who loved the people had any immortality: he alone reached backward into the past and forward into the future.

Democracy was the struggle of society to fulfill itself. Education was but the process of that fulfillment. And up to this moment the haphazard education of the masses had been sealed and sanctified by blood. Oh, the pity of the struggle of the crowd against the class-mind. Oh, the horror of shattering life, in a passion for freedom, larger spaces, and ideas, against organized and powerful ignorance.

Cosmus felt himself—his projects—shrink down into their true proportions. This sweeping view of the whole—the pitiable struggle—the past—was exhilarating, and yet it dulled the fine edge of effort. Something was gone. It was hope. He knew that success would not come to-morrow or the next day. They—he and Kuhns and youth everywhere—all were but skirmishers in the eternal army.

As he went on in the moonlight, thinking these things, the sweet male voice of some worker broke the silence, in a plaintive song, that Cosmus followed into the night. It was an old song, but until now Cosmus had never understood it.

"Mine eyes have seen the glory of the coming of the Lord."

The music ceased on the edge of the factory which, stained with color, shouldered up in the mist, all its daylight ugliness gone—a thing of strength and beauty. This creation of the strong—industry—the new empire—what had democracy to do with it?

Democracy, it seemed to him, after all, was but the promise of the strong not to exploit the weak!

When he went back home, he called up Sarah Blackstone, to ask if he might call and be forgiven.

"For what?" she asked.

"For my rudeness!"

"Oh, were you rude?"

After a few commonplaces, she said casually:

"By the way, I have been thinking all week of going to France."

She, too?

Strange that all the world—individuals and races—were seizing upon the war as an instrument of self-fulfillment! They were but moths in a flame! But Sarah was not going. She *must* not go. He would not let her.

19 Margaret's Father

Margaret found that events record their changes but gradually. The sense of loss, of difference, that had crept into her mind the first morning after the major experience of her life, had vanished; then it appeared again with keener sting, after Raymond's indifference over the telephone. She now found that it was a constant companion, boring ceaselessly into her consciousness. Things were no different; the difference lay only in her attitude toward them. For the first time she was thrown upon herself, and she found herself helpless. What had she to do with thoughts? She became morbidly conscious of functions that were merely normal. She heard blood pounding in her ears; her heart seemed to beat in her throat; she thought she heard bells ringing; and her eyelids twitched nervously. She couldn't study; she could not play. Her old self-assurance was gone. If she went to a dance, she trembled when she danced, grew confused, and missed her step. Gayety was but forced, halting and conscious.

When her girl chums noticed the defection from her old manner they nudged each other, and said, "Mag's got it bad." Or they came to her, teasing. "What's wrong, Maggie?" they asked. "Have you heard that Ray's going for sure?"

And she would answer, trying to smile,

"Wait till you get as old as I am, then you'll understand!"

Then she would catch herself wondering if she were getting old. Did age come this way? Old, and never married!

With all this self-examination, Margaret felt no guilt because of responsibility to society; and she felt no remorse because of a responsibility to a Higher Being, who, having invented desire, then contrived social institutions to curb it. Calvinism held no sway over her.

How revealing of changing standards it would have been to know what empty meaning Margaret would have found in that epic of an earlier day, "The Scarlet Letter." Surely, austere self-torture, in the presence of an unseen, angry God, was not a part of her reaction. And as for the law—Margaret would have been willing to stand up before Iron City at any moment, with Raymond, and say, "This is my man," or go off with him, without so much as paying a license fee at the county clerk's office. But why this sense of loss? It must have been because Raymond despised her.

In her way Margaret suffered.

In spite of her precocious knowledge of sex, she was innocent. Sophistication was instinctive, not acquired. And, too, she became morbidly curious about this mysterious extra-equipment of her body called sex. She craved more knowledge about it. There was something pitiable in her feeble research methods. Cut off from her mother, and from any scientific treatment of the subject, she seized upon the few words that came into her mind laden with meaning, and began to trace them by cross references, from dictionary to encyclopedia. This task had engaged her the night she became sick at the library. She had suddenly come upon a plate depicting vividly all the naked truth of reproduction, under the caption, "Obstetrics." She plunged into night, ineffably alone; she waded through seas of sickening darkness. Would that unspeakable experience come to her? God! She couldn't stand it. She was too young, too much alone.

The next morning at chapel she was acutely aware of what the organ said. It seemed to roll billows of black sound over a bruised and tortured body—and to bellow dismally of lost things. Loss, loss, loss. Margaret leaned her head on the back of the seat in front of her and trembled like a craven. John Cosmus, seeing her at that moment, thought that she was praying. When the organ ceased, Margaret knew that she must tell her mother. Confidently, a half hour later, she went into the living-room, where her mother sat sewing, and said,

"Mother, I've something to tell you———"

Then she could get no farther; she could utter no other word; she combed her mind for some sentence—some fragment of news—to interpolate at this point, and all she could say was,

"Well, I forget what it was now. Isn't that funny?"

Then began a battle—a miserable struggle—to tell. She knew she must, and she knew she would. She became obsessed with the notion that she would some time blurt out the whole story before her father, or before some guest. She tried to formulate a laconic message that would reveal all, in unshocking terms.

Finally one morning, she said abruptly, "Mother, you'd better get Raymond Sill to marry me."

She had done it.

Mrs. Morton looked up from her sewing, understood, but did not answer. She went to the telephone and called for Carl Morton, and then for Doctor Carr.

"Come to my room, Maggie; I'm going to bed. I'm afraid I shall have to have an operation."

"Oh, Mother, don't."

But Mrs. Morton had fainted.

Carl Morton, living with facts all his life, thought until the moment he discovered his daughter's training had been inadequate to meet the stress of her generation, that a fact was the hardest foe in the world to face. But now it was not the fact of Margaret's seduction, but its unreality that crushed him. He could not believe it. He could not accept it.

He was always seeing his little girl as he wanted her to be, never as she actually was. Margaret looked no different; indeed she was more beautiful, if any thing—and more considerate. She hung over his chair at night, with a light for his pipe, as he had longed to have her do; he sat back luxuriating in the comfort of it, and immediately the Great Shame which was so unreal became the bitterest reality of his life.

Carl said no word directly or indirectly to Margaret that led her to believe that he knew her trouble. Some delicacy—some sentiment—made him mute in the presence of this fact. He tried hard not to let it make any difference in his relations. For a time he succeeded so well that Margaret inquired of her mother, now confined to her bed, whether her father really knew.

"Yes, he does—and you have nearly killed him."

One day when Margaret came down to the living room, she found her father, not reading as was his custom, but sitting very still, his hands gripping the arms of the chair fiercely, and his eyes dull and distant. She knelt down beside him, laying her head on his knee.

"Oh, Father, don't. Please don't. Do you hate me?"

He got up hurriedly, with a swift gesture at his eyes, and walked quickly out of the room.

After that, he seemed farther away from her than ever; something of her mother's resentment seemed to show itself in him.

To make matters worse Carl Morton was dispossessed of all normal functions. The men at the factory thought that "the Strike had got the old boy." It had not, but it had left him free to brood over personal troubles. He was torn between two courses, the desire to succor his little girl, and his respect for law and custom. Margaret, now that trouble had come to her, seemed to need him more than ever; she was like a child again. At the same time the weight of custom, that brutal collective opinion of the mass, to which he was so acutely sensitive, grew in his imagination, to some gigantic monster standing ready to ruin them. He must not be tender to Margaret, for that would be encouraging social crime; and yet, always, he saw her as a child reaching out tiny, supplicating arms to him.

So he struggled pitiably—until the chronicle of his suffering showed itself in his carriage and face. The four weeks that followed Margaret's confession Morton spent pretty much alone at home, trying to convince himself that the Trouble was real. There was no work for him to do at the factory; it was shut down. Morton did not understand his master. He had gone to Sill early in the strike, and had shown him how they could run along with half force and seventy per cent production. Sill had replied,

"By God, no! This town is going to get its belly full of strike—and they'll never want another one." And Morton saw Sill thrive on the struggle.

One afternoon Morton, driven to confusion with the thought of Margaret's disgrace, suddenly came to a realization of its reality. In one of his brown studies, as Mrs. Morton called them, there floated up from the deeps of memory a picture of the past. He saw, with the sharpness of first impression, the first time that he had performed all the rites of motherhood for the baby. It was Sunday, and Mrs. Morton had taken suddenly to bed; from the pillow, she directed him, as he awkwardly bathed and dressed little Margaret. His fatherhood, hitherto so shy, warmed with tenderness, and he felt for the first time that the baby was his. That very afternoon a cousin of Mrs. Morton's had come in, bringing her son, not quite three. In the course of his rompings, the boy had struck little Margaret upon the head with a stick. The blow seemed to fall a hundred times upon his own head.

There was an impulse to rend little Billy limb from limb, to snatch up his own child and flee, and still he smiled at the guest, and pretended that the blow had not much hurt the baby. Sitting there this afternoon, he reëxperienced, with redoubled pain, the force of the boy's assault upon Margaret.

Groaning audibly, he found his hat, and dragged his feet out into the street. He went straight to the factory, and found R. Sill. As Sill saw his foreman, wild eyed and haggard, stumble into his office, his mind at once jumped to his own affairs.

"Why, Morton, what have you been doing to yourself—worrying about this strike? It's as good as won. Do as I do; thrive on it."

Morton sat down feebly in a chair and said bluntly,

"Raymond's got Margaret in trouble, Bob—"

"You mean?"

Morton nodded his head.

"Why, the damned fool."

That was all from Sill.

To tell the truth, R. Sill was not greatly surprised; his real concern was for Raymond. What inconvenience would this escapade entail? Now that he had his son comfortably settled in the Efficiency Department, he didn't want to send him away.

In the silence that intervened Sill got up and called Raymond.

He said significantly to Morton,

"Say nothing; I'll handle him."

In a moment, the young man stood before his father, entirely ignoring Carl Morton, like a soldier at attention in the center of the room.

"Well, what is it?" he said defiantly.

"You know very well, Ray," answered his father.

Raymond was startled for a moment, then he recovered his composure.

"Well," continued Sill, "what are you going to do with this problem?"

Raymond had no trouble in finding words.

"I don't know what this man has been telling you, Father, but I don't see that there *is* a problem. He'd better get the others first."

Others!

That word fell on Morton cruelly.

"That's an insulting lie, young man"—he snapped and he sprang up, roused instantly from his lethargy.

"No scene here, Morton. That'll do, Ray."

When Sill turned from the door that shut Raymond out, he saw Morton dejectedly looking at his feet, tears running down his cheek. He did not know that it was only years-old respect for himself—the master—that had kept Morton from braining Raymond with a chair.

Carl began agitatedly,

"You won't believe him. You can't believe him, Bob. Margaret loves him. Margaret's innocent. I'll bring her here to tell you herself——"

"Now, now, now, man," growled Sill behind up-raised hands, "don't get excited, Morton. This, like all problems, must be approached coolly."

"But you'll make him marry her!"

"Sit down, Morton, sit down—let's go over this together."

"Think what people will say."

"People be damned." Sill leaned back in his swivel chair, picked up a paper weight, measured its proportions carefully, then said reflectively,

"Morton, you and I are back numbers in these matters; time was when the fuss you are making would be just about the thing, but people are seeing things different now."

Morton looked as if he would contradict him.

"No, don't interrupt till I'm through." It was the master talking. Morton kept silent, humped in a chair like one who is old and freezing.

"Life is a fight, that's all. All this rosy mythology about the brotherhood of man goes very well in churches, but between men it don't go. Why, you know how it is in business; the strong win, don't they? You and I have been through enough scraps together to understand that, haven't we?" This he said expansively with his heartiest note of comradeship.

"Now I figure," he continued, "that the young people haven't lagged behind, and are seeing life pretty much as it is these days. They're older at sixteen than we were at twenty-four and they know very well that love hain't only a matter of holding hands."

Morton was not following very well, for Sill's analysis of the world he was living in ran so counter to Morton's own conception that he could not grasp it.

Sill went on.

"With divorces, and small apartments, the home ain't what it used to be. Why, I remember that grandfather's house in Vermont had thirty rooms in it. The family meant more then. Just take the case of Raymond and your girl. I bet she is not all cut up about this, is she now?"

"It made her mother sick."

"Your girl probably understands better than you—"

"You mean, what?"

"I mean that I can't make Raymond marry her. It isn't necessary."

Morton sat speechless, his eyes on Sill's face.

"Love is a fight, too," Morton's master went on, "and the strong win." He turned out his hands. "Of course, I'm sorry it hit your girl, Morton, but it needn't; we can fix that. She can go away for a few months, and we can fix up the bill."

Morton's confused mind did not completely grasp the fact that the philosophy Sill was expounding so fluently, was merely that through which they both had gained their power. Sill was expressing what he saw everywhere around him, the invasion of the home by the economic law of the survival of the fittest. Morton himself had been a lieutenant in many great struggles; but from a higher motive than Sill, out of respect and admiration for a friend; therefore, he would not be expected to see all so clearly. But something of Sill's truth he began to grasp, and he found it changing the shape of his whole world. For some inexplicable reason he found himself thinking of Walt Kuhns. Rising, he said wearily,

"I don't want your money, Bob, nor your counsel either. You know that."

"Well, we understand each other anyway, don't we?" Sill demanded.

Morton evaded the question. "After the strike is over, Bob," he said curtly, "you better look for another man for the forge room. I'm done."

"You're a fool, Morton."

"I'm done."

He went out tremblingly. Margaret might better be dead! How noisily an empty life runs!

What a tragedy it is to build a life upon another life, only to find both shattered because of one. What prolonged agony may lie beneath the seamed face and quiet manner of the man next you in the car, or facing you in the street! Walt Kuhns was such a man, perhaps.

"Here's your cap, Mr. Morton." It was Mr. Sill's stenographer. How sweet she looked! How clean!

"Thank, Miss Effie."

And Carl Morton found himself on the street.

Perhaps Margaret was not serious about going to France; at any rate, she made no effort to leave college and to enter war work. That atmosphere of ideas that had enfolded her like a fate, gave her another toss into bitter experience the night after Carl's interview with R. Sill.

In the hope of regaining some of her old happiness, Margaret went to the Green Jewel with the girls. From the moment that they entered she, tense and fearful, was unable to take her eyes from the screen. The play was "Adam Bede."

Through the medium of the play Margaret now began to see that she had taken her affair with Raymond too lightly, whereas the proper thing, the inevitable course, was to destroy herself. All heroines did that. She must die.

She made that resolution and afterwards she was filled with exultation. The girls found, on the way home, that Margaret Morton had recovered most of her old gayety.

20 Iron City's Citizens' Alliance

"What we need is a Horse-Thieves' Association."

It was Haskell speaking at a conference of the leading citizens of Iron City over the "appalling state of our fair city due to the blind greed and voracity of certain workers, misled by mercenary and brutal walking delegates."

The last phrases were those of Senator Matt Tyler, in whose office had gathered Sill, Boyne and Haskell.

Haskell continued,

"When I was in Idaho, I saw just how effective such a little alliance could be. We all belonged—from editor to bar-tender; and when we caught the thief, zip, he was strung up."

Perhaps Haskell was not serious. What he lacked was imagination. The fatality of the class-mind is to forget that those outside the charmed circle are human beings.

"But you didn't have to face two thousand thieves," said Boyne, who was inclined to be pessimistic.

"There's only one," Sill's big voice boomed.

"Kuhns, of course," Haskell explained, anxious to bring the meeting into his own hands again. Sill did not answer. He despised Haskell for dealing in the obvious.

"But we can't hang him," Boyne continued.

"Still there is a strong point in Haskell's suggestion." Senator Tyler always considered his particular function to be the judicial.

"Well, we're got to do something," Boyne continued; "in spite of optimism in some quarters (this was meant for a thrust at Sill) the strikers have had the best of the bargain, and are carrying the sentiment of the town."

"That's because of Cosmus—young fool," put in Haskell, "but they're not carrying sentiment outside of the city."

"Thanks to the *Republic-Despatch*, I suppose," sneered Boyne.

"Listen here"—Haskell went on, ignoring Boyne's thrust. "This from the *Trinway Globe*!

" 'Iron City is enjoying unusual prosperity with all the luxuries thrown in. Strikes are daily occurrences. Hundreds of men with families are anxious to work and pay for their homes; but the powers that be say 'no.' Trinway is content to go a little slower and manage her own business.'

"That ought to fetch 'em. I am running that on the front page tomorrow. If once the public sees that the strike is ruining its——"

"Gentlemen," R. Sill inquired, "is this a meeting of the Ladies' Aid?"

It was the signal they were waiting for. The balance of power in any assembly always gravitates to the strongest will. With alacrity Boyne, Tyler, and Haskell made themselves attentive, and the conference took on an air of greater formality. They all knew that Sill carried the solution to the problem behind his ears; and instinctively they knew that the battle lay now, and had lain, between just two champions, Sill and Kuhns.

Sill, unable to conceal his satisfaction in his own power, spoke again.

"I suppose you know that the core-makers asked to go back to work this morning."

"Is that so?" asked Boyne.

"Bully!" Tyler exclaimed.

"Like whipped dogs," chuckled Haskell.

"That, gentlemen, is the close of the first stage of our campaign. It means that our method of attrition is working; if the core-makers are sick of the strike, the merchants and the public soon will be. And let me point out that some gentlemen, you remember (Sill was looking directly at Boyne) were anxious to stagger along for months on half an output, and give the strikers the satisfaction of seeing us stagger; that would have been mere foolishness. Nothing short of complete paralysis of trade would be effective."

Sill raised his voice slightly, "I repeat, this is no mere local disturbance; this is a nation-wide movement, and we'll teach the country how to rid itself of these jackals. I venture to say, gentlemen, that after we are through with them there will never be another strike in Iron City."

He lit a cigar and Tyler, clearing his throat, said,

"We find in the interference of the constitutional rights of citizens by organized labor, that the freedom of individuals has been restricted and personal liberty assailed."

Sill turned gratefully to Senator Matt Tyler; he found that Tyler never failed to clothe his beliefs and practices in the high sounding language of the legal tradition. It was as if the toga concealed the brutal sinews of a war-god in its softening folds. For this, Sill found Tyler indispensable, and loved him as a comrade and brother.

"That's just it, Matt, and you're the man to put that across to the people. The second step in our campaign is to take advantage of the restless sentiment of the public against the strikers, and crystallize it into action. Yes, you're right, Haskell, we need a Horse-Thieves' Association. What do you think of an Iron City Citizens' Alliance?" He turned to Boyne. "When once we get the public behind us, we can go the limit, and even hang Kuhns!" and Sill smiled grimly at his own humor.

Everywhere in this materialistic civilization of ours we see evidence of the mathematical imagination at work. Bridges are built, canals dug, abysses spanned, buildings lifted—the great and terrible cities laid down—by the vivid precision of the scientific mind. But what we lack is poetic imagination, that kind of insight which lets us into other lives. This faculty and this only may make our civilization safe and democracy real.

Sill had mathematical imagination; he lacked woefully the poetic. Perhaps he was not serious when he spoke of hanging Walt Kuhns, only blind.

There followed more discussion. Sill made clearer his plans. Tyler was to draw up the manifesto, which would serve as the keynote speech, for the formation of the Citizens' Alliance. A young lawyer chosen to be vice-president, would deliver the speech and Senator Tyler would lend his name to the movement as president. The alliance would seek to embrace all the manufacturers and merchants of the city. But first they must be won, and the only way to win them was to show them that the strike had ruined trade, and had blackened the fair name of the city.

Pens and paper were brought out, and soon in neat longhand, Matt Tyler, U.S. Senator, was drafting page after page of eloquent argument.

Sill leaned over the table.

"One word, Matt. This Alliance must be entirely democratic."

"Of course, coincident with the ideals of the nation."

"I was thinking," returned Sill, "that we could use some such plan as this. We could vote according to establishments, say, each establishment to have one vote for every four employees. Let's see, that would give you, Boyne, three hundred, and me one thousand."

"We can fix that."

There was more scratching, and more consultation, and then, at length, with dignity and formality, Senator Tyler arose and read:

"The Alliance concedes the absolute right of all persons to organize for the protection and furtherance of their common interest by proper methods, but it denies the right to organize for an unlawful purpose by unlawful means. If the purpose of any organization, whether of capital or labor, is to hamper or restrict the freedom of the individual to follow what association he will, to coerce other persons to become members of such organizations and to come under its rules and regulations, under penalty of a loss of employment or of business, then such organization is unlawful, is contrary to the spirit of our government, and to the spirit of American institutions."

When Tyler reached the last phrases he mouthed them melodiously.

There was a rustle of applause. Haskell, lean and fulsome, was clapping his hands softly, even Boyne caught something of the spirit of the attempt, while Sill was visibly elated.

"We find in the interference of the constitutional rights of citizens by organized labor, that the freedom of the individual has been restricted, and personal liberty assailed. Men have desired the right—our merchants and tradesmen—of managing their own business affairs and they have doubtless, as a matter of policy, submitted to this, and more than this, have paid tribute, by way of advertising, through channels which sought to forge the chains tighter and tighter, and further encroach upon their legitimate rights and liberties as men and citizens."

As Senator Tyler was moistening his lips to proceed, there came a rattling knock on the office door. The Senator frowned, but as the summons continued, he walked resentfully across the carpeted room and threw open the door.

On the threshold stood Walt Kuhns. The Senator looked embarrassed. Haskell blessed "Jesus Christ!" under his breath and began to laugh as boys do who are caught in mischief. Boyne was preoccupied with something out of the window. Then Tyler, having brushed his hair three times with his unencumbered hand, opened his lips to speak, but Walt Kuhns, who was standing at ease in the hall, anticipated him.

"Is there room for a representative of the press, gentlemen?"

Sill, alone unperturbed, his eyes glittering and keen, answered as a general should,

"Men have been shot for an intrusion less insulting than this—press or no press."

Kuhns never flinched, though the words were bitter.

"Oh well," he answered smiling, "please to remember that if you happen to be interested in unions, gentlemen, the 'Labor Defense' is at your service, and the Trades Council keeps open house."

"Shut the door, Tyler," commanded Sill, bluntly.

The door was closed, but to a keen observer, something close to admiration for a moment flickered in the eyes of R. Sill, then was gone. Tyler marched back to the end of the table, while Haskell, pale and trembling, began to curse.

"He'll give me hell in that sheet of his now—the black-hearted——"

"Don't swear, Haskell, are you afraid?"

Tyler began again,

"The sacred and inalienable rights of citizenship——"

"All right Senator," Sill broke in, "that will do very well. We understand each other," and picking up his hat, he strode out. The meeting was over.

Three days later at a mass meeting at Johnson's Opera House the Iron City Citizens' Alliance came to life. Cosmus, a spectator, in the back of the hall, was interested to see on the platform, between Matt Tyler and Martin Boyne, President Hugh Crandon of Crandon Hill College. The meeting was unreeled as rehearsed in Tyler's office a week before; the young lawyer, mouthing Senator Tyler's words, drew applause from the audience at the proper moment, so that R. Sill at the vantage point behind the scene, surveying the whole drama, as the mover of the strings, knew that the second battle of the campaign was duly won.

The following Sunday, Reverend Mr. Dingley, of the First Congregational Church, preached on the text, "Be of the same mind, one with another."

Although the strike had been in progress for two months, and Iron City had writhed in anguish, this was the first Sunday that Reverend Mr. Dingley had referred to the subject so near to all hearts. Now he said:

"Organizations have underestimated the rights and the place of the individual man, whether in the form of a mob of lynchers, or trusts or labor unions. Labor unions have underestimated the relation of religion to the individual man, and have chosen to shape their movements in the saloon rather than under the protecting mantle of the Church. Perforce, union men—for we may think of men only as individuals—have been misguided, and have mistaken violence, rather than love, for an instrument of persuasion."

Over at St. Peter's, Father Gregory, after reading this union pledge: "My fidelity to the union and my duty to the members thereof shall in no sense be interfered with by any allegiance that I may now or hereafter owe to any other organization, social, political, religious, secret, or otherwise—" thundered, "No Catholic taking such an oath can receive absolution from me or any other priest."

Only two men arose and walked out.

By these signs public sentiment, always fickle, was due to veer and Walt Kuhns, lashing back coolly and sagaciously in his paper, burning in his cause, threatening here, imploring there, was telling the strikers that their cause was won. But in truth it was lost the moment the public, moving along habitual channels— press, the church, and the school—transferred its unstable allegiance.

21 The Strike

At the college, that other channel of public opinion, the strike was taboo. No word concerning it appeared in the college paper, though two students, Weaver and Jenkins, catching its meaning, became sympathetic followers of the working men. President Crandon once referred to the "horror and vulgarity of violence and of narrow-minded anarchism." Professor Charles Henry Clarke spoke on the "beauty of self-control, and the ill-fated French Revolution"; while Dean Georgia Summers rhapsodized over "that idyllic time when the rustic and artisan would rejoice in their noble share in the labor of the land."

Watching anxiously, John Cosmus found that Iron City considered the strike monotonous. It was not so interesting as a baseball game. Nothing happened. There was no violence. Day after day, the men picketed the empty factories in a grim effort to rally flagging public attention. One by one, some of the workmen grew discontented, and dropped off, moving away to other towns for work. But the majority were faithful—the six hundred held true behind their leader. Him Cosmus found always vivid and interesting. As he saw more and more of Walt Kuhns, he was astonished to find him possessed of the very qualities that made Ezra Kimbark so attractive. What friends these two vagrants, lost to the church, would have been if the gulf of class feeling had not opened between them! Kuhns was everywhere imparting his spirit to the men. He implored them to respect property and to use no violence. He strove to lift the strike into the abstract realm of principle. He had confidence enough in this riff-raff of human life to instruct them in "the art of striking in order to focus public opinion on the justice of their cause." And he succeeded! There had been no violence and no destruction of property. Picketing was peaceful. A negro, said to be a worker, had been beaten up because the men had learned that all the former negro workers were still in Sills pay, waiting for the factory to open. This was the only instance of violence. Haskell's paper made much of this assault of doubtful significance.

Cosmus was scarcely more than a benevolent spectator of the struggle. Once or twice he contributed letters to the "Labor Defense" and brought disapproval down upon his head. He did not see Kuhns often because Kuhns was too busy. But the glimpses he had of the man won him to loyalty. The labor leader was no selfish demagogue, but a far-seeing, fearless, patient patriot. Cosmus marveled at his patience, coolness and deep capacity for indignation.

Inseparably linked with the strike in Cosmus's mind was the war. Both upheavals—the stupendous there and the miniature here—were but manifestations of the same spirit beneath; both represented destruction of barriers, and the perceptible union of large masses of men. Inevitably the war was to mean internationalism—was meaning it, as nation after nation in alliance groped toward each other for understanding. How was Iron City, then, ever going to become a part of that glorious post-bellum world, if it could not accept understandingly mass movements at home?

There were the usual drawn faces of men, who found themselves in the midst of an ordeal severe beyond their calculation; there were patient, sharp-tongued, conservative women, eager for the comforts that the strike would bring, but hating the cost; there were children with puzzled faces, and aching bellies; there were men made bitter by the sharp sense of difference between those who were up, and those who were down and under; there were men grown cynical, convinced that there was no justice or kindness in the world and that conditions could never be bettered; there were men grown vengeful and cruel, eager to hurt and destroy; and there were men ready to make their leaders suffer for failure which had come too soon.

To this spectacle of woe, Iron City was indifferent. Jealous of its reputation, interested only in business, blind to principle, it prided itself on the respectability of the strike. It rejoiced in surface sight.

Cosmus saw one day a little girl in clean pinafore eating refuse from a neighbor's garbage pail. Here was symbol enough of the social order.

"Here in America, metaphysics have fallen into disrepute. The science once described as the 'search in a dark room for a black cat that isn't there' is quite too impractical for the modern world. Yet, in so far as metaphysics means passing beyond the physical, seeing beneath the surface, democracy rests upon it. Only when men become metaphysicists to the extent of seeing principles behind masses, and quivering, palpitant minds beneath externals, may democracy become actual."

As usual it was Sarah Blackstone who shared Cosmus's doubts and hopes during this period.

One day in the third month of the strike R. Sill called up his friend, Senator Matt Tyler.

"Can't you come down, Matt?"

"What's up now—victory?"

"Better than that—revenge."

In a half-hour Tyler's roadster stood in front of the factory and Tyler was mopping his brow in the quiet office of the manufacturer.

Lighting a fresh cigar, R. Sill took from a strong box, the key of which hung to his watch chain, a legal looking document; he patted it fondly, and then said, handing it to his friend.

"There—ain't that a beauty?"

Tyler's quick eye ran over the paper. Amazement shone in his face, then admiration, and fear. He whistled incredulously.

"Aren't you going too far, Bob? Be careful."

Sill leaned back in his chair, as he had done when he talked to Carl Morton several weeks before, and the same proud look of power came into his face. But now he was jubilant.

"Stand up, ye great barrister, and be catechized. Who maketh the laws of the state?"

"Public Opinion."

"Who executeth the laws of the state?"

"Public Opinion."

"Of course, and we have carefully prepared Public Opinion for Judge Dunbar's injunction. Read it."

Senator Tyler began to read. The injunction, issued by Judge Dunbar, of the Circuit Court, named Walt Kuhns, Jerry Mulvaney, Mary Levinsky and Wilson Grover. The plaintiff was designated as R. Sill and Son. There were seven clauses, and as the Senator read them, Sill exultingly translated them into the concrete.

"From at any time, in any manner, or at any place interfering or meddling with any persons whomsoever who may desire to enter into the employ of the plaintiff, R. Sill and Son."

"That's for Mulvaney and his pickets."

"From threatening or coercing——"

"That's for the low-down guy who beat the nigger."

"From gathering in bodies, or coercing or accosting——"

"That's for Wilson Grover, and his anarchists——"

"From publishing or causing to be published——"

"From writing or distributing——"

"That's for that Cosmus."

"From boycotting——"

"That's for that he-woman."

"From committing any acts of which the plaintiff, R. Sill and Son, complains."

"That for the whole gang—no matter what they do. What do you think, Tyler—ain't she a beauty? Just about air-tight. Eh?"

Senator Tyler wrinkled his regal nose and frowned disconcertingly.

"Yes, if you don't care what you do. Extremes usually act as boomerangs. You'd better get Dunbar to ease it up a bit. That's my advice."

Sill put the injunction carefully back in the box, and the box into the safe. Then he turned and faced Tyler.

"Oh, well, Matt, you see I'm not running for the Senate or anything, and I guess that'll have to stand as it is."

"When do you spring it?"

"At the psychological moment."

But Tyler, on his way home, still shook his head and muttered,

"That's going too far, quite too far." Perhaps the Senator had babbled so long about the inalienable rights of the people that he had come to believe in them.

*   *   *   *   *

When John Cosmus came around the corner approaching the factory, he heard laughter—epic laughter—the great tittering of a good-natured crowd, ending in ragged calls and bickerings. As he drew nearer, he found instead of a few pickets—the quota of strikers in the past—a large irregular patch of men, gaunt and severe. They stood carelessly about before the gate of R. Sill and Son's plant, laughing in derision. In a few minutes, as he joined the men on the outskirts, he discerned Kuhns among the men, and a few women and children hanging on the edge of the crowd. Standing in front of the gate was a man who, one could see at a glance, by clothes and manner, was not of the strikers. He was evidently the object of the laughter and evidently between him and the crowd was passing much talk and banter.

He was saying,

"I can lick any ten of you."

Replies came thick and fast from the crowd.

"Lick Sill's boots."

"Who let you out?"

"Dust off your think-tank!"

"You've got dirt in your carburetor!"

The man answered.

"If any of you think you can keep me from work, step up like a man, and try it. I can lick seventy-five of ye, fed up on bad whiskey."

To this more laughter. Cosmus was surprised at the good humor of the crowd—its discipline. He knew that Kuhns must be proud of these men, his disciples of non-resistance. Soon John had the satisfaction of seeing the man pass into the factory. Thinking the incident closed, and seeing Jenkins and Weaver on the other side of the street, he was approaching them, when he heard that peculiar raucous dissonance, somewhere between a murmur and a shriek, which issues from a crowd in anger. It was a terrible noise, and he saw, as he turned, the men, like black ants, coalesce by instinct to form a human battering ram. What had happened? He mounted a stone, and leaped to a fence, holding to a branch of an overhanging tree, to steady himself and looked.

His limbs trembled beneath him as the crowd, fast taking on the beastly exterior of the mob, was flowing toward the factory gate. Cosmus saw that a man—a much larger man—in the posture of challenge and defense, had taken the place of the first decoy. It was evidently his presence that had worked the change in the strikers.

Cosmus saw Kuhns, too, rush from the side to intercept the crowd, motioning them back like a traffic policeman. There were shouts,

"Get him! Get Daggett! Get the skunk!" mingled with the threatening roar of mad men; the crowd enveloped Kuhns, passed on and stormed the gate. The lone aggressor waited to take one lunge at the foremost assailant, then slipped into the safe precincts, of the yard. Stones began to fly. Curses, maledictions, the terrible moody buzz of mob anger and impotence, beat in Cosmus's ears. He saw futile battering with bare hands against barred doors. Then the gate of the factory opened and the snouts of two fire hoses emerged; from them heavy streams of water began to pour. Cosmus was dazed. The water was hot. Steam arose as it met the air. Strikers were rolling on the ground, shrieking and cursing. Women and children screamed; he saw Kuhns run back and forth before the wavering line of men, as if to push them into the street by sheer physical force. But the men did not heed. Twice they charged the gate in the face of the steam, and then tumbled shrieking to the pavement. Then seizing stones and sticks, they hurled volley after volley, in impotent anger at the conquering foes. The water never failed—two streams of sizzling rain, cut a circle about the factory gate three hundred feet back, ringed around by murmuring, threatening men; Walt Kuhns stood just without the fluid shot, facing the crowd.

Suddenly the water ceased. Then Cosmus saw the women and children on the edge of the crowd dash to the curb, and where they parted, running, he saw up the street, an oncoming automobile, at full speed, swaying back and forth almost from curb to curb. It had set up a loud honking, but nevertheless it came on, deliberately, straight for the factory gate; preempting the street as its right. It was a blind thing, for it narrowly missed a child as it swung on two wheels around the short corner and bore down upon the crowd of men. By magic the crowd parted and Cosmus was thanking God that the way was so easily cleared, when something happened. The water had wet the street. The wheels skidded, the car leaped a tangent straight for the mass of men, who scattering, scampering, parted again.

Another cry from the crowd! This time of pity and dismay. The machine seemed to swerve and then stopped tremblingly, glued to the pavement by heavy brakes. Cosmus jumped down and ran where the crowd was thickest; elbowing through, his breath bothering him, his imagination over-wrought. Expecting to see death, he at last fought his way to the machine. The automobile was clogged by angry strikers. White and distraught, Raymond Sill sat behind the wheel. In the arms of two men was the limp form of Walt Kuhns, blood running from a still mouth.

Before Cosmus could show pity or resentment more machines appeared, and officers pushed men and women, now thoroughly cowed, back to the pavement. The sheriff took command and howled orders.

"Line up, Mulvaney; line up, Kuhns;" and then, paying not the least attention to the wounded leader, the sheriff served his injunctions and made arrests.

Suddenly Cosmus found his tongue, in a high and squawky voice,—he cried,

"My God—such law; don't arrest Kuhns. There's your man— he's a murderer." And he found himself the center of an excited throng, for he was shaking his finger in the white face of old Sill's son.

Without a word the sheriff motioned the strikers down off the big Stutz, muttering something to Raymond about "getting out of here." Raymond, still white and trembling, slowly drove the car toward the factory gate, which opened as if by magic to receive him. Contemptuously, bitterly, silently, the crowd let him go.

Awesome stillness settled down over the street. At the summons of a whistle a police ambulance, the one which had once before carried Walt Kuhns, nosed its bleak, black way into the crowd.

"Officer, I protest," Cosmus said, his voice still husky. "This man is not fit for the police station."

"Who said he was?" the sheriff answered gruffly; then turning to the driver he directed, "To the Emergency Hospital."

The limp form of Kuhns was lifted not untenderly into the ambulance. Cosmus turned away, sick with the pity of it all. He saw the women, with aprons at their eyes, little children clutching frantically at their mothers' skirts, men cowed and sullen. Suddenly somewhere in the factory, a whistle began to blow—shrill and long, and there was the sound of revolving wheels. Sill had won. Industry—the world's business—had been resumed. "That is industry's voice," thought Cosmus. "Shrill, superior, soulless. And these men are soulless, too."

He saw the strikers dispersing wearily, and as he turned at the end of the street beckoning, there was the River of Wires reaching toward the cities and beyond.

A hand on his shoulder brought Cosmus to the realization that the student Weaver was trying to say something to him.

"Don't you want to come with me, Professor, to the Iron Works—there's more trouble down there, they say."

"Where?"

"At Crandon Hill Iron Works."

That brought Cosmus up with a jerk. Sarah! Riot! The two students saw the professor dash madly after a jitney, relieve the man at the wheel after emptying his own pockets of coin, and drive off at a speed something in excess of all limits.

Cosmus lurching back and forth in the unsteady seat, had time to curse all strikes and violence—that touched the innocent; and he received at the same time the blows of his own merciless intellect as it saw and measured the law of compensation. "That's what you get," intellect was saying, "for preaching strikes; the woman you think the most of shall pay."

He drove the car on furiously. Once he saw a traffic man, gesticulating wildly, but it did not occur to him that it might be he whom the policeman wished to stop, until he had left the blue-coat, semaphoring foolishly far behind.

The Crandon Hill Iron Works were built close to the pavement at the intersection of Fourth Avenue and Fifth Street, and as Cosmus wheeled around the corner he came suddenly upon the crowd, beating at Boyne's windows and doors. He saw at once the futility of trying to press through that throng, and turned away from the shouting mob, up a side street. He sped off to the left upon the railroad switch track, that cut the Iron Works in two. Within the factory's great yard, he found no manifestation of excitement. The place was still. No guard was at the wide door of the foundry to bar its entrance, and he threaded his way through the deserted shop, not without a sense of the pathos of abandoned and disused things which the stale coal-scents invoked. He managed finally to come out into a narrow dark passageway, that opened upon the wide marble corridor, where mahogany doors glistened. Here Cosmus was upon familiar ground, and he had no trouble in finding the luxurious offices of the president, where Sarah worked.

He threw open the wide door, the guttural complaints of the strikers, cruel, soulless, and urgent, came in through the broken windows from the street. Was the office empty! Undisturbed, save for bits of shattered glass, and scattered stones and cans, the large room had never seemed more attractive; and even in the midst of his excitement Cosmus felt break over him, surge after surge of tender feeling, and welling memories of Sarah. The great office—throne of might and injustice—meant to him only her! It was the place where Sarah worked.

It was irony that he saw Boyne first,—a crumpled figure caught between the brick jamb and the half-closed French window that opened upon the narrow portico overhanging the street;— Boyne's head dangled sickeningly toward the floor where black blood had clotted. Cosmus glanced away, to see Sarah lying clear and beautiful behind the desk. As he bent over her, he noticed an ugly, discolored bruise above her right eye. But for that, she seemed asleep! Thank God! And comfortable.

Cosmus turned around quickly, answering impulse, and lifted Boyne clear of discomfiture, which though only apparent, nevertheless was so pathetic. It eased him to see the limp figure lying straight and still. "He must be dead—he is so limp," he thought.

As he did so the mob beneath, as if detecting the movement at the window, set up a swelling howl of anger. For a moment, something like fear and hatred beat at Cosmus's heart. He hesitated. Some impulse drove him toward the portico to thrust out at that violent thing in the streets.

Then, turning away, he lifted Sarah in his arms and lurched into the hall. She was heavy for him and he staggered but he knew infinite satisfaction in that moment. Beneath excitement, conflicting ideas, physical exertion, he was aware of the sweet appeal of her person. Saddened, exultant, he staggered down the long hall, into the passage way, and threaded the maze of deserted walks of the foundry to the yard, where the Ford still panted. He lifted her in, started abruptly, stalled his engine, and pushed futilely at the self-starter. Then pillowing her tenderly with his overcoat, which he stripped off, he whirled the engine into action, jumped in, backed daringly over the tracks, and wound his way out of the yards again. Soon they were in the street, and Cosmus dashed off through an alley into Jenkins Street, now empty, toward home.

In her own room, under the wise administration of the land-lady, Sarah opened her eyes. There was no wonderment—only weariness and pain in that look, Cosmus thought. But she smiled, too, up at him.

"I'm all right," she said, "it was you who came?"

They made her comfortable.

"I must tell you," she said, "when the men attacked, Boyne and I rushed to the window. I think they shot him, and a stone or something hit me," her lips trembled.

"Oh, John, I never want to see another strike again."

That night, with Sarah recovered, Cosmus on his way to the hospital to see Walt Kuhns, saw an extra *Republic-Despatch*. Black lines flared across the page.

JUDGE DUNBAR PUTS END TO REIGN OF TERROR

Serves Injunction on Violent Mob Outraging Public Decency

ONE STRIKER SERIOUSLY INJURED IN FRACAS—MAY DIE

Boyne, President Crandon Hill Iron Works, Shot, but Will Recover.

STRIKE REGIME OVER: PUBLIC REJOICES!

Cosmus read; paused and wondered. So Walt Kuhns pays.

How the city streets swarmed! and he heard the sound of careless laughter!

22 Passion's Wake

One evening soon after the ending of the strike Raymond came home from the factory by foot. He was disturbed. He knew that Margaret had recently seen his father, and that she had made a plea for Mr. Sill to use his influence to keep President Hugh Crandon from discharging Cosmus for his part in the strike, and that, strangely enough, she had succeeded. He was aware that she had been impertinent—brazen his father had characterized her—and he had concluded that Margaret must have threatened to expose him publicly. He had received, too, a note from her saying that if he did not take her to the dance at the Country Club she would come alone and "make a scene." These facts were unpleasant, but they did not account entirely for the deep sense of foreboding which he carried home with him that night. There was something profound and ominous in the gloom which enveloped him—something beyond his mind to control. And he had not ridden home; in fact he had not ridden in a car since—since the ending of the strike. Somehow he could not go near the big Stutz. It made his nerves jumpy. He did not go in to dinner, but went straight to his room, where his mother found him soon after.

"Son boy," she said, "are you ill?"

"No, Mother. Just plagued tired."

"Would you like a cup of tea?"

"No, Mother. It keeps me awake. I guess that's what does it," and he tried to speak naturally.

"You're working too hard," his mother said anxiously.
"Yes, Mother."

With a deprecating gesture of impatience, his mother moved toward the door. Before turning the knob, she paused and said,

"Hazel said she would go to the club dance with you."

"I am glad, Mother."

When she was gone, Raymond threw off coat and collar, sank into a great chair, and smoked cigarette after cigarette. At 10:30 he went to bed.

He awoke with a clear mind; through the open window came the sound of singers trailing home through the misty night; a lively wind was stirring in the trees, and when the college clock struck some minutes later, he counted, "One, two, three"—only three hours to lie awake, he thought.

"Four, five"—and so on to twelve o'clock. Then he remembered what had awakened him so soon. It was a dream. He was in a court-room thronged with familiar faces. He saw them from the prisoner's box. In front of the Judge's bench was a black coffin. He was being arraigned by some one whom he thought was Cosmus, but when he looked up—there was Margaret, clad in black crying "murderer, murderer." The sound of that awful word had wakened him.

He shivered under the covers. The wind crashing among the autumnal trees came to him freighted with notes profoundly hostile. Nature seemed some sardonic machine, and in the rhythmic pause of the wind, he heard the clang of the machine of his father's creation on the other side of the town—and he wondered about the men working there. It would be almost good, he thought, to be there with them tonight!

He tried to bring his mind around to the point of realization that the world outside, the factory yonder, the wind clattering dolefully in the trees, his room here filled with shadows, were just the same as they were by day. But he could not. They were not the same. By day the world was open; the houses of the town, the people, enveloped him in friendliness. Now the night, save for the din of the factory, shut them out. He was alone.

As one who clambers fearfully along a crumbling edge for one peep into the troubled depths of a volcano, Raymond peered into himself. What he found there made him lie sleepless, and stare through fear at the wall of darkness above him. . .

About four, before he fell asleep, he had resolved to go to Margaret and offer some kind of reparation. . . . But Walt Kuhns?

When Margaret Morton arrived at the Country Club on the trolley alone, she found the great stone house aglare. The last party of the season in late October was often the gayest, and to-night Iron City, as if feeling released from the bondage of the strike, had gathered as if by agreement, in a finale of social splendor. A long line of glistening limousines, open cars of every type and model, including Fords, denoted something of the size and catholicity of the crowd.

Already the orchestra was crashing out a two-step in syncopation. Rag-time from its barbaric lairs in South America, for the first time, seemed out of place to Margaret. Outside the night was still, save for complaining leaves, rustling dryly along upon the heavy current of damp winds. As she went up the path, past the leaden lagoon now smeared with blurred images of vari-colored lanterns from the windows, she shuddered. The pool looked very cold and very deep.

"I hope they have a fire," she thought.

When she entered she saw that logs were crackling in the two big fireplaces in the ball-room; she paused in the hall a moment, sweeping the room from length to length, letting her glance rest on jeweled and brilliantly gowned women, and soberly attired men. Then she saw Raymond with Hazel Tyler. An ineffable sense of loss, the vanishing of youth and the staleness of the world cut through her icy calm. She trembled; tears came, and she set her lips to keep back sobs. Too soon the fullness of life had flown. In that look—cut off as she was from all pleasure that she loved—Margaret realized remotely the staggering price one pays who precociously yields herself to the urge of sex.

She did not go to the ladies's retiring room. She found, instead, as she had hoped, the library unoccupied. No fire had been kindled in the narrow grate, but she did not hesitate to enter. She kept her heavy cloak muffled around her, and without flashing on the lamp, sank down in the Morris chair, just outside the zone of light cut by the chandelier in the hall. Here the blatant music, and the ting-tong of merry mingled voices came to her, and here she had time to think.

In the last months, during which Iron City had been convulsed with the strike, Margaret had passed into a kind of sublimation of grief. Save for spasmodic wildness, such as her championing of John Cosmus before R. Sill, much of her old gayety of manner had returned. But it was the gayety of tragic exultation. In the perception of a solution to her problem, she had become elated but morbid. To herself, she seemed two persons—one bitterly suffering, the other a solicitous witness of grief. All her acts were dramatic. It was this theatrical sense which had elements of danger, for it would sustain her in participating in roles of even tragic outcome to herself.

In the few minutes in which she sat alone in the cold room of the club, she thought bitterly of her father. Carl Morton had not weathered the storm; he sat at home even now, feeble and old, plunged futilely in treatises on education. Would he never take her back again? It was the look of mute appeal in his eyes—puzzled, searching, dog-like—that gave her nerves. He ought not to look that way! He ought not to take on so! He never could see things as he ought to.

And Raymond?

She had come to see Raymond; she must find a maid and send for him. She arose, and stepped into the hall. At the other end, she saw him alone peering about as if looking for some one. She beckoned and he came towards her.

"I was looking for you, Mag; I have come to take you out of this." The words were decisive, prompted by deep feeling, but it was not given these two thus to recover so easily by a phrase the alluring rapturous world which they had lost, for Margaret misunderstood. Highly strung as she was, she thought it was some scheme of his to get her out of the way that evening,

"Oh, no, you don't," she answered. "I am going to stay. And what is more you are going to dance with me."

She had raised her voice in excitement, and during a lull in the music and dancing below, it sounded unnatural and too loud. He glanced nervously around, and she, seeing his perturbation, thought that her suspicions were confirmed. Raymond had come up to intercept her, to keep her away from the ball-room.

"Come in here," she said, "if you are ashamed to be with me."

Ignoring her tone, he followed her back into the library; she shut the door behind them, and after fumbling at the curtain at the window, switched on the light. There were cigar stubs and ashes on the table—and the room looked cold and uninviting. Raymond snatched up the waste basket, emptied its contents into the grate, throwing in a few magazines for good measure, and struck a match. She watched him narrowly. How wasteful he was; the fire gave out only a little heat and a sickly light She coughed; and he glanced at her apprehensively.

"How have you been?" he demanded "Sick any?"

A gleam of satisfaction shone in her face. He was concerned about her then.

"I've been in bed a lot," she answered.

"Well enough to travel?"

"That depends on where."

"Anywhere," he continued, "away from Iron City. I hate it. I keep the plane out here, you know. Here at the County Club there is a fine field for landing. We'll find some place, Mag. You don't know how sick and tired I am of this efficiency business Dad gave me, and of this Walt Kuhns mess."

He spoke without passion, mechanically, and his words and tone made Margaret almost pity him. He did not seem very much like a lover. But when she answered, she was precipitate.

"I don't want to go away, Ray. I won't go. You're ashamed of me. You know it. We ought to stay here together, be down there dancing, happy like the others."

He stretched out his hands toward the flimsy ashes in the fireplace as if for warmth, then turned toward her, his eyes awake, and interested.

"But I thought you were sick and couldn't."

"Maybe you did and maybe you didn't. You could have come to see me, couldn't you?"

His eyes shifted.

"If you'll go with me, Mag, I'll make it all up."

"But you can't make it up—that way. There's only one way,—to take me down there."

"But you can't go when you're sick."

"But I am not sick; I'm just like I was."

He turned to her eagerly.

"What do you mean?"

She said again emphatically,

"Like—I—always—was."

He understood, and suddenly he felt warmly happy, happier than he had been for months. Life, after all, was as it ought to be; he did not need to pay for that blind moment in the church. There were no consequences to be met. The great God Law had slipped its orbit. There was justice in the world at last. His manner changed. He arose and stood leaning against the mantle, something of his old dashing spirit returned.

Before he spoke, Margaret saw the change in him and began to cry. "There is nothing to cry about, Mag. We're well out of it now, and—" Without finishing, he sat down beside her on the couch, and drew her close to him.

She pushed him away questioningly, searching his face.

"Don't," she said.

The one thing which had sustained her for weeks—had eluded her in the moment of her need. The dramatic in this scene with Ray had vanished. He, not she, was playing the grand role—and going free. She wiped her eyes clear of tears, and said very simply,

"Ray, I have decided to kill myself unless you own me before the others."

She had rehearsed those words many times in the last few weeks, nevertheless they came spontaneously now. They sprang out at him with vivid force, and they seemed alive to Margaret, too. It was as if some inner urge had uttered itself through them. She saw Raymond start, look queerly at her, and tremble.

"You just couldn't be such a fool, Mag. You were as much to blame as I, and you have not suffered more."

"Look at me, Ray."

She waited until his eyes met hers.

"Now do I look as if I meant it?"

"You couldn't be such a fool," he reiterated spiritlessly, his face white and drawn, his whole frame trembling; he was thinking of the last time he had seen Walt Kuhns.

Margaret did not enjoy her triumph; she had thought she would. In her the sense of loss renewed itself. Could the world ever again be as it was?

Suddenly Raymond turned on her meanly.

"You fool, you'd like to make me a murderer, too, like that God damn Professor Cosmus."

"Oh, Ray!"

They could hear the music of the dance and feel the timbers of the whole house swing in rhythm to the lilting feet. But something had whisked them afar off from all that merriment.

After a moment, Ray said,

"Well, damn it, why don't we go down?"

He arose and stood facing her.

She saw him in that moment in a new light—the bullet head, the narrow eyes, the well-kept mustache, the figure somewhat squat—all seemed hideous—repulsive as passion always is. Then she knew that it wasn't Ray that she wanted. He did not cure the insistent sense of loss. She began to understand that it was an inner rather than an outer loss and must be a permanent one. What was she going to do now? What if he did consent to go down with her—even to live with her, could she be happy? It was not Ray that she wanted, and the realization left her weak and distraught.

She arose quietly, and drew her cloak about her tightly,

"No, I'm not going down. You go, Ray."

"Come to your senses, have you?"

"Yes," she said simply. "Go."

He shrugged his shoulders, drew out a silver case, selected a cigarette and jabbed it fiercely between his lips. He did not light it. With the bearing of one who is well rid of a bad situation, he strode out.

Margaret stood for a moment thoughtfully, then she turned out the light. Going to the French window, she unloosed the clasp, and stepped out on the balcony. The night was dull and dark, and the lagoon, save for splashes of color, seemed as leaden and unfathomable as ever. She followed the balcony around to the steps that led to the ground on to the tennis court. Then she went hurriedly and purposefully through the wet grass, brushing the sere bushes as she passed, to a solitary bench by the water. Here she sank down gratefully. The sky had opened, and a star or two, and a crooked moon showed themselves. Afar off as in a daze, she heard the clang of brass, the clinkle of strings and the creak of floors under swinging feet.

She was honestly trying to understand the situation; she was groping as well as she might with her imperfect equipment, toward a solution of this dilemma in her young life. Hurried into maturity by precocious passion, she was confused by the unexpected paths that distended from passion's center. She could not choose.

There was her father;—he had once so loved her. That congenital affinity which from baby-hood seemed to unite them, had suddenly snapped and left them groping. The great outer world of convention had drifted between them, and she could not understand how he could care more for a social law than for his own daughter. And now his eyes hurt her. His broken efforts to be as he always had been struck terror in her heart. His allegiance to a social standard of another day remained inexplicable to her. To her it seemed that her father had never known about life. He had wanted her to have happiness, but he had not shown her how or where to find it. All he had ever said was, "Don't, don't, don't," until her ears ached. All the pretty world of pleasure had seemed closed by "don't." Then there was her mother so spiritless, so utterly lost to life. Margaret, as she thought on those two quenched lives at home, was filled with pity and resentment and the hopeless futility of turning back to them for aid.

She sat gnawing her nails, torn by the music from the Club, and the swish of leaden waters before her. She heard, too, above and beyond the brass and strings, the pervading monotone of industry—the whisper of wheels and whine of whistles—expansive and dim, the faint note of her environment. She had known that factory all her life—and only during the strike had she ever failed to hear the beat of its wheels. Could she look to it for help? Her hands clenched at her face and she turned hot at the recollection of old Sill's arrogance. How she hated him. His factory had sucked her father dry and then scrapped him!

As usual Margaret was not thinking. She could not think; only aim to, and beat about in futile efforts to reason. She was drifting hopelessly along on the river of images that flows through the subjective world.

From the factory her mind flowed to that other group of buildings on the hill, still and calm, under the young moon, so aloof from the life that surged around it. How impotent to help her the college seemed in this complex crisis in relation with other humans and with herself. Strange, when she thought of the college, she always thought of Cosmus.

She recalled that meeting long ago on the road east of the city, and his suggestion that they go to the secluded cabin. What if she had gone? Would life have been different? A wave of self-pity broke over her, and she leaned against the cold bench and sobbed. Cosmus had not helped her; no one had. She was alone,—lost.

With sudden resolution she stood up, and threw off her heavy cloak. Her limbs were tense, like an animal's, ready to leap as she stood looking down into the pool. It was deep here she knew, for the heavier launches came up from the river. She wondered how quickly it would be over, whether she would struggle; then as the cold wind struck her, she put her cloak on again. It would help drag her down, she thought.

Calmer now, she had turned to leap into the water, when her ear caught the persistent drumming of a motor. Was a launch coming up the river? No, it seemed behind her. Just behind. Just above. Suddenly against the open sky she saw a flying shadow; and then a floating rag against the moon and stars; and then a vast leaf wafted eastward. Raymond in his plane! She followed his flight, all vibrancy. Suddenly his motor seemed to stop, the great leaf swerved, veered and disappeared in shadows behind the trees across the river. How dangerous to fly at night. Why wasn't he going toward the city?

Margaret sat down on the bench trembling. A light broke in upon her. Perhaps Raymond was running away. She was all resentment toward him now. Until this evening she had thought that she wanted to make him suffer; but she had suddenly realized in that last interview that after all what he felt or thought no longer made any difference to her. She hated him for his selfishness and for what he had done to her life, for what he had made her suffer—alone! If only he were really gone she could forget and begin again; she need never be reminded of what had happened. After all, what did it matter—a little slip like that? There was to be no baby—no one need ever know.

If only he were really gone! She looked up in the sky where he had disappeared—suddenly she felt free—suddenly she chose to live.

Some one must have opened a window in the house, for the

music blew out to meet her mood. She must be free! The moon and stars, the orchestra said so! How she wanted to be happy! How she loved life! Far away the foolish thought of death receded. She knelt softly by the lagoon, and dropped her handkerchief into its waters, and bathed her burning face.

It made no difference. Who would say it did? Who was to deny Margaret this easy egress from her problem? After all it was not a matter of bad and good. Only a simple matter of discrimination. It was not what Margaret had suffered, it was only what she had missed.

She went exultantly toward the house. On the balcony in a patch of shadow, a woman was standing looking into the night. Margaret craved human intercourse.

"Oh, aren't you happy!" she cried impulsively.

"No, child, I can hardly say that I am," a voice replied.

And then Margaret saw that it was "that Sarah Blackstone."

23 A Letter from France

It was broad daylight in Cosmus's room, clear and quiet like the rare days of childhood. The postman had just brought the mail. At the top of the letter when he opened it he read in a strange handwriting, "Sergeant Ezra Kimbark died with honor in the recent offensive at ————."

Cosmus held before him the saddest of all war's ironies, a letter from the dead to the living. It seemed to be poor Kimbark's daily jottings, made into a letter. He had written:

"I know your insatiable appetite for war stories; you have read them all, so I am not going to entertain you with any close-ups of the front. My case is pretty typical. War is all body. That I have found out. I find myself overeating, lusting and undersleeping. The first relief I get from service, I gorge myself on chocolate or wine and cakes—if I can get them; and I have a hard time turning away from the women that infest all camps—even the best. Life is cheap—as nothing else in the world, and therefore one can't have very much respect for himself. It is only during the infrequent lulls in the battle—when an unbelievable silence floats down on a fetid world, and peace glides in—that I ever seem myself; you wouldn't know me.

"One dream has recurred nearly every time I sleep. Myself falling in a charge. I always see him,—Ezra Kimbark, that was I,—from the outside. I am the spectator, never the participator in the battle—and always I fall from a bullet, face forward toward the enemy's trench.

"Yesterday when we took ten yards of trench, I saw a French boy refuse to plunge his bayonet into the breast of an enemy, when he cried 'kamerad,' and lose his life from a bomb from somewhere behind. I bent over him. 'Don't stop,' he cried, 'I'm just a little out of luck. Go on, go on.' He tried to wave his arms.

"Sometimes one has insistent visions—these come at the most impossible moments; in an interval of quiet, or in the rush and stir of charge.

"The other day when the Germans drove us back I was filled with the hallucination that I was accompanied by a figure that was large and paternal, sheltering me. I knew it was an illusion, and yet I liked it. And more strange, I saw just behind me the materialization of a picture I once had seen of Lincoln—high hat—shawl about his shoulders, large and paternal. We had not eaten anything for nearly three days; got caught between fires, and you know they say hunger produces visions.

"And yet I am not sure this Lincoln wasn't an objectification of my recent musings. All my life-long I have been trying to find America, my country, and it has only been in these few days of horror that I have come into any realization of what America is to me. I flatter myself that this is not merely the usual experience of the expatriate, but peculiar to me. The guns have pounded something into my head at last, John.

"The tangled truth of the war reveals this fact: Nations will no longer exist because of geographical boundaries, or the natural bonds of race and tongue. America is not fifty states, or the central part of North America. She isn't even a language, or a form of government. She is a current of ideas—nothing more. The Germans did right in emphasizing 'kultur' at the beginning of the war for kultur, and not the 'Uber Rhein States,' is Germany. And American kultur is America. All that this movement toward internationalism can mean, is reinterpretation of nationalism.

"We have been thing-minded in America, and imagined that a pseudodemocracy and a million square miles of pay-dirt made us America. We have neglected, too, the great embodiment of our 'kultur' in our native genius. Lincoln with his passionate vision and his practical power, his 'malice toward none' and his ability to prosecute the Civil War to a successful conclusion, is American 'kultur' incarnate. America, formed of the liberals of the world, has shown a propensity for putting into practice the loftiest concepts acquired through world-experience. And the whole question at stake is whether we prefer Lincoln to Frederick the Great. This *is* a war of kulturs.

"What of America and the war?

"Turned a preacher, haven't I? why shouldn't I? That you at home should see this in time is worth something more to me than my miserable life.

"I have thought a good deal lately about my talk with you just before I left, my whining and groaning—all that sort of thing. I guess I must have been 'weepy-drunk'—and I have concluded that I was not so much of a poet as I thought I was. If I had been, I should have created something in spite of the Sills and Crandons that rule America. And yet I still hold a grudge. I had as much genius as John Hay, born ten miles from my home, and he succeeded. All of which seems petty in the light of this candle, here in this dug-out, amidst the bellowing of these guns."

Here the scribbling stopped. The letter remained unfinished. There were enclosed a few details from the sender about how Kimbark had met his death, his popularity in the squad, and his unfailing good humor. That was all.

So Kimbark was dead! The news was not a surprise and yet it was particularly disconcerting to Cosmus. It seemed at the moment of its coming, the last straw of grief in a burden of heavy sorrows. Cosmus was sick at heart.

There are some natures who find their happiness in the farther reaches of the spirit; in patriotism and in religion, and love of humanity. Cosmus was of such disposition. It seemed more important to him that justice triumph than that his own body be comfortable.

Unfortunately the modern world furnishes such a mind as his with a medium for watching the progress of justice in the world; the newspaper with its chronicle of events is but a mirror of human society. With a perverse gift of imagination, Cosmus lived through every event recorded until his mind was a convulsive heap of tragic stories. Rape of Belgium, German atrocities, Armenian disasters, strikes, riots, plagues and poisonings; the continual thwarting of the wish of the majority by the few, the cunning, the bribery of the ruling class; an impending national crisis of portentous implications, restive classes, and at home in Iron City, Walt Kuhns, mangled and broken; the city gagged by the patrol of injustice. Now Ezra Kimbark's death!

Tears? John Cosmus had not cried for years. His grief was not of that sort, but he felt the brooding, smoldering sorrow of intense contemplation.

His mind was seismographic in its recording of world tremors; and the incoming year of 1917 seemed full of grave forebodings. This weight of the universal, resting heavily on his mind, told on his physical strength. He found himself going home from classes utterly fatigued, and Sarah Blackstone told him he looked ten years older. He could not rest. His sleep was broken and fretful. His mind was a cinema of frightful close-ups. More than ever he craved amusement, relaxation and play, and yet every effort to get away from the sorry circle of ideas he counted wasted. He took pleasures guiltily.

His only reading was newspapers. Newspapers obsessed him. Through them he watched every move of the opposing armies on the Western front, and when the morning paper was read he waited for the noon edition, and passed, after its perusal, to anticipation of the evening.

In keeping with the popular vogue of *vers libre* he became addicted to the habit, and drolly conscious of his unscholarly effort, set down lines to "The Newspaper." They were of no interest, except as representative of his intimate union with the world. He wrote:

"I rush out of my house,
And drag you in,
You foul thing:
Reeking with the sweat and filth,
The putrid slime of all the dirty world.
I devour you through my eyes,
Incorporate you into my life:
Incorporate you into our composite life.
Why do I lust after scandal, and you.
Man's poor failures, miserable delinquences, tragic
horrors—and you.
Why can't I rest until I have brought you in!"

Cosmus did not show his "poem" to any one; it might have been better if he had. He was fast losing grip on social principles, and he needed the steadying experience of laughter—at himself.

He went to see Walt Kuhns, who gave him deep concern. He was allowed to be with the leader of the strikers only for a few minutes and the visit was unsatisfactory. Though Kuhns had recovered consciousness in the three days intervening, he still was weak and still spit blood. He seemed pitiably insensible to the fact that the strike had utterly failed. On the table was a pad of paper and a pencil.

"I'm glad you came, Comer," he whispered. Then seeing Cosmus's questioning glance, said, "*The Defense* comes out just the same, you know." But it didn't, Cosmus knew. That was only a merciful fiction which the nurses had fabricated.

From the hospital that night, he went forth outwardly calm, but inwardly troubled. It's so hidden—this tragedy of daily life— this slow invisible burning at the center of personality—with no outward vent. One can carry grief and transact the surface duties of daily routine, with no more manifestation than quickened pulse, heightened blood pressure or unchanging color in the cheek. Even these evidences were not present in Cosmus. His trouble manifested itself only in hopeless wrath, deep enervating anger, at forces that pinioned Kuhns to his bed; in a petty aversion for the crowds and jungle of the city.

"God! what a noise!" he thought. "The people are so aimless. They push so! There is no room on the sidewalks. Those mustard colored coats are hideous. Women will show their ankles. I must get out of this quick, or I'll smother."

He turned off Main Street, and thought of home. Then, he knew he would not sleep. He must go on. He must tramp, tramp, tramp until he was tired. He was not tired now, only nervous. And he had a headache, too.

He craved something. What was it ? Ah, he knew. A talk, a rousing talk with a friend on some such abstract theme as "Is suicide ever legitimate?" With a friend? Say, with Kimbark.

Then his mind jerked back to the letter he had received that morning, and to the bitter realization—more keen than at any time that day—that Kimbark would not ever talk with him again.

His mind resumed its pounding. Yes, the war had brought changes even in the city. There's millionaires' row yonder built out of munitions. Every brick in those mansions is a human life. And Mrs. B——says, "If the war holds out another year, we'll be multimillionaires."

But this will not do. One's mind must have rest. Play is an excellent tonic. One should play. He would go and get Sarah Blackstone. He retraced his steps, turned up the chief residential street, and in the course of ten minutes stood before Sarah's door.

Once there, he could not go in and he felt a strong resentment toward her. He had been quite right, Sarah was all mind. She lacked warmth, humanity, body or something. But he loved her. Yes, he loved her—but he would not marry her. Some one, perhaps Sidney Haynes, would do that. He turned back and went over to the park and sat on the bench beneath the statue of R. Sill, the first, where they had sat together the first night three years ago. They had seemed so near then, and now their relations were just a long series of vain gropings toward each other. But he wanted her. He needed her.

Why couldn't she be like his mother? Why couldn't he go to her to-night—now—and creep into her arms and feel the quietude of deep maternity? Instead, if he went she would make him think, and arouse his will to action and make him feel that he must do something at once or the world would tumble, a black cinder, into a sea of oblivion.

No, he didn't want Sarah tonight. He wanted rest.

He sat on the bench in the deserted park for perhaps an hour. "Trying to relax," he called it, and then a loaded street-car jangled by; above the wheels he could hear the laughter of people in pursuit of pleasure, and he could see that not all were going home from toil. In that moment the crowds seemed identified with himself in want, and hunger for something, they knew not what.

He arose, and followed the path, crisp under foot with bronze oak leaves, down through the hollow in the park, across the street, through a darker street, across the railroad tracks, out into the open country. Near a creek, that found its destination in Bass River below, he discovered a sycamore tree, ghost-like, in the dark, its roots spread out like a woman's skirts. He sat down on these roots in utter fatigue and waited.

His mind worked in and out of problems, experiences, memories and impressions. He thought of the day now nearly ten years before, when he had climbed the telephone post, tapped the trans-continental wire, and had got his inspiration to go to college. He thought of college, graduate school, his hopes for education, Margaret Morton, Raymond Sill, Walt Kuhns, Ezra Kimbark, President Crandon,—these vivid personalities that crowded his life—and then the factory—whose faint clangor he could still detect in the night; and the war. How different, how vastly different the world was now from the world as it then seemed to be!

In some moment of this thinking he became aware of the vast night stretching around him, the earth so wide and patient, the stars, infinite and tender, the expansive stillness of the world. The valley yonder, the heavy speech of the running water, the city lights behind—they, too, were part of the peace of the wider upper universe. Behold, the night was paternal and enfolding.

Suddenly as he sat there all fatigue was gone. It slipped from him mysteriously. He was strong, capable. Even the war—that inexplicable orgy—seemed potential with good. Somewhere in his thinking, some idea, some raveling of feeling, had brushed his soul clean of fear, anguish and hatred. He had let go and slipped into Life.

At length he remembered: that cleansing thought was the thought of God.

Behind him, breaking the stillness, he heard a voice calling— far away, indistinct, then nearer. Rested, he arose, and went toward the city. As he approached, he could detect the words borne by the voice: "Extra, Extra."

Should he buy a newspaper? Yes, he was strong to face reality again. An extra edition of the *Republic-Despatch* gave another start to Iron City's jaded attention. The headlines read:

MILLIONAIRE'S SON MISSING

Raymond Sill, Only Son of the Head of Iron City's Premier Manufacturing Establishment, Disappears

NOT SEEN FOR THREE DAYS
FOUL PLAY ON PART OF STRIKERS FEARED

WALT KUHNS MAY HAVE INSTIGATED REVENGE—WILL BE PUT UNDER SURVEILLANCE

"Here is hell to pay," Cosmus thought. "If Walt Kuhns is held in any way responsible for this, all human justice fails. How utterly, how criminally preposterous."

But what was to be done? Who dared to affront the law, or who was subtle enough to thread the webby forces that lay behind the

Law? "That damned Raymond Sill, he deserved all he got, whatever it was. He was wicked all through," Cosmus thought resentfully.

But did that touch the problem? In searching for a solution, he thought of Hugh Crandon before he saw his tall form ahead of him in the thinning crowds. It took but a minute to overtake the president, present his request, and march along with the affable gentleman to his palatial office.

24 The Genteel Tradition

"Do you smoke?"

With a flourish President Crandon took a box of fine cigars from his desk and offered them to his caller.

"I keep these here for my trustees when they call; of course, I don't use the weed."

Cosmus declined the luxury, and wondered how any one could imagine that Crandon would taint his elegant lips with tobacco.

"Look over this, then, will you for a moment, Mr. Cosmus? I was just on my way to the office when you accosted me, and I should like to get some work out of the way first."

President Crandon was handing a copy of "The Classical Ideal" toward his guest. Cosmus took the book, opened it casually, but occupied his mind with his own reflections.

The office of President Hugh Crandon always seemed so impossibly shiny, so unused and unusable, so formidable and uninviting to John Cosmus that he smiled at his own temerity in approaching the head of Crandon Hill College. Yet he did not about-face.

Something had happened to him that night. The deep emotionalism into which war and the death of Ezra Kimbark had plunged him, had passed at length into fighting spirit. If this office, finer even than R. Sill's, was just like its owner, showy and formidable, still it could not turn Cosmus back from the job in hand. Walt Kuhns must be saved the least inconvenience now;

and it was time, moreover, that Cosmus make himself felt in this institution. He was beginning to forsake the rôle of spectator, for that of actor.

Piqued, too, by curiosity, a curiosity that had never forsaken him in these years at Crandon Hill College, Cosmus was anxious to peep behind that mask of immobility that President Crandon wore.

What was this Puritan's will to power? What logic could sustain the actions of this petty monarch of this little world?

Cosmus, student of society that he was, had his own pet theories about President Hugh Crandon. He had evolved them months previous when he learned that Reverend Mr. Crandon had called on a young instructor and demanded that he have children, and that he, Crandon, often dictated just what the few women teachers should wear. The era just past, the student of society cogitated, was especially conducive to growing a variety of despots in the national garden. Men addicted to the disease of power were common; what R. Sill was in civil life, Crandon was in domestic. R. Sill chose to dictate public morals, Hugh Crandon to regulate private manners. For to Cosmus, Crandon had always seemed bent on weaving and preserving a network of personal relations. Form, manners, the machinery of life,—never its spirit and principle,—seemed his chief concern. He chose his faculty from among the husbands of his wife's friends, or from the sons of eminent professors, who had gone before; and he strove with all that in him lay to preserve that fine mass of college traditions which finally resolved themselves into personal reminiscences of the history of a few illustrious families. Many a time Cosmus had heard the president of Crandon Hill tell how he had won the allegiance of so illustrious a financier as R. Sill to a noble institution. There was no out-looking vision in his educational addresses.

President Crandon seemed utterly suspicious of an idea. An idea was so impersonal. It usually cut through the fabric which he was energetically trying to erect and worse—it was no respecter of persons. When Cosmus had gone to the president with a plan for reaching the aliens in the city with elementary courses in social hygiene, he had answered, "Well, now that is a very novel idea, Mr. Cosmus, very novel indeed, and I shall keep it in mind."

This mind must have been an inward-opening storehouse, for no ideas ever got out. Cosmus often thought, if an idea could be properly sexed, clothed in immaculate linen, and presented at an afternoon tea, or at a meeting of the board of trustees, then Crandon might accept it, especially if it appeared with proper references. But usually ideas appear in such gross nudity, at such unexpected times, in such outlandish places, it were best to taboo them always. The old, the tried, the well-bred—these must be the custom of the college. At whatever cost, the fabric of personal relations must not be rent.

And yet, when Cosmus saw President Crandon turn toward him with the engaging smile which he knew so well how to use, so infectious was the charm of the man that he wondered if he had read the riddle of his personality aright.

"And what can I do for you?" he asked. "It's a pleasure to have you come in this way. I always crave frank relations with my faculty."

This was disarming. If Cosmus had expected coldness and deceit, he was to be disappointed.

"I have come about the strike—that is, the disagreeable aftermath of the strike."

"Yes, yes, it was very unpleasant, indeed vulgar and damaging, wasn't it? Iron City has been very fortunate up to this year to have no such disgraceful labor disturbances. But it is all over now, I understand, and quite localized. No doubt, we can congratulate ourselves on our successful emergence from this chaos, Mr. Cosmus."

Cosmus was astounded. Though he was armed with previous impressions of Reverend Hugh Crandon, still he could not adjust his mind readily to the president's easy acceptance of conditions as they were. Surprise prompted him to put his remark in the form of a question.

"So you, too, think it as spasmodic?" He was thinking of R. Sill.

"What else? The working man has never been so prosperous, so well-informed, and I should say so content. It is only when he is tampered with by well-intentioned but misguided reformers, who urge him to break the law, that he becomes a nuisance. We must have, therefore, laws to discipline the reformer. And we will, no doubt."

Was this some colossal jest? Fresh from the sight of Walt Kuhns, from the reality of war in Ezra Kimbark's death, as Cosmus was, to him President Crandon seemed some poor automatic thing chanting platitudes. The riddle of his personality was more tangled than ever. Cosmus had not lived long enough to know that men can be good local citizens, and know nothing of national problems or responsibilities. He did not know that President Crandon gave widely to charity, and was the donor of the very room at the free hospital where Walt Kuhns lay. He did not know that he was the greatest authority on Church Law in America. How could he gauge the struggle and heart-burnings that Hugh Crandon had suffered to keep alive this institution in an inimical industrial environment? All Cosmus could feel was indignation and despair; the impulse to strike, and the temptation to flee, and his only thought was, "Can all this suffering be for nothing?"

There was abrupt silence in the room, for Hugh Crandon was waiting for his caller to speak. But John Cosmus did not speak. Instead he arose as if to go, hopeless of presenting his plea to such a judge. Then the president said:

"I am glad you brought up the strike, Mr. Cosmus, for it gives me an opportunity I have long wanted."

He paused; Cosmus braced himself. "If he rebukes me," he thought, "I'll flail him."

"Of discussing," Crandon continued, "your connection with it. It has been a matter of great pain with me, with all of

us—faculty and trustees alike, that you have transgressed—
though not maliciously, I know—the noble traditions of the
college by abetting law-breakers. But I have been patient. I have
remembered your youth, and your ability, and in the face of
strong opposition have clung to you, for I have been confident
that in the end you would put yourself in harmony with the large
historical background of the institution."

President Crandon was almost warm in his manner and he
allowed the ghost of a good-humored smile to flit across his
impassive countenance, as he continued:

"You see, I am something of a radical after all. I include
radicals. When I find a man opposing me, I draw a circle and
take him in. I can't hate him, you know; that wouldn't be
Christian."

"The genteel tradition in American life," Cosmus inwardly
commented, "is here embodied admirably in you, and is this the
key to your riddle?" But he answered innocently:

"Couldn't you draw a circle, and take Walt Kuhns in, too?"

Crandon's placidity snapped.

"No," he answered sharply, "he is outside the law—and all
human respect."

"But he stands for the new day."

"That's just it. The new! The new! A man is sufficiently
condemned nowadays if he does not seek to put into practice
every random idea of an irresponsible tramp. A man is nothing
nowadays unless he is in accord with the new era—an era of mad
chaos, cheap morals and ugly manners. A man is subject to the
criticism of every callow youth if he does not familiarize himself
with every fashionable cult, every social theory, every literary
whimsy, every transient morality—whether they run counter to
age-old principles or not. What would become of the world if it
were swayed by every vagrant mind? This institution, Mr. Cosmus,
stretches back into the past for over a century; I expect it to
stretch forward into the future, endlessly. Can it endure if it flirts
with ignorance? Should it shuffle off its heritage to take on the

social theories of a Walt Kuhns? I have received this institution as a sacred trust from the hands of noble ancestors; I have slaved under its burdens, in the face of a thousand crises, to hand it on untouched by the ephemeral to the future. Colleges must embody the tried, the right, the eternal—I love this college, and by God! I shall protect it from all adventurers."

Cosmus was deeply impressed for the moment by the president's earnestness. For the first time he had peeped behind the mask which Hugh Crandon wore. But the imperturbable institutionalism of Crandon was not sacrosanct to youth.

He answered hotly: "It is either hypocrisy or stupidity that can make you pretend that democracy is not an age-old, well-tried principle; and Walt Kuhns represents the new democracy and out yonder in the world that you ignore, masses of men are preparing to burn this sacred institution down about your ears, if you don't listen. Education is for all, not some."

And he turned on his heel and walked out. Then, pausing in the hall, he retraced his steps to add another word. In the doorway he paused. The form he had left so proud and defiant was crumpled in a chair,—old wrinkled hands pressed tightly against forehead, eyes closed, lips mumbling as in prayer. Had the cause of Walt Kuhns won? Cosmus backed out thoughtfully.

Cosmus did not leave the administration building which contained the office of Hugh Crandon without a sense of awe at the unavoidable pain of the world. He could not soon forget the anguish on the old president's face, and he would have willingly spared him that but there was a new generation—the breed of Walt Kuhns—which must be looked after. Youth, impatient and strong. Ah! there is nothing so cruel as youth save, perhaps, old age.

It was not yet ten o'clock when Cosmus turned in at the Y.M.C.A. At the desk the clerk told him to call 2440.

2440? Who was that? Then he remembered—Margaret Morton.

"How long ago was this call rung in?" he asked.

"About ten minutes ago—and she seemed awfully anxious."

Cosmus called Morton's and had Margaret on the wire at once. She wanted him to "come up—now—at once—please." With some reluctance he decided to go, not without misgivings, however. He remembered; and as he walked along he discovered that the old fragrant charm of Margaret still lingered near him.

She opened the door before he could ring the bell, and ushered him into the dim empty parlor. He looked around expectantly, and she explained that her father and mother had gone to a neighbor's.

"They don't go anywhere any more unless I urge them." She paused. Cosmus was conscious of the murmur of her silken skirts. "And besides, I wanted to talk with you alone."

Cosmus marveled at her. Her face was paler and thinner, and she looked older, yes, and her figure was matured, but the old unfathomable witchery of eyes, bosom and hair had not faded in the slightest. Margaret Morton would always be a beautiful woman, yes, and a dangerous one. She sat easily on the edge of the chair, after the first conventional greeting, not embarrassed (Margaret never was) but sunk into thoughtfulness—a state quite unnatural to her. In his heightened imagination, she seemed like a gay butterfly, water-soaked and wind-blown in some dark retreat. Suddenly she explained why she had sent for him. She said, without perturbation save for a quick fluttering, sideways glance:

"Oh! Professor Cosmus, I'm afraid Raymond Sill is dead."

"Dead? What do you mean?" he answered.

"Killed. I've always been afraid he would be. He was so reckless. I've warned him, but he paid no attention. He said he had a hunch he couldn't be and all that. Now I'm afraid he is dead."

"You're excited and perhaps just imagining it. What makes you think so?"

"No, I'm calm," she answered, "and I think I'm glad. You see, he was not very good to me."

Then she told him, not too coherently, of when she had last

seen Raymond three nights before at the Country Club: she said nothing of their quarrel, but she told him of the aeroplane against the moon, tipsy, careening into the shadow of the trees.

"You see, I thought it always flew that way until I read this." She held up the extra edition of the *Republic-Despatch.* "And then I remembered it did seem funny even then and how something took hold of me here inside, some fear—some joy. Oh, to think he may be lying out there now!"

"This is serious, Margaret. Have you called up the police?"

"I didn't dare. Maybe he's in Chicago,—only gone away, and then he would laugh at me."

"But a man's life might hang on this information; perhaps ____"

She looked up, startled.

"Raymond's, you mean?"

"No; some one must be held."

"But I want you to go and look for Raymond. It's just out Trimway Road, next to the big hill. Can't you go, won't you go, now? At once—early in the morning?"

"I'll go on one condition, Margaret—that I can notify the police of my intentions. Let's see—to-morrow's Friday. I have only one class, but there's regular faculty meeting. Still, I'll go. Of course, I'll go."

"I knew you would help me."

He made her go into details as to the approximate position of the falling plane. "Wait, couldn't you go with me?" he interrupted.

She shrank back, visibly startled.

"No, oh no. We might find him."

The look on her face—the fear, awe, amazement, were almost laughable.

At the open door they paused for a moment, looking out. The mild December night, the same that had enfolded John two hours before in the bliss of solitude, enfolded them both now. How responsive nature can be, colored by human moods. The night, which two hours ago seemed to him paternal, now was palpitant with passion.

"Almost like spring," Margaret said, "and there's a moon."

"It's been a wonderful day," he answered.

She came close to him and looked out. They stood for a moment crowded in the frame of the door, thinking of other such moments, and the might-have-beens of the yesterdays. She laid a warm, soft hand on his arm, and said:

"Do you think, Professor Cosmus, that a girl who has committed a great, great wrong, ever has a right to marry?"

Somehow the question did not come as a surprise to him. It was the kind of a question he would expect of Margaret. She was looking up at him eager, deep-eyed, receptive; he marked how her bosom curved under the sway of her breath. Margaret was serious.

"Why, of course, all of us sociologists believe that, provided ——"

"Provided what?"

"Well, that she doesn't make the same mistake over, is refined and chastened by her first experience, and perfectly frank in her confession of fault."

"I confess, then," she answered softly. "Raymond was the man, and if you find him dead——"

He did not get the full significance of her quick retort at first, and when he did, he trembled wonderingly, drew back, afraid of her challenge, and pushed past her to the walk. He stopped there, for she was saying almost with something of her old gayety:

"Aren't you going to say good-night?"

"Good-night, Margaret—and don't marry too quickly, not unless the right man comes along."

She did not answer. He heard the door close behind her.

In his room, a quarter of an hour later, the open letter of Ezra Kimbark recalled the grief that had started the day. He threw himself, without undressing, full length upon the bed.

"What a day it has been," he said.

It seemed to him that he had experienced all things in that narrow cycle of twelve hours—grief, exaltation, hate, love—no, not love—he had not seen Sarah Blackstone.

Hours later, when he arose to undress, he could see from the open window the streets below, and far across the city, above the silent houses, in the moonlight, the expansive fields and the hills so enduring and so still.

25 The Haunted Wood

The next morning Cosmus donned his corduroy hunting suit, took his gun, and after a light breakfast set out to follow up Margaret Morton's clue. He stopped at the police station and placed his evidence before the chief. Contrary to his expectations, he found the officer more than interested.

"I never did believe that the strikers had anything to do with the boy's disappearance. Kuhns wouldn't have stood for it—it hain't like him anyway," Chief Garrigan said.

"You know him, then?"

"Every one does."

"And the strike has fallen through completely?"

"They closed the *Labor Defense* office yesterday."

Chief Garrigan was giving orders as he spoke, and two officers and a machine soon stood at the door. The men were introduced as Officer Clark and Officer Stillson. Cosmus at once agreed with them that they should all part company at the Stillwell farms, which lay across the river from the Country Club, and comb the land thoroughly for sight of the fallen plane. All three were to keep in touch with each other by reporting every hour or so by rural telephone to Chief Garrigan.

Iron City was hardly awake when they left the town and followed the winding river road north. As they climbed the ridge they saw across the still water Sill's factory smoking at their feet and Cosmus wondered if Raymond's father had gone down to work yet. Of what was the great power thinking now?

Clark and Stillson, not inclined to include "the perfesor" in their talk, were discussing that very point.

"The old man," Clark was saying, giving his stiff thumb a jab toward the factory, "don't say much, but I guess he feels it, though."

"I heard he laid it on the election," answered Stillson maliciously. "He thinks the world is coming to the end, now that Hughes got it in the neck."

"He told Daggett yesterday that he would have rather lost the strike than his boy."

"I suppose so, but he didn't bring him up right. That boy ought to have been in France this very day."

"Then he would have been a sure enough goner."

"But that's different."

The machine had cut down through a valley where a few banks of snow choked the hollows, and had left the smoking factory behind. The morning was clear and still, the crows flapped over the brown fields, and Cosmus was conscious again of the teasing wires running along ahead of them, in undeviating lines, on and on. What did the River of Wires mean to him? Was this common thing his beauty? He concluded, "Every one must have his moments of mysticism and those wires give mine to me."

At the Stilwell farms, the officers were inclined to kid "the perfesor" about his gun.

"Perfesor," said Clark, "I have a feeling in my bones that you will find the corpse. You won't get scairt, will you, at the sight of a body, being not used to it? A dead body gives queer feelings, you know."

"Oh, you forget the gun, Stillson," put in Officer Clark.

"If I find it, gentlemen, I shan't need the gun, you know."

"Save for the crows; they're nasty birds," Stillson returned.

"And say, Perfesor, there are some old quarries off there near the river; don't you be falling into them, and breaking your neck."

Cosmus replied pleasantly: "To be frank, men, I don't believe any of us will find Raymond. After all, Miss Morton has very little reason to believe she saw the plane fall. It's what you call a hunch, you know. Now, look, it would be that spot over yonder, according to her description. Just in line with that old sycamore tree."

They made for that section of the field lying along the wood, but they saw only bare ground. Farther on they saw something which looked like debris, but it proved to be only an old white log. They moved off from this center in diverging radii, scanning every foot of ground. It was slow and harrowing work. John could see that the officers even in spite of their jocularity were sobered by the thought of coming upon the soulless body of a man. John himself felt uncomfortable, and the thought crossed his mind that this must be the way scavengers feel; crows were flapping blackly across the white hollows of the wood. He did not allow the distaste, however, to decrease his watchfulness. Conscientiously, rod by rod, he scanned every field and wood in turn, moving far off from the others until about noon, when he came upon a farm house.

He entered and called Chief Garrigan. The chief advised him to come in.

"Clark and Stillson have been in for half an hour," he told Cosmus. "They said that they had combed their two sections with a fine-toothed comb, and found nothing. We'll send a machine for you."

"Never mind about the machine and tell Clark," Cosmus replied, "that I was wise after all about the gun. For if I can get a bite to eat, I'm going hunting. I'll send him some game."

The farmer's wife had already set out ham and eggs and buckwheat cakes with thick corn-syrup on the table, and when Cosmus had satisfied his hunger, he went out into the fields again with none of his old feelings of awe. He was done with this gruesome business, and the sun was glistening on river and field and wires and he was strong.

As he walked along he thought of Walt Kuhns. He must devise a way of saving Kuhns from any implication in a murder for vengeance. But how? He racked his mind in vain. After an hour of fruitless devising, under the spell of rhythmic walking, he slipped into a more pleasant vein of thought. Receding far behind him were the city, the strike, the war, and he carried something of the sense of aloofness to life, a mood which had come to him so vividly the night before when he had sat alone under the sycamore. He saw that Walt Kuhns was not to be greatly pitied even if the strike had failed, for his day was coming, was dawning, even as Sarah Blackstone had declared. He saw, too, more plainly than he ever had before, that Kuhns had within himself the profound potentialities of happiness. He was self-urged, and nothing—no, not even Sill, or the defection of the strikers—could touch the leader. It seemed, too, to Cosmus as he recalled Kuhns—so noble in form—that nature itself had favored this man whom society had cast out. From these thoughts he passed to Sarah again. He had seen her only once in the five days since the fracas at Boyne's shops; she had recovered from the shock completely, but she was not going back to Boyne's office. "I just can't, John," she had said. Cosmus remembered these words vividly now, and the look of pure helplessness in her eyes. "I've been a fool," he thought. "I'll go to her to-night. How lovely she is."

He must have been walking two hours, and he had reached a large knoll; as he looked back he could see no sign of the city, but strange to see, caught in the contour of the hills, there was the Country Club miles away. And when he turned to look forward he saw beneath him a road and beyond a gray valley, bare save for a great clump of tamarack trees, the kind that appear occasionally in the Middle West.

He had not once thought of Raymond Sill or Margaret Morton since noon. As he came down the knoll, he remembered them; but he had dismissed them from his mind again by the time he reached the fence that bordered the road. There was not a human being nor a house in sight. Gray stillness—not quite peace.

He put his hand on the fence post, to leap over, but did not leap. A thought, irrationally emerging, arrested him. It was of America. He had been watching Washington narrowly since the recent election of Mr. Wilson, and he had detected an unwonted nervousness on the part of the administration. What did it mean? Then the thought, which had arrested his leap. "What if Germany resumes unrestricted submarine warfare?" He leaned against the post. "War! But would America be ready?"

He clambered over the fence, and crossed the road, for the first time aware that he was tired. If he were going to get any game, he had better get it quickly. He decided to skirt the tamarack grove on the left, but found it much larger than he had thought. He left the road behind and was about to plunge into the woods when he came upon two country boys. They seemed to be doing nothing.

"Any game hereabouts, boys?" he asked.

The older answered:

"Yes, in the woods, but you mustn't go in."

"Doesn't your father like to have hunters?"

"He don't care."

"Then why shouldn't I go where the game is?"

"It's haunted."

Cosmus smiled.

"Father told us all about it. A great white bird was shot through the heart while it was still in the air, and when a bird on the wing is shot through the heart, its body flies straight up and its spirit comes down to stay in the woods."

"But why should I fear the bird?" John answered, "when I want a rabbit? Is there a road on the other side that will lead me back to Iron City?"

"Sure, but it's shorter to go back that way," the little boy answered, pointing over his shoulder.

John smiled, and started off pushing the bushes aside with one arm. It was a good place for a ghost,—green and still, and now snow-covered. He had not gone far when suddenly he was out in a circular clearing,—and he saw what he did not want to see. The sight almost stopped his breath. There in the white snow was something not snow or brush, with something dark beneath it.

Shocked, he ran forward. Raymond Sill was lying there. The fragile airship was now but a heap of rags and staves; its occupant had evidently loosened the straps, which held him in, and when the machine struck, had fallen, dead before he lit, face forward, one arm beneath his head as if asleep. There was something pathetic in the posture. Cosmus bent over the thing that had been life. Raymond's face was bruised and grim and terrible.

The gun had fallen from the hunter's hand, and he stood upright, wondering and helpless. He saw for the first time why men praise the living after they die. In truth it is but praise of death. This mysterious going-away of the breath, this subtle thieving of motion, light and energy—one can not come into the presence of this with evil upon his lips. Let the black world of wrong recede far away from this all-mastering mystery. The hunter looked around, and was aware of the beauty of Raymond's sepulcher. The falling plane had barely scraped the trees above and brought the wayward occupant into a haven, still and immortally green. But the loosened straps? Had Raymond taken his own life?

Cosmus's thoughts went back to the morning, to what Officer Stillson had said: "That boy ought to have been in France this very day." That was the pathos of it, the pathos of unfulfillment. Raymond, the parasite, was parasite still. How different all would have been, if he had been Pilot Sill of the French Aviation Corps!

These flashing thoughts left Cosmus with the realization that some one was tittering behind him.

Startled, he turned; it was only the two boys he had left at the edge of the wood.

"Does it stink?" they called, and ran back tittering. But one was pale and sick before he reached the covert of the trees.

"Boys, boys," Cosmus called, "have you a phone at your house? No, don't come back here. Lead me to it."

He glanced again at the corpse, and then started with the boys across the fields. They did not talk much. The boys confessed that they had known that the body was there. "We found it three days ago, but was afraid to tell Dad, and Mother is sick of the fever." That was all.

The winter's day was almost ended as they hurried across the fields. The boys had to run to keep up with Cosmus, who was busy with his own thoughts. His mind, though clear, was not untroubled. He was thinking; this heap of rags and sticks and bones, was this all there was left of the proud human bird, which sat upon a cloud and rode the ranging winds? How like a fable of all our civilization; the vanity of flight; the lofty fabric of man's scientific imagination brought down to this overpowering bathos!

In a few minutes he was talking to Chief Garrigan

"I've found him," Cosmus said.

"What? The king of the Jack-Rabbits?" the chief bellowed good-naturedly.

"No, man, Raymond Sill—dead."

"Honest to God? Where?"

"At Burgund's place six miles west of Stillwell farms. Send an ambulance and help."

In two hours the sad cortege entered Iron City. What the other men thought, Cosmus did not know, but all he could think of was who was to tell R. Sill.

At the police station, besides the chief there was Margaret, a very pale and restrained Margaret, and her father, Carl Morton, dim and sad.

"Margaret thought that you would find him," Morton said, "though it seems impossible."

"Has any one telephoned Mr. Sill?" Cosmus asked.

The chief and Morton looked at each other significantly,

"No doubt the chief has," Margaret answered.

"No," Carl Morton said slowly, "I told the chief that I would go up. Mr. Sill has not treated us well, but he's a father, too, and

I'm going up to him."

Carl said to the men hovering hesitantly around the back of the ambulance, "Wait a few minutes, then bring the body to his house." And Cosmus, somewhat amazed at the turn events had taken, saw the foreman fade away in the gathering darkness.

When he had told the chief the particulars of the search; the accidental discovery of the body; when he had described the spot in the tamarack wood where the corpse lay; retold the story of the two boys; and had offered the hypothesis of suicide, Cosmus added thoughtfully:

"At any rate, chief, this clears Walt Kuhns."

Garrigan's eyes met his sharply for a moment and turned away; then he answered gruffly.

"Well, that won't make a damned bit of difference now— Kuhns is dead."

Cosmus wanted to say "No, no, that's unfair; that's unjust." But he only looked blank and asked, "When? How? I thought he was getting along all right."

"Just kind o' faded away, I guess. A nurse found him sitting up in bed, leaning against a pillow, stone dead, an hour ago."

"I'll go over there," Cosmus answered.

On the street, a few minutes after, he found himself caught in the five o'clock rush, but gratefully he plunged into the current of humanity sweeping by. He welcomed the contact with life. He enjoyed touching elbows with living men. He delighted in the faces of joy and eagerness flowing past. He felt the old primordial joy of gregariousness, the sense of companionship in time of trouble, the mystic union through words unspoken, or hands untouched, with brother souls everywhere.

How good, how common, how joyous was this great turbulent sea of the general life.

And for the first time Iron City did not seem indifferent to Walt Kuhns. It was Walt Kuhns, and he was it.

The hush of carpeted corridors, the swish of muffled doors, the tread of padded feet at the hospital fell upon his senses with peculiar poignancy. It was almost as good a place to die in as Raymond had had yonder in the evergreen grove. Like a shuttle, Cosmus was weaving these two lives, so estranged, together. Of this office he was conscious. Some sudden flood of meaning enveloped life. The events of the day were no longer mere links in a nightmare of death, but great realities. Are all men thus lifted out of the commonplace at sight of death?

A nurse explained to Cosmus that the hospital had been trying to get in touch with him by telephone for an hour; that Kuhns had died much as Chief Garrigan had said. She concluded,

"He must have been writing when his heart stopped. We have left the papers just as he had arranged them for you to see. You can come in."

She led the way to the room, which bore the plate, though Cosmus did not know it, "The gift of Reverend Hugh Crandon, LL.D."

He was grateful for the screens around the bed that shut out the sight of the still thing behind. The nurse left them alone.

Half-guiltily, he glanced at the papers. They did not seem to be of much importance, just scribblings, in the nervous, weak hand of a sick man. One seemed to be an editorial. It was headed,

"WHO KEEPS THE LAW?"

Then followed a brief statement that R. Sill had taken back to his factory all union men, provided they made affidavits to the effect that they had severed their allegiance to any and every labor organization.

Following this, in cold irony, was a section from the injunction which Judge Dunbar had granted to R. Sill, which had been served on the strikers on that fatal afternoon of the riot.

"Or who shall coerce or compel any person to enter into an agreement not to unite with or become a member of any labor organization as a condition of his securing employment or continuing therein, shall be punished by a fine of not more than

$500 nor less than a hundred dollars."

That was all.

Cosmus sought another page. Scrawled feebly across its face was—

"My eyes have seen the glory of the coming of—"

The words trailed off into indecipherable marks. But they had power to recall to Cosmus eight months before, a night when he had heard a voice—a man's voice—singing through the darkness. Had that voice been the voice of Walt Kuhns?

Cosmus went softly into the hall and found a seat in the shadow, where he could be quiet for a moment. He saw the nurses, like white dreams, slipping silently in and out of rooms. He heard a suppressed groan; subdued laughter; hushed whispers. He caught the cloying sweet of ether. He was bent on bringing his mind back to normality, on seeing things as it was fitting for a college professor, a student of society, to see them.

He was surprised to discover how little he had seen of Walt Kuhns; he was startled to find how near the man was to him. That outlaw dead was to him like a brother. In his death there was no pain, only the full sense of possession, of having gained something. He remembered the first time he had seen Kuhns at the factory, cursing; he remembered the man's inability to remember his name; "Comer" he would say invariably instead of Cosmus; he recalled his passionate allegiance to his Master; his patience, his capacity for indignation, his cool logic, courage and fairness; he remembered his eloquent face with the scar, and the crown of gray hair. Cosmus found that he knew this man better than he knew all his colleagues at the college with whom he had daily intercourse. What was Walt Kuhns's power? Was it giving all he had for a cause? And his charm? That was a deeper problem which belonged to the incalculable powers of personality. But it was probably his gift for gregariousness. He knew better than all other men the common touch. And the common touch? Who had it? Who in this onrushing age of cities and internationalism, dare be without it?

Cosmus's meditations were broken by the shrieking of factory whistles. They drove into that subjective word of his the iron wedge of reality. Who dare be without the common touch? Such men as R. Sill and Hugh Crandon? He, Cosmus, himself lacked it pitiably. He himself lacked all of Kuhns's virtues, his passionate surrender to a cause, his gift for gregariousness. But he would lack them no more. He could give something, too, to the age that was yet to come.

It was about 5:30; there was a faculty meeting that night, and he had time to bring Walt Kuhns to Crandon Hill.

As he went down the hospital steps, he met a line of workmen from the factory, and they seemed, too, almost like brother men.

26 Bonds of Class

Just as he was, in hunting suit of corduroy, fresh from the deaths of Raymond Sill and Walt Kuhns, with their profound significance, John Cosmus entered the meeting of Crandon Hill's faculty. He was unaware that his tardiness and unusual costume and his eerie appearance seemed singularly out of place in that dignified assembly. He had forgotten completely about them. He sat down in an obscure corner trying to collect his thoughts, staring somewhat blankly at the painting of Professor Mather, deceased, lately added to the walls, beside those dim Puritanic faces of the other Mather, first president, and the old philosopher, Professor Jason. To Cosmus, there was encouragement in the benignant face of Professor Mather.

Across the room, Dean Georgia Summers was whispering to her neighbor, "It was just like that Mr. Cosmus to plan this dramatic entrance. He is always seeking the unusual."

For a moment Cosmus thought that the faculty had deviated into a discussion of some essentials of education, for he heard many grandiloquent words concerning the "welfare of our students," the "psychic factors in education," "the amenities of human life," "the *sine qua non* and *raison d'être* of." But as he became more familiar with the controversy, and as his mind lost the edge of its excitement, he discovered that the question in hand was whether class-bells should ring ten or seven minutes before the hour. Over this all-important question, the faculty of the college was divided, and the learned school men were having the time of their lives. The somewhat fragile nature of the subject did not deter them; they showed no pity; they allowed the glitter of their minds to play in and out of the delicate fabric with all the brilliancy of fine needle-like instruments.

Cosmus heard explained the science of bell-ringing, the philosophy of bell-ringing, the psychology of bell-ringing and the social etiquette of bell-ringing. No one could question the excellence of the minds thus employed; here was masterful logic, splendid imagery, and subtle reasoning. Here was the learning of twenty centuries, lifted to a crowning height by the sheer intellectual force of thirty well-trained intellects, and dashed upon—a flea. It was as if Darwin were writing his immortal book on whether five or six o'clock was the best time for dinner; it was as if Plato, lost in the maze of scholasticism, were discussing the question of how many devils may dance on the point of a needle; or as if Jesus were sitting with the Pharisees in the temple drawing up a code forbidding the plucking of corn on the Sabbath. It was all of this and more. It was solemn, it was pompous, and bitter—with never a glint of the salt of humor.

But human nature is not made of iron, and after a while the contestants wore themselves out, and the ball of controversy, put so vigorously into play, came back to rest. The resolution was laid on the table.

Then President Crandon, who had sat quietly through the debate, asked passively if there were any more business. There was a moment of silence in which Cosmus suddenly found himself upon his feet looking around into the faces of his colleagues. They were not sympathetic faces nor even comprehending faces; most of them were openly hostile or contemptuous. And for a minute, he looked uncertainly and timidly around, as persons acting upon impulse often do when facing an audience and found himself wondering foolishly and futilely, "Why am I standing up here?" And he moistened his lips and said nothing.

But President Crandon had recognized him. Then, gasping

as one suddenly plunged into cold water, Cosmus began to speak quite automatically and with the first word, uncertainty in his mind, like clouds, rolled back and disclosed a discourse so orderly in plan that he was surprised that it was his.

With the first sentence, he regained assurance, and when Professor Erickson, on the other side of the room, began to whisper and titter, he stopped short and said:

"Mr. President, have I the floor?"

"You have."

"Then, if I am disturbed again, I shall take the interruption as a personal insult, and by all that's decent, I'll act accordingly."

There was no more disturbance.

It was not an oration that Cosmus was giving, but a plain talk. It lacked the polish of either Professor Clarke's or Professor Erickson's set speeches. Often it was disjointed, but as he progressed he found that they were listening—in spite of themselves.

*"Fellow-teachers, Americans," he began. "Goldminers in the Klondyke fields of Alaska have looked across the frozen thread of Bering Strait, this winter, and seen the great plains of Siberia towering away in the distance. The farthest verge—the last frontier—of this new world has suddenly come upon the back door of the old; and for once, for the first time, in the history of mankind, we are one world geographically. The frontiers of the world are gone. Where are the New Zealands, the Australias, the West of these United States? Where are the new worlds for Europe? Suddenly we people of this age are turned in upon ourselves, face to face with the problem of human relationships. No more, as our fathers did, can the democrat secede from a native autocracy and seek a new world, there to build a happier home. Democracy, liberalism, cooperation—all the virtues of the pioneer—must fight now for existence throughout the world. The frontiers are gone!

---

* There is here no attempt to report John Cosmus's speech in full.

"Geographically one, the states of the world are also a commercial unit. Interlocking directorates, vast shipping interests, swift couriers of electricity and steam, a flood of books, explorers and travelers, have leveled all distances and made Peking a suburb of London.

"We citizens of Iron City—God help us—have been given not a town but a world to live in. The citizens of Berlin, Hull and Bordeaux have been given the same world."

He paused and was aware of the stillness of the room, and he wondered why his hearers did not interrupt. Their faces showed displeasure; but no sound came from them. The president lounged tolerantly in his deep armchair.

"And we have no more known how to adjust ourselves to world-relationships than children would. The world is geographically, commercially one, but the world's people are more various than the world's races. They are separated by corroding prejudice, and superstition, by medieval symbolism and prehistoric impulses, by barbaric ideals and predatory interests. The art of erecting bonds between men, which is education, has not yet kept pace with the art of destroying barriers between men, which is science applied.

"In the first experiment of living together we have failed utterly, failed miserably, made angels weep, and fallen to scrapping like school boys over the ruins of the world.

"For Germany, the bully, with all gift for organization, has learned first how to live in gangs. An expert in socialization, it has socialized more error than truth. A super trust, it would monopolize all trade. A great community, it would Germanize the universe by means of the sword. It is the narrow, local mind of the village butcher nationalized. It is the apotheosis of class-thinking. It is the dog-in-the-manger trying to ascend a world throne."

Here a thin rustle of applause blew about the room. The audience seemed less impatient, less hostile, but only for a moment.

"But not all Prussians live in Germany, not all Prussians are Prussians by blood. We have Prussians in Iron City, in America. All men who stand for class are Prussians. The misguided manufacturers, who broke the strike with the heavy rod of privileged law, and destroyed Walt Kuhns, are Prussians. We who in our Pharisaism closed Dover Street to the traffic of aliens are Prussians. All men who are not respecters of human personality of whatever color, custom, race or religion are Prussians."

Dean Georgia Summers was fumbling with her hat; Professor Erickson was drumming almost audibly upon his teeth with the frayed end of a lead pencil; President Hugh Crandon was sitting up straight—with flushed face. But no one interrupted.

"It is plain, gentlemen, that what is needed is a deep abiding liberalism—a flood of ideas—of truth—that will make class-mindedness impossible. We must erect bonds between men as fast as science destroys barriers. We must increase justice. We must lay bare the sham of democracy, the hypocrisy, that makes us talk of the land of the free and then deprives men, however humble, of the right of free labor. Our only hope is to make our colleges evangels of world-mindedness."

Cosmus saw Professor Clarke raise his head as if to deny, and his hands twitch nervously.

"Ah, yes, we speak of liberal education, better say illiberal. How can this college be liberal, when R. Sill, if not in name, is in actuality the president of this institution? How can the Crandon Hill of Professor Mather be liberal if it closes its gates to Serb and Slav and Italian because they are not New England born? Are we the protector or betrayer of the average mind?

"We are seeing this world thrown into a crucible, the old barriers leveled, the old lines erased, and we are presuming that the world will come out with pretty much the same patterns traced upon its face. It can not; it will not. All the barriers of race, color, geography will be burned away. Out of this world war will come just two peoples—the people who believe in all, and the people who believe in cliques; the liberal minded and the class-minded; the kaisers like R. Sill, and the common man like Walt Kuhns. Out of the world struggle will come one or the other—as victor.

"Americans, it lies with Crandon Hill College to bring the world to Iron City. Provincialism, once the virtue of American life, is now its curse. If America is to endure, it must leave America and go over to the world. We keepers of ideas must forsake machine-made formalism and go over to life. We must forsake the past and go over to the future. Yes, gentlemen of the faculty, we must adopt the Chautauqua brand of education, if that means reaching the people with world-ideas, for on such education real and not fancied democracy depends."

He paused, there was a rustle of skirts and Dean Georgia Summers had haughtily swept out of the room. The speaker grew confused, groped for some conclusion, failed, and sat down glowing with an inward sense of relief.

"Any further business?" snapped President Crandon.

"Mr. President, I move we adjourn." The voice of Erickson was impatient and severe.

The motion was seconded, and before it could be formally put, every member of Crandon Hill's faculty fled out of the room without so much as a glance at John Cosmus. Once Cosmus caught the eye of Professor James, disciple of Dewey, flashing encouragement; but the little professor, too, passed out.

"Five children and a debt on a house make a man cautious of expressing opinions. Thank God! I'm free," thought Cosmus. Then he was alone.

But with solitariness came reaction. He felt lonely and useless. All action seemed futile. He sat down in the empty room foolishly staring at his hands, and past them to the hunting suit; in that moment he got the other man's point of view. He saw the faculty as they streamed out into the dark, warm with the sense of well-being; he experienced with them the acute sense of difference between them and him; he saw them as they saw themselves, the tried guardians of the tried, backed by the authority of the past and the prestige of the great universities, and of public opinion; he saw them glowing in the sense of comradeship, arm in arm, thirty to one, sneering and indignant. He could hear them say, "How utterly sophomoric." He saw himself in contrast a mere boy projecting an untried revolutionary scheme. No wonder he had failed; the difference made him laugh. Some day, he consoled himself, some great crisis will shake them out of their lethargy.

He found his hat, and went out. Loneliness did not disappear in the darkness. In his mind, he followed his colleagues home to smiling wives and cheerful hearths; and the thought did not make him stronger. Did it pay? Did discrimination pay? Long ago, he might have been on the road to a scholarly, cloistered life, with no problems, save lovely hypothetical problems of pure mathematics. And a wife.

Like a sensible young man realizing that he was hungry, famishing, he went *not* to the little Bohemian cafe where he and Sarah had had so many cups of tea, but to the hotel and ate as youth should. After this meal, in spite of languor of body and mind, he went out into the streets again, because he could not face his lonely room. He went straight to Sarah's house. She alone seemed capable of destroying this loneliness, and of uniting him with men again. He would be very kind to Sarah to-night. With this resolve, he ran up the steps and impatiently rang the bell. He could not believe what the woman who opened the door told him—that Sarah had left town.

"She has gone to Chicago, I think," she added, "as much as three days ago."

Cosmus stood a moment indecisively at the gate, smiled, shrugged his shoulders, and said softly to himself, "Damned if I care." But care he did; before he reached his room he had resolved to go to France.

27 Two Funerals

There were two funerals in Iron City on the same day. R. Sill, with Carl Morton and Margaret, sat together before the great crowd at the First Church, mourning Raymond. His funeral was the most costly and grand Iron City had ever seen. There was pomp and ritual.

Out Osgood way, Walt Kuhns was buried in the negro cemetery. Cosmus went. There he met for the first time, Mary, the Lithuanian woman, Duke, the negro statesman, Grover, and Jerry Mulvaney. There were many others whom Cosmus did not meet or know; he had not realized before that there were so many strange faces in Iron City. Girls, who looked as if they were stenographers, or shop clerks; men who might have been book-keepers; the entire chapters of the carpenters, barbers and tinsmiths unions; scores and scores of workmen from Sill's plant, which had shut down in honor of Raymond; every one of the city's thirty nationalities was represented; a few merchants; these made up the assembly. They stood with uncovered heads out under the gray sky, and listened to a deacon in the Greek church chant a simple requiem. A chorus of men's voices sang "My eyes have seen the glory of the coming of the Lord."

Jerry Mulvaney, a chastened and sombered Mulvaney, in a melodious voice read a psalm, and a verse or two "from a poet," he said; Cosmus recognized the lines as Whitman's "I Dreamed in a Dream." That was all. No, not quite all. In truth, there was no pomp and ritual but every love has its ritual, and the love of these men for Walt Kuhns expressed itself in a rite, which may have lacked beauty, but not sincerity or dignity. As the plain coffin was lowered into the grave, Jerry Mulvaney said:

"Friends of Walt Kuhns, in recognition of his services to us all, and in the faith in him and in his cause, with its ultimate triumph, I have pleasure to inform you that I have here for distribution mementoes of our noble and honored brother."

With that he distributed from a basket into eager hands buttons from Walt Kuhns's coat, locks of hair and other souvenirs. Then the damp sand was dashed upon the coffin, and the crowd solemnly dispersed.

As Cosmus turned away, with the full sense of Kuhns's final triumph, Jerry Mulvaney whispered in his ear.

"Say, Professor, we've handled Daggett all right. He is on his way now by foot to Dayton, where he can find fellows more to his liking."

That night, on his return to town, John Cosmus wrote the following letter to Sarah Blackstone:

Dear Sarah,
(That was the first and fifth salutation that he had penned. The other three were, "Dear Playmate," "Dear Friend," "Sweetheart." The separate notes to each salutation were in harmony with the keynotes he struck.)

I was surprised to hear that you had left Iron City, and I am writing to ask if you are to return. If so, when?

You will be interested to know that I have made my one grand effort "to make them see," and that I have failed. Now Iron City is a tomb.

There seems nothing for me to do, but go to France. But before I go, I must see you.

Yours ever,
COSMUS.

He waited three days for an answer, and then he wrote again.

In those three days he tasted the bitter fruit of social ostracism. The boycott set up by his colleagues, on the evening of his talk at faculty meeting, was of long duration. At first Cosmus tried to convince himself that the coldness he detected in his acquaintances was fancied, a projection of his own mood. But after he had tried to break through it several times, he could not doubt its reality, or its sharpness. Nothing was going to happen as a result of his speech, save ostracism, and that was worse than open hostility.

Cosmus was hardly honest enough to acknowledge the justice of this punishment. He did not at once see that he had boldly cut across the precious bonds of class, and yet that he still expected his colleagues to include him amicably in the pleasant circle of social relationships. He had failed to show proper respect for the age and honored service of Reverend Hugh Crandon, president of the college. He, a mere youth, a teacher with only an instructor's rank, had taken upon himself to instruct his superiors and seniors. To his colleagues, he was a kind of vagrant tramping the highways of the world, indifferent to the ties of family, church and state. To them, he seemed intent merely on destroying, not on creating. Suspicious ever of ideas, they suspected the bearer of them. They could not exonerate him from ulterior selfish motives. And yet, they were not strong enough, they were too thin and watery in feeling, too utterly lacking in conviction, to strike at him openly, and to dislodge him. There might be something in what he said after all!

Cosmus was in danger, too, he saw now, of becoming a mere Abstraction, a thin bloodless Idea striding menacingly across the world. That was the trouble of espousing principles, one was likely to forget all human ties, all the lovely, joyous personal relationships which made life not a mere battle, but a song.

He might have known the passion of sacrifice for a cause; or the brotherly abnegation that a comrade might lift the flag one hillock higher; or the solemn lunacy of surrender to an ideal beyond greed and grasp; but could he know the exquisite spirit of sit-and-talk, which unites friends, the gentle blending of spirit in spirit, which is the fine flavor of all family companionship? There was Ezra Kimbark, cut off from him too completely by a devotion to a romantic past, and Walt Kuhns, dead before his time; had he made enough of these chances for human companionship?

By some such reflections as these Cosmus came to see, by means of the truly painful ostracism of his professional coworkers, something of what he was missing, and when he did see it, he was filled with bitter remorse that he had not bound Sarah Blackstone to him by more lasting filaments of friendship. Passion—the warm grasp of hands, the impact of lips—these are the winged messengers of the intellect and soul, and these must leap between lovers before they really may become friends.

He recalled all the happy moments he had spent with Sarah and he remembered with positive pain the many times when her joyous, child-like spirit had seemed crushed by the too weighty problems of the world, which he had mercilessly laid upon it.

"Sarah, Sarah," he thought. "Have you been a child all this time, longing for play and laughter?"

He knew that it was more necessary than ever that he see Sarah Blackstone before he went to France, but all he could do was to wait and suffer, for much genuine misery is wrapped up in thwarted social instincts. He had almost decided to go to Chicago and seek her when he received a note, postmarked Iron City, stating that she was at the home of Mother Curtis.

28 Understandings

"I just ran away from all this," Sarah said simply. She and John stood on a hill which had not yet lost all its heritage of winter snow, overlooking the city. The slate hues of a March twilight were sifting down over the spires and stacks of the town; to the north the sky was all red—almost like blood—from the furnace fires of the Sill plant. They could see railroad trains and interurban cars slip in and out among the trees, and farther on, disappear into the precincts of the town itself, but they did not catch the murmur of traffic or industry where they stood. All was silence, peace.

Sarah finished, "though I must confess that it does not look so hideous now from the hill."

"It never seemed so beautiful to me," answered John.

He glanced at her questioningly. Somehow their first walk, since her return, had not been a complete success. He had not found it easy—no, not so easy as formerly—to confide in her. Constraint tied their tongues, and missing the speech of hands intertwined, these two speechless lovers were tossed rudderless upon the untried sea of passion. This afternoon they had not welcomed silences. So Sarah was saying hastily:

"I just had to hear some good music. Do you realize that music, the one art that is peculiarly nonclass, is wholly a class project in America? One can't hear anything save ragtime outside of the large centers."

John was not especially interested in sociology at that moment.

"Some day," she continued, "the government will realize that it is more essential to control the arts—music and the drama—for its people than it is to carry mail."

He nodded assent, absentmindedly, wondering if he and she would ever find that moment of understanding for which he knew they were both groping. And he despaired. She seemed too impersonal; and yet, he could vividly recall those moments in the past when their spirits somehow had met and merged. She seemed to be the only human being who shared with him union with the general life. Perhaps that was all. Perhaps Sarah was just another comrade like Walt Kuhns?

She was saying, "How dark it is already. Hadn't we better be going?"

"I suppose we had."

It was over then? This was the end? He looked away from the town across the fields, and suddenly his eye was arrested by a path which led to the wooded hills beyond. It seemed to invite exploration and to offer escape from the town and problems into the passionate quietude of love.

"Are you tired?" he asked.

"No, but I thought you were—of my talk."

He ignored her petulance.

"Let's stay out a while longer, then. Will you, Sarah?"

"If you want to."

And so they turned to take the path.

Sarah was vaguely angry and hurt. In fact, without in the least understanding the dark tangle of her own moods and impulses, she felt deep resentment toward Cosmus. He seemed to hurt her intentionally. He was entirely self-centered, and at times she was almost certain that his passion for people was just another manifestation of his selfishness. This accusation was going pretty far, and she was wise enough to count it a momentary aberration of mind, but she did not know that it was due to some stirrings of the thwarted sex self deep down in the folds of personality. No woman can be won by an abstraction. Arthur or Launcelot?

Inevitably Guinevere will make the age-old choice. For the tragedy which shadowed these two young persons as they followed the path together in the fast falling twilight was not new; other souls best capable of being friends have been tragically incapable of mastering the intricate riddle of sex.

As they tramped the hills, something in the mystery of dawning spring, innate in the dying winter, the shell-gray sky, trees soft with mystery, gave a fluttering promise of better things. For the first time that day they found silence unembarrassing, and when they spoke, it was with the consciousness of intimacy. To them, it seemed in this new mood as if just beyond the hill, at the end of this staggering path, a new world lay—a world of certitude, and smiles, the haven of lost and forgotten things. But when they had nearly brushed its domain with their feet, they, not it, fled away into the work-a-day world. Sarah broke the silence.

"I wonder if the war will ever stop?"

"Did you see today's paper?"

"Yes."

"It looks as though we should get into it," Cosmus said thoughtfully.

"John," she answered gravely, "I think I should be glad, for them and for us."

"Yes?" he answered uncertainly.

"Have you ever sung in a large chorus, and expressed yourself through some great harmony fully, in unison with many other voices of your kind? There is no other emotion like it. It has nothing in common with the herd-instinct of fear; it is sublime, cleansing, empowering. That, I fancy, is what war is like. The mistake that the pacifists make—is that they have associated patriotism with the vulgar herd-instinct, not with this choral experience."

"In spite of the horror and blood?"

"In spite of the horror and the blood," she answered.

They had entered the wood, and they seemed to have passed suddenly into darkness. They lost the path and dropped into an unfamiliar land, a land of rolling hills and many valleys, out of sight of town and all human habitation. They turned to retrace their steps, but in the darkness, they found themselves walled in by rough hills carrying the sound of falling water. They came together by instinct and grasped hands, and walked breathlessly in silence. Were they lost? They fumbled about here and there, hoping to find the opening that had let them into this unfamiliar land. They grew confused, and tried to resume their conversation where they had left it, each hoping to hide from the other the concern that was rising in their minds.

"And you really think war a good thing?" John asked coolly.

"Of course not. How could I? It is hideous. But it does bring the sluggish mind into contact with the general life."

They stopped to listen instinctively, thinking perhaps to catch some sound that would guide them back to town. But only the heavy silence of the out-of-doors met their ears. They must have come upon one of the hilly sections south of Iron City, but they could not determine now which was south and which was north. To make matters worse, a shifting wind swept a heavy mist, almost like rain, across the world, blotting out all common objects, and bathing the landscape in mystery. They suddenly found themselves in a sublime world of vast shadowy proportions, unfamiliarity and soft sounds.

Sarah laughed nervously. "How vexing," she exclaimed "I believe we're lost."

"I've known that for the last half-hour," Cosmus admitted. "Funny—we can't be two miles from the city, and yet for the life of me I can't find a path out of this pocket of hills."

"It won't be so funny if we have to wait until morning," and Sarah made an effort to laugh.

He tried to see her through the mist. All he could discern was a shadowy form, very opaque, without any distinct features. He did not answer, but he redoubled his efforts to devise a way of regaining their bearings. Once when they stumbled down a path, they found themselves ankle deep in water.

"We must keep walking," he whispered. "Are you cold?"

"Oh, no," she answered, but he could feel her shiver.

As they threshed about in the mist, up hill and down, they were aware suddenly of a great light dawning in their faces. It permeated the mist, made radiant the dreary, dripping world, for all reality like a rising sun. Some dread took hold of them for a moment; though not superstitious, they felt the shudder all men feel at the sight of the supernatural. Spellbound, they watched; then they saw and understood. What thrilled them so mysteriously was only the headlight of a common interurban car. But was it going to or coming from Iron City? After a debate, they decided that it was going to the city and they made off in that direction.

Feeling relieved at the prospect of finding their way home, they threw off all concern, and raced along hand in hand like children. Wet branches of low trees beat their faces, and they found themselves pushed together as they twisted and turned to avoid this rock or that clump of bushes. Suddenly, without warning, Cosmus took Sarah in his arms and kissed her again and again.

Then he half-flung, half-pushed her from him, for he found her stiff and unyielding in his embrace, her mouth turned from his, her bosom heaving with sobs.

"God," he cried, "I hate you."

He half-staggered, half-ran in the opposite direction, anywhere to be rid of her. Sarah heard him stumbling through the bushes, dislodging stones as he went; then she heard a sound as if he had fallen, and what sounded like a groan.

"John, John," she called, "Come back."

No answer. She cautiously felt her way after him, came to a ledge, let herself down carefully, feet first, and landed beside him where he lay.

She leaned over him, and spoke his name. At first he did not answer. And before he did—in that fleeting moment—something happened to Sarah Blackstone.

All the old weight of loss and longing, wistful disappointment fled and she knew peace. There was something infinitely good in being here, in the still dark, dripping night, bending over him. New life stirred; something dead broke from her and slipped away. A great current of Life pinned her to the ground, made her a part of the growing things, and the deep, maternal earth. She seemed to be opening door after door of meaning. She was enfolded by the presence of her mother and for the first time she understood the wild out-reaching passion of her mother's death-bed letter. It was as if she were her mother. Her mind went joyously free, rollicking among childhood memories—old orchard days, hollyhocks and pansies, and dolls—had she ever played with dolls? It was as if she had known nothing else as a child but dolls, for she felt tearing at her bosom the old ecstasy of early girlhood in mothering dolls.

She reached down and began to rub John's hands; she bent over and kissed him. He did not stir or speak.

She tried to bring her mind back to the present, to understand the seriousness of the silly predicament in which they found themselves; lost within a mile of the city, in the cold and rain, the possibility of an all-night vigil, her reputation gone, and John hurt. But in that first moment before he spoke, all these considerations were brushed aside, and she only knew that it was well with her. She was saying, "That kiss has made him mine. I am alive. I am happy. There is no death, war or grief. Life is entrancing. I shall go on opening happy doors forever."

Something had indeed happened to Sarah Blackstone.

Then John said heavily, "It's my leg, I think."

"Can you stand?"

She helped him to his feet, but the minute she withdrew her support, he was down on his knees again with a groan.

"You must leave me and go back for help," he said.

"Listen," Sarah exclaimed, "isn't that the bark of a dog?"

Somewhere not far distant over the hill a hound was baying. She called loudly several times, vainly. For a bad three minutes she was afraid she had silenced the dog, but again they heard its welcome baying.

"We must follow it," she said. "Come."

She took his arm and drew it over her shoulder, and together, slowly and painfully they skirted the boulder in front of them and scrambled up the hill. It was painful work for John. It was pleasure for Sarah. She never flinched when he stumbled and threw his whole weight upon her. She stood up tremblingly, but strong. Now and then they paused to rest, or to wait for the dog's howl. Over hill and hillock until, when they had climbed the highest hill of all, they came suddenly upon a little house and barn. There was no light. The dog's bark changed to snarls. Sarah could see the beast bristling and fierce against the wall of mist. She was afraid to go in. She called out, as she remembered girls did in books.

"Hello, the house! Help."

After repeated calls, a dim light flickered at a window, and the back door cautiously opened. Sarah explained quickly that Mr. Cosmus was hurt, and that they needed a carriage to get back to Iron City.

"Tain't far," said the man. "Wait till I get my shoes on."

He came out in a few minutes with a lantern, and hitched an old horse to a family carriage. He was gruff but not unkind, and gently helped Cosmus into the back seat.

"Will you ride with me, Missy, in front?"

Sarah answered simply, "He may need me," and climbed in beside Cosmus.

The farmer clucked to his mare, the carriage rattled forth, through the barnyard, out of the gate, down a long, dark lane, and then upon a road they both knew. Lights flickered now before them, danced in their mist-blurred vision, and soon they caught the sound of the city. They did not talk. Cosmus was in pain. Once he said:

"It's broken, I guess," referring to his leg.

Then he ignored the pain and his companion. He lay back

thinking, "I've been a fool, that's all; this is the end."

And Sarah was thinking, "This is only the beginning; it will go on like this forever. I'll tell him tomorrow."

And so they came to the hospital.

But the next morning, in the glaring daylight, Sarah found it harder to tell than she had thought. The whole affair looked different. If she had followed her desire, she would have gone to Cosmus, and begged to nurse him as her right.

But the world of broad daylight is not the world of romance; reason entered, and convention. She telephoned to the hospital, cried a little when she learned that his leg was broken; sent him flowers, wrote him pretty, stiff little notes. But in the days that followed she did not see Cosmus, or hear from him. Although she had found love, she began to wonder whether she had not found it too late.

29 Into Whose Hand

Groping in the debatable lands of experience, John Cosmus during the weeks that passed, while he was convalescing, knew the bitterest failure. He had come to a point in his career, he vaguely realized, where events come in full cycle, but within or without himself he could get no new impetus forward. Sunk in deep negation, nothing made any difference. He was like one set adrift in an open boat, too loyal to life to leap to death into the black waters, to passive to raise a signal of distress for safety. He lay for hours in his bed in the hospital, still and calm, and even flippant, but never enkindled, never himself. The accident, which had enforced this idleness, seemed to him the last affront from a particularly enigmatic and malevolent world. And like many another modern in this era of stress, he had erected a shell of stoicism about a nature perhaps over-ardent and sensitive, and was playing the snail.

To be sure, at the seat of all this trouble was Sarah. If he had had her, he argued, the rest would have been bearable. Studiously avoiding sentiment, he still was forced to admit that she was necessary to his happiness. Together, they might have ignored the world and built an ivory tower above and beyond all this stress. . . . But he was without her. That *was* the end.

At this time Cosmus's world was walled around by the lurid fires of war. War was the most real reality of his life—as it was all men's. And he, like so many men with broken anchor, was being held firm by the routine of common work.

But not for long; one day after he had been in the hospital a couple of weeks, he received a note from President Crandon. He wrote:

Dear Mr. Cosmus:

Please accept regrets from me in behalf of the whole college. I am sure you have been missed from your accustomed place.

It is my unpleasant duty to inform you, however, that the trustees are forced to dispense with your services henceforth, due to certain retrenchments revealed as necessary at the close of the last fiscal year. Your salary will be continued until you are out again.

Believe me,

Sincerely yours,
HUGH CRANDON.

This letter evoked only derisive laughter from Cosmus. He was now, he told himself, practically cut off from all human society, for the newspaper—drab thing—united him only with war.

So days passed in which his mind lay fallow, and his heart was torn by pain.

One April morning he had a visitor. Much to his surprise, Samuel Curtis, sad and dim, bobbed in through the door.

"Glad to see you gitting along so well, Professor. You'll be out soon?"

"I could go out now, I suppose," Cosmus answered, "but, you see," and he spoke somewhat bitterly, "my salary stops when I go out, so I guess I'll just keep this room, and bunk here for life." Then, seeing the perplexity on his caller's face, he continued: "You see, I'm fired, Mr. Curtis; you were right; I'm not fit to teach on Crandon Hill's faculty."

Curtis was not disturbed by this earnest exposition. His eyes merely shifted from the table to the window.

"Pretty day. You ought to be out—would do you good. Suppose I hitch up the old mare, and bring him around to the door.

You can drive out alone, if you want to."

Cosmus's mind leaped back to that September day four years before when he had arrived in Iron City. There came to him in a flash all the aims and hopes and dreams which he had had then and which were now shattered and gone, and he was smitten with fear and pain; fear that the world was but a mad place, and pain at his failures. To himself more than to Curtis, he said:

"Has it been four years since I rode behind the old mare? My God, and Iron City has not changed one bit."

"Oh, yes, it has—much," Curtis answered quickly.

"You mean, it's bigger and richer?"

Curtis did not answer directly, and in the silence that intervened a joyous bird-note floated into the room, and charmed away all sadness.

"Say," Curtis said finally, "that Walt Kuhns wasn't such a bad fellow, was he?"

Was that the old man's answer? It was mighty decent of him to have come in, anyhow.

"You know, Mr. Curtis," John said, "I never held it against you that you put me into the street."

Curtis did not answer at once. Instead he said,

"Will you go for a ride, Professor? The mare's outside now."

"Outside now? Why not go? Why fester in bed?"

"Surely, I'll go," Cosmus spoke heartily.

Crutches were brought and he limped down after his lugubrious caller. They emerged from the dismal hospital. April! with rich earth scents, feathery leaves, broad sunshine, and vibrant currents of hope in the air. Cosmus gulped the freshness in greedily. Then he saw who was in the Curtis phaeton holding the lines over the broad back of the old red mare. Sarah!

Slowly it dawned upon him. She had sent Samuel Curtis and she had come for him then. Perhaps, perhaps? He allowed Curtis to help him into the phaeton and as in a dream, he and Sarah drove down the shadowy street, out the sleepy road. The world seemed a very decent place to live in.

They drove in silence. Black birds tinkled in downy covert, farmers were turning heavy furrows in the fields; pigs grunted, roosters crowed in the barnyards; the soil awaited the seed; and over the hills and fields glinted the River of Wires. Once again he felt contact with the general life; and he knew this common sight as America, his Country.

"Stop a minute, Sarah, won't you?" he said finally. "There on the hill. For the first time, I know what those wires are saying. All my life long they have been teasing me to guess their meaning. Now I know. How simple. They mean this, 'There are no races, nor countries, only brotherhoods of men. We unite the world. Shall it be slave or free?' Think of that, it's the old fight, ever the old fight."

Sarah turned the mare's head into a flowery lane. He was half-sorry that he had broken the silence, for he feared she might vanish before his eyes. He asked,

"Where are we going?" fearful lest they be going home.

"To my Symphony."

For a moment he did not remember; then he recalled that other day long ago when they seemed to have entered a child-like world guilelessly, and had found each other there. He turned toward her eagerly.

"Sarah!"

"Wait," she said, "I hurt you very much that night when you broke your leg, didn't I?"

"Let's not think of that now."

"Let's talk it out, John, first, while we can. That's always been the trouble with us. Our tongues have been so awkward."

"What is there to say? I love you."

"It's been my fault all along," she answered, trying to recover the reins that had dropped from her hands when John had taken them; "you see, it was my bringing up, I guess. I was locked so into myself. I was not complete, whole, I never could give myself to any one. I drove you off. Sidney Haynes was just another part of my loneliness. I made him up. He existed as a mythical love."

How sad, John thought.

"And then, that night when you broke your leg, it seemed as if I had changed." She paused. "John," she added decisively, "it was as if all at once I had found my body at last, had found the joy of living, had found life." She turned to him slowly, her face suddenly shy for all its radiance. "I love you," she said breathlessly. And he took her in his arms at last.

They rode for a long time together, and saw the descending sun tint the half-awakened earth with beauty, until at last the long beams shattered themselves against the mystery of dark-blue woods and a tender twilight, upon whose bosom a young moon fluttered, fell like a lullaby over the land.

They found still roads where no hint of other human souls penetrated; little private roadways, theirs alone, down which the old horse seemed to trot delightedly. Sometimes like all lovers they did not speak in words for minutes; but mostly they talked passionately together; of life, love, experiences, and dreams, each trying to impart to the other something which grew more inarticulate at each word.

Once as the road skirted a wood and mounted an upland, they looked down upon a valley where waters twinkled through white mists, and impenetrable shadows lay. Something formless, even abysmal, in the prospect struck in them a mood of wonder. It was as if they looked upon the twilight of a world-dawn, upon the first creation, they, the first man and woman. Perception awakened in John.

In that moment he seemed to become a part of the race as it had been and is and was to be. And he knew himself a part of all Life. He drew Sarah to him passionately,

"You will want children, Sarah?" he asked.

"Will I!" she answered. "Oh, John!"

A moment later the horse drew the phaeton around a turn in the road and they caught the sound of the city, until this moment unheard. Sarah could not restrain a shudder. She thought of the children which were to come, and of the world of cruelty in which they were to have their life. Even he, as he heard the undertone of trade, felt return upon him the weariness of the morning, the pain, the impotency and despair. Why deceive themselves by the romance of love?

Whither sped the old world while they, with young hearts, clattered along in an antique shay of another generation? Whither drove they? This they knew as they sat with clasped hands; that it was into a turbulent world. And they were sad. For them there were just two facts: the perennial wrongness of cruelty and greed, and the eternal rightness of love.

Oh, if they could only know to whose hand the future would be committed!

FINIS